Readers love Lord Mouse

"Please just trust me when I say this writing is a joy with which to spend your precious reading hours. The dialogue, the descriptions, the unexpected twists and turns, and revelations. Every story should be so lucky as to be told like this."
—Prism Book Alliance

"*Lord Mouse* was a welcome surprise and I found myself appreciating nearly every minute of the book."
—Joyfully Jay

"It's so much fun when I try a new author, and they blow my socks off with a well written story that is so full of twists and turns that you have trouble putting the book down. Such is the case with *Lord Mouse*."
—The Novel Approach

"The action was exactly as promised, and I loved the relationship between Garron and Mouse as they slowly moved from forced companionship to friendship, and eventually to something more."
—Just Love: Queer Book Reviews

By Mason Thomas

The Witchstone Amulet

LORDS OF DAVENIA
Lord Mouse
The Shadow Mark
Mouse: Scoundrel at Large
Three Tales

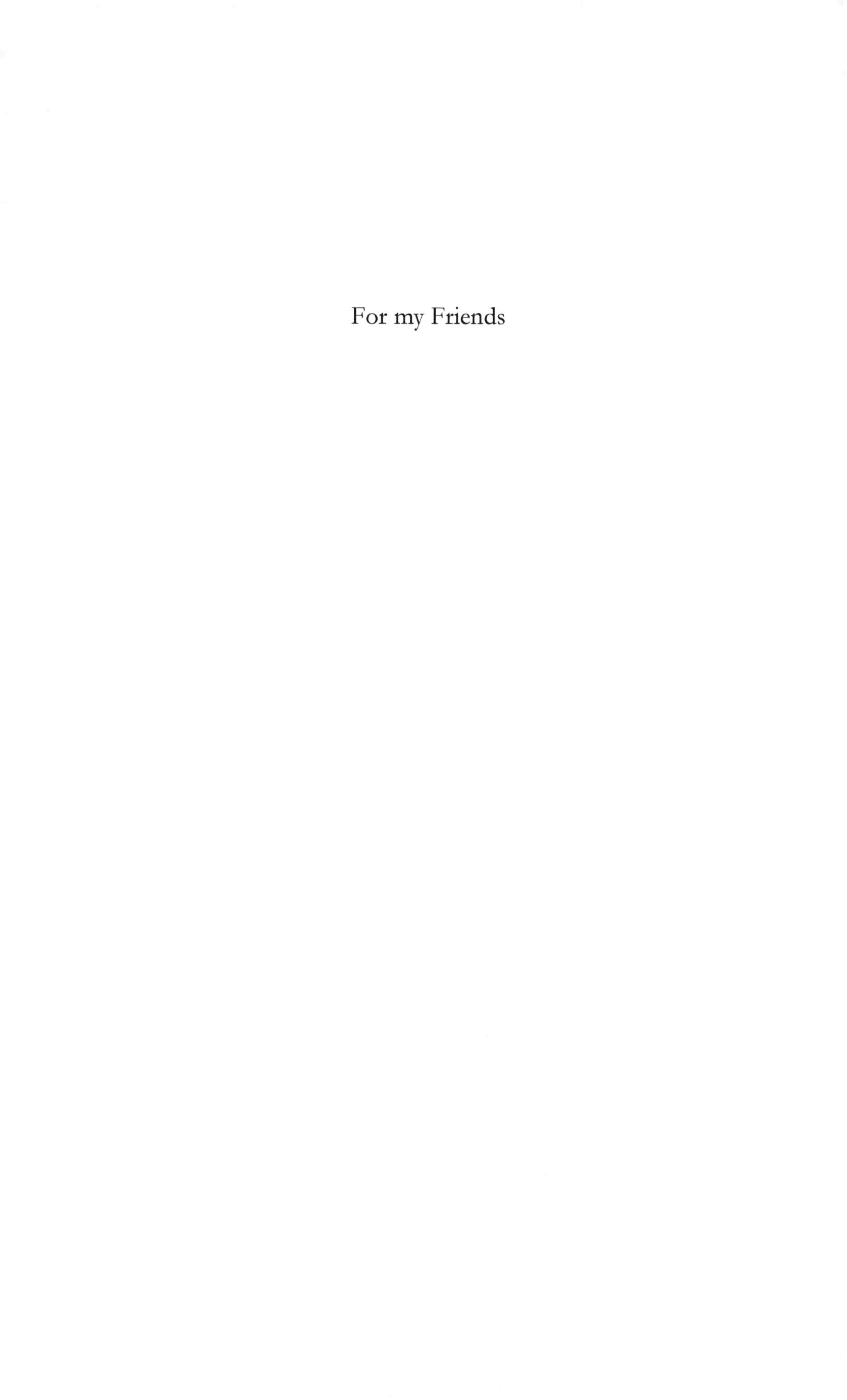

For my Friends

MOUSE:
SCOUNDREL AT LARGE

MASON THOMAS

1

THE TRAP on the little wooden box was laughable and obvious.

Mouse scoffed at the shoddy workmanship. Rudimentary at best. And poorly hidden to boot. It was borderline insulting, really. One would have thought a merchant of such means could have afforded a better lockbox. Squinting, he slid his thinnest hook pick into the tight gap between the lock's edge and the wood of the box. A slight tug, and he disengaged the spring that would have ejected the poison tipped needle into his hand if he had attempted to fuss with the lock's keyhole.

Disarming the trap wasn't necessary. Not really. Knowing the lock was strictly decorative, an obvious fake, there was little chance of triggering it. Mouse had seen the trick before—would-be thieves would be lured in by the showy piece, eager to stick their tools into it. In doing so, they would ignore the rest of the box. But Mouse wasn't *any* thief. And he had no intention of sticking anything into that particular hole. The actual locking mechanism was hidden elsewhere.

In truth, he disabled the trap for the satisfaction of thwarting the incompetent dolt who built it.

The poison wouldn't have killed him. Probably. It was more likely to render him unconscious. Those that are burgled by professionals like himself appreciate an opportunity to interrogate the thief, perhaps find out who hired them. Mouse had no interest in waking up in a dungeon and facing the prospect of thumbscrews or the pear of anguish expanding his nether orifice until he talked.

But time was pressing. It took longer to sneak away and make his way to Trivot Agata's private wing on the second floor than he anticipated, and the festivities downstairs were showing signs of decline. Agata would not wait to see the last of his guests out. When it became clear the energy of the evening had flagged, the great master of the estate would decide he had consumed too much wine and beg off to retire, likely with one of the acrobats he'd hired to entertain.

The last thing Mouse needed was to be discovered mucking about in his dressing chamber.

Mouse could still hear the distant thrum of music and laughter through the floor. The hall wasn't directly beneath him, but close. But he could also hear an increase in footfalls in the corridor beyond the drawing room. Out-of-town guests making their way to the guest rooms.

An indication it might behoove him to speed the matter up.

He could, of course, simply take the whole box with him. Smash it to bits outside—which felt like cheating—or figure out how to open it at his leisure. Or hand it over to Jardem and let him figure it out. That option had appeal since Jardem would only get frustrated and demand Mouse do it, anyway.

But the missing box would alert the esteemed master that he'd in fact been relieved of his items sooner than was convenient. Mouse was too much of a stickler to follow that route. He preferred things done properly. Best to get it open, make off with the item he'd been hired to pilfer, and leave

Agata in the dark about his misfortune for as long as possible.

The creak of floorboards and voices in the corridor pricked Mouse's ears.

Fuck. Box tucked under his arm, he scurried to the door of the bedchamber.

Someone was just outside the door to the corridor. The voice was louder than a standard conversational volume. Drunk? Maybe. Entitled? Definitely. Not Trivot Agata, Mouse decided. *His* voice had a grating nasal quality that the voice in the hall lacked.

Whoever it was, they needed to keep moving.

Stepping back into the bedchamber, he turned the wooden box around in his hands. The quality of the wood inlay was adequate, Mouse admitted. Begrudgingly. It was cleanly assembled, even if the design itself was uninspired and bland. The creator had been a woodworker first, not a locksmith, one that enjoyed assembling the object.

Which meant the lock would be hidden in the wood itself.

Mouse bit his lower lip as he used his fingers to probe around the sides, pressing at each of the individual pieces of wood that made up the box's design. The surface seemed solid, unyielding, everywhere he touched. But instinct drove him. He knew he was right—the answer lay in the design.

The voice was still outside the door. Still unnecessarily loud. He was berating someone. Mouse couldn't tease out the complaint. The words were slung together in a spirit-induced gush and muffled by the thick oak door.

Then, Mouse heard the sound he dreaded most—a key turning in the lock.

He closed his eyes and grunted. Why couldn't people just enjoy themselves at a party and not make his job more difficult?

His fingers moved at an accelerated pitch now, pressing each fragment of beech or oak as if he were attempting to play a squeeze box. It had to be there. He wasn't wrong.

Mouse froze for a moment, ears straining. He heard the distinct squeal of hinges as the door was pushed open. Someone had been given access to Agata's private chambers.

He kept at it, pressing on all the different sections of inlay.

"—happy to wait—."

"No need," a voice replied in a forced singsong tone, slurred by drink. Mouse caught the note of irritation and impatience beneath it. "I shan't be a moment. I know precisely where I left it."

And the door closed.

Mouse rolled his head back. "Fuck," he grumbled under his breath.

Clearly, not Agata. Mouse recognized the voice, of course. The intruder was none other than Trivot's peacock of a stepson, Pravis, the oldest child of Trivot's new wife. He had flitted about the party like a garish butterfly, landing on every colorful flower in the room. He sought any attention he could garner, but all his attempts to woo were roundly rebuffed.

His advances were as indiscriminate as they were indelicate. They ranged from the daughters of the richest guests to the lute player and each of the four jugglers. Everyone responded to his attempts with an expression like they were smelling swamp gas for the first time. Despite being newly brought into the Agata family, he had yet to be accepted into the society of Har Tesera.

Mouse moved into the dressing chamber again, putting two rooms—Agata's personal drawing room and the bedchamber—between Pravis and himself. Mouse made mental calculations about how long it would take for Pravis to drift in this direction.

Mouse was trapped and still didn't have what he came for.

The only windows were against the opposite wall of the bedchamber. He'd inspected them earlier should he need a hasty exit. Large, cumbersome things with rusty hinges.

They'd make noise if he tried to open them.

He considered crawling into the wardrobe. He could pick the lock in the dark. Probably. If he could find where it was hidden. But he'd be trapped in there, too. Likely all night.

Unacceptable. Too many things could go wrong. Agata might notice the box missing. A servant might go into the wardrobe for any reason…

He had to find a way into the box.

Slow footfalls crossed the floor of the drawing room, muffled by the rugs. Pravis was circling the room. He, too, was looking for the box. Why else would he invent a reason to sneak in here without his stepfather's knowledge? And he didn't know where his father kept it.

Mouse kept at it, inspecting with his fingers.

As he turned the box around to examine another side, he felt the slightest shift when his thumb slid along the edge of the box's corner. His whole body froze, the frenzied search halting like the slam of a door. He'd found it.

He turned the edge upward toward him. Lips tight, he pushed with his thumb and slid the corner section down. It glided smoothly to reveal a metal plate and a tiny oblong hole.

"Clever bastard," Mouse growled. The woodworker was more skilled than he had first given him credit for.

He dropped onto a stool and gripped the box between his thighs, corner facing upward. Rake and hook tools pinched delicately in his fingers, he went to work on the small hole.

In the other room, he heard the clink of fine crystal. Someone was taking the opportunity to raid his stepfather's fine spirits while he conducted his inspection of the room. The creak of floorboards suggested impatient pacing about the room.

Mouse closed his eyes to concentrate. The lock was stubborn, the apparatus inside unfamiliar. It took him more time than he wanted to catch the pins within and determine the direction they moved. And the hole was made for a very small key. He didn't have a lot of maneuverability.

His eyes popped open when the creak of floorboards stopped. Sometimes there was more danger in not hearing anything.

Working a lock couldn't be rushed. He closed his eyes again and, by feel alone, went back to visualizing the mechanism inside. But his ears remained fixed on the activity in the other room.

Gently, he negotiated the pick through the row of pins. Lifting, turning, holding in place.

Movement. Something inside slipped, and Mouse heard the satisfying click of the mechanism inside the lock.

He released his breath. There was no sound more beautiful to his ear and no sensation like it when he had access to the forbidden. His face flushed. His body quivered.

A sudden marching of feet—over carpet first, then hardwood. The footfalls had a determination about them; a decision had been made. The harder clap of boots on wood told Mouse that the intruder had entered the corridor connecting the drawing room and the bedchamber.

Caution and delicacy were no longer required. He flopped the box onto his lap, threw open the lip and rummaged inside. The contents were a varied collection of documents and letters, some tied together with ribbon, and a few gemstones that Mouse was tempted to pocket for himself.

Jardem told him the patron promised extra if Agata was unaware of the theft until much later—to give the patron time to escape the city safely with the prize. Not that Mouse was gullible enough to believe he'd see one additional coin. Jardem liked to dangle that possibility, but Mouse wasn't fooled.

Still, Mouse liked a job done right. Reputation was everything in this business, and swiping more than you were hired to was against guild policy. It caused unnecessary risk. And he didn't need to give Jardem any excuse to cut his share. The stones would fetch a nice price if he could sell them in secret, but he'd also gain Jardem's wrath if Agata discovered too soon that he'd been burgled.

So, he let them be. He located the folded documents with the red wax seal that were buried at the bottom and tucked them into his boot.

Perhaps, on a night he was free, he'd come back and liberate those beauties for himself.

The clomping of boots was getting closer. Mouse threw the box onto the shelf, took a moment to position it just as he'd found it, and dashed out of the small chamber.

As Mouse bounded into the bedchamber, the door swung open. Fighting to regulate his breathing, he took a position next to the bed, then drew back the lavish bedcoverings.

"What are you doing here?" The voice from the doorway was dripping with privilege and condescension.

"Turning down the master's bed linens, my Lord," Mouse replied. He added a lilt of fear to his tone for effect. "He is said to be requiring the chamber soon."

Pravis, Agata's stepson, stood in the doorway, palm still on the handle.

Despite all his other failings, the young Pravis was one of the most smartly dressed in attendance. It didn't do enough to tip the scales in his favor, unfortunately. Fine clothes did not make one less insufferable.

He was a slim man, with narrow hips and slight shoulders. His lips were pressed in a perpetual displeased glower, and his eyes were dark and belittling. He dressed all in black. His coat was lavish, with an intricate brocade, finely interwoven with iridescent black beads at the breast and around the very high and very stiff collar. Rebuffing the current fashion of three-quarter length doublets, his ended dramatically at his waist where his wide belt and very tight velvet trousers showed the shape of his hips and legs. A medallion hung from a red ribbon at his throat. Against the immaculately white chemise that encircled his neck, it was a punch of brilliance, like the sun breaking the horizon.

Pravis's crown was a chaos of wispy brown curls that looked like he just come inside from a windstorm, and the slightly too long rust-colored muttonchops followed the shape of his delicate jaw.

One hand still on the door handle, the long thin fingers of Pravis' other hand drummed on his hip. His white gloves were tucked into his belt. He stared down at Mouse with a mix of surprise and displeasure. He obviously hadn't expected his unauthorized search to be interrupted.

"Who are you?" he snapped in that imperious tone that only the privileged could manage so effortlessly. "I don't know you."

"Jiri, my Lord," Mouse replied, pulling in his shoulders in a submissive hunch and looking away. "I'm new to his master's estate. Did I do something to offend you, my Lord?"

Pravis stepped into the room with way more shoulder movement than was necessary. His mannerisms were oily and superior.

"New? And already assigned to my father's suite?"

Mouse donned his most effective woeful expression. "I am a prize, my Lord. Won during cards from Master Bouradon of Har Serena."

Pravis lifted a brow. It was a name he would certainly know. Bouradon was at the party earlier but had already departed. "An indentured, then."

"Yes, m'lord."

"How did you get in here?"

"Unlocked for me, my Lord. By your father's steward—"

"*Step*-father," Pravis corrected with a sharp edge of disdain. Those two simple words did enough to tell Mouse how much love the two of them shared.

Mouse bowed his head. "Of course. Apologies. I was not aware…but I will remember."

Pravis had clearly not been granted unfettered access to Agata's private chamber. From the decidedly masculine decor to the missing traces of a feminine wardrobe or accoutrements, neither was Pravis's mother, Agata's new wife. She may be an occasional visitor to this chamber but did not sleep here. Mouse had spotted her downstairs. She spent most of her time on the terrace with a few of the other wives, leaning in close and whispering in conspiratorial tones.

It was easy enough to conclude that Agata's recent marriage was a sham. Mouse had no idea what Agata had acquired from the arrangement, but Pravis's clandestine arrival here made it fairly likely he and his mother were after the same thing that Mouse currently had hidden in his boot.

Whatever it was.

Mouse had gotten his hands on it only just in time. Pravis had had the same idea—filch it while the old man was entertaining. Although this peacock was likely not bright enough to figure out a way into the box. Perhaps he'd already procured a key. But considering where the actual keyhole was located, he would have with near certainly ended up unconscious on the floor, victim of the poison.

Mouse regretted that not happening. It would have been entertaining to steal the document while this fop was out cold on the floor.

By getting here first, Mouse had practically saved his life. Maybe someday he'd send Pravis a discrete note letting him know how very close he came to disaster.

This scrap of parchment had exchanged hands several times already, Mouse had learned. A popular item, indeed. What warranted such coveting?

A question for later. Now, he had to slip away without triggering Pravis's suspicion, and be free of the estate before Pravis, or his *step*father, discovered the document had already been nicked.

"The steward has the key," Mouse said. "Regretfully, I have not yet been informed of her name, but—"

"Tanja Vo?" Pravis cut in.

"Ah. Yes. Many thanks, good Lord," Mouse replied with a bow. "Mistress Tanja Vo directed me to prepare the chamber for the master's retirement. He is expected to be…entertaining."

"Hmmm," Pravis grunted, deep in his throat. He stepped in, sat on the bed, and crossed his legs. The tip of his boot did little circles as he leaned back and braced himself with one arm. His eyes attempted to make a casual sweep of the room, searching. "He is to return soon, then?"

"As I understand it, yes my Lord."

"I'm no noble-born, so you can cease with that." He sounded like it pained him to admit that. Rich, but no title or true influence. Oh, the trials these young members of the merchant class must suffer.

"Apologies," Mouse replied. This was taking too long. He had to get out of here. With the sheets turned down and the pillows arranged, it was time for his exit. "I will leave you to your interests, *master*."

Pravis was still sweeping his gaze around the room. Mouse circled around the bed toward the door.

"You know," Pravis cooed, as he rose from the edge of the bed to stand between Mouse and the door. "My bedchamber could use some attention as well."

Mouse groaned inwardly. He knew that tone. And the hungry look in Pravis's eye. After a night of rejections, Pravis now resorted to propositioning staff. Mouse kept his face turned, acting subservient and demure, but in truth, looking directly at Pravis's sultry gaze threatened to empty his stomach.

Under different circumstances, Mouse perhaps would have considered bedding him. If there was something to gain by it, of course. He'd reap no enjoyment from it, certainly. Pravis was comely and well-formed, had all his teeth and had fine skin free of pox scars. But this entitled prig felt everything was his for the taking, even his stepfather's personal servant boy. Believing he was indentured, Pravis didn't care that Mouse couldn't refuse the advances without consequences. Mouse understood what it meant to feel powerless, and disgust burned inside him like a kiln.

Pravis pinched Mouse's chin with his fingers and steered his face to force their eyes to meet. A lascivious grin broke the corner of his mouth.

Mouse considered his options.

Anyone else in the guild would simply kill the fucker. Mouse didn't hate that option. The world would be a better place without this vile grease bucket that felt it was acceptable to take advantage of the helpless. But that wasn't his style. And he'd have to do something with the body and the inevitable blood stains.

He could go ahead and let the cretin have his way with him, of course. He'd endured worse. Much worse. But time was pressing here. The longer he remained about the manor, the more likely Agata would learn his precious document had been pinched. And there was always the danger, albeit slim, that Pravis might discover the document on him when they disrobed.

Mouse opted for the more pragmatic approach.

He turned his eyes away and donned his most bashful smile. "I am at your bidding, my Lo—I mean, Master. It would bring me the greatest pleasure to prepare your bed." Mouse paused and let his eyes lift for a fraction and connect with Pravis's. "For whatever pursuit you require it for this evening."

Pravis chuckled low in his throat. "Such an agreeable servant. You will do well in this house, I wager."

"I know my place, master. And I exist only to fulfill the will of those more worthy than myself." He managed to say the words without choking on the bile chewing at the back of his throat.

Pravis let a knuckle trace the length of Mouse's jaw line.

"I must report to Master Agata that his chamber is prepared. But, if it pleases you, I will go directly to your chamber after and…have everything in proper order for you." He turned his eyes away again. "That should provide you ample time to conclude your interests here."

Pravis's hand froze by Mouse's chin.

"My report to Master Agata could take time," Mouse added. "As much time as you require."

He could feel how every muscle in Pravis's body stiffened.

"Clever, clever, boy," Pravis replied. His tone was laced with suspicion.

Boy. Mouse suppressed a smile. The assumption that Mouse was still a youth, balls barely dropped, always amused him. He was likely the same age as Pravis. And with a larger cock. Mouse braved another look into Pravis's eyes. This time, his own gaze was confident and calculating.

"I am astute enough to recognize the real power that exists in this manor, Master," Mouse said. "The official master of the house is aged, doddering. But it is easy enough to see who is running the business here."

"Gleaned so quickly, in so short a tenure?"

"Call it a talent, Master. And I assume you are to inherit my indenture when…when the time comes?"

Pravis made a slow nod, and there was a hint of a telling smile. "Sooner than later, one hopes."

"Then doesn't it stand to reason that your satisfaction should be my primary concern?"

"You are indeed a wise lad."

"I have many gifts, master. As you will discover. Do you have any specific requirements for the preparation of your bedchamber?"

"Surprise me," Pravis replied.

That was easy enough. He'd be surprised all right.

"My master will not be disappointed."

"He better not be." Pravis tapped the side of Mouse's face with his palm a few times before he returned his attention to the chamber. "Now, off with you. Keep my stepfather busy and your reward will come. And then come again."

Mouse fought down a gag. Why did those with power always feel their prowess in the bedchamber was unsurpassed?

"As you wish," Mouse said as he glided around Pravis toward the door. As he did so, he let the back of his hand graze against the hardened cock restrained within Pravis's trousers. Then he slipped from the chamber and was gone.

The poor fop was due for a slew of devastating disappointments.

Too late he would realize he'd been duped, and he wouldn't even be able to inform his stepfather that an intruder had been in his bedchamber—because that would mean admitting he'd been there himself.

Mouse exited Agata's suite of rooms, leaving Pravis alone to conduct his fruitless search. He took a set of back stairs toward the servant's wing, well clear of where the festivities were taking place, where he could slip out a back window unseen.

2

MOUSE LINGERED in the shadows outside the estate to make certain his exit had gone unnoticed. Not that he had doubts, but now wasn't the time to get sloppy. Sounds of merriment still wafted out into the quiet of the street, but he caught no signs of alarm or spotted anyone combing the grounds within the high iron fence.

The street was, for the most part, quiet and vacant, save for the sporadic departure of attendees climbing into their carriages and being wheeled away, and the lonely pair of city guards that looped past every so often. Street lanterns cast wide, warm circles of light on the cobbles. The wealth of any neighborhood was directly proportional to the number of lantern poles and the number of missing stones in the street. Here, there was a lantern in front of every residence, sometimes two, if the estate's grounds were large enough. And there were no missing stones in the street along this stretch of manors. This neighborhood was well-monied indeed.

But Mouse knew that. A good many of the residents in this neighborhood were in attendance inside. But not exclusively. The well-heeled from all over the city and even the kingdom were inside. Some were noble-born, those with selective business investments or who were broad-minded enough to be seen at an event most nobles would see as beneath them. It was attended mostly by those who'd managed to accumulate wealth and power on their own.

The itchy servant's garb was balled up and tossed behind him, and he was relieved to be back in the comfort of his own clothes—a light tunic and jerkin. Shoulder against the side wall of a storefront alcove, he tugged out the cork from a half empty bottle with his teeth. He'd snagged it from the kitchens on his way out. Spitting it aside, he tilted the bottle to his lips. He was no expert on fine wines—he was content with a mug of ale or mead. But this felt smooth as it glided into his throat and made the tip of his tongue tingle. He could get used to drinking this.

In the distance, a cluster of hulking shadows shifted at the margins of the lantern light. A group of three, maybe four, skulked in an alley. The Scourge, Mouse concluded. Sworn enemy of the guild, and menace to anyone on the street. They were lying in wait for drunken and unsuspecting partygoers who made the ill-informed decision to walk home on this warm night. Or to ambush a carriage that rolled past.

He caught himself stepping deeper into the shadow of his alcove and was irritated by the sudden and all too familiar twist in his stomach. He wasn't that helpless street rat anymore, the one tormented by thugs like them. He had no reason to fear them anymore. But those survival instincts were embedded deep in his gut.

He grunted to himself and took another slug from the bottle.

No one was searching for him. That was clear enough. But he hung around longer than necessary, if only to prove to himself he wasn't scampering off because the Scourge was about. He tossed the empty bottle aside and strolled off, staying clear of the lanterns' light.

He headed south toward the docks. His head spun a little

as he padded along. Not from the wine. The thrill of a successful job always left him heady and reeling.

The Night Fingers Guild occupied a sizable old warehouse squeezed between the industry quarter along the river, the docks, and the southern boundary of the merchant district. Years ago, the guild had received the building as payment from a client who found himself short the coin he'd promised. A new appreciation for where his hands were located on his wrists persuaded him to find an alternative method of payment, and the deed was handed over.

Mouse spotted guild muscle patrolling the streets as he drew closer. The perimeter was always well guarded, as there were plenty of organizations set on seeing the guild's downfall—and not just the Scourge. Yet Mouse, on principle, preferred to enter the facilities undetected. He wasn't worth his salt if couldn't sidestep the ale-soaked lumps that were put out on patrol.

He had a preferred route, of course.

He'd become well-practiced at this path—it hardly required any thought or effort anymore. He could execute it as easily as if he were walking the street. Which, of course, meant it had grown exceedingly dull. So, Mouse started looking for new ways to evade the guild's watchers and get inside unseen.

He approached the guild from the north. Of course, this neighborhood had few lanterns, and even fewer were lit, and the street was missing an impressive number of stones. No well-heeled residents were around here to fund the repairs, and the city certainly wasn't about to invest coin in a neighborhood infested with miscreants that didn't pay taxes. The guild muscle ambled about, trying to look casual as they circled the perimeter, but they looked more like wayward bulls trying to find their way back to the barn in the dark. He recognized them, even in the dark, though he never bothered to learn any of their names.

None of them would know who *he* was if he danced a nude jig right in front of them.

Guild protocol dictated he was to approach, give the signal, and be recognized as an official member. Only then would he be permitted to proceed. Mouse wasn't much of a protocol enthusiast. Rules chafed him in all the wrong places.

He mapped out his path and launched into motion. First, he scaled the wall of a tenement building to the east to a second-story balcony. Then he leapt to the roof of the abandoned guardhouse in the middle of the intersection—a remnant from a time this region was more affluent and flush with those who warranted such protection. Official guard posts had to bear the city and kingdom flags. The great pole that once displayed those colors was still mounted atop the roof, although the flags were reduced to sad scraps of shredded cloth. Mouse shimmied up the pole to the orbicular finial at its top and crouched upon it like a perched crow. The pole swayed like a ship mast on rough seas. He encouraged the movement by carefully leaning, and when the position was right, he sprang onto the narrow sill of a boarded-up window on the second floor of the warehouse. From there, it was quick work to scale up the crisscrossing wooden beams to a higher window and slip inside.

Straddling the window ledge, he made one final glance at the street below and chuckled before he ducked his head inside. The guild muscle still blundered about the streets, oblivious as always.

A part of him debated with himself if he should eventually say something to Jardem. Guild loyalty and all that. If Surev was still in charge, Mouse wouldn't have hesitated. But with Jardem at the helm, the answer he landed on was always "maybe later."

Inside, Mouse pulled closed the warped, ill-fitting shutter. With a sigh, he leaned his back to the wall and rubbed one bloodshot eye with the heel of his hand. He was at it for hours inside Agata's estate, and the tension was catching up to him. This last climb sapped any reserves he had left.

He hated to admit, but he was relieved to be back. Not

happy. It was never good for him here in the guild. At least, not anymore. But now, tired as he was, it felt something akin to returning home. He could rest now. Since he'd evaded the witless sentries below and made it up here without detection, he was free to snag a couple of hours of sleep before surrendering the document to Jardem.

With a grunt, he pushed off the wall and delved into the dank and creaky corridors of the upper levels of the guild. His secluded hole was on the opposite side. He didn't need light to find his way. He knew his way by touch and feel, how the air moved and smelled, which floorboards groaned beneath his weight.

"Hole" was how he described it to deter the curious. The clever lock he installed on the trapdoor helped curtail any prying as well. Sanctuary was a more fitting title. He'd equipped the once dismal space into something almost cozy. A stolen rug, an improvised mattress, discarded tapestries covering the bare walls, a traveler's chest with a lock—all of it made it something he could call his own. A rarity here, and one he protected fiercely. The ceiling was low, but for him, that wasn't a problem. He could move about freely. Summer heat could make it oppressive at times, but on nights like that, Mouse preferred to sleep on the roof, anyway.

The other established thieves didn't live here at the guild. They resided elsewhere, somewhere private. Mouse wasn't afforded such a luxury.

He neared the final corner, then slowed. Light washed the wall ahead.

On instinct, his hand dropped to his dagger. Vigilance and caution were imperative. For all the talk of the guild code, a knife in the rib was not unheard of. Guild members weren't known for their cool heads, and grudges lingered like a pus-filled infection. Petty disputes led to retribution. There were plenty here who had some beef with him. Admittedly, a hearty spoonful of it was earned.

But then again…those intent on causing trouble didn't

announce themselves with a lantern.

He moved his shoulders back and stepped around the corner, keeping his hand near the hilt of the knife. Whoever was there already knew he was coming. He'd made no effort to dampen the sound of his boots on the wood flooring.

The short corridor ended at the makeshift ladder that led to his space in the roof. But on the floor, her back against the lowest rungs, waited Zelianna. The lantern next to her cast its warm light on her smooth walnut skin. She had one knee up, and her tattooed forearm rested on top. The brown bottle in her delicate hand swung loosely as if ready to drop.

"Took you long enough," she grunted. She lifted her dark eyes, and her gaze landed hard on Mouse.

It shouldn't have surprised him that Zel knew the location of his secret lair. She knew the inner workings of the organization better than anyone. In many respects, she was the one that kept it running.

There was good reason she was the top paid thief in the guild and third in line to the throne. Her reputation for success was unmatched—even by him, though in his defense he was younger by several years. She was treated like nobility among the rank and file. Very nearly worshiped by Jardem. What did surprise him was that she had made the effort to climb all the way up here to meet him.

Mouse forced his expression to remain neutral as he took a few tentative steps closer. He didn't sense any danger, but Zel was a master at cloaking her true intentions. Something he hoped to learn from her someday.

Unlikely, that. Zelianna never had time for, or interest, in Mouse. More reason to be surprised by her presence here. She rarely ever acknowledged him.

"Wasn't aware I was on a schedule," he said.

She set the bottle down next to her, still gripping its neck. From the hollow clunk, the bottle was nearly empty. Her eyes had a slightly unfocused quality as she held her gaze on him. She'd been here a while.

"The job was completed hours ago."

Mouse didn't want to know how she knew that. "Ran into some complications. Wanted to make certain I wasn't followed." A lie, of course. And she likely knew it was a lie too, but she didn't challenge it.

She rolled the bottom edge of the bottle on the floor for a moment, her lips pressed in pensive thought. Her eyes remained on Mouse. Then, in one flowing motion, she rose to her feet. Even slightly inebriated, she managed it with the grace of a heron taking flight.

"I was instructed to find you. See to it you went to Quickblade directly. No diversions."

Mouse grunted inwardly. "Well, you found me."

"Quickblade wants you to report to him." She stepped in, shrinking the distance between them. "Now."

Mouse forced himself not to look up to meet her eyes as she towered over him. His insides knotted. Damn it. He hated that she intimidated him.

So much for any shut eye first. She wasn't about to get out of his way, and she would report to Jardem that he *had* returned if he didn't show up at his door now.

Zel lifted the bottle to her lips and drained what remained. With a harsh exhale and a rough smack of her lips, she tossed the bottle behind her. It landed with a thud but didn't break. It rolled on the uneven floor to rest against the wall.

"Quickblade seems unusually keen on hearing if the job was a success," she said.

Her tone had shifted to something more dangerous. Her reputation included more than her ability to get the job done. She didn't suffer anyone getting in her way.

"You could have told him yourself," he replied. "Apparently, your spies have already informed you of that."

In the dark corridor, backlit by the lantern, it was hard to read her expression fully, but he saw her brow lift on one side. "That is your job to report on. Not mine." Her eyes lowered to her fingernails, as if something about them caught her attention. "Curious. Such an important job, yet he assigned it to you."

"I come cheaper."

The reply needled her for a reason he didn't understand. He could feel the heat of her ire rolling off of her. "Little Mouse," she whispered. "What is your game, I wonder."

"Is survival a game, Zel?"

She chuckled softly and took another step closer. "I will caution you to watch yourself. And to remember your place."

"My place," he repeated. "My place is in a smelly hole in the rafters while others dine on fresh meats and sleep on full mattresses without bugs."

"Sounds like where a little mouse belongs, if you ask me." Zel smiled down at him. It was unsettling. "You may think you have talent, but you have yet to cut your teeth."

This was the most she'd ever spoken to him at one time. Mostly, she'd ignored him since his arrival at the guild. "Odd. I was told there were opportunities for someone like me. Someone with talent."

"Talent," Zel repeated, her tone dripping with scorn.

"Surev—"

"Surev is gone. And talent is not skill. You need to remember that. Opportunities come with time. When you've proven yourself."

"I've not proven myself? No failed jobs—"

"Out of a few dozen, maybe. I have hundreds. People are starting to ask questions, little mouse. Wondering how you've managed to become Quickblade's new little pet."

Mouse's insides hardened. He couldn't let anyone know. It would only make his life worse if more found out what Jardem had somehow discovered. "I'm not his pet," he growled.

"You are taking jobs from those more worthy than you."

So, that's what this was about. Mouse's work in the guild was cutting into other thieves' profits.

"Who determines worth, Zel? Maybe your time has passed, and you just haven't realized it yet."

Her hand lunged out and caught Mouse by the throat. He gasped as the fingers constricted. But the dagger's point pressing into her ribs quickly redirected her attention. She looked down and saw the blade Mouse had against her gut. It hadn't broken through the fabric of her tunic, but the slightest additional pressure would pierce it—and her skin. Her grip loosened, but she didn't release him. Mouse held the dagger firm.

"Are you suggesting," Mouse said casually, "I refuse Jardem? Tell him 'no, thank you?'"

Her expression was dark and dangerous. "These jobs he hands you. They're above your status. More experienced members should have them. What influence have you on him?"

"Influence?" Mouse burst out a laugh. "I thought you were sharper." He was pushing her to her limit, he knew, but he wasn't about to cower beneath her. "He pays me nothing, and I still get the job done. Maybe it's your cut you should reconsider. You've priced yourself out of jobs."

Zel leaned in, snarling. "The guild doesn't pay my share. Clients pay my share."

Clearly, Jardem was charging the same amount for the jobs and keeping the bulk of it in his own purse. Because he could. Zel should have figured that out herself.

"Well, you have regular access to his ear. Maybe this is something you need to broach with Jardem, not me. If he's lost faith in you—"

She chuckled darkly. "He knows precisely what he has with me."

"No doubt. And I am, as you are quick to point out, a low rung on this ladder."

She released his neck with a shove. "You are being watched. Closely."

Of course, he was.

Enemies weren't anything new. But he naively hadn't anticipated finding more of them among the more powerful members of the organization. Zel was not to be trifled with, and he had no idea how many others felt as she did. Mouse had somehow made himself a threat. He would have thought Zel was above such petty jealousies.

He kept his narrow gaze locked on hers as he slid the dagger back into the belt, making certain she saw no fear on his face. Then he backed away.

A knot had formed in his stomach. Fuck. A complication he didn't need. And one that would be impossible to rectify.

The thing was…he respected Zel. Of anyone in this organization, she was perhaps the only one he looked up to. Admired. She had built herself up from nothing to be the top thief here. She was respected. Feared. Surev had been her mentor too. Just like him.

It stung to know she loathed him. He could have used an ally.

With a sigh, he worked his way back down the dark corridor, this time toward the rickety staircase that would take him to the lower levels of the guild. The whole time his mind was consumed with one idea: how many others saw him as she did? As a threat. A problem that needed fixing.

3

WITH SLEEP denied him, he shuffled his way down the convoluted levels of the old warehouse down to the second floor where Jardem had claimed his office. His muscles felt soused with fatigue, and it ate away at him from the inside. His head was a fog, thoughts refusing to coalesce. *Make this quick,* he told himself.

Surev, in his day, had kept an office barely bigger than a wardrobe. It was all he needed, he claimed. Jardem's office was obscene in comparison. He'd commandeered what had been the space used for gambling, relegating that activity to the main open area of the first floor with everything else.

Chelka sat on the floor outside Jardem's office, knees up and a small wooden horse tumbling about in her hands. Her legs had outgrown the child's shift she wore. The bottom hem barely covered her knees now, and it was much too tight in the shoulders. She glanced up as Mouse shuffled up the corridor and released a bored sigh.

"Finally."

Mouse found the strength to smile at her. "On guard duty, are you?"

"No," she said with a roll of her eyes and scoffed at him. "Told to wait here until you arrived and tell you to 'stay put until you're called for.'" She said it in a surprisingly accurate lampoon of Jardem's voice and inflection. "He said he's busy." Her attention returned to the toy horse.

So, hurry up and get here, now wait.

"Careful," Mouse warned. "The walls are thin here. He's likely to hear you." He extended his hand and gestured with his fingers to give up the toy. Chelka hesitated only a heartbeat, then placed it in his hand. Mouse turned it about. "Where'd you get this?"

"Found it."

A vague answer, colored with a tint of defensiveness. Stolen, then. Guild rules were clear—anything nicked was to benefit the guild. But she wanted this for herself.

Mouse lifted his eyebrows as he inspected it. "Well made. You could sell it in the market and get good coin for it."

"I don't want to sell it. I want to keep it."

"Then, you should." Mouse handed it back to her. "Keep it hidden. Others will recognize its value and not care that you've claimed it."

She frowned and held it to her belly as if someone at that moment would swoop in and snatch it.

Like him, she'd been recruited from the streets. The guild was always on the lookout for new talent, and Chelka had shown enough to catch someone's eye. Just like he had done all those years ago. Guild life was an improvement over life on the streets in many ways—they got a roof over their head, a dry bed, regular meals, training, some protection from brutal rivals like the Scourge—but it was never what they were promised.

The selling point that roped most in was the illusion that they'd be part of a family again. Every lost soul was swindled on the idea that, if they joined, they'd be embraced by a slew of brothers and sisters. And to the lonely and hungry, belonging was a powerful elixir.

But life in the guild was a far cry from the shimmering wonder promised to them. Belonging came with a price. Signing on meant relinquishing liberty and independence and becoming a slave to quotas and allocations. And it never took long for the new recruits to discover their adopted family was little more than a motley collection of broken and twisted souls who thrive on cruelty and malice. New members were an easy target, and their behavior against them easily justified. For weren't they treated the same when they came on? It was all part of the same perverse and ageless cycle of brutality.

Chelka's experience would be no different. Those in charge of her training hadn't even bothered to get her something to wear that fit her properly yet. He'd take care of that tomorrow.

He stepped past Chelka and approached the door to Jardem's office. Light stabbed through the gap under the floor, and he could hear the hum of conversation from within.

"He said to wait until he was ready for you," she whispered nervously.

"Hear that?" He tilted his head and cupped a hand to his ear. "I think I heard him call for me. Better not keep him waiting." He winked at her, then pushed open the door, not bothering to knock.

Jardem Blacksworn was known by many names. Quickblade was the most common, but also the Ghost of Har Tesera, Lord Night, and a few other even more cringe-worthy ones. Mouse himself had never been privileged enough to see for himself how these grandiose monikers had been awarded to him. He'd not been in the guild long enough to learn of Jardem's talents firsthand. But he couldn't help but wonder if they'd been self-branded.

Talk among the old guard seemed to support some of it. Jardem was a respected thief and a cunning spy. As head of the organization, it was harder to read what the pervasive opinion was. Members were less open to criticize. He had a way of finding out. Mouse suspected he knew how.

He stepped inside.

The room was almost comically large for its purpose, and Mouse made exaggerated marching strides to cross the wide gap between the door and the desk at the far side. The room was made to appear vaster by the lack of furnishings. A monstrous desk sat at the far end, with a few high-back chairs facing it, and a few padlocked cupboards stood against the side wall, but that was the extent of it. The walls were covered in art—paintings and tapestries, but also what looked like the tribal art of the Vardic barbarians to the west. Masks. Animal totems.

Jardem had a particular fascination with the barbarians. Perhaps it was their rumored brutality, or maybe their tribal government reminded him of guild life, but whatever the reason, Jardem's interest bordered on obsession. Mouse always thought it strange. The art was notoriously hard to obtain and wildly expensive. Stolen, certainly. Even as head of the guild, there was no way Jardem could afford such valuable luxuries. Yet theft for personal gain was against guild policy, but it was typical of him to thumb his nose at centuries of established practice.

Displaying a king's fortune worth of art on his wall was the peak of arrogance.

Unless they were all forgeries. But Mouse couldn't imagine Jardem settling for anything but the real thing.

The oversized desk was more suited for some high noble. Jardem had it covered with various appurtenances of business to give the look of a proper and professional workspace. Currently, he had his chair pushed back on the rear two legs, and one boot was propped against the desk's edge. As Mouse approached, Jardem's eyes shifted from the woman who sat on the edge of the desk opposite him. She glanced over her shoulder, following Jardem's gaze, her expression neutral.

Mouse didn't know her. She was comely and well-presented, dressed in breeches, a black tunic, and a sleeveless, leather doublet. All fine quality.

Client? Or something else? Mouse wondered.

Ludvic, second in command of the guild, leaned against the wall, looking bored. One arm rested over his midsection, the other propped up with his elbow on his wrist. He was picking at his fingernails with his teeth.

Ludvic was never a thief himself. Didn't have the talent for it—or the intellect—and for most of his tenure in the guild, he wasn't much more than a head-cracker. Despite being rather dim, loyalty to Jardem had cleared an unlikely path for him. He weaseled his way out of the organization's sewers and nabbed a healthy portion of the guild's power for himself. He outranked even Zel, which Mouse knew must needle her.

The unknown woman lifted her buttock from the desk's edge, her eyes still on Mouse. "We'll resume this later," she said with a lift of her brow. Her voice had a deep and sultry timbre.

She scooped up her cloak from the back of the chair, draped it over her forearm and glided past Mouse. She left the door open.

"You were told to wait," Jardem said as Mouse approached the desk to stand between the two chairs.

"I was bored," Mouse replied with a shrug. "Did I interrupt something important?"

Jardem lifted his eyes to the ceiling. "Politics," he said, his voice a low grumble. "This time, the interruption was welcome."

Pity, thought Mouse.

Jardem's gaze passed to Ludvic, and with a barely perceivable tilt of his head, he signaled his loyal dog to leave the room. "Check on progress," he said.

Ludvic grunted, pushed himself from the wall and followed the woman out the door. When the door closed, Jardem pulled his boot from the desk's edge and let the chair drop with a soft thump on the rug under him. He swept his ruddy hair from his eyes. "Well, you're here. Don't stand there like some lost mooncalf. Sit down."

Mouse moved closer but remained standing. Distractedly, he lifted a small wooden bust from the desk and turned it about. The male face of the statue had the sharp features and high cheekbones of a noble-born.

Jardem reached over and snatched it from his hand and set it out of his reach. He narrowed his dark gaze at him as he leaned forward. "Took you long enough. This better not mean you fucked it up."

Mouse felt ire zip up his back. When had he ever fucked up? He kept his jaw clenched as he reached under his jerkin and pulled out the sealed parchment. The edges were bent a bit at the edges from being in his boot, and the stiff parchment crinkled in his grip. The red wax seal glared up at him like a demon's eye. Whatever was in here meant trouble, the kind of trouble that brought the attention of rich and powerful people. He should be glad to be rid of it, but he hesitated.

"Come on, then, hand it over." Jardem mounted his elbow on the desk to prop up his hand. He snapped his fingers twice and flattened his palm.

Mouse reached over the desk and dropped the documents in the open hand.

With a smirk breaking the corner of his mouth, Jardem inspected the seal. "Yet unbroken."

"You thought I'd peek?"

"No. Expected the current holder would." Jardem's eyes lifted. "Were you tempted?"

"That wasn't the job."

"Ah, the famous Mouse integrity. The 'honor among thieves' drivel is an invention, you know. Honor doesn't drive this guild. Fear does."

Surev didn't think so. He believed honor and respect inspired loyalty. "It's why you sent me, is it not?"

It did not escape Mouse in that moment that the leader of the thieves' guild was advocating chaos and lawlessness within his own organization. Next, the noble-born would be volunteering a portion of their allowance to feed the street rabble.

Jardem grunted—it landed somewhere between a scoff and chuckle. "I sent you because I own you." He turned the sealed parchment about in his hand, inspecting it. "And if you don't return with the results I want, I ruin your life. You certain this is the right document?"

"The emblem in the wax—"

"Yes, yes. I know the king's seal when I see it. That doesn't mean it is the document we seek."

Mouse pulled in a calming breath through his nose. "It was precisely where the intelligence claimed it would be. Well protected. And…I was not the only one looking for it."

That made Jardem look up. "A problem I need to worry about?"

Mouse stared back at him with a level gaze.

Jardem grunted noncommittally. He lifted the lid to a box on his desk and dropped it inside.

"So, my payment?" Mouse pressed.

"I'll deal with it in the morning."

The leader of the Night Fingers (gods, how he hated that name) knew Mouse was watching where the document landed. Moments after Mouse stepped from the office, it would be placed in a secret location—Jardem was smart enough to not let Mouse know where.

"A valuable document. Clearly," Mouse said. "The client will give a hefty purse for it, certainly. I want to know what my share is."

"I'll tell you in the morning," Jardem repeated, sounding like a parent speaking to a badgering child. His patience was clearly thinning. "Or afternoon. Or whenever I fucking decide to. Must calculate your expenses first. Lodging, food, cost of your indenture…" He ended with a widening sneer.

"Jardem. You agreed. This time—"

"Did I? I don't recall. Were you not listening when I said I own you? You're beneath indentured, Mouse. A slave is even above you. You are…chattel. A tool to be used until dulled beyond worth. Then discarded."

His leer clung to Mouse like bad pipe smoke. Mouse could almost smell Jardem's putrid arrogance on him.

Mouse yanked his eyes from Jardem's face. It was the only way he could avoid the murderous rage threatening to shred him apart from the inside. Looking any longer at Jardem's smug expression, he'd be sparked into doing something singularly foolish. He knew what would happen if he ever attempted to harm Jardem.

Jardem had made that clear. He always had a contingency plan. Always.

He hadn't wrestled control of the guild by licking the dirt. He was wily and exceedingly well-informed. His network of spies and informants was unsurpassed. And now Mouse was his hostage.

"Off you pop, little mouse," Jardem said, reaching for a parchment and quill. "Now that you did a proper job of it, I have work to do." He dipped the quill into the ink well and lowered his head over the parchment.

Mouse was dismissed, already forgotten.

He left the office but intentionally left the door wide open. A few moments later, he heard Jardem shout. "Gods roast you, Mouse. Close my fucking door."

Mouse grinned, relishing in the petty pleasure of it. Jardem wouldn't forget this when he considered his cut for the job, but at the moment, Mouse didn't care. He pretended to not hear him bellow as he wove through the guild hall.

Chelka was gone, having fulfilled her duty. Off to find a quiet hole to sleep in, no doubt.

She was like him in so many ways. Like him, she was plucked from the gutter and dropped into this chaos, only he'd been older when his offer came. Like her, he was alone, with no hope of finding a way off the streets on his own.

And she had talent. She was clever. Quick.

Something washed over him, then. Like a shift in the wind that carried a memory. No…not a memory. More like the presence of a ghost, a lingering sense of some part of himself that once was.

The sensation was fleeting, but that single heartbeat brought him back to those days on the streets. Those days of endless uncertainty.

He had scraped by somehow. Even during those early days, when he knew nothing about life on the streets. He found food when he really needed it, though hunger was a frequent companion, and he had a dry place to sleep. He could nab enough coin to purchase some necessities. And, most importantly, he was adept at staying clear of the brutal and ugly muscle that owned the streets at night. Likely, it was that slick mastery of evasion that Surev saw as the potential in him. Days drifted by, the next one no different from the previous one, and eventually they added up into years.

He survived. It was what he did best.

Surev had groomed him to be a master thief, to take a leader's role in the upper ranks of the guild. When he died, all that ended.

Chelka had had no such mentor. Even in the beginning. She'd been left to fend for herself with no guidance and little training. And she didn't seem to have the drive to want more. She seemed content in the shadowy muck where she'd landed. Maybe she didn't have the will for it, the same hunger that Mouse had. Maybe, abandoned for so long, she could imagine no other path but the one she was on. Mouse did what he could to help her, but…

But he had his own concerns.

He never figured out how Jardem had learned of the murder. Didn't really matter—what was done was done. But it always dug into Mouse like a dagger's tip. Perhaps Mouse had said too much after too many ales at a tavern. Jardem had ears everywhere, always listening. But Jardem had learned of all of it—how Mouse had killed Marcan. An accident, but in the eyes of the king's law, that mattered little.

Marcan, the son of a Lord, had been visiting Mouse's village for the summer to visit with a distant relation and, as Marcan put it, be out of his father's hair for a time. Being boys of a similar age, the two of them bonded quickly despite their difference in status and spent each day together from first light until they were called back home when the fireflies arrived. On hot days, they'd swim naked in the river and sun themselves on the sandy shore of a secluded spot. It always felt deliciously wicked to be naked together. It was their secret.

On one such day, ribbing turned to playful shoving, which turned to wrestling about on the banks. They laughed and hurled insults at each other as they rolled about. Marcan pinned Mouse down, sitting on his chest, hands pressed against Mouse's elbows. In the back of his mind, Mouse knew he should be squirming to get free, but Marcan's bare ass was on his waist, his cock and balls resting on Mouse's belly, and Mouse didn't want this situation to change.

He looked up at Marcan's grinning face. Sunlight ignited his hair as it was tossed in the wind.

Mouse didn't know what came over him. He simply gave into an impulse—and lifted his torso and kissed Marcan on the lips.

It was foolishness on his part, Mouse knew now. Wishful thinking that Marcan shared the desires he'd held secretly just beneath the surface all summer.

Marcan's face went crimson with fury.

Mouse was never sure what precisely drove him to such rage. Was it simply that such a relationship was loathsome to him? He never signaled he was against such things. He doubted it was a novel idea. Even in his small village, Mouse had known such attractions existed. Marcan had been betrothed to a girl since the age of five, but he never spoke of her or showed the slightest interest. He was, however, fiercely intent on pleasing his father, who had arranged the future marriage. Or did Mouse overstep his place in the world and insult a noble-born with a base advance? Marcan was proud of his station, but he'd never once lorded it over Mouse or wedged his title between them.

Mouse would never have his answer.

Marcan attacked him. With Mouse still pinned on the ground beneath him, he unleashed a flurry of fists, striking him again and again—on the head, the body. Mouse tried to deflect the blows, but they came at him too fast and too hard. Marcan had always been the stronger of the two. In an act of desperation, Mouse brought up his leg and braced it against Marcan's chest. With a frantic thrust, Mouse kicked him off. Marcan flew backwards and was impaled on a protruding branch of a log.

It was an accident, of course. But that didn't matter. Marcan was noble-born. Mouse's intent didn't matter. And even at this young age, Mouse knew killing a noble-born meant the axe. Not just for him but, in accordance with the king's law, for his father as well. A deterrent to all who might consider murdering nobility.

But they would have to find him guilty first, and to do that, Mouse would have to be apprehended and tried. He had no choice but to flee—leave the quiet village and his idyllic life in order to protect his father.

That was how he'd ended up on the streets of Har Tesera.

Jardem had unearthed all of it. The murder. The name of his father. His village. And now, Mouse was Jardem's pet. If Mouse ever disobeyed him, all the information Jardem possessed—which included documents, apparently—would be turned over to the king's guard. It would mean not only Mouse's execution, but the execution of his father.

And Jardem had a safeguard, as well. Even his death would not release Mouse.

Mouse had done everything he could to hide his true identity, all to protect his father—he'd abandoned the only home he'd ever know, let his father believe he was dead—only to have the information fall into the hands of evil itself.

It was only an indenture, Jardem had sworn to him. He'd dangled the promise of freedom, vowed he could earn Jardem's silence in time. But Mouse knew better. They were lies designed to mollify him into compliance. Jardem would never willingly give up the power he held over him.

He was Jardem's puppet for as long as he remained master of the guild.

4

WITH THE document handed off, Mouse was finally free to wend his way back up to his nest in the rafters. He marched back through the corridors, his footfalls hard claps on the wood floor. Jardem, of course, had blackened his mood, robbed him of the thrill and satisfaction that came with a well-executed job. Without fail, every encounter with him was an infuriating reminder of his captivity. It always ended with loathing simmering in his gut, burning away at his hope that his standing might ever improve. Tonight was no different.

Even worse, actually, if that was possible.

The prospect of any sleep was now distant. His mind was grinding like a millstone, and his skin prickled with a craving for chaos. He needed to exorcize this dark energy somehow. Drink too much. Get into a tavern brawl. Strip down to nothing and scream in the middle of the street. Throw rocks at The Scourge.

His baser impulses urged him to leave the guild and hit the streets again, but he knew it'd be pointless. By this hour, tavern owners were shooing the last of their stumbling patrons toward the door. The optimal window for causing trouble had passed. The only city district with any remaining life would be The Stakes, and Mouse had no interest in engaging in that trap. His hunger was for something messy, not calculating. Not organized.

He stopped, sighed, and reversed course.

This late at night, the only real option to satisfy his petty need for rebellion was raiding the best food from the kitchens—quality foodstuffs intended for Jardem and the mysterious guests he entertained in his office, like a Lord receiving dignitaries. Mouse knew where they were stored, knew where to find the key, and knew how to avoid the traps.

Mouse also knew it infuriated Jardem, who threatened to castrate the perpetrator, which only added to the satisfaction. Rummaging through Jardem's private stash of overly expensive grub would have to be enough to scratch that itch for causing trouble. Besides…he *was* hungry. He had pilfered a few of the morsels served at Agata's party, but that was hours ago and not anything close to a meal. Most of it was inedible. Delicacies, they were called. Mouse called them vile.

Raiding the kitchen came with an unfortunate pitfall—it meant descending to the ground level of the guild.

Since Jardem had commandeered the room formally used for gambling, the brutes and heavies of the organization had adopted the main space on the ground floor. What had been the quiet common area for all members of the guild was now little more than a gambling den. It didn't matter what time of day or night Mouse braved the area, it was filled with the unwashed, flatulent rabble that did all the head smashing for the guild. And regardless of the hour, they were loud, drunk, and angry about how much of their coin they'd lost to dice.

The kitchens were located at the far end. There was no other way to reach them.

He avoided the lower level when he could. Most thieves of his caliber enjoyed some respect among the guild membership, but Jardem's contemptuous treatment of him was a public normalcy, so Mouse wasn't awarded any such courtesy.

The lower dregs of the organization saw it as license to take out their petty frustrations on someone that they thought had more than they deserved. Those in the upper tiers of the organization—the proper thieves and spies—were perceived as something akin to royalty, untouchable and granted everything, while those at the bottom fought for scraps. Making matters worse, the upper echelon was rarely around. The dormitories were beneath them. They earned enough to hold their own flats and only graced the guild with their presence to claim their cut, peruse the contract board, or train. It was no surprise to Mouse, who was listed among them in title but nothing else, became the focus of their jealousy and spite.

Mouse's size also invited attempted harassment and intimidation, and it didn't matter how many noses or fingers Mouse broke in defending himself in these endless attempts to punish him. The assaults kept coming.

He wasn't afraid of the lower levels. Not anymore. He was simply exhausted by it.

Soft footsteps approached from behind.

"I can hear you, Cassar," Mouse said.

"Gods. How do you always know it's me?" the voice behind him asked.

Mouse slowed his pace. "Your left boot. The heel's loose." It was complete fiction, and it made him grin thinking about Cassar spending hours inspecting the heel of his boot. He shook his head as Cassar stepped in next to him. "Your stealth still needs work." It was an annoying habit, trying to shadow him around the guild.

"I get by well enough," Cassar replied, his tone defensive. "Not everyone has your ear. You're not heading to bed, I see."

"How astute. What are you doing here, Cas?"

"I know how you get after your meetings with our beloved guild master. Making sure you aren't about to do something singularly stupid.”

“I’m fine,” Mouse lied.

He let his eyes pass over him a moment as Cassar kept pace with him. He was younger, sixteen perhaps, but taller by a hand’s width. Thin as a reed, it was as if his body only knew one direction to grow. His skin was pale as birchbark, and his long white-blonde hair was a flood of soft waves that landed on his shoulders. His face was thin and delicate.

His gentile ways and soft features made the brutes of the organization wary and uncomfortable. That, and everyone suspected he was a guild spy. Which he was, of course. He and Jardem were the only ones who knew of his uncanny ability, but something about him put everyone off. Perhaps they were anxious of revealing their own secrets to him. As it stood, Mouse was the only one who would talk to him. The two pariahs among the membership had formed an uncommon bond.

Cassar lowered his voice and leaned closer as they walked. “I worry that one of these days, Quickblade is going to have had enough of your shit.”

Mouse stopped mid-step and faced him.

“Wait. Were you listening?”

Cassar closed his eyes and sighed. “Not through you. I know how ratty you get about it.”

“Because I don’t like you in my head without my knowing.”

“I’m aware,” Cas replied dryly.

“How do I know you aren’t scrying in my head when I’m taking a shit or…or taking care of some, you know, private business?”

“First of all…ew. I’m not depraved like you are—.”

“And how do I know you’re not sifting through my thoughts or my memories?”

“Because it doesn’t work that way.” Cas lifted his eyes. “And even if I could, I’d not expose myself to that nightmarish prospect anyway—.”

"Hold on." Realization was setting in. If not him…He looked around the corridor and dropped his voice. "You scried through *Jardem*?"

"I didn't have much of a choice after Ludvic was dismissed, did I?"

"That was bold."

Cas shrugged noncommittally. "Like you said, no one can tell."

Mouse grunted and started walking again. He wondered at times if Cas wasn't being completely honest with him. He could typically sense when someone was lying. Cas was more difficult to read.

"So, you heard it all?"

Cas didn't reply as he kept pace with Mouse. That was a yes, then.

The muscles of Mouse's jaw clenched. He growled through his teeth. "Colossal fucker, that one. You must understand why I detest him. And why I can do nothing about it." He couldn't even wish him dead—because that meant disaster. Cas never hinted he knew what Jardem had over him. And he never asked.

"Doesn't help when you provoke him like you do."

Mouse scoffed. He wasn't wrong. "Well, I'm not going to roll over and just let him fuck my ass dry, if that's what you're suggesting," he grumbled.

Cas studied Mouse's eyes a moment before looking away. "So how to do you intend to get even with him tonight?"

Mouse glanced at him with narrow eyes. It was disturbing how well he knew him sometimes. "Raiding his private stores, if you must know."

"He'll know it was you."

"I hope he does," Mouse answered defiantly. "Feel free to bugger off now."

Cassar sighed but didn't take the cue to leave him be. "Of course, make him want to punish you further. Great plan."

Mouse scoffed but didn't answer.

A bit of the edge around Cas's tone softened. "Maybe if you were more…nuanced with him. Instead of taunting him, like when you call him by his name in front of others—."

"Because it's his fucking name. I won't call him Quickblade, or Lord Night, or Super Spy, or whatever new horseshit name he dreamed up for himself."

"This is what I'm talking about. It only drives him to kick you back down. I worry one day—"

"Stop wasting your energy fretting about me, Cas. I don't."

"This storm that engulfs you will spark his wrath one day."

Mouse glanced his direction with a tight gaze. "More wisdom gleaned from your witch eye." It was a targeted attack intended to sting. Cas hated when Mouse called it that, but his prodding and unsolicited involvement in his business made Mouse's skin twitch with growing irritation. He wanted to be left alone.

Cassar frowned. "No. Anyone that spends half a day with you can see it."

Mouse grunted low in his throat. He needed to change the subject. "Something's off about this last job. I can't put my finger on it, but Jardem was…edgy. More prickly than normal."

"That was your own doing."

"No, he had to have it straight away. Even sent Zel after me. Couldn't wait until tomorrow."

Mouse clocked Cassar's subtle reaction. Cas wasn't aware of that, and that detail surprised him.

"And I sensed something when I handed the document over. Once he had it in his hand, he visibly relaxed. He tried to hide it, but I could tell. What's the gossip about it around the guild?"

Cassar's expression closed up like a shame flower when someone gets too close to it, and he took a new interest in his feet.

"Oh, come on, Cas. Fuck, I know you scry on half the guild and report—"

Cassar made a quick, nervous look around to see if anyone was in hearing range. "Gods, Mouse. You trying to get me killed?"

"No one heard—"

Cassar scowled. "Fuck, you're insufferable in this mood. Not sure why I bother…."

"Me either," Mouse clapped back.

"Just keep your voice down."

"How do you do it?" Mouse shook his head. "How can you stomach feeding him that information? About members of the guild?"

Cassar made a sad chuckle. "I have a choice?"

"You don't have to tell him everything."

"Who says I do?"

Mouse wanted to laugh but held back. He wasn't convinced Cassar had the spine for lying or, even, omitting the truth. "Whatever. So, spill it. What's being said?"

"This will not improve your mood."

"What does?"

"Fair." Cassar sighed and ran fingers through the white waves of his hair and took in a long, defeated breath. "Few were happy it landed on you."

Zel had made that bit clear enough.

Cassar continued, "The client is said to award a fine prize for the retrieval." Typical professional jealousy. Mouse knew he'd see little of this boon. If any. It would all end up in Jardem's greasy hands and in his own fattening coffers. "Fewer still thought you'd succeed. None are happy you did."

The confidence in him was heartwarming. "What is it? Anyone know?"

"You're the only one who's had access to the thing. If anyone would know, it's you."

Mouse glared from the corner of his eyes. "That seal was royal, Cas. Issued from the king himself, I think. Despite your low opinion of me, I'm not daft. A broken seal might have affected its payout, and I wasn't going to hand Jardem yet another excuse to not pay my share." Not that it mattered, really. Jardem had enough reasons stored up.

The two of them reached the stairs heading down to the main floor of the guild. Mouse started down the rickety steps, which groaned and swayed as he descended. It was only a matter of time before the entire structure collapsed. No measures would be taken to repair it until it did. Jardem wouldn't spend a single crown to fix it beforehand.

Below them, he could hear some of the bruisers arguing drunkenly about something, probably someone cheating at cards and getting caught, but at this hour, most of the regulars had likely passed out. A quick slip past them into the kitchens should be easy enough. Grab a jug of hard spirits, a plate of some stewed meats and bread, then off to his bed.

The rank blend of sweat, grease, and piss rose to meet them and stung the insides of the nostrils. One more reason to escape this cesspool as quickly as possible.

Cassar kept pace with Mouse, one step behind. "No one knows what the document is. Or at least they're not saying." At the landing halfway down, Cassar grabbed Mouse's arm and pulled him to a stop. He dropped his voice to a whisper. "I admit, that's the odd bit. No chatter. None. Plenty of grumbling about you—"

"That's nothing unusual."

"—but no speculation about the document itself. Not even from Zel or Ludvic."

Mouse frowned. He stood with one foot on the next step, one foot on the landing, a hand still on the railing. A lantern hung from an iron hook nailed into a post, illuminating their position. Anyone below could easily spot them. The exposure made him uneasy.

Mouse bit his lower lip in thought. Most commissions were to steal objects of some import. Jewels. Art. Weapons. The target might be valuable on the dark market or simply a family heirloom whose ownership was in dispute. It might even be an item of power, crafted by mages and given peculiar properties. Magecraft unsettled him. He knew little about it and stayed well clear of it.

But a mysterious document was an unusual commission. It would surely drum up interest and plenty of curiosity. The guild should be buzzing about it.

"Orders from the top to not discuss it," he said quietly.

"Sounds likely," Cassar replied.

"That *is* curious." Mouse resumed his trek down the stairs and out of the light.

The ground floor of the former warehouse was filled with a hodge-podge of furniture. Tables for eating—now annexed for gambling—a dusty old settee, and various workbenches for attending to weapons, repairing equipment and such. A few lamps still burned. The rest had run out of fuel.

A table toward the back was occupied by four brutes. Whatever they were arguing about earlier had apparently been settled. They were all friends again and back to slapping cards on the table between them. The rest of the space was quiet.

He moved to the shadows along the wall and crossed the chamber.

Something caught his eye. He stopped again. "Also, curious…" he whispered under his breath.

Cassar, a step behind him, turned his gaze to where Mouse's eyes pointed.

Across the open chamber, a bruiser sat alone. He was seated on a stool, back against the wall. His head was lobbed to one side, his mouth hanging open like a snoring fish. Asleep. His position next to a door was intriguing in and of itself. The sword at his belt made it noteworthy.

Bad form in the common area. Standard rule: unless being tended to at the workbenches, weapons were stored away in private lockers. Gambling, drinking, and blades were a volatile combination.

But not this brute. Stationed next to a random door.

"Cas, where does that door lead?" He didn't remember the door, but that didn't mean anything. He didn't spend enough time down here to be all that familiar with the lay of the land.

Cassar's face crunched in thought. "Cellars, I think?"

There were cellars under the guild? How did he not know that? "Have you ever known Jardem to post a guard anywhere in the guild? He doesn't even keep one outside his office."

Cassar narrowed his eyes at the grunt stationed there. Then, his eyes shifted to take in Mouse again. "Whatever you're thinking, it's a terrible idea."

"All my ideas are terrible. If they were someone else's."

Cassar shook his head. "Your arrogance, sometimes." He narrowed his look at Mouse. "You think this has something to do with the document you pinched." It was more an accusation than a question. "Don't you?"

"Stay out of my head."

"No one needs to scry that to see that. It's on full display all over your face."

"Seems a bit too coincidental. Strange guard outside a cellar door on the same night I hand it over to Jardem?"

Cassar rolled his eyes. "And what if it does have something to do with it? That isn't our concern. Surely Quick—"

"Don't say it," Mouse cut in with a pointed finger.

Cassar let out a long sigh. "Surely *he* has a good reason, and he doesn't need to clear it with *you*."

"It's highly unorthodox," Mouse said as he tugged on a tuft of incomplete beard on his chin. "And insulting. It's against the code of the guild. A stationed guard? Here? That denotes distrust, Cas. Distrust for his fellow members of the guild—."

"Gods, sanctimonious is not your color."

"You don't find this at all peculiar and unsettling, Cas?" Mouse pressed. "There's an *armed guard* stationed in our guild!"

Cas pursed his lips at the snoring lump. "'Guard' seems a stretch. But, to your point…you're not entirely wrong."

"Which is your way of saying I'm right. Something's foul. I told you from the start I didn't like the smell of this."

"If you're caught—"

Mouse closed his eyes and released an exhausted sigh. "Cas, I just infiltrated the highly secured manor of a very rich merchant and stole a document of extreme value right out from under him without being detected," Mouse replied sourly. "I think I can manage slipping past one sleeping thug doused in ale. I'll be in and out in without a soul knowing."

Cassar threw up his hands. "Well, I'll have no part of this."

Mouse grabbed his wrist. "Oh no, you're going to keep watch for me."

Cassar tugged his arm free, his brow tight. "Absolutely not."

But, Mouse noted, he stayed where he was. If he was fully against the idea, he'd be walking away already. "Payment for eavesdropping on my conversation with Jardem. I still haven't forgiven you for that." He lifted one brow. Mouse wasn't above petty manipulation to get his way. "Come now. You're curious too. I can see it in your eyes."

"If he finds out I was involved—"

"How would he?" Mouse laughed. "Literally no one else in the guild, maybe even the city, can do what you can do. If you're asked, say you were scrying on the idiots fighting over the game."

Cassar grunted, his lips pouty. "He can tell when I'm lying."

"Now you're being paranoid," Mouse replied. But he was probably right.

"The cellar would be cut from solid rock. Not sure I can penetrate that."

"Quit looking for excuses. You're helping me and that's

final." He made a quick scan of the room, making sure no one had noticed his presence yet. "Simply tip me off if someone's coming." Before Cassar could protest further, he crossed the open guild hall toward the sleeping guard and the door.

5

THE KITCHEN raid would have to wait.

He circled around and kept to the thicker shadows, more out of habit than concern of being noticed. The brutes at the far end of the common area were focused on their game, and drink had undoubtedly dulled them into being barely sentient.

He edged himself closer to this mysterious door he'd never noticed before now. The irony, of course, was he would have continued to overlook the damned thing had Jardem not posted this buffoon out in front of it. But the damage was done. It was something irresistible now. Like a siren's call, it beckoned to him. Mouse wouldn't sleep a wink if he didn't know what was being protected behind it.

Why, he wondered absently as he rested a shoulder on the wall to observe, *were these mystical creatures that lured men to their deaths always female?* He, frankly, wouldn't be tempted in the least if he was called by one to follow her and her fishy body into the depths of the sea. Now were it a man…well, the story might end differently. But he considered himself more selective than that, frankly. He liked men with all their bits. And legs. He did enjoy a strong set of legs.

Did sirens come in a male form? Curious question, but it didn't matter right now, he supposed. He brought himself back to the task at hand and would contemplate that mystery later.

He pretended to bite at his nails while he gauged the room. The card game continued unabated. The thug at the door continued to snore, drooling into his beard, and appeared ready to fall from the stool and onto the floor at any moment. Cassar, elbows on the railing, continued to leer at him from the landing.

Mouse stepped closer, putting his weight on his toes.

In front of the door and close enough to slap the snoozing guard, he stood with his hands on his hips and shook his head at the brute. Pathetic. He was tempted to kick his boot a little to see what it would take to get him to stir him awake. Maybe after his innocent perusal of the cellar he'd do him the courtesy before Jardem or Ludvic discovered him like this.

He rested his thumb on the door's latch and pushed down. It depressed with a clack—he could both hear and feel the lever arm lift on the opposite side. The door wasn't locked. In a building full of thieves, that would be pointless.

Normally, he'd have a tiny flask of oil with him to address the hinges. They surely required a well-needed dousing of lubrication, but the job tonight didn't necessitate his typical thieving kit, and those supplies were back in his hideaway in the rafters, anyway. He had no choice but to risk it.

He pushed, keeping his eye on Snoozy. The door swung inward, releasing a high-pitched squeal, like a rat caught in the jaws of a cat.

The guard grunted and wiped at his slobbery face with the back of his hand but otherwise didn't budge. No surprise, really. Bashing heads all day was grueling work. He needed the sleep. Poor baby.

Mouse stepped into the dark corridor and eased the door closed, holding up the latch arm until the door was in place against the jamb again. Then he lowered the arm into the groove of the receiver.

Well…that was easy.

He waited, listening. More out of habit than any real concern. It would likely take a full assault on the guild to stir that idiot awake. Mouse could hear his pig-like snorts through the door. Jardem should really vet his shady coconspirators better.

Mouse's heart thumped with the thrill of defiance. This was certainly better than stealing some fancy foods that he would likely throw out the window, anyway.

A part of him itched to be caught down here. He'd plead ignorance, of course—how was he supposed to know it was off limits? He wondered what Jardem would do when he learned that Mouse knew whatever secret he kept down here. Jardem would punish him for sure. But how?

How far was he willing to go to keep this secret?

Mouse inhaled slowly, breathing deeply in the dark. It was thick and sticky, filling his head with the smell of mold and decay. Strange, this little hole had eluded him—though, in fairness, he avoided the turmoil of the ground floor whenever he could.

Hand to the rough wall, he shuffled blindly into the corridor. In short order, the floor disappeared under his foot. Confident, he lowered his foot down. It landed after a short distance with a crunch of loose stone under his boot. A step. It was a stairwell heading down.

Cassar was right. A cellar under the warehouse.

And down he went. He followed the spinning passage like he was descending the thread of a screw. Soon, a faint light dusted the wall ahead.

He slowed and silenced the sound of his boots on the stone. Nearing where the stairwell ended at a corridor, he put his back to the wall and held his breath, listening. Voices resonated off the stone. Male voices. He couldn't discern the words, but it was a relaxed conversation. Two men, maybe three.

He frowned. No, one voice seemed elevated, more agitated.

A single tallow candle, tucked in a carved-out nook in the wall, cast a frail and flickering light across the grim corridor. It was clear this cellar had been used for cool storage back when this was a warehouse. The space was as primitive and unfinished as possible. The walls were rough, and black beams shored up the length of the ceiling.

Again, Cassar had been right; the cellar was cut from solid rock, like a mining tunnel. Mouse suspected that maybe Cassar knew even more than he had revealed. What else had he kept from him? And was Cassar's concern was justified. Might his witch eye not be able to reach him down here?

It didn't matter, at any rate, he told himself. He'd already committed.

Dark recesses on either side of the corridor ahead told of doorways to darkened rooms, but at the far end, a steadier, warmer light splashed from an opening onto the floor. The voices emanated came from there.

At a crouch, he slipped into the corridor and approached the lit doorway. Shoulder to the wall, he eased his head around the jamb, made a quick inventory of the room, and pulled back again.

From side wall to side wall, the room was divided in two by a row of metal bars, set vertically from floor to ceiling. The black metal was unmarred. It reflected the lamp light without signs of rust or age. This had been constructed recently. The entire back half of the room had been converted into a cell. A simple gate framed in iron was at one end. Mouse noted the heavy chain and lock that kept it secure. Two large men were in the room on Mouse's side of the bars, silhouetted by the lantern on the floor by their feet. Their backs were to the door.

A cell? Here in the guild? Mouse's insides constricted. The guild did not take prisoners.

Mouse hadn't spotted anyone in the cage, but no one guarded an empty cage. Plus, he'd heard more voices.

Whoever was in there was against the far wall, hidden in shadow.

Mouse risked another glance.

Two brutish types had their heads close together, chatting quietly with each other. Mouse could make out only fragments of the exchange, but it was enough to tease out the gist of it. The prisoner had refused to answer any more of their questions. And like all tormenters drunk on their power, the brutes were simply amused by the emphatic stance. With their attention on the cell, Mouse took measure of the room.

Movement from inside the cell offered a brief glimpse of the figure within. By the size, Mouse assumed male. He wore something pale blue or green.

Not a typical color scheme of those in his business. This was not someone from the guild, kept here for punishment.

Anger smoldered in Mouse's gut. Was this a new policy? Was kidnapping now part of the Night Fingers' menu of services? It shouldn't surprise Mouse that Jardem would consider expanding the guild's repertoire but ransoming off prisoners wasn't sanctioned. This cell was built in secret, so that told Mouse that Jardem knew that.

"Contact me if he decides to sing again," one brute said as he stepped away. He picked up one of the two lanterns on the floor and turned for the door.

Mouse groaned inwardly. Ludvic. Of course. Jardem's faithful dog didn't act without permission. So…this *was* guild business, after all.

Mouse ducked out of his line of sight just in time and sprang into the dark room across the corridor. The sickly sweet smell of rotting flesh was pungent here. Mouse swallowed down the surge of bile that chewed at the back of his throat. Something dead was in the room. He heard scurrying in the dark behind him. Rats, feeding on whatever it was.

Ludvic stomped heavily out of the room, down the corridor and up the stairs. Mouse waited for the lantern light to shrink to nothing in the stairwell, then he eased out of the dark room, breathing through his mouth. He could taste death on his tongue.

Mouse considered leaving, but he needed to know who the prisoner was first.

Based on the glimpse he'd caught of his clothing, Mouse guessed rich merchant or noble-born—yet the latter seemed too bold, even for Jardem. Noble-borns were highly protected under the king's law. Merchants less so, but they had their own way of inflicting justice on those that wronged them. Either way, it was a dangerous game Jardem played. What was he up to?

Again, crouched in the corridor, Mouse spied into the room. The remaining thug squatted onto a low stool, eating a lump of hard bread and cheese. Mouse wanted to gag. *How could anyone think about eating in this stinking pit?* The taste of decay was still on his tongue. He'd need a large pint of ale to wash out his mouth the minute he left here.

The lantern light reached the brute's face when he sat down. Mouse recognized him. This wasn't the usual sewage rat that polluted the lower level of the guild, one that spent his time guzzling down cheap ale and tossing dice whenever they weren't out bashing skulls. No, this one had a polish about him. He carried the scent of competence with him.

One of Jardem's personal stock. A former city guardsman, once in the Duke's employ, likely brought low by some scandal or misconduct. Jardem was quick to scoop up these fallen servants to the crown. There was always room for such offenders in the city's underground—if they were willing to divorce themselves from any moral code and virtue. Not that the city guard was flush with scruples, anyway. He was likely happier here. Less wear and tear on the boots, and the pay was better than what the duke handed out.

His sight having accustomed to the dark, Mouse could now make out the general shape of the prisoner at the back of the cell. He was sprawled out on a cot. With the lantern on the floor, the light didn't reach his face.

A sudden buzzing behind his eyes snapped him from his scan a moment before a distorted image commandeered his sight. It was as if he'd been transported back to the common area of the guild.

Cassar.

His unique talents could go both ways. He could scry and experience a scene through someone else's senses, or he could project what he witnessed into the mind of another. From the angle, Mouse knew Cassar was still on the landing of the staircase where he'd left him.

Jardem and Ludvic conversed outside the cellar door. The formally sleeping guard massaged his jaw. Someone had punched him awake.

Jardem took the lantern Ludvic still carried. Even at this distance across the dark common area, Mouse could tell Jardem wasn't happy. He pushed through the door and headed into the stairwell.

Jardem was coming down.

Shit! Mouse tensed involuntarily. Thankfully, Cas had managed to give him a modicum of warning.

Regret now weaseled into his gut. Perhaps this was a horrible idea, after all. He would never admit it to Cassar, of course. Remaining undetected from Ludvic was easy enough, but Jardem was a different story. The fucker was crafty and always alert. He didn't get where he was by licking the dirt.

But the larger problem now was that the dolt stationed above would be wide awake on his duty outside the door. Or Jardem would replace him with someone more competent altogether. Getting out undetected was going to be very tricky.

He darted back into the putrid smelling room. It was vile, but it still gave him some access to what was happening in the room with the cage. The rats squeaked their displeasure at their meal being interrupted.

The sound of confident footfalls on the stone floor echoed through the corridor. Cas's warning had come just in time.

Jardem marched through the corridor with the poise of a king and entered the prison chamber. "Well now. Comfortable?" His voice had that irritating lilt of self-importance and conceit that Mouse loathed.

"You know the answer to that," said the voice in the back of the cage.

It was husky and deep. On the surface, the self-assuredness matched Jardem's. The privileged always had a way of sounding convinced of their own importance. But Mouse could hear something lingering beneath it. Fear perhaps. Or uncertainty. But not weakness.

"You've ensured my comfort is at a minimum," the prisoner added. The rich tone reverberated off the stone like the dulcet hum of a prayer horn.

Mouse couldn't help himself. He had to see who owned such a voice.

He slunk further into the corridor again and craned his neck to gain a peek. Jardem was at the bars, his back to the door. The guard on the stool remained focused on his bread and cheese, looking bored.

Mouse didn't need to see Jardem's face to know the fucker was grinning like a drunken idiot.

He risked moving farther. If he made a noise, he'd be in plain view of the guard.

"What have you done with…with…" the prisoner trailed off.

"How touching," Jardem replied after a moment. "You don't even remember his name, do you? Well, rest assured, your hired man is safe. He exhibited as much loyalty to you as you apparently have for him."

"Where is he?"

"We set him free," Jardem said with a lift of his palms. "That's how it works. He gave me the information I asked for, and he was released."

Mouse looked back over his shoulder at the room. Well, that explained the smell. He was freed, alright. Freed from the toils of this world and now safely in the next.

"I hope you didn't spend much on him," Jardem continued. "I recommend, in the future, you spend your coin more wisely. Good protection doesn't come cheap, and you were absurdly easy to capture."

The prisoner remained quiet.

Jardem stepped closer to the bars of the cage. "Now, Ludvic tells me you are still stubbornly refusing to talk to us."

Jardem waited, but the prisoner still said nothing.

"You disappoint me," Jardem purred. "I was hoping that you'd had a change of heart since our last discussion."

"Sorry to ruin your day," said the prisoner from the shadows.

Jardem clicked his tongue. "Unfortunate. It will be so much easier on you if you just tell us."

"Why would I do that?"

"Because I would let you live. Other players in this game will not think twice about slitting your throat."

"Don't insult me with this act of being reasonable. I'm well versed in the games of your kind." The amalgam of both contempt and confidence in the man's voice made Mouse's skin tingle with excitement. He was an immediate enthusiast of anyone that spoke to Jardem like that.

"I doubt that," said Jardem. "You have no idea what I'm capable of."

The prisoner scoffed. "You think you're the first villain I've encountered?"

"Villain," Jardem repeated with a cold chuckle. "My client is highly motivated. Willing to pay quite a hefty sum for results. Which means I'm willing to go as far as necessary to achieve those results."

"And what makes you think I know anything?"

Jardem chuckled. "Because my informants believe that you know more than you're saying. Despite your proclamations to the contrary. And I trust *them*." He pulled out the document from his belt and turned it about in the air. "Look what we've acquired tonight."

The figure moved out of the shadow into the light of the lantern and Jardem's flickering torch. He glided up to bars of his cage.

The man was about the same age as Mouse. Twenty perhaps, or a year or two older. The fine doublet of pale green and gold buttons was filled out most agreeably. Not the form Mouse expected from one of the entitled classes. The body looked like it belonged more to a dockworker. His hair was black as the shadow, and his blue eyes caught the torchlight and sparkled like gemstones.

Mouse forgot himself. He could only stare in wonder. The face was so finely sculpted it belonged on a statue. The solid jawline, the thoughtful brow, the fullness of his lips—all accentuated by the warmth of the torchlight, which made his skin glow like bronze.

The man gripped the bars of the cage. "Worthless…as is."

"We're aware." Jardem tucked it back into his belt. "But it is only a matter of time before we find it, Master Tenric."

Master. Not Lord. Merchant class, then. By the quality of dress, he was from a well-established family.

Tenric's eyes shifted. Only briefly—but his gaze turned directly to Mouse. He saw him skulking behind his captors. The eyes flickered a moment in confusion, then returned to Jardem.

"You're no different from them, you know," Tenric said.

Jardem seemed confused. "From whom, Master Tenric?"

"Your client. Whoever's paying you. They're thugs with fine jewelry. Petty thieves with fat bellies. Feeding on the weak and always lusting for more power. Just like you."

Jardem laughed. It had a cutting edge. "How exciting to meet someone so quick to know my measure."

Tenric scoffed. "You want to know what I think? You have no intention of passing that document over to your client.

You want it for yourself."

Jardem was silent a moment. "And can you imagine the possibilities, then? What a scandal that would wreak, yes?"

Not a denial, Mouse noted.

Tenric's expression changed, as if he was suddenly exhausted. "What if I'm telling the truth?" He let go of the bar and stepped away. "What if I don't know where it is?"

"Then that would be most unfortunate for you." Jardem chuckled. "It's late, Master Tenric. And I tire of this. I'll give you one more day to consider my offer. It is more than generous. Your life for the location. Simple as that." He paused, waiting to see if Tenric replied. When none came, he began to turn. "One day."

Mouse's stomach leapt to his throat. He was out in the open, completely exposed. He hadn't expected the conversation to end so abruptly.

"How do I know you're telling the truth about any of this?" Tenric spat out. His eyes made a barely perceivable shift from Jardem to Mouse. "That I can trust you."

Jardem stopped and turned back to face Tenric. "Do you have a choice but to trust me?" He attempted to affect a compassionate tone, one intended to show he cared, but it reeked of trying too hard. "You have an opportunity to salvage some of your life here. Perhaps not the one that you'd hoped to gain. But that life is reserved for others more deserving than you."

Mouse forced himself out of his momentarily stunned state. Had this rich fop snagged Jardem's attention so Mouse could duck back into hiding?

He eased back across the corridor as Tenric leaned his face against the bars and stared fearlessly back at Jardem. "Honestly, I don't care if it ever comes into my possession. But I will stop at nothing to ensure it never finds its way into your soiled hands."

Mouse couldn't pull himself away entirely. He watched as the two men stared each other down through the bars. The guard looked up finally from his bread and cheese. His body tensed, expecting something to happen. Silence followed. Mouse could hear the slow intentional drawing of a long breath, the sound Jardem made when someone dared cross him. His exhale came out as a low laugh deep in his throat as he reached a hand between the bars and traced a knuckle down the side of Tenric's cheek. "We'll see about that."

Mouse slipped into the darkness as Jardem spun on his heel.

Jardem departed, lantern swinging cheerily in his hand, leaving the sole guard behind chewing on his bread. Mouse peered around the edge again.

Now what?

He'd gained the information he sought, but it came at a price. He couldn't ignore the unfortunate fact that the guard would now be wide awake. He wouldn't dare nod off again, or he'd be flogged and thrown out on his ear, for sure. Mouse was well and truly trapped.

He padded up the circular stairs, rejecting each idea that came to mind as to how he might escape the room unseen. Every option would end with his being spotted. There was no way to escape the cellar unseen.

He slowed as he neared the top and took in long breaths. He had no choice but to step out and try to lie himself out of it. Sent to deliver a meal. Ordered to give Ludvic a message. These lies might work now, get him out in the short run—but it would reach Jardem's ears, eventually.

Then he would pay.

While he stood in the dark, drumming his fingers on the rough wall, a new image overtook his vision. The guard outside the door was awake—but had a look of panic face. His back was straight, and his head darted about. Up, down, side to side. He waved a frantic hand in front of his face. Then he bolted to his feet and waved his hands about until he reached the wall.

Cassar had blinded him.

Mouse's vision went black also as his own sight returned in the lightless corridor. He chuckled to himself as he blindly felt for the latch. Crafty fucker. It wasn't something he knew Cas could do—he'd inquire on this little trick later.

He needed to act before the dolt started screaming in his panic. Less concerned about making noise at this point, Mouse tugged open the door and slipped out in a crouch. The guard, gasping in heavy breaths, fumbled about against the wall.

When Mouse was a safe distance away, Cas released him. The guard froze mid-flailing and looked about, confused. His chest heaved. Slowly, he drifted back to his post in front of the door, righted his overturned stool, and flopped back onto it. The entire while, he searched around him to see if anyone in the room had noticed.

"You're an idiot!" Cassar said as Mouse climbed the stairs to rejoin him.

"What?" Mouse exclaimed, feigning a perplexed look.

"Once again, you're lucky I didn't abandon you."

"*Would* you really abandon the only one in the guild that doesn't find you odd and disconcerting?" He said it with a smirk but knew the barb would sting. He appreciated Cas's assistance, but he wasn't about to listen to any of his sanctimonious rot.

Cassar's face flushed. "One day you may test that notion one too many times."

Mouse scoffed. "Nonsense."

Cassar scowled and leaned his elbows on the railing, looking out over the common area. One of the card players had passed out at the table. The other three slid his stack of coin away from him and continued to play, betting with his coin. "And was this reckless endeavor worth it?"

Mouse raised an eyebrow at him. "You weren't watching?"

"Watch the door *and* you at the same time? If I had kept my eye on you, I wouldn't have spotted Quickblade—"

"Gods burn me!" Mouse said, throwing his head back

"—coming to the door. Though the gods know, you need someone watching you at all hours."

Mouse grunted. "I manage just fine, thank you."

Cassar pulled a face. "So out with it. What is so important down there that it requires a guard?"

"So, you *are* curious?"

Cassar grunted.

Mouse put his elbow on the stair's railing and leaned in. "A prisoner."

"A prisoner," Cas repeated, sounding dubious.

"In a cage."

Cassar's eyes narrowed. "We have a cage?"

"Apparently, we do now," Mouse replied dryly.

"That seems counter to our purpose here," Cassar said with a frown.

The implications of this news were obviously not lost on him, either. The guild functioned within a very narrow window of lawful tolerance. Thievery, in the eyes of the dukedom, or even the king's guard, was often dismissed as petty and unimportant. Investigating some rich widow's lost bauble was beneath their interest. If something was burgled, the blame typically went to the victim for being careless. As long as the guild didn't interfere in city business, it was largely overlooked as a nuisance, sort of on the same level as the city's rat population.

Wealthy nobles or merchants getting pinched was also a chance for lowly servants in the king's livery to get in a chuckle at their plight. Everyone enjoyed witnessing the well-heeled take a hit.

But other crimes were less tolerated and harder to overlook. Crimes that upset the nature and function of things in the city tended to garner more attention.

"I agree," Mouse replied.

Cassar turned inward. For a moment Mouse thought he might be trying to scry into the cellar, but he couldn't unless he knew specifically who was down there.

"What does this mean, Mouse?"

Mouse stepped closer. "It means I think I found a way to bring down Jardem and break free of this fucking guild."

6

CASSAR REFUSED to look at him. Elbows on the railing, he continued to stare out over the shadowy common area.

"You have any idea how insane that sounds, Mouse?"

Mouse looked down at his feet. "I can't stay here, Cas. You know that. Not like this. This is my oppor—"

"It's going to get you killed."

Mouse took in a long breath and let it out slowly. "Remember when Surev was alive?"

Cassar grunted in a way that said the question was absurd. He'd known Surev longer than Mouse had.

"He had a way about him." Mouse's voice dropped to a soft hum as he reminisced. "You felt like you were part of something. Like you belonged. He made you feel—"

"Like you were part of his family," Cas answered for him.

Mouse nodded. He didn't remember much of being in a family anymore. It was just sort of a vague, warm feeling he couldn't pin down. But the time in the guild when Surev was alive was the closest he'd come to having that feeling again.

"Everyone worshipped Surev, yes," Cas said. "But he

was old, Mouse. And things change."

"Surev believed in me," Mouse said in little more than a whisper.

Still looking out over the common room, Cassar rested his head against the stair's support post. "I remember," he said with a laugh. "I was still pretty little when you were brought in. I was just figuring out what I could do. I watched you through Surev."

Mouse couldn't hide his shock. "So…a long history of cheek."

Cas glanced over at him. Even in the dim light, Mouse could see the warm smile break the corners of his mouth. "It wasn't like that. Surev encouraged it. He said he wanted me to know how the guild was run." Cas looked away again. "You were so…angry."

"Living on the streets can do that," Mouse said. He diverted his eyes to the floor.

"And Surev was so patient." The memory softened Cassar. "He knew exactly how to earn your trust. And he always knew what you'd become."

"But now there's Jardem," Mouse said. He dropped down and seated himself on the first step off the landing, his back to Cas. "Now I'm nothing more than a dog he can kick…and send to fetch things. I am one of the best here, but I get no recognition or respect. From anyone."

"That's not true, Mouse," Cas said softly. There was little strength in the words, as if he struggled to believe them himself. "Everyone knows how good you are."

Mouse scoffed, and a thick silence descended between them.

"You…you can't defeat him," Cas said. "He's too smart. Too…*informed*."

And Cas played his role in that. Keeping him informed. Had Cas given information to Jardem about him? His gut told him he wouldn't, nothing important anyway—Cas had to keep himself safe, too. But the question always nagged at him.

Mouse heard Cas sigh.

"Say what you will about Quickblade—"

"Fuck, stop calling him that."

"—but he knows what he's doing."

Mouse wasn't in the mood for Cassar's spineless logic and reason. He was always too cautious. Too careful. The result of always sitting safely in the shadows, watching events from afar. He assumed no threat. If he'd spent any time in the middle of the danger, like Mouse did every day, he'd learn about the necessity of taking risks.

The opportunity was there. Mouse was going to take it. "Who is the client that wanted the document?"

"I don't know," Cas protested. His voice sounded uneasy.

Mouse leapt to his feet again and spun on him. "Stop trying to protect me, Cas!"

"I don't know!" he repeated, louder this time.

Mouse wasn't sure he believed him. He fell silent as he chewed his lower lip. Something ate at him, but he couldn't tease it out from where it was lodged in his head. Some piece of what he'd heard down in the cellar. None of this was normal guild business.

He could feel Cas's eyes on him.

"Mouse…" Cas began and stopped himself.

"He's up to something."

Cas sighed. "He's guild master. I'm sure he's up to any number of things. It's his guild to run as he likes."

"But there are rules, Cas. Rules that have stood for a century. Jardem isn't working for the guild. He's out for himself. I feel it."

"Ah, so you fancy yourself a seer now," Cas grumbled sardonically.

"No. This is instinct. I'd bet my ball sac that he's double crossing the client that hired the guild for that document."

"Why would he do that?" The skepticism was thick in his voice.

"Because there's something out there of even greater value than that document. He and the prisoner were talking about it."

"What is it?"

"No idea. But Jardem wants it for himself. I know that tone in his voice when he covets something."

"Do you honestly think he'll risk the reputation of the guild—"

Mouse chuckled. "Don't be naïve. Jardem doesn't give a handful of steaming shit about this guild. He reeks of ambition."

"And you're some guild loyalist now all of a sudden? Going to save the guild from him?"

His eyes drifted to the table of card players. "No. Guess I don't care that much about the guild. But I've never betrayed it, either." He stepped closer to Cas. "This ploy of his could be my chance. I could leverage my own freedom from this dung heap."

Cas turned around and leaned his back to the railing and looked at his feet. "And leave me behind."

Mouse felt his stomach tighten. "Cas, you belong here. I don't."

"You said it yourself. No one trusts me. They think I'm a fiend."

Guilt squeezed his insides. "I shouldn't have said that. I'm sorry. It's not true—"

It was Cassar's turn to scoff. "It is. I don't need you to protect me from that. I understand all too well how I'm perceived here." He paused to take a breath. "This *will* end you. He'll not let you survive if he discovers you've crossed him."

"He'll not kill off his best thief. Besides, he'll never know I'm on to him—until it's too late."

"Gods, you're arrogant."

Mouse stood. "That fucker thinks he owns me. I've been waiting for my chance to prove to him what a mistake that is.

And this is it."

Cas was quiet a moment, studying Mouse. "What does he have on you?'

"Never mind that. The fewer that know, the better. But he'll regret that he ever tried to use it against me."

Cas wouldn't look at him. "Mouse…I don't think I can be a part of this. Don't ask me to help you."

"That's your choice, Cas," Mouse replied, hearing the ice in his tone. "But don't interfere in mine." Before Cas could say another word, Mouse started down the steps. "Food, wine, and a few hours of sleep. Then, time to get to work." He headed towards the kitchens, knowing Cas continued to watch him from the stairs.

After a meal of boiled eggs, figs, and a full earthenware jar of pickled fish and onions that he scooped out with his fingers, he dozed for a time on his pallet in the rafters. But his mind wouldn't let him sink any deeper. When he closed his eyes, grim images swooped in like crows to pick at his consciousness. Vague sensations of pursuit and bondage cycled through his thoughts. They weren't dreams, but some strange affliction plaguing his unsettled mind.

Eventually, he gave up and threw himself from the pallet. Rest wouldn't come until he learned more about what Jardem was up to. He tugged on his clothes again, cinched his belt around his waist, and descended the ladder. Slipping out the closest window, he lowered himself to the street and snuck away.

Dawn had gained a foothold on the horizon as Mouse hit the vacant streets of Har Tesera. The city was still tomb quiet. Only packs of dogs and rats roamed the cobbles at this hour, but birds were knelling out their warnings that all creatures of the night should go to ground. By force of habit, Mouse kept clear of the main thoroughfares and plazas, instead taking the web of alleys and streets too narrow for carts and wagons. A few times, he scurried up to the rooftops and traveled in a more direct line than he would ever be able to below.

Mouse could get from the North Gate to the South Gate faster than a city guardsman on horseback.

He cut through the Hollows, the oldest district in the city, now largely abandoned.

There was always an endless swirling stew of lore about that dark corner of the city. Every toothless sage with a beggar's cup would warn travelers to give it a wide berth—as if they might stumble into it somehow.

It had a convoluted history. No one seemed to know what really happened in that district, but every version of the tale was seeped in magecraft and evil doings. Mouse, not prone to superstition or mania, understood the reality was likely something far more mundane. From what he was able to discern himself, teasing out the embellishments and inflation, the district was struck a century ago by a plague. A terrifying one, no doubt. The tales spoke of the dead rising and roaming the streets. To protect the rest of the city, the decision was made to seal off the district. All those inside were left to fend for themselves, ill or not. What happened after is murky— there is no record of what went on inside the district, but the imagination of those outside was strong and inventive.

The district was left abandoned, long past the end of the plague. The entire area was deemed cursed and troubled by tortured and angry spirits. Understandable. If it had been him forsaken and left to die in that district, he would have been one extremely pissed spirit that would stop at nothing to make all the living miserable.

Even now, a century later, no one would live there, and no business would claim the forsaken properties and buildings.

But as is the case with all things abandoned, the vermin are the first to return.

Despite the long endurance of those frightening tales, the Hollows steadily became a hive for dark activity. The stigma of evil was diminishing, the fear of curses weakening, and since most of the city's inhabitants still avoided the area, it was the obvious place for the seedy to take root.

But at this early hour, the district was vacant and oddly tranquil. The vermin had slunk back into their holes to escape the judgment of daylight. Mouse cut through the streets among the ruins, feeling like he was alone in a crumbling and uninhabited world. He aimed for the soaring tower of the Academy District, silhouetted against the dawn sky.

After slipping through a section of crumbling wall, he veered south and plunged into the Commerce District. A few twists through web-like streets landed him in a circular common enclosed with a half-dozen inns, all vying for attention with flashy paints and elaborate flags. The stalls that choked the center of the plaza were currently all boarded up or emptied, but a few venders had rolled in with carts in the pre-dawn to begin stocking the shelves in their tents.

Mouse wove his way through to the opposite side, then slipped into a side alley. Back in the shadow, he shimmied up a drainpipe and stepped over the iron railing of a narrow ledge that pretended to be a balcony. It had just enough room for a squat little stool and a few emptied wine jugs and not much else.

He guided one window shutter open with his palm. It squeaked in protest. Mouse winced and waited, but only heard a tiny coo in response. So, he swung it open wider. With enough room to slide though, he invited himself into the small room.

The rising dawn cast enough light through the window for Mouse to make out the figure enshrouded in a blanket in the middle of a bed. One figure. Not two.

Mouse kicked off his boots as quietly as he was able, then shred the rest of his clothes, leaving them in a pile on the floor. Naked, he crawled on all fours across the bed.

It squeaked under his weight. The figure grunted and squirmed under the covers. Mouse froze in place until the figure quieted again. Once positioned at the figure's back, he lifted the edge of the blanket and gingerly slipped under it.

Sticky warmth enveloped him. Mouse pressed up against the silky skin. One arm snaked over the torso, and one leg bent over the hip.

"Mouse, what are you doing?" Taurin grumbled into his pillow.

"Oh, this is how I'm welcomed? I take time to visit—"

"You're lucky I recognized your smell. I could have easily stabbed you in the neck."

"You know my smell?"

Taurin grunted sleepily. "That wasn't a compliment. Now cut the bullshit, Mouse. What do you want?"

"This," he said and kissed Taurin's neck. His cock was stiffening quickly. He wiggled his hips a little. "And maybe a little of this."

"I had a late night, Mouse—"

Mouse tightened his arm around him as he continued to kiss his neck and back. "Is that a no?"

Taurin sighed. "I hate you sometimes," he said, but he shifted and pushed his firm ass against Mouse's groin. "Fine. If you promise to let me sleep after."

Mouse grinned. "Promise." He moved his cock into position between Taurin's cheeks. "So nice when you are pre-greased. Saves time." He maneuvered his hips a little in small circles and gently pushed. For a moment, there was resistance, but with a slight pop, he entered Taurin, who pulled in a quick breath through his nose.

"Gods, you're horrible," Taurin replied, but there was mirth just beneath the surface of his tone.

Mouse chewed on Taurin's ear while he rolled his hips in a slow steady rhythm, like he was churning butter. He drank in the feel of Taurin's body against his own as he hugged him closer. He glided his palm over the curves of his torso, cupping the pectorals and pinching the nipple between his fingers.

"How do you do it?" he whispered.

"Do what? Taurin replied between gasps.

"Your skin," Mouse breathed. "Your tone."

"Occupational obligation."

"Perfection." Mouse slid his hand southward across sweat glazed skin, passing over the rippled belly that spasmed under his touch. Fingers combed through the tight curls of hair before Mouse scooped his palm around the tightening sack under Taurin's hard cock.

Taurin moaned low and buried his face into the pillow. "You're a scoundrel."

"You wound me sometimes with these cruel accusations," Mouse whispered.

Taurin let out a small chuckle of surrender. "Just get this over with so you can tell me what you want."

"If you want me to hurry…"

Taurin reached around and put his hand to Mouse's cheek and pushed him harder inside. "Don't you dare."

Mouse laughed as he continued to thrust his hips against Taurin. Gently, he encircled Taurin's shaft with his hand and ran his hand along the length of it, twisting slightly as he passed over the head. He pinched the end of the foreskin between his fingers before gliding his hands down again to expose the head.

Taurin's cock was a fine piece of art. Unappreciated by most of his clients because they were more selfishly concerned with their own cock and reaching conclusion. But it was the perfect size, in Mouse's view. For all possible activities. It extended straight out like the pole for a hanging shop sign and had the most beautifully shaped helmet Mouse had ever seen.

Mouse kept his hips at a conservative pace so as not to trigger his own finish, allowing Taurin to direct their progress. Mouse didn't have to wait long. Soon, Taurin was panting, his body squirming with each rise and fall of Mouse's hand on his cock. Mouse felt the scrotum contract into a tight ball against his knuckles just before Taurin cried out and threw his head back against Mouse's shoulder.

The cock pulsated in his hand. He avoided the head—

Taurin was sensitive there when it was his time. Thick globs of white fired out with the force of a ballista. Taurin's entire body spasmed. The weaker spurts toward the end covered Mouse's hand.

"Well, that was impressive," Mouse hummed into Taurin's ear. "Been a few days, has it?" He picked up the pace of his own hips, but it didn't require much. Feeling the sticky ejaculate running between his fingers was enough to send him to his own completion. Taurin moaned again as Mouse emptied himself inside him.

Mouse licked his fingers with a dramatic flourish while Taurin buried his face in the pillow and laughed.

"Better?" Mouse asked.

"Better," Taurin replied with a nod.

Taurin's clients usually didn't give him the opportunity to finish himself. Some expected it of him, but most wanted to shoot their own arrow and then hastily leave. Mouse always made certain Taurin had his opportunity.

Energy flagged from them both, and for a time they simply lay there spooning, enjoying the warmth of their bodies under the blanket and ignoring the sticky wet between them. Mouse left himself inside Taurin until he lost the erection and it slipped free on its own.

He peeled himself away and sat on the edge of the bed.

"There are linens on the floor," Taurin said groggily. "They may already be soiled, though. Not sure I have clean ones."

"I grew up on the streets, lovey." He lifted a wadded piece of fabric from the floor. "That sort of thing doesn't bother me. I've wiped my cock on worse things."

"I've no doubt," Taurin replied dryly. "I hope you appreciate that you get for free what rich men in this city pay good coin for."

"I am always immensely grateful." Mouse used the basin of water on the side table to wet the soft cloth, then ran it around his groin and inner thighs, then tenderly cleaned up

Taurin as well, front and back.

Taurin slid toward the center of the bed away from the wet spot, rolled over onto his back, and slipped his hands behind his head.

"So, what is it you want?"

Mouse tossed the wet cloth aside, then spread out next to Taurin again on his side. Elbow on the mattress, he propped his head up with his hand. "Seriously, Taurin, must you wound me so?"

"Spare me the indignant routine. You forget I know you better. So, out with it. You came for more than…that."

It amused Mouse that Taurin would talk openly about his experiences with clients, but when it came to sex between the two of them, he was oddly demure. In one fluid movement, he sprang off the bed, crossed the room, and dropped himself into a cushioned chair. "Well, since I'm here, I may have a question or two."

Taurin exhaled and lifted his eyes.

Mouse leaned his elbows on his knees. "I will have you know I can get all the information I need from just about anyone in this city. Perhaps I prefer to get it from you because I appreciate—"

"Gods, enough! What is it?"

Mouse smiled at him while he tugged at the beard on his chin. "Fine, then. Considering some of your clientele, I would value your insight regarding a recent contract I completed."

Taurin waited, eyes narrowing slightly. Mouse knew he would never divulge any information specific to his clients— especially the more powerful ones. He knew better to even ask. Trust was an important component of Taurin's arrangement with his clients. Many appreciated having someone they could talk to after their official transaction had been concluded. Taurin took that confidence in him seriously.

"A *completed* contract," Taurin repeated. He sat up a little in the bed. His curiosity was piqued.

"I am curious about the details of the job. The object I

was asked to acquire was…unusual."

Taurin rolled his hand in the air. A gesture to get on with it.

Mouse took time to explain the basics of the job, Jardem's reaction after, and the prisoner underneath the guild.

Taurin groaned at the mention of Pravis.

"You've had the pleasure?"

Taurin scowled. "Unfortunately. His privileges here have been revoked. He is no longer welcome."

That didn't surprise Mouse. He resisted asking what he'd done to get himself banned. He decided he didn't want to know. "The document is valuable enough for a wealthy merchant to keep it hidden and locked away, but it is also worthless without something else. Some other object."

"Are you asking me what this document was? Not my area of expertise, and certainly not enough information to go on."

Mouse bit his lower lip. "No, but I was hoping you could lead me to someone who might have some ideas, though."

"Why the interest? Not like you to care about a job once it's completed."

"Jardem. It's his involvement in this. It's…curious."

Taurin frowned. "Gods, I know that look."

"What?"

"Mouse, leave it be. Jardem is dangerous. Perhaps even more than you know."

The fact that Taurin knew that should have given Mouse pause. "If I know what the document is, it will help me understand what he's up to."

"And do what with that information?"

Mouse hesitated, wondering how much he should say. "I'm not sure yet. It's my way out—"

"Mouse—"

"Jardem's plotting to double-cross the client. I feel it. Maybe if I can prove it, confront him with what I know…well, his leverage over me will end."

Taurin sat up in bed, propped up by his muscular arms. The covers rested at his waistline, exposing his finely sculpted chest and flat belly. He stared at Mouse a moment, his expression serious. "Your plan is to blackmail the blackmailer? Mouse, I strongly encourage you to rethink this."

"I can't have my father used to control me," Mouse growled. Taurin was the only one Mouse felt comfortable sharing the leverage Jardem had over him with. "I don't know how he learned of my…" He stopped himself. No need to say it around Taurin. He knew the whole story. "This extortion will not go unanswered, Taurin. I will see that he suffers for it."

Taurin sighed. "You could press Pravis for the details. He clearly knew what it was if he was looking to snag it, too. The weasel would cave quickly if you applied any pressure…"

"Considered that." Mouse leaned in, putting his elbows on his knees. "But getting access to him again might be tricky. I poisoned that well, I think. I'll use that as a last resort."

Taurin fell quiet. His lips tightened, and he stared unseeing at the ceiling for a time.

"There is a scribe that visits me on occasion. When he manages to scrape up the coin. Even still, I give him a discount with the understanding that I might need his help someday. He's rather talented and well-connected, I'm told." He made a weak shrug. "I won't ever need him, to be honest, but a part of me feels for him. He works for a magistrate in the Academy District, so he's well informed in matters pertaining to law."

Academy District. Mouse wasn't the type to be able to just wander into that office. "Where can I find him?"

"His urges are more robust than his salary, so he supplements his visits with me with an alternative venue. How familiar are you with the goings on in the Hollows?"

Mouse couldn't help but grin. "Spent enough time there to learn a thing or two."

"Why am I not surprised?" Taurin said with a lift of his eyes. "Well, this scribe frequents a place that was a former textile factory and warehouse. Lots of individual rooms."

"The Hollows' Ball," Mouse said.

"Of course, you know of it," Taurin replied dryly. "Frequent visitor, I imagine."

"Actually, no. But I keep tabs on a number of people that do visit regularly." Jardem wasn't the only one who valued intelligence.

Taurin made a low, disapproving noise in this throat. "This fellow is a quirky sort and follows a strict routine. When not visiting me, he attends the ball on the eve of his one day off. Which is…" He lifted his eyes in thought. "Tomorrow, as luck would have it. A word of caution. He's timid and will scare easily."

"Noted."

"So, try not being an asshole."

"I can be charming."

Taurin scoffed and leaned forward. He shook out the dark curls atop his head with his fingers, which made the muscles of his shoulders and biceps swell and form delicious curves. "I have errands to run and no clients until this evening. Sleep here if you like. You look like you could use it."

"Thanks," Mouse replied wryly.

"Quieter here than at the guild, I imagine. You really should get your own flat."

"If Jardem paid me for the work I do, I would."

Taurin shuffled to the edge of the bed and dropped his feet to the floor. He looked askance at Mouse as he reached for his trousers. "I'm actually glad you came by, Mouse."

"Me too." He gave Taurin a salacious grin.

Taurin didn't seem to notice. His mind was elsewhere as he stepped into the trousers, stood, and pulled them up to his waist. "It saved me the effort to getting a message to you. I've been meaning to tell you something."

Mouse frowned. "And what is that?"

"Madam Diamond wants to expand her business. Open new establishments in other cities. She's asked me to run the first one in Har Orentega."

"Orentaga? That far flung backwater?"

"It's growing. And there's currently no formal competition. I am to have full control."

"You're to be a madam."

Taurin chuckled softly. "I suppose that's true."

Mouse kept his face neutral. "Well, what an enormous opportunity for you."

"Yes. It is at that." Taurin opened the doors to the wardrobe and started to dress. "Not ashamed to admit I'm rather looking forward to the change in role. Madam Diamond feels I've the mind for it. And I agree."

Mouse was busy looking at his hands. When he looked up again, Taurin was pulling on his boots.

"Maybe you could arrange a visit. Help me get established."

Mouse made a noise low in his throat. "Doubtful Jardem would allow me the time away." He felt Taurin's eyes on him, but he didn't want to meet them, so he kept his eyes on the floor. "How soon?"

"Not sure. But soon, I think." Taurin put his hand on the door latch. "Look, I have to go," he said quietly. "Get some sleep. We can…speak more on it later."

Mouse didn't answer as Taurin stepped out of the room. Once he no longer heard the boots in the corridor, he left through the window the way he'd come.

7

MOUSE HEADED west for no other reason than it was not the direction of the guild.

Taurin was right; he needed sleep. His mind was a fog and his muscles felt gummed up with sticky day-old porridge. But he no longer wanted to be in Taurin's space. Not now. Not after what he'd learned. And he had no interest in running into Jardem or any of the other Night Fingers.

By providence or intent, he ended up in the northern part of the Merchant District, a quarter known as the Workbench, and he stumbled into Rharden Square. The plaza was choked with motley-colored tents in preparation for a market, with Rharden's large stone head peering over them from the center. Mouse had never learned who the man had been or why he deserved to have his likeness so prominently displayed here. No one else in the city seemed to know, either. Or care. His statue had been rudely treated for years. The stone was barely visible underneath the layers of graffiti and postings glued to its body like armor made of parchment.

At the far side of the plaza, in front of a temple, stood the bell tower. It was the highest structure not only in the plaza, but in all the Workbench.

Folks were already drifting into the square while venders rolled up their tent flaps and burdened tables with their wares. The early crowd, wading in among the tents with coin purses in hand, was keen to get the first picks of the merchandise and produce. Vendors were more than happy to sell directly from the crates.

Mouse kept to the perimeter, staying close to the buildings that formed the square. He circled around until he lingered at the base of the bell tower. The door faced the old temple. Strange that as many times as he'd been here, he never bothered to find out what god resided there. He never concerned himself with such things. Seemed fair since the gods never concerned themselves with him.

Pretending he was relieving himself against the door, he waited until no one was close enough to notice his actions, then slipped out his tools and worked at the door's hefty padlock. It looked old and rusty, but Mouse knew the insides still functioned well. Only because he kept it well-greased for occasions like this.

He doubted there was even a key for it anymore. Or, if there was, if anyone knew where to find it. The tower had been abandoned after it was struck by lightning, which broke the bell loose. No one seemed interested in fixing it since it was a relic of a past age. The bell was supposed to warn citizens that the city was under attack, something that hadn't happened in over a century.

So, like everything else that didn't concern them directly, the Duke and all the city's elite ignored it. All the better for him.

Lock picked, door opened, he slipped inside. The stone floor was broken into pieces and dented from the impact of the fall, but the bell was long gone, its metal reallocated. He took the stairs that clung to the wall, a narrow scaffolding of wood. His body remembered which of the steps were rotting and unstable, and he stepped over them without conscious thought.

At the top of the stairs, he stepped onto the platform. The center of the floor here was gone, taken out when the bell dropped. Somehow, despite the ravaged hole in the middle, the warped and twisted floor that remained was stable. Mouse believed its rickety appearance kept others away, but he'd spent enough time up there to have faith it wouldn't give way and drop him to his death. He took in a long breath at the top stair—the climb had winded him.

Nothing had changed. It was as if he'd only abandoned it yesterday. The woven mat and pine box were still there, untouched since the day he joined with the Night Fingers. The undisturbed nature of it felt like some pathetic shrine.

This had been his home back when he'd spent his day pilfering food from the markets, rummaging through rubbish behind the rich merchants' homes, and lifting the odd coin now and then when people weren't paying attention.

He'd been here only a handful of times since the day Surev convinced him to give up his life on the street—even so, it had been years.

He took a few steps in, close to the wall. The floor creaked and seemed to bow inward toward the open center. Maybe it was his imagination. Maybe it was more unstable than he remembered.

An unexpected sorrow took root in the pit of his stomach as the ghost of his past loitered about the place. How long had this been his refuge? And he'd been lucky to discover it. Others fending for themselves on the street were far less lucky. Those difficult days were a blur in his memory now, yet still the feelings in his gut were as crisp and fresh as an apple taken from the tree. Fear and uncertainty had saturated the stone and wood of this place, and memories of cold nights bit at his skin. Yet how strange that the memories of what he was were not what brought on this unhappy temper. Instead, it was what he had become.

He was free in those days, though he didn't appreciate that at the time. Free. Not trapped as he was now. A prisoner.

And the memory of those days when his life was his own stabbed cruelly at his insides.

Mouse leaned his elbows on the window ledge, staring blankly at the sprawling market far below. It was in full tilt now, people flowing among the stalls and booths in this swirling tide that reminded Mouse of sand caught in an eddy along the bank of a stream.

He watched, unfocused for a time, lost in his thoughts. How long, he couldn't say.

"Dolt," he said aloud to himself finally and pushed from the window ledge.

In the pine box, there was the blanket he knew would be there. He put it to his face and inhaled. It smelled exactly as he remembered.

He reached into his boot and pulled out the dagger. His father's dagger. Strange how it felt so light in his hand. He remembered the day he took it—it seemed to fight him as he'd removed it from the box. Now, it felt a part of him. It had guided him all these years.

Now would be no different.

He wadded the blanket up as a pillow, positioned the knife under it, then spread out on the musty smelling mat.

He was asleep in moments.

The sun was well past its zenith when he woke again. He'd slept nearly the entire day. By force of habit, he folded the blanket and tucked it away in the pine box. One never knew when he'd be out on the streets again. Could be sooner than later, considering what he was planning.

At street level, he combed the market, looking for anything and nothing at the same time. He sidled up to a food booth, straddling a stool, and bought a few dry and overcooked meat pies to break his fast. Or was this dinner?

Jardem would be wondering where he was. He'd have the next contract for him by now. Mouse imagined Jardem screaming from his office for someone to hunt him down. But if Jardem wasn't going to pay him properly, he could fucking wait.

His threats only went so far.

He shoved the empty tin plate away like he was angry at it and left the booth. The crowds had thinned some, thankfully. Mouse meandered through the tide of people. Rough characters loitered about between tents, watching. These weren't guild members. Several gangs infested the streets of Har Tesera. The guild ignored them for the most part, unless they overstepped and targeted anything larger than a few crowns' worth at one time. Then the guild heavies would step in and remind them of the rules. Private contracting was discouraged and the threat of losing fingers or getting legs broken was typically enough to keep petty street thieves from drifting into guild territory.

The gang members were quick to measure him as someone not here to shop and eyes dropped to his hand for signs of affiliation. When none came, they scowled. He was an enemy.

Mouse paid no attention to them. None of them would dare act against him publicly in the daylight.

He took his time wandering the stalls, looking at the wares, wondering what it would be like to have the coin to purchase any of it. Most of it was items to fill a home—something he would never have any use for, apparently. Venders eyed him warily when he fingered the merchandise. He didn't look the part of someone interested in expensive textiles or fine porcelain serving pieces from Har Orentega.

He was stalling, of course. Wasting time instead of returning to the guild. Out of spite. He wanted to make Jardem wait. He wanted him angry.

But the merchandise here wasn't enough to hold his attention. In fact, it only served to irritate him, reminding him of what he'd never have.

He lingered in a booth that sold leather mugs tooled with

intricate designs. They were beyond what he'd be willing to pay—it was a frivolous expense, and it'd likely get stolen from his kit the moment he left it alone—but there was a seductiveness to it, a small dream of a *someday*, a day when he could spend coin on an inconsequential trinket of no real value.

While he turned one of the mugs about in his hand as if weighing if it was the one to purchase, something caught his eye. In a nearby tent across the way, a man dressed in a long emerald doublet and yellow stockings was running his fingers through a collection of chains hanging from a wall of pegs. He had a pinched face and his grey hair was pulled back tight against his scalp and confined in a tidy braid behind him.

The man did nothing suspicious per se, but what snagged Mouse's attention was the quality of the chains he inspected. The man was well-attired, clearly able to recognize and afford fine garments. But the chains he admired were cheap. Not the type of thing this dandy would pay any attention to.

Mouse bit the inside of his cheek. His imagination? Possibly.

He glanced at the man's shoes.

Shoes were the first thing to give someone up. Mouse could tell a person's income by the shoes they wore because people did not spend coin on good footwear unless they had it to spend. It was one thing people were not likely to notice if you cut a few corners.

It was also an indicator of one's taste.

This man's shoes would cost enough to feed Mouse for a year. He would not be looking at those cheap chains with the interest he appeared to have.

Mouse made an overly obvious grunting noise that signaled the mug was not for him and left the booth. He swung through a few other stalls without really looking at the merchandise. He paused at an incense shop and put his nose to the jars while he made furtive glances over his shoulder.

A few booths behind him, the man in the emerald doublet

was now looking at carved wooden toys. The man was subtle, smooth. He never once was caught looking at Mouse directly. Mouse still wondered if he was being paranoid—but his instincts screamed no, he'd picked up a tail.

Mouse's heart thumped as genuine unease settled in his gut.

This was new. He had no idea who this man was, nor could he think of any reason why he pursued him. Mouse's value to the guild was his anonymity. No one really knew of him, which made it easier for him to slip in and out of places. Frankly, Mouse preferred that. He'd always favored the shadows to being out in the open. Yet even inside the guild, he wasn't regarded as having much importance. On the street, it was even more so. He was invisible.

So why follow *him*?

With a satchel of incense still held to his nose, Mouse frowned. Whoever he was, he was of considerable means. What could possibly be his interest in a common street rat like himself? Was he a client of the guild? Former client? *Disgruntled* client? Mouse searched his memory of jobs he'd done recently, reviewing each of them one by one in his mind. This man didn't trigger any memories.

The notion bloomed in his head that this man might know Jardem. Perhaps even be working for him. Mouse needed more information.

He chose his next vendor carefully—a larger tent with some of the side flaps down. A dressmaker. The tent was heaving with women's garments of every sort, from extravagant to simple. Mouse wove his way past the tables and through the crowd of hay-stuffed tailor dummies that looked like they'd been swiped from the archery yard. They displayed the shop owners more striking offerings. In the back of the large tent were smaller tents, spaces for women to try on prospective garments with waiting attendants to help dress them.

A quick coin to the dressing room attendant, and he was

granted access to the changing tent. He wiggled under the canvas sides, reaching the outside and circling around.

When Mouse peeked around the corner, the man in the emerald doublet was in a pipe shop but showing signs of distress. His eyes darted from booth to booth while at the same time pretending he was interested in a long pipe shaped like a phallus.

He'd lost his mark.

Mouse grinned inwardly as he slipped the dagger from his boot and crept forward.

He was behind the man in an instant and had the dagger pressing into his ribs.

"Ah," the man said. There was no fear or apprehension in his voice. "You *are* clever."

"I'm also in a spiky mood. Why are you trailing me?"

The man in the emerald doublet chuckled. "A fair question. Perhaps we could go somewhere to speak more privately. Over a drink perhaps."

"Or I could stick you right here in the square?"

"Master Mouse, if I could locate you this easily, do you suppose others would not be able to do the same? And my death would bring a price on your head that would make every assassin in that guild salivate."

He knew his name. That was disconcerting. Outside of the guild, no one knew who he was. Who was he dealing with here?

"Are you familiar with the assassin's guild here in Har Tesera?" the man added with lift to his haughty smile. "Would you recognize one of them if they were…say, ten paces from you?"

Mouse felt cold. "Who are you?"

"My own name is not important at the moment."

Mouse pursed his lips. "I'll decide what's important."

"I am merely a messenger. An envoy. I am here to represent an interested party, Master Mouse."

Interested party? "Do messengers often stalk the

recipients of their message from the shadows?" Mouse asked.

"Shadows?" The man chuckled as made a show of looking around. "Simply waiting for the right opportunity. That's all." He made a sad little sigh. "Now, I implore you to reconsider where that dagger is placed. I'd hate to have this fine garment damaged." There was entirely no fear in the man's voice. He was calm and composed. "Do you think, dressed as I am, that I would brave this market alone?"

Mouse closed his eyes and took in a slow breath through his nose. "How many crossbows are pointed at me right now?"

"Three. Stab me and you won't make it two steps."

Mouse pulled the dagger from his side and slipped it back into his boot. The man turned around, and a smug smile broke his thin lips.

"Clever and wise," he said with a condescending lilt.

"What do you want with me?"

"A conversation. That's all."

Mouse eyed him intently. A part of him wondered if the crossbowmen were a bluff. He fought the urge to swing his gaze over the rooftops. "Fine. Talk."

"Master Mouse, this is hardly the venue. Important business discussions do not take place in such a public forum as this. One must take precautions from unwelcome ears."

"First, dispense with the 'master' treatment," Mouse replied dryly, making sure he sounded unimpressed. He couldn't decide, though, if it was meant to flatter him or was condescending mockery. "I'm granted no such title."

"Your reputation would suggest otherwise."

Flattery then.

"Second, if you think so highly of my skills, you cannot really think I'd consider wandering into some dark alley with you?"

The man smirked. "Do I look like the type to conduct business in an *alley*, Master Mouse?"

"Is this guild business?" Mouse asked.

A cold seriousness infected his voice. "No. *We* wish to

speak with you. Not the guild."

That was oddly intriguing.

"I'll meet you somewhere public," Mouse said. "Less crowded perhaps. Out in the open. No private residence."

The man made a sideways dip of his head in consent. "I invite you to the Golden Flute. Meet me there in an hour."

"The Flute?" Mouse couldn't help but laugh. "As if the likes of me would ever be permitted in there."

The stranger made a knowing smile. "I'll see that you are welcomed most hospitably. You'll be escorted to a private table towards the back."

Mouse hesitated, then nodded.

The man smirked again as if he'd won some challenge. "One hour, Master Mouse. I suggest you not keep us waiting." And, still smiling, he turned and walked on.

Mouse stared dumbly after him.

The Golden Flute? Who was this man?

Mouse knew of the tavern by reputation only. Located in the High District—where exactly was uncertain—it was an establishment for the wealthiest citizens. Mostly nobility, but some of the more connected merchants were permitted as well.

Whoever this man was, he was connected to some extremely powerful people.

It would take him the hour to get across the city into the High District and track the place down. With an exclusive membership, it wasn't the type of establishment that trumpeted its exact location. Finding it would be tricky, and someone that looked like him wouldn't likely be given a straight answer if he asked. He'd considered asking the man in the emerald doublet where it was exactly, but he didn't want to appear foolish.

He had sources for such information. But they themselves would require locating.

With a sigh to collect himself, he wound his way through the market toward the perimeter again. Before he exited the market's tents, he heard his name as a hard whisper behind him.

He froze. What now?

A boy, no more than ten, jogged to catch up to him. Juri. A pickpocket assigned to this square.

Mouse spun on him. "Never use names outside the guild," he growled.

Juri blanched. "Sorry. Forgot myself." He made furtive glances around to see if anyone had heard. *Rather late for that*, Mouse thought. "But we was all told to give you a message if we spotted you. Was afraid I'd lose you."

Seemed everyone was keen on talking to him today. How'd he become so popular?

"From Quick—"

"Don't!" Mouse held up his palm. "Don't say that name."

"Right, right. No names."

The lad was a mixture of awkward and reluctant—as if he didn't want to talk to Mouse but felt compelled to. He was the unlucky guild member to locate him first. Mouse could tell the lad felt unnerved just being in his company. What lies had the guild woven about him to the point even the youngest of members were uneasy around him?

Mouse pinched the bridge of his nose. "Just give me the message?"

"You're bade to return to the guild with the greatest urgency. Qui—someone seems desperately angry that you remain unspoken for today."

Mouse grunted. He didn't have time for Jardem today. And he wasn't interested in not getting paid for another contract.

"You didn't find me," Mouse told him and turned to walk away, but the boy grabbed his sleeve.

Mouse stared at the hand as if it burned.

"No disrespect, but I'll be whipped and turned out if I was caught lying. Or worse."

Mouse let his head drop back. He didn't have time for

this. "Would some coin cloud your memory? Enough to meet your quota for the day?"

Juri gaped for a moment, but then considered the proposition with a lift of his eyes. "If there was a bit extra for a fruit pastry, might not have run into you today at all."

Mouse scowled. He dug into his purse and pulled out the coin and slapped it into the boy's hand. This would put himself short now. He'd have to resort to pickpocketing himself for a decent supper. "You never saw me."

"Mouse who?" Juri said with a laugh as he scampered off.

Mouse headed off toward the High District with a nagging concern in his gut about what had Jardem so desperate to have him back at the guild. Well, it would have to wait. He had a date to keep.

8

FOR ALL its exclusivity, The Golden Flute was unassuming from the outside. Mouse expected a peacock, but the exterior was decidedly more peahen. From the street, the building looked more suited for lenders' offices than for an upmarket drinkery. The inside, Mouse was certain, would more than make up for its reserved outer countenance.

It explained why it had escaped Mouse's notice. He knew the city well—though, arguably, the High District less so. This establishment didn't preen for attention. Unlike some festive ball at the Duke's court, the intention here wasn't about being noticed. More the opposite. It was about being welcomed inside.

Mouse approached the rather simple door and gave it a confident knock, one that announced that he belonged there. His gut felt like a nest of spiders. Few things in the world caused him discomfort, but interacting politely with the wealthy and powerful always put his teeth on edge. Stealing from them was so much easier than trying to have a conversation.

The door opened almost immediately. A man dressed

entirely in black stood at the threshold. He had a narrow, rat-like face. Dark eyes raked over Mouse, and his nose wrinkled like he smelled the gas from the sewer as he held the door's latch with one hand, his other hand smartly positioned behind his back.

"This is a private establishment," he said. His voice was haughty and dismissive.

"I've been invited, apparently. Ensured you would be most welcoming and accommodating upon my arrival." After the effort it took to find the place, his curiosity got the better of him. He needed to see the inside. In the back of his mind, Mouse wondered if this was some elaborate prank, and he would not be granted entry after all.

The man blinked. "Ah, yes. The unconventional guest known as Mouse."

"At your service," Mouse replied with a bow.

The servant drew his eyes from boot to head as he considered Mouse. "Doubtful," he replied dryly. "I can think of no service I'm in need of you'd be qualified to satisfy."

"I might surprise you. I am a man of many talents."

The man grunted. "You were expected earlier."

"Your establishment isn't easy to locate. Hard to even find anyone willing to point the general direction." Mouse also didn't want to send any message that he worked for those who invited him here or was afraid of them.

The man made a noise low in his throat as he pulled the door open wider to allow Mouse entry. It clearly pained him to do so.

Mouse wanted to laugh. A servant was a servant—whether it was for a country lord, a rich merchant, or a barkeep in the West Gate. Wiping the ass of someone with heavy coffers still made you an ass wiper, even with arguably finer garments and better food scraps. Mouse never understood their elitist superiority. They always acted like they shared their master's power and influence. The truth of it was they could be turned out at the slightest misstep. Their masters granted them no loyalty for their servitude.

Beyond the servant was a dark hallway, walls painted with a rich wine color. A chandelier hung from the high ceiling, alight with five thick candles. Mouse could hear the hum of conversation and music rolling out into the street from deeper inside.

Mouse refused to display his unease. He marched inside with a confident step of his boots, though the plush carpeting absorbed the sound. Once Mouse was past the threshold, the door was quickly closed, as if more undesirables might somehow wander in given the chance.

The man gestured to a side room. "In there, quickly before any of our legitimate patrons see you."

Mouse scowled but complied. He stepped inside a small square chamber furnished with a long bench against the wall and a round table in the center.

The man stood at the threshold. "Garments have been provided. There, on that table."

"Something wrong with what I'm wearing?" Mouse sneered.

"If your intention was to murder us all, no. But to dine with us, we require something more…civilized."

Dine?

"Place your current attire in the box under the table. Or I'd recommend you toss them into the fireplace, which seems a more appropriate option," he added with a lift of his eyes. "And your weapon goes in the box as well."

"It remains with me."

"Sirrah, you are a guest in this establishment, granted access by those better than you, and you do not have the authority to decide this matter. It remains in the box. It is perfectly safe, I assure you. No one here would covet the quality of knife that you could afford."

Mouse kept his lips tight. It was best to let the prig believe that.

"Clean yourself thoroughly from the basin. A generous

application of scented powder would not be unwelcomed either. Dress yourself—I assume you know how. Knock when you are ready."

Mouse congratulated himself for having the force of will to not to stab him in the neck.

The servant pulled the door closed, shutting him in. With a sigh, Mouse did what he was told. He peeled off his garments and shoved them into the box. Standing naked at the basin, he washed his body with a soft cloth and water that was surprisingly still warm. When he was finished, the water in the basin was opaque and grey.

He ignored the powder. The Flute's gatekeeper outside and the rest of the patrons would have to suffer his body's natural bouquet. He would have to go back to the guild eventually, and if he returned smelling of rose petals, he'd be murdered on the spot.

The garments chosen for him fit surprisingly well for the most part. Somehow, his size had been accurately messaged to the gatekeeper before he arrived. The doublet provided him was an innocuous blue. Simple but of fine construction, the fabric substantial yet soft. The linen tunic had a heavily starched collar that scratched his neck, and the buckled shoes were stiff and pinched his toes.

He rapped on the door to signal he was ready.

The servant stood at the door a moment with pressed lips and crossed arms to critique the result. With a sigh that conveyed it would suffice, he spun about and led Mouse down the rest of the hallway and through a door at the far end.

Mouse had been in a number of taverns and drinkeries around the city. Each was as unremarkable as the next, and the insides were wholly interchangeable. People generally called on the establishment closest to their own flat or on their way home from where they were employed. This made the stumble home in the dark both easier and safer. The food or entertainment at one might encourage a longer walk to a different tavern on occasion, but ambiance was never a deciding factor. At least within the circles he ran in.

The dining room of The Golden Flute shook Mouse's notion of such a thing. This was a destination, a place one would cross the city to visit. The idea of it was revolutionary. The room was extravagant, but not grotesquely gaudy as he would have thought—like a good many of the rich homes he'd burgled. Coin and taste were rare bedfellows. The walls were the same wine color as the hall, but these were adorned with fine portraits of bloated old nobles long dead. The tables were covered in white linens, a flickering candelabra centered on each. Gentle music came from somewhere, but Mouse couldn't determine the source. The musicians were hidden away.

The chamber had a calmness about it, but Mouse forced himself not to submit to it. He stayed vigilant. There was more danger here than in a drunken street brawl. He would have to tread carefully.

A few tables were occupied, but the tavern was largely empty. It wasn't yet the typical hour for supper. Mouse couldn't tell if there were patrons here early to gain access to the best table or if they were holdouts from a late noon meal. Conversations tapered to a standstill when he entered, and they all eyed him curiously as he crossed the room. A fine coat was not enough to disguise him as anything but a pretender in this place. He announced his base self by just walking.

Mouse scowled inwardly, resenting their quick judgment of him. Something he needed to learn, he told himself. He would find what it took to pass for one of them. Become one of them.

With a wave of his arm, the servant gestured to a nook in the far back corner of the chamber. Mouse frowned, feeling the uncharacteristically cold grip of uncertainty. He was out of his element here. Nothing felt familiar. The chamber suddenly felt like a cage, and he was the exhibit. He forced a nod. With his duty concluded, the servant strolled back across the dining chamber and disappeared again behind the door, leaving

Mouse in the middle of the chamber, still feeling eyes on him. He pulled in a slow breath and approached the nook in the corner.

It was a tiny three-walled room with an intimate table tucked inside. Lush blue curtains were drawn back on either side of the opening and tied with gold rope. Sitting with his back to the far wall was not the man he encountered in the market.

Mouse stood at the opening and waited for the man to notice him. It gave Mouse a brief opportunity to evaluate him.

He was large but fit. That was the first thing Mouse noted. Broad shoulders and a full chest filled the fine cream-colored doublet. He was also comely and flawlessly manicured. The loose curls of his short chestnut hair looked as if they'd been arranged to look just so. He had a thinly trimmed mustache and beard that cupped only his chin, darker in tone than the hair on his head. The flecks of grey at his chin and temples put him at about twice Mouse's age.

The man looked up from a document he was scanning and spotted Mouse standing there. He rolled up the document and set it aside.

"Ah. You've arrived at last," he said. His voice was deep and gruff. It wasn't warm, but his tone wasn't unpleasant either. It was absent of emotion or position. It was skillfully neutral. He gestured to the chair opposite him. "Please. Join me."

Mouse forgot how to use his legs for a moment.

"I assure you. You are in no danger here. Sit."

Mouse stepped forward, withdrew the chair, and settled into the cushioned seat. He felt more than saw the curtain behind him close, shutting them in.

He also felt the absence of his dagger and regretted leaving it in the box.

"Appears an hour on the street differs from what I have come to know as an hour," the man said.

Mouse could read nothing from the tone. He couldn't tell

if the man was being playful or if he was angry to be kept waiting. Perhaps both. "You have me at a disadvantage, my Lord. I expected to meet with someone else."

"No such honorifics, if you please. I'm not noble-born and detest anyone treating me as such."

Mouse felt the compulsion to apologize. He choked it down. The man's very presence oozed power. Mouse refused to succumb to it.

"Call me Savir," he said. "Master Savir, if you must, but I don't require it. Not here, at any rate. I confess, I thought you a page or an errand boy when I looked up. You have a very…young countenance."

"So, I'm told."

"My son is taller than you, I'd wager, and he is but fourteen. What is your age, if I may inquire?"

"Twenty." Or so he believed. He was rather foggy on the actual number.

Savir leaned back and stroked the small beard on his chin. "Remarkable. I took the liberty of ordering a meal for you. I trust you are hungry."

It took a moment, but Mouse found his voice. "If this is on your coin, very."

The man smiled thinly. "Of course." He snapped his fingers.

The curtain opened briefly, and two women stepped in, each with a plate. The meals were set in front of each of them and the women filed out without a word. Another woman stepped in with a silver tray loaded with crystal chalices and a richly painted carafe of dark wine. The tray was set between Savir and Mouse, the chalices filled with wine, then she, too, departed.

Mouse looked down at the meal. A whole roasted bird filled his plate along with roasted vegetables. It was too small to be a chicken.

"Grouse," the man said, answering his unasked question. "No objection, I pray."

"Well, it is the third time this week, but I'll suffer through it, if only to be polite." The sweet smell wafted up with the steam and turned his hunger on in an instant. His stomach betrayed him and took that opportunity to growl absurdly loud.

The man smiled again—this time seeming more genuinely amused. With a forefinger and thumb, he picked up a cut piece of root vegetable Mouse didn't recognize. "We are not at court. No need to stand on any prim etiquette." He popped the section into his mouth. "As my father used to say, 'lay back your ears and get to it.'" Without waiting on Mouse, he started in on the bird, taking it apart with his hands.

This was all to put Mouse at ease, he knew. To disarm him and make him feel more comfortable in this foreign world of the extremely wealthy. Mouse wouldn't know the first thing about the proper use of utensils at a fine table, and Savir knew this.

Mouse gave into the demands of his stomach. He twisted off a small leg and bit into the flesh. Sweet juices ran down his chin. He closed his eyes while he chewed. It was the most delicious thing he'd ever eaten.

Savir sucked the grease from his fingertips after setting a bone down on the plate. Mouse marveled that not a single spot of grease had landed on the cream doublet. "I apologize that you were not better informed of who you were sent to meet. Vosaf should have been more direct with you."

Mouse fought against the habit of wiping his fingers on his trousers or coat. Instead, he used the linen covering the table. "Why was he following me? If he knew who I was, why didn't he simply approach me?"

Savir looked up. "To business, then? I prefer to enjoy my meal before such talk, but I understand your earnestness. Very well." He took a sip from his chalice. "Try the wine. You'll find it exquisite, I'm sure."

Mouse wanted to shout, "cut the bullshit!" This lack of pretention, this congenial effect, was fiction. This was a man who enjoyed considerable power. He reeked of it. And yet he wasn't a noble. Curious.

Savir set down his chalice. "My associate has been studying you," he said matter-of-factly, as if it were the most common of occurrences.

"To what end?" Mouse asked while he chewed.

Grouse, it turned out, was delicious. He intended to eat the entire meal. No sense in letting any of it go to waste. He'd never eat like this again. So, when this meeting ended, he was intent on making sure there would be nothing left uneaten on the plate but bones.

Savir smiled again as he took a bit more wine. "It is essential to understand who one intends to do business with."

"Business? Do we have business to discuss?"

"I daresay we do." Savir's tone turned serious, and it lowered to nearly a whisper.

Mouse stopped mid-chew and look up. "Well, that sounds particularly foreboding."

Savir recovered and affected a weak smile. "Master Mouse—"

"I am also not largely in favor of titles. Mouse is adequate."

Savir dipped his head. "I am part of an organization. One widespread about this great kingdom. One graced with more influence than you can imagine."

Mouse's brow narrowed. "Are you somehow part of the king's service, then?"

Savir leaned in on his elbows. "Not all power comes from nobility, sirrah. In fact, the king would be loath to admit it, but we wield more muscle to bring about change in this world than perhaps he does himself. Certainly more than any of his individual dukes."

Mouse was quiet a moment. "A heady claim." He did not believe this to be some idle boast.

"An accurate one, none the less."

"And what is this organization, pray tell?"

"We are known by many names, Mouse. Within our fraternity, we have a name we call ourselves, but that is a closely held secret known to only those who've proven worthy and have been granted admittance. Those outside of our association generally refer to us as the Shadow Elite."

Icy spiders danced along his spine. Of course, he'd heard rumor of them. He wasn't even certain he believed they existed. And he certainly never dreamed he'd encounter them.

"You've heard of us?" Savir asked, clearly gauging his reaction.

Mouse swallowed and fought to maintain his composure. The meat sitting in his stomach was now dangerously close to coming up again. "You've been mentioned a time or two in conversation."

"Our organization is responsible for more of how this kingdom functions than you may realize. The noble-born think they grip the helm of governance, but I will tell you they don't know the half of it. My association manages the flow of money. Of commerce. It is through our efforts that citizens thrive."

Thrive? Mouse bit his tongue. The Shadow Elite had some work to do if they felt the common folk of Har Tesera were "thriving." But Mouse wagered that now was not the best time to challenge Savir on that.

"So, why the interest in me?" he asked.

"You were part of a certain contract, I understand. To obtain a document."

Ah. Mouse leaned back in his chair. "I've participated in many contracts of late. You will need to be more specific."

Savir frowned, and some of his congeniality dissipated like pipe smoke. Mouse caught his first glimpse of who was behind the mask of calculated pleasantries.

"Let's dispense with this dance. You know of what I speak. It is now in the hands of your leader at the Night Fingers Guild. What do you know of it?"

Mouse thought about bluffing, but he didn't have enough

to really mount a good lie. He decided for once to stick with the truth. "Very little. I did not break the seal, and Jardem doesn't share such details with me."

Savir nodded in thought. "And Jardem has not yet given the document over to the client."

"I do not believe he has."

"That wasn't a question."

Mouse pursed his lips. Savir knew what the document was and knew who'd hired the Night Fingers to steal it. If Mouse was to guess, the individual who'd hired the Night Fingers was not part of the Shadow Elite. But Savir was not about to share any of that information.

And Mouse understood why he was here. He forgot about his meal.

"You want me to steal the document from Jardem."

Savir acknowledged this with a single slow nod. "I want it so it can be destroyed."

"Why not return it to the individual who has claim to it?"

Savir's face darkened. "It should not be in the hands of anyone. Not the original owner. Not your guild leader. No one."

Mouse had hoped for a name slip—but Savir, of course, was too savvy for a mistake like that. "From what I understand, in its current state, it is worthless."

Savir swirled the wine in his chalice a moment. "Until it no longer is."

The missing piece.

"You will be rewarded handsomely should you acquire it," Savir said after draining his chalice. "You've proven yourself capable. Stealing it from Agata was aptly done. Shows you are as talented as I've been told."

"Perhaps you've been listening to the wrong people."

"Doubtful."

Mouse sighed. "The hardest person to steal from is another thief. Jardem will have it well hidden and well protected. I won't promise anything. It would be easier if I destroy it myself—"

Savir sat straighter in his chair. "No, you must bring it here. To me. I will need proof that it was destroyed, and the only way I'll be satisfied is if I do it myself."

Mouse donned a smile. "Of course. I completely understand." This fucker wanted it for himself, too.

"I'm pleased to hear it." Savir pushed back his chair. "The hour grows late. I must depart. But I trust we have an accord? You will acquire the document for us?"

"I've made no such commitment, Savir."

Savir looked up in surprise, brow tight. "A promise of payment—"

"Was nebulous, at best." This was a man not accustomed to someone saying no to him. "I will require a drawn contract, no different than you would draft when dealing with the guild directly."

Savir's lips tightened.

"Recognize," Mouse continued, "I could be jailed—or worse—for working outside my indenture to the guild. It is strictly forbidden to take contracts independently. I would be taking a great risk."

"Your involvement will remain our secret—"

"Until it no longer is," Mouse replied coolly.

Rich and powerful men remained rich and powerful by not parting with their coin. Mouse was far beneath this man. He would not think twice about denying him the promised payment due to some manufactured wrongdoing.

"This contract," Mouse continued, "will need to ensure proper payment is made to me when the job is completed. I'm sure you will offer a fair amount." He held up a finger. "And it will need to protect me from any legal consequences should my name become known—"

"I am not certain that is possible—"

"If you are as powerful and influential as you insist you are, I'm certain you can find a way to see it done."

Savir's frowned. A rare show of emotion. "Mouse, you

need to recognize that time is of concern here—"

"Master Savir," Mouse interrupted. "With all due respect, your concern about this document does not make it my emergency. I will make no effort to retrieve it before an agreeable contract is signed. How quickly that happens is entirely up to you."

He forced his expression to remain stoic and in control, but his heart fluttered like a captured starling. The back of his mind chided him while the words spilled from his mouth. He couldn't believe he was speaking this way to someone with more power and influence than most nobles—perhaps even more than the duke. Savir knew his name, knew how to find him. Mouse could be dead by morning if Savir wished it.

Savir stood and ran his hands down the front of his doublet to straighten the creases gained from sitting. "A word of advice, young Mouse. A legal contract can be a messy and restrictive affair. It sets limits. Creates tensions between individuals when the wording is ambiguous. You know how these lawyers and magistrates are." Mouse wanted to laugh at that. As if he encountered them daily. "Yet without such restraints, it is very likely you would achieve more than what was decided early on and scribed on a page. Mutual trust, Mouse. That is what I speak of. Trust that could spark a relationship that extends beyond this one task."

Mouse smiled up at him. "Would here be an appropriate location to pick up the contract?"

Savir dropped his linen napkin on the table and stepped through the curtain without another word.

#

Alone in the small room, Mouse could breathe again. He finished his dinner. Then, he moved over to the chair that Savir had occupied and ate his unfinished meal as well. Then he drained what was left of the wine.

Feeling fat and a little tipsy, he drifted through the dining chamber, back toward the changing room. Gatekeeper was in the hallway, admitting an older man and his much younger companion. Mouse recognized her from Madam Diamond's establishment. Gatekeeper looked sternly at him as he walked by.

"It's about time."

"Everything better still be there," Mouse said.

"I could say the same to you. Need I check your pockets for pilfered utensils?"

Mouse lifted his arms and gave his body a shimmy. "No jingles. But you are free to inspect me," he added with a smirk.

"I'd rather not, thank you," Gatekeeper replied with a grimace.

Mouse stepped into the room. "Can I keep the doublet?"

Gatekeeper sighed and rolled his eyes. "No," he said, and stepped away, leaving Mouse to change back into his own clothes.

Mouse took it anyway, along with some finely inscribed cards with the Golden Flute emblazoned across the front of them in gold ink.

9

AS DUSK settled over the Hollows, Mouse, from his rooftop perch, spotted the glow of candles and lanterns coming alive inside the abandoned warehouse. Only a few at first, but the numbers were increasing. The first attendees were arriving and staking their favorite locations within the old labyrinthine building. The Hollow's Ball had begun.

Mouse had arrived hours earlier and monitored the street below. A few people had wandered inside in the late afternoon hours, but they were quick to depart. *The curious*, Mouse thought. *Here to see if the rumors were true.* Or the anxious and unsure, coming to scope it out while it was still light out. But now that darkness was thickening, a steady flow of hopefuls was disappearing inside.

It was time to drop down to street level and join in. With no idea who he was looking for, Mouse certainly wasn't going to spot his scrivener's arrival from the rooftop. With any luck, he was already in attendance and easy to identify. He didn't have much to go on.

Mouse would need to mingle like all the others.

He stepped through the collapsed northern wall, the grand entrance to the Hollow's Ball, though there were other ways in as well. Someone had created a bridge of sorts over the berm of old debris and dirt, a pathway of overlapping wooden planks. No one lingered here—it was too open, too exposed. Everyone stole to the upper floors.

There wasn't one type that attended the Ball. Some were older. Some younger. Body forms ranged from the fit to those that were less so. Some were well-to-do (though they tried to disguise it), some low-born, and everything in between. But they all fell into one of two groups—those that wandered like a beast on the prowl and those that hunkered down in a secluded site and waited.

From the little that Taurin had said about this scribe, Mouse's instincts told him he was the latter. Which suited Mouse just fine. He preferred the prowl and wasn't keen on waiting around for something to happen.

The Hollow's Ball wasn't something widely known in the city. Those who had heard the rumors of it usually had the wrong idea about those that attended. It was assumed that the attendees were unable or unwilling to accept the inconvenient attractions the gods had seen to fix within them. It was believed that most were married with families—perhaps they were arranged marriages and they had no say as to who their spouse was to be. And when their wanton desires reached a crescendo of heat, they came here to experience what they craved for a brief time before returning to the lives they were trapped within.

Which wasn't at all true.

That *did* exist, of course, but it was only one fragment of the varied stories that made up the Hollow's Ball.

Some of the attendees just desire the anonymity of it, participating in base pleasures without commitment or obligation. No names. No costly courtship. They walked away with the benefits without any of the trappings. Others were addicted to the thrill of it—the hunt and the public nature of it.

Not to mention the variety. But still others were simply not suited for courtship, for the struggles of finding someone compatible to talk to and spend time with. The heft of expectation was just too great.

So, they brought themselves here, where they were not expected to conduct themselves in any socially appropriate manner or participate in such grueling tasks such as conversation.

Mouse circled about the second floor, investigating who was there. Some wandered about with him, like shoppers checking out the wares at a market, uncertain what booth they should descend upon first.

Mouse drifted in and out of spaces to gain a glimpse of who waited there, sometimes triggering hope and then disappointment as Mouse made his exit without an exchange. Sometimes he stepped into an activity already in progress. A few of these had acquired an audience of sorts, standing silently in the shadows. He was even encouraged to join in one of the larger groupings, but he begged off with a lift of his hand.

When he didn't find what he was looking for, he made his way to the next floor and continued his search. The danger was the young scrivener would find what he was looking for before Mouse found him—and then leave when the encounter was concluded. If he didn't find him in time, he might have to wait another week and try again. Mouse didn't have that kind of time.

He was growing more discouraged as he took the rickety stairs to the fourth and final floor of the building. Up here, the integrity of the floor seemed less certain, and it was more unlikely he'd find the man in question so far from the rest of the night's activity. The more popular locales were down below.

Light filtered through the spaces between the wall planks up ahead. Mouse followed the corridor until he located the door and stepped through it. The room was large, but half the outer wall was missing. At some point, it had collapsed to the street below. A cool night wind blew in through the hole. The state of the room was disconcerting, but the view over the dark streets of the Hollow, dusted blue by pale moonlight, caught Mouse in the throat.

Someone leaned against the wall in the corner, a lantern at his feet.

Mouse took a casual step into the room to make sure he was visible. Mouse could feel the man's eyes on him. He had his hands tucked under his arms, and he certainly looked the anxious type.

"Quite the view," Mouse said. "I can see why you've chosen this spot."

The man didn't reply. Instead, he looked at his feet and not at Mouse.

"Salutations," Mouse added, wielding his most disarming smile. It paid to use big words when trying to charm the educated. He stepped closer and offered a cheery lift of his hand, close enough to get a better look at him.

The man lifted one hand in a small wave. His fingers were blackened with ink stains.

It was the confirmation he was looking for. Mouse stepped over debris in the center of the room—a portion of the ceiling that had collapsed.

The scribe looked nervous enough to bolt, so Mouse took it slow, heeding Taurin's warning. The scribe watched the approach with eyes like a rabbit spotting a wolf across the field. Mouse considered that he might appear too young for him—though a few here made it clear that was their preference—so he moved more into the lamplight so his beard would be visible.

The scribe seemed to consider the question as if pained him. "E-evening."

Gods, this guy was nervous. "Care for some company?" Mouse lifted a metal flask from the inside pocket of his cloak. "I brought us a beverage. Care for a nip?"

The scribe nodded.

Mouse twisted the cork off the flask and handed it over. The scribe took it in his ink covered fingers and raised it to his lips, his eyes still on Mouse.

He was older than Mouse, but not by much, and his appearance was a bit slovenly. His clothes were ill-fitting. Tufts of dark hair stuck out from under his coif bonnet, and his beard was in desperate need of a barber's attention. He didn't seem to care much how he looked. But despite that, he still carried a wholesome charm about him. An innocence. He was comely in a sort of accidental way.

"What's your name?"

Again, a long pause. As if he debated with himself whether to answer truthfully. "Othmar."

"Pleasure. You can call me Mouse."

Othmar's lips broke into a small, sweet smile at that.

Mouse stepped in closer until they were nearly touching, and he slipped a hand along the small of Othmar's back. Othmar stepped back as if startled. "No."

Mouse held up his hands. The last thing he wanted to do was spook him, so he moved back and gave Othmar space. Everyone spent time at the Hollow's Ball for different reasons and had different inclinations and interests. Mouse only had to figure out what he was looking for.

Othmar, for his part, looked embarrassed by his own reaction. He turned his head and closed his eyes. Mouse waited, wordlessly. Then, without warning, Othmar lowered to his knees and began the work of loosening the drawstring of Mouse's trousers.

Mouse understood. Submission was the objective here. Othmar's only interest was providing another with pleasure. He sought none for himself. His own satisfaction was met by using his power to bring someone else to conclusion. Mouse was to provide no physical stimulation in return. The only expectation on Mouse was to overtly show he enjoyed the experience.

Othmar tugged Mouse's trousers to his knees. He pulled in a sharp breath and stared at Mouse's strong legs in wonder. His quivering hand rested on Mouse's thigh and followed the contour up his leg, then circled it around to palm his ass. His other hand cupped Mouse's sack as his cock swelled to life.

Then Othmar took Mouse fully into his mouth.

Mouse gasped, and a groan escaped his throat. His head fell back, and he involuntarily placed his hand on the back of Othmar's head, raking fingers through his hair—acceptable contact since it denoted Mouse's enjoyment.

Mouse let it continue for a time, then pulled his hips back to remove himself.

"Wait…wait," he said, shuffling backward. "Not yet. I was getting too close."

Othmar, sitting back on his heels, looked disappointed as Mouse pulled his trousers up over his hips. The stiffened cock remained out. It would be too uncomfortable to tuck it away into his trousers.

"We're not done. Just…need a breather. That all right? I'm not ready for this to be over."

Othmar nodded and stood again, wiping his spit-soaked beard with his hand. The two were silent for a time, both catching their breath. Othmar's eyes shifted to meet Mouse's and his mouth opened to speak.

"You're—" he began, then struggled to continue, stuck on the same sound before he managed to finish. "Beautiful."

Mouse smiled warmly back at him. "Thank you. As are you." It was the truth. "You are also quite talented," he added with a smirk.

Even in the poor light, he could see Othmar blush.

The stammer explained everything about him. Writing was how he best communicated, which was why he'd pursued a vocation as a scrivener. And he came here because there was rarely a need for conversation.

Mouse took his hand and inspected it. "You're a scribe, then." Othmar tried to pull it away again, but Mouse did not let it go as he massaged the palm with his thumb. Eventually, Othmar relaxed and let Mouse work the muscles in his hand.

"Why do I find that…enticing?" Mouse asked.

Mouse let the silence between them linger for a time while he massaged Othmar's hand. His writing hand. Othmar's eyes closed in pleasure. He likely hadn't ever felt that kind of relief to the overworked instrument he depended on.

"Funny," Mouse continued. "I was going in search for a scribe tomorrow. I had questions." He chuckled dourly. "But no," he said. "I've no wish to ruin our encounter with such mundane matters."

Othmar bit his lip. "I can."

The eagerness in him made Mouse's insides twist. "No, it's all right." His voice turned sober. "I've no wish to cause you unease. Another time, perhaps."

Othmar held his eyes on Mouse a moment, lips pressed, then lowered to a crouch. For a moment, Mouse thought he might try to resume the earlier activity, but instead, he reached into the small haversack on the ground. He pulled out a leather-bound journal, quill, and inkwell. He sat cross-legged on the floor and put the journal in his lap, open to a fresh page.

"You carry that around with you always?" Mouse asked, a smile creeping back onto his face.

Othmar nodded. He took the quill and ink and began to scribble onto the page. When finished, he turned the journal so Mouse could see. Mouse, having softened a bit, tucked himself away into the trousers and sat down next to him. It was still uncomfortable; his cock squeezed against the loosened drawstrings of his trousers. He positioned the lantern so he could read the words on the page.

You can read, then? Othmar wrote.

"I can, actually," Mouse said with a laugh. "Does that surprise you?"

A little. Othmar smirked and made a little shrug.

"I'll forgive that assumption," Mouse replied.

"Considering."

This will be faster. Then I can get back to doing what I do best.

Mouse couldn't help but laugh again, even louder this time. "I can tell you're being modest. I agree you are very good at the other activity, but by your pen, I can tell you are a talented scribe as well."

Othmar shrugged but still wielded a shy smile. *Ask your questions.*

"Very well. I need to know something about a document."

What kind of document?

"That's the problem. I need to know what it is. All I know is it is very valuable." Mouse gave him a skeletal account of how he came in possession of it.

Othmar narrowed his eyes at him in a judgmental fashion, but then wrote, *If I am to discern what it is, I need more detail. Tell me what you know of it.*

Mouse relayed what he knew, which wasn't much. How it was locked away in a rich merchant's bedchamber closet, how the head of the guild had someone locked away in a cellar, how the Shadow Elite had an interest in it. He also told Othmar how there was something else people were looking for—that the document was worthless without it.

Another document?

By now, the outside was fully consumed in darkness. The sky, viewed through the hole in the wall, was a rich indigo and dotted with the first intrepid stars. Mouse had to tilt the journal toward the hooded lantern to make out Othmar's words. "No. I got the impression it was an object of some sort."

Othmar slammed the journal shut and launched to his feet. He stomped across the room scratching at his shaggy beard.

"What is it?" Mouse asked, rising to his feet, too. "Do you know what it is?"

Othmar didn't respond.

"No one knows I'm here talking to you. You're not in danger." Mouse hoped that was true.

Othmar chuckled and looked over his shoulder at Mouse. With sudden conviction, he crossed the room again and dropped to the floor and picked up the journal again.

I can't be certain. Understand?

"Of course."

Othmar scribbled for a while before he passed the journal over. *The missing object in question is likely a royal signet rod. It is a misconception that the king only uses his ring to officiate legal documents. Too many require his seal. So, his highness entrusts a number of stewards to wield signets that are carved in ivory. They are called the Crown Notaries, and they are used to conduct the king's business.*

"What makes you think this object is one of those signets?"

Because one is rumored to be missing.

Mouse frowned and bit his lip as he thought. Possessing the royal seal would be of tremendous value. But also, a dangerous thing to possess. "How did it go missing? I'm certain it was something well-guarded. Who would have the balls to steal something directly from the king's palace?"

Not all the king's business is conducted at the palace, Mouse. The Crown Notaries travel all over Davenia on the king's business.

Mouse had never considered that. He had no concept of the inner workings of the government or of commerce. He was a street rat that knew how to lift shiny things.

The notary that lost his signet was en route to somewhere with it. Possibly to here in Har Teresa, but that is not known for certain. The carriage was set upon by bandits on the road. Supposedly.

This sounded fishy. "Why 'supposedly?' You don't believe the tale?"

Othmar made a weak shrug before he started writing again. *The notary would be accompanied by the king's guard.*

And few know of their schedule ahead of time. Seems unlikely to me.

Made sense that the movement of these rods was kept under wraps. "Inside knowledge? A traitor or spy within the palace tipped the bandits off?"

Othamr made a face, as if to say, "Possibly."

"Or they saw the pretty carriage and attacked the protective retinue, thinking it was filled with a fat noble and his riches. They discovered the Notary and took off with the signet rod."

Attack the king's men? Rather foolhardy.

Mouse scratched his beard. "Desperate folk will try all kinds of foolishness for the promise of coin. And it's not as mad as you think, besides. There are plenty of skilled robbers out there on the road with the numbers and the talent to pull it off." Mouse knew several personally that would attempt it without a second thought.

Othmar considered that, running his blackened fingers along the edge of his quill.

"The signet rod and the document were both taken when the carriage was ambushed, then?"

Probably not. They were likely separated.

"Good point." The document was probably already at the destination awaiting the Crown Notary and the official seal. Mouse bit his thumbnail and made it snap on his front teeth as he considered this. "So, this document everyone is after was supposed to receive the king's official nod." Mouse sat back on his heels. "What could possibly be that important?"

Othmar smirked knowingly as he turned the journal to Mouse so he could read. *Impossible to say for sure. Could be any number of things. The king wields the power to grant almost anything. Land. Pardons for crimes.*

Mouse bit his lower lip. Until the document received the signal seal, it was only a sheet of parchment. Jardem had his eye on it for some reason. Savir said he wanted it destroyed. Didn't want it in the wrong hands, he said. But Mouse didn't trust him. He was still convinced Savir wanted it for himself.

The conversation with Savir still unsettled him. He was alarmingly well informed. He knew who Mouse was, knew he was involved in the theft of the document, *and* was able to effortlessly locate him in his old haunt in Rharden Square. What else did he already know?

He'd played a dangerous game with Savir. But at the moment, he couldn't shake the feeling that if he went along with him, he'd only trade one pair of manacles for another. The man was too guarded. Too in control. And Mouse didn't trust anyone he couldn't read. His instincts told him Savir would betray him if it suited him—regardless of any contract they'd signed. A contract was meaningless if one of them was dead.

He'd done what he could to buy some time. Now, he needed to learn more about what was happening. If he was going to expose Jardem, he needed more.

Like finding out who the young merchant was in the cage beneath the guild. And what had he done to make him the intended recipient of the king's favor?

Othmar poked him, jarring him from his thoughts. He put the journal back in Mouse's hands. *I have answered your questions.*

Mouse smiled and glanced up. Othmar was watching him with raised expectant brows. "Indeed, you have. You've been more than accommodating."

I feel I am entitled to some recompense for these added services.

"And you shall be granted that reward most willingly and enthusiastically." Mouse lifted to his feet, and as he did, he held onto the waistline of the loose trousers. The trousers rolled off his hips and ended up inside out and hanging roughly off the edge of his boots. He extended his arms, offering himself to Othmar.

As Othmar set the journal aside and shifted onto his knees in front of Mouse's exposed lower half, Mouse held up a finger. "But—"

Othmar eyes narrowed at him. He was tired of delays.

"I feel there may be times I'm in need of a talented scribe. One not unlike yourself. Don't know what your wages are, but I could put a few more coins in your purse on occasion. Interested?"

"Very," Othmar said. He scribbled something more at the bottom of the journal page, tore it off and handed it to Mouse. The location of his tenement.

Then he commenced with his earlier pursuit, and Mouse made no effort to stop him. It was late in the night by the time Mouse took his leave of the Hollow's Ball. Mouse had fulfilled his end of the bargain, giving Othmar the full sum of his desired payment.

Twice.

10

OUTSIDE THE Ball, on the street, a cluster of men had gravitated around a makeshift brazier made from a large, broken earthenware vat. Someone had brought a jug, and it passed from hand to hand around the fire. They laughed and shared their exploits from the night, like returning warriors bragging of their time on the battlefield. How many arrows they'd shot. How many times they'd took an arrow. They reveled in this secret world and weren't yet ready to return to their lives.

The relaxed nature of the gathering told Mouse this was a routine event. The men clearly ran in different circles within the city, but none of that mattered here. The Hollow's Ball had a strange leveling effect, and their common purpose had created unlikely alliances—even friendships. For Mouse, the comradery they shared stabbed at him. He was tempted to join in.

For a time, at least, he might not feel alone.

He forced himself to keep walking and wended through the abandoned streets, unsure where he was headed. The Hollows became the haunt for a different form of creature come nightfall, and it was unwise to linger long among these gloomy streets, especially alone. But his mind whirled.

Othmar's insight gave him much to ponder over—and fret about. The seal had already told him of the connection with the king, but part of him assumed it was some sort of missive. Knowing it was some royal decree requiring the formal seal was disquieting.

He was used to pinching shiny baubles that a spoiled merchant's wife coveted. This felt beyond him. He had, in a sense, pilfered something owned by the king himself.

Was the king aware this document had fallen into nefarious hands? The last thing he needed was the king's guard poking around, too, asking him questions.

What if…what if it was what Othmar suggested? A king's pardon. If he found the missing signet, could he use it himself? Clear his name? A quick spark of hope made his heart lurch.

No…Savir could afford his own pardon if he needed one. He wouldn't desire it as he did. It was something else.

A noise in the shadows yanked him from his thoughts and made him flinch. Rats, probably, but his mind was expecting an ambush.

He sighed and cut down a new street that led to the Hollow's wall. Time to leave. This place had real dangers this time of night, and he wasn't paying attention to his surroundings. He knew better than to wander these cursed streets, distracted as he was. Trouble would find him.

He scaled the crumbling wall and crossed the plank bridge to a nearby roof.

Back in the city proper, he took to the narrow streets, hood over his head, his cloak pulled in tighter against the night's deepening chill. He let his legs choose the direction. The streets here were not his usual haunt, but he knew generally where he was, knew what direction to move. But as he drifted back, his thoughts again drew him deeper within himself.

He'd been absent from the guild the entire day now.

Jardem was going to be furious with him. A part of him didn't care. Another part of him relished in causing it. Eventually, he'd have to head back and face Jardem's tantrum. But he wasn't ready yet.

The only thing that drew him back to the guild hall was the handsome young prisoner Jardem had in the cellar. Mouse needed to talk to him again. At length. Othmar had stirred a hundred more questions that only the rich fop could answer.

The sound of footfalls on cobbles cut through his thoughts and landed into his consciousness. Several pairs of boots. Behind him. The pace was steady, unhurried, not unlike his own. He grunted, irritated with himself. He'd fallen too deep into his thoughts again—he had no idea how long this group had been behind him.

Paranoid? Perhaps. But he wasn't taking chances. Savir's spy had put Mouse on edge. And who else was on the list of those wanting their hands on this document?

Or it may be as simple as a hungry pack of Scourge, hoping to prey on someone alone and unprotected. Damn his foolishness. He knew better.

He quickened his pace, and his mind riffled through his options.

A quick scurry to the rooftop? A dash down an alley? Both risky if he didn't know where the danger was. He could run right into them.

He turned a corner onto another wide street, well-lit with the steady light of street lanterns. To test if this was paranoia or instinct. His pursuers turned as well.

A sound drew his attention upward. Onto a rooftop. The clang of boots on clay tiles—a sound he knew all too well. A shadowy figure ducked out of sight just as his head cocked upward.

They were attempting to surround him. Cut him off.

His rooftop option was off the table now. If there was one up there, there were more.

Fuck.

It was an ambush then. Whoever it was, and whatever their aim, he had no intention of loitering about.

He made a quick inventory of the buildings around him. Most of the street was shuttered and dark; homes and businesses were closed up tight for the night. But up the block was the elegant stone façade of a temple, with towering pillars supporting a grand portico. Two braziers burned warmly on either side of wide double doors.

Temples didn't keep a merchant's hours. Their doors would be open. He'd cut through and find another way out. Hopefully, his pursuers would have enough of a healthy fear of the divine to enter a temple after him.

As he jogged up the marble steps, he glanced up at the elaborate stone relief of the portico—a dramatic scene of battle and carnage with a striking nude figure at the center, head near the point of the triangle, face looking to the sky. Mouse still had no clue what god was worshiped here, but he took the giant naked warrior as a good sign.

He pulled open the heavy door, which groaned on ancient hinges, and he slipped inside. Then he pulled it shut again with a thud.

After a short candlelit vestibule, the temple opened into a large octagon. The chamber was basked in golden light. Fires crackled within shallow braziers that hung from the domed ceiling on thick silver chains.

Mouse's footsteps echoed eerily as he stepped onto the intricate tile pattern. It was unlike anything he'd seen—not that he frequented such buildings. It was a dizzying swirl of burgundy, black, and blue, over-lapping spinning vortexes that made the eyes blink. In the center of the chamber was a statue of the same nude man that was on the relief outside, only here he gripped a spear in one hand, its end planted into the floor, and had a helm tucked under the other arm, pressed to his flank. The grand sculpture was surrounded by eight reliefs carved into the walls—all depicting unrelated scenes that included this striking nude man.

Eight stone benches formed a circle around the statue.

He circled around to the opposite side. Another short corridor led to a door. Locked from within. No keyhole for him to pick.

Fuck.

He pulled the dagger from his boot, sat on the edge of a bench, and waited to hear if the door opened.

The snap of a latch was followed by the creek of stiff hinges. Mouse's body stiffened. But it wasn't the massive doors across the chamber that opened. It was the smaller door nearer to him.

An acolyte stepped into the warm light of the chamber. The devotee had a shaved head and wore a long burgundy robe that matched the tile on the floor. Mouse blinked at the figure. The face was beautifully formed with soft curves and had bright grey eyes that flickered in the light.

Mouse couldn't tell if the acolyte was male or female. The features seemed to lack any of the markers that might hint to gender and instead swam somewhere between them.

"I thought I heard the arrival of a late-night worshiper," the acolyte said. The eyes shifted to the dagger in Mouse's hand.

Mouse quickly slid it back into the boot, for reasons he didn't understand, feeling embarrassed. He didn't know what to say, so he lifted his hand in an awkward half-hearted wave.

"Ah. I've startled you. My apologies." The acolyte made a gentle bow with closed eyes. "Forgive me, but you've the look of a man with a nest full of troubles."

Mouse's face flushed. "I'm fine."

"Are you?" asked the acolyte. "Well, you're safe here, if that is your worry. I can assure you of that."

Mouse wasn't convinced. His eyes kept shifting toward the entrance to the temple.

"Feel free to stay here and contemplate these trials you face as long as you wish." The acolyte's eyes shifted to the statue. "Inir is here to guide you. Many have found the answers they seek by simply meditating on his image."

Mouse cleared his throat to stifle a clumsy chuckle. "I've seen worse things to stare at," he managed to say.

"Indeed," said the acolyte with a glimmer of a smile forming on their lips. The acolyte stepped closer, making no sound.

Barefoot, Mouse assumed.

"By all means, you *should* admire him," the acolyte said. "Because he is as glorious as the rising sun. The Whirling is not opposed to weaponry. Only…there is a time and place for such things."

"The Whirling?"

"My order. We follow the will and teachings of Inir. Protector and martyr of Yene Prosaeno."

Mouse knew none of those words. "Ah," he said.

The smile widened. A knowing and gentle smile. "But I see you are ill-informed about our faith. Inir in his wisdom has guided you here."

"Uh…the door was open." Mouse was beginning to wonder if this was a bad idea.

"As it always is. Stay and admire Inir as long as you wish." The acolyte turned to leave through the door they'd emerged from but stopped and turned back to face Mouse. "My name is Etar. Share your name if you wish, but it is not expected here."

Mouse considered remaining quiet, but he answered, unsure as to why. "Mouse."

Etar bowed again. "Honored to meet you."

Usually his name brought questions, but Etar accepted it without even a lift of eyebrow. Perhaps the acolyte thought it wasn't really his name.

"It is not often," Etar said, "that we are visited by a member of the thieves' guild."

Mouse's mouth dropped open. He wanted to deny it, but he knew there was no point.

"There is an aura about you, Mouse. One I find familiar.

The way you move, the way you breathe, the way you watch."
Etar slid up a sleeve to reveal a tattoo on the forearm. "I am
acquainted with the ways of the street. And I am familiar with
your kind as well."

Mouse knew the tattoo. The Scourge.

"You seemed surprised. Does it shock you that someone
with a past like mine could choose this life?"

"I suppose it does," Mouse said.

"The way of Inir is not like others within the pantheon.
Which is what led me here in the first place." Etar reached
under the neck of their, grabbed a chain, and withdrew it. A
large emerald dangled at the end. "Look at this jewel.
Beautiful, is it not?"

It certainly was. And the value of it staggering. Mouse
would not have expected such a treasure to be casually on the
neck of an acolyte.

"Would you find the same beauty or value in it if it
remained just an unpolished chunk of rock? It is the facets cut
into the stone that give it is value, yes? The beauty in the world
is not made of one type of soul, Mouse. It is an amalgam of
souls all making their way in the world."

"And that includes thieves, like me."

"It does indeed. And former killers like myself."

Mouse's insides clenched. He did not expect that.

"We all have our role to play in the Whirling. Should we
fault the wolf for killing the rabbit? Survival is blameless."

"Is it?" Mouse asked softly, diverting his eyes from the
intensity of Etar's dark gaze.

Etar was quiet a moment, head cocked slightly,
considering Mouse. "So, these troubles you ponder. Are you
the wolf…or the rabbit?"

"Depends on your perspective, I suppose."

"Fair. And refreshingly honest. Most would label
themselves the victim in their troubles. Yet you did not. You
intuit the complexity in the Whirling."

Mouse bristled at the notion of labeling himself a victim.

He caught himself glancing toward the entrance again and listening for the grind of old hinges.

Etar's eyes followed the direction of Mouse's attention, then swung back. "No one will enter the temple now. I've seen to it."

Mouse immediately stiffened at the thought that he was trapped inside here. Etar didn't appear to be a threat, but the admission of being a killer—former or otherwise—gave him pause.

"In your former life, before you joined here," he said quietly. "What were you? Wolf or rabbit?"

"Neither. I was the scorpion. I would strike, not out of survival, but out of anger. Out of contempt. And I would relish in watching my victim suffer and die." Eyes drifted back to the massive naked statue. "Inir saved me from that life. I now embrace my part of the Whirling." Etar's voice never gave a hint of emotion. Hands and forearms lost in the wide sleeves, Etar seemed enshrouded in a state of peace. "It is one of the tenets of our faith that we provide help to whoever requires it. Inir, however, teaches us that to help those who do not ask for it is the highest offense. Be it through pride, foolishness or confidence, all are entitled to attempt to save themselves if they are able. We will not take that agency away from any. But if it is our help you desire, you must ask."

Mouse scoffed. "I doubt you can do anything to help me."

"Help comes in many forms, Mouse." Etar shrugged. "Inir did guide you here. Perhaps, for once, trust in something other than the dagger in your boot."

Mouse frowned. He didn't say anything for a time, and the space between him and Etar was growing thick.

"Make your ask if you wish to," Etar pressed with a cold gravity that sent waves of icy down the length of Mouse's arms. "Or not. It is up to you."

"Very well, acolyte of Inir." Mouse said. "I am interested in your help." He spat the words out quickly, like pulling dressing from a wound fixed to the skin with congealed blood. It surprised him how hard it was to let those words leave his tongue.

Again, the sly smile broke the edge of Etar's mouth. "Speak the way I might be of service to you."

There was an oddly sexual undertone to the way Etar said the words.

"Very well," Mouse said. "Grant me the advice I require."

With no real overt changes in Etar's expression, Mouse did sense a momentary sign of satisfaction he couldn't qualify. Etar glided soundlessly across the tile to take a seat on the edge of the next bend over from where Mouse sat. "Speak your dilemma, then."

Mouse thought a moment. He didn't trust this Etar…not yet. "I have a client. Trapped in an indenture by a powerful man. He aims to be free of it, but the one who possesses the document of indenture has intelligence that will destroy my client."

Etar nodded. "A tragic yet not entirely unfamiliar story. Go on."

"The client believes the powerful man is involved in some…illicit activity within an organization he runs."

Again, Etar nodded their close attention to these details. "As are so many. And you've been hired to find evidence of this criminal enterprise?"

"I have," Mouse replied. "But the situation is thorny, Etar." The details whirled around Mouse's head. It was too complicated to spill all the details here. He kept to the main problem. "If Jardem finds out about my attempts to dig up what he's up to, it will trigger retaliation." He realized too late he'd said Jardem's name. His eyes darted to Etar to search for a reaction, recognition, but nothing registered on their calm face. "If…my client reveals the evidence and attempts to extort his freedom, there is nothing stopping the man from still retaliating."

"No. Nothing."

Mouse was convinced this peaceful and somewhat disconcerting acolyte could see right through his fiction. As he uttered each word, he tasted their falseness in his mouth, and he was certain they had the same ring in Etar's ears. But he pushed on, regardless. "And a powerful third party is also involved, complicating matters further."

"A dangerous sort?"

Was the Shadow Elite dangerous? Was the king dangerous? Mouse kept his sarcasm tucked under his tongue and only nodded.

Etar filled the silence that followed. "They want in on this criminal enterprise, no doubt."

"You are disturbingly astute, acolyte."

It was Etar's turn, considering all that Mouse had revealed to him, to make a glance toward the door, and this time the acolyte frowned. The gesture sent a roll of icy prickles down Mouse's arm. "Ah," Etar said, with a hint of new comprehension. "So, you are in the process of finding proof of this involvement. But you are unsure what to do when you find it."

"Yes," Mouse said softly. "That is my dilemma."

"Well, I'm pleased to report to you, Mouse, the solution is rather obvious," Etar said with a lift of palms to the ceiling. "Praise Inir."

Mouse looked up, astonished.

"First, your client must never reveal the information you discover to the one holding this writ of indenture. That would end in disaster." Mouse was ready to cut in that that was obvious, but Etar anticipated his interruption and lifted a finger. "They instead reveal it to the organization he runs, removing that which shores up his power."

Mouse stared back dumbly. Of course. It was obvious. If Jardem was disgraced for breaking the long-established rules of the Night Fingers, he'd be removed as head of the guild. Perhaps even ousted from the guild entirely. If Mouse's involvement was unknown, Jardem wouldn't retaliate against him. Mouse was both suddenly giddy and angry he hadn't thought of it himself.

"You must be very careful," Etar warned. "This man—Jardem, you called him—must never learn of your client's involvement in this. Choose wisely who you pass the damning evidence to. Make sure they are willing to topple the man's power and have a hunger to claim, even if for themselves."

Mouse lifted to his feet. His head swam a little. "That…that could actually work."

Etar stood as well and bowed their head. "I am truly honored that I was able to provide you aid. It is safe for you to leave now, by the way."

"Was it not earlier?"

Etar said nothing, but instead drifted back toward the door from which they'd come. Before disappearing from the chamber, the acolyte turned again. "I'll add a warning about the…third party that has shown investment in this endeavor of yours. They are more dangerous than you realize."

"I know," Mouse said. "I've met them."

"I fear you are still widely ignorant of the perils you face." The stoic face shifted with disturbing speed into a smile that carried little warmth. "When this business is concluded to your satisfaction, I invite you to return to us and perhaps honor us with a token of your gratitude. Whatever it is you feel is appropriate." And Etar disappeared through the door.

Mouse stood in the now empty temple.

No longer at the helm, Jardem's power over him would cease. He'd be free. It was a dicey plan. But it could work. The wheels of his mind were churning, already spinning all he'd learned into the threads of a design.

He took one last look at the towering beauty of Inir before he pushed through the front door. He half expected it to be locked, but it swung open on its tired hinges. As he descended the wide marble steps, glowing golden from the braziers that still burned even at this late hour, he noticed dark stains on several of the steps. He didn't recall them being there as he came in. Perhaps in his rush to find safety, he'd failed to notice them.

But he didn't think so.

11

EXHAUSTION WAS setting deep in his body as he shuffled through the finely maintained streets of the Merchant District. It had been a very long day, and the thickening fog of weariness in his head muddled his thinking like he'd been drugged. Yet his stomach reminded him he hadn't eaten since the Golden Flute. Big as the meal was, his stomach was empty now and demanding more.

A meal and to bed.

He aimed his trajectory back toward his old haunt by the bell tower. He'd take a meal in a tavern that knew him and knew to leave him be. All he wanted in that moment was to submerge himself in the isolating din of a crowded room, mug in hand, and to mull over all he'd learned.

Then, he'd sneak into the tower for the night. He still wasn't ready to face the guild or Jardem. He'd see how he felt in the morning.

He landed at The Three Swords, a grungy establishment riding the twilight between the Merchant District and the bank of warehouses by the river. It was a favored lair of the dockworkers. Mouse liked to eavesdrop on the gossip that rolled in from the other duchies via the merchant ships. Dockworkers were the first to hear any news from abroad and quick to compare notes. When he entered the tavern, the dockworkers were already knee deep in their revelry. They were at the song-singing stage of their bibulous entertainments.

> *Keep your balls in your right hand*
> *And two fingers in her bum*
> *Wiggle the one and tickle with two*
> *And ya both are sure to—*
> *Come on up, and take your turn*
> *The bailey's called the front*
> *You grease up the pantry, sir*
> *And I'll butter up the—*
> *Country boys have joined the queue*
> *All doffing off their kits...*

Mouse took a stool at the bar and pantomimed to the barkeep that he wanted an ale and a meal. No use attempting to yell over the full-throated singing of twenty-odd sailors. He slapped coin on the smooth wood counter and a foaming mug was plopped in front of him soon after.

The song ended, and the room exploded with a hearty cheer and raucous laughter. Some men leapt to their feet, hands up like champions at a tourney, while others fell off their stools and rolled about the floor. Then, an unseen wind shifted, and the merriment lost its momentum. The fun was over, and the dock crowd descended back into their ale and their banter.

A serving wench dropped a wooden plate in front of him as she dived back into the crush of bodies, and the aroma hit his empty gut. It was a generous portion to be sure—and far cheaper than the posh meal he'd had at the Flute: a few cuts of roasted pork, a mound of broad beans, a wedge of boiled cabbage, and a hunk of bread. He tore off a piece of bread and sopped up the juices pooling on the plate.

As was his habit, Mouse kept his ear to the room while he tore off pieces of meat with his fingers and popped them into his mouth. Easier now that the song portion of the evening had passed. One never knew what information would be useful.

Some noble-born's vessel had docked that day. No one of high standing based on the quality of the crafts, and no one could state with any certainty whom the craft had delivered. The arrival of nobles wasn't anything unusual or noteworthy, really. Traffic in and out of a city as large as Har Tesera was commonplace.

But there was other talk, whispered talk. Mouse couldn't quite grasp what it was about. But something of interest had happened at the docks—and the dockhands were more reticent about sharing the details.

Orno, the barkeep, abandoned his post at the keg taps and leaned a hip and elbow on the bar across from him. He had the look of a brutish man that had allowed time to catch up to him. His shoulders and arms were still thick and strong, but the belly beneath his apron was the size of one of his kegs. His thick beard was flaked with unruly strands of white, and his head was shaved to the scalp. When the lantern light hit his head just right, Mouse could see a shadow of new growth above his ears.

"Ah, the winds of turmoil bring the ill-famed back into my fine establishment," Orno said.

Mouse glanced around the room as he took a swig from the frothy top of the tankard. "Strong wind, indeed, by the look of the crowd."

Orno laughed. "Welcome back to the Swords, young Mouse. Not seen your face here since that scuff with the Scourge brawler."

Mouse groaned inwardly. He'd forgotten about that. Maybe he'd chosen the wrong tavern. "He had it coming, Orno."

"Ah, no argument here. It's why I didn't send the bill for

the smashed table to that guild of yours. Happy to see that cunt get his what for.”

Mouse tore off a piece of bread and sopped up the juices pooling on the plate. “Then, is this meal on the house as a way to show your thanks?”

“The chair cost was more than that slop you’re inhaling.”

Mouse shrugged. Fair enough. “Worth a try. Lots of whispers here tonight, Orno. What’s got these dockhands tittering like handmaidens?”

Orno lifted his eyes. “Rumors about some rich merchant gone missing. Not really paying any attention to it, honestly. Some saying he was murdered. At some inn. Along with his personal guards.”

“Why would dockhands be concerned about that?”

Orno shrugged. “His private craft is moored at the docks. City guards were by to inspect and secure it. The boys are taking bets on who comes to claim it now. I can fill you in on the odds if you want in on it.”

Mouse wasn’t interested. Orno shoved off to return to his taps as more orders came in. Mouse pushed his empty plate away, downed the last of his second ale, and left the tavern.

The streets were vacant now, the merchant district all but abandoned. Mouse cut into the plaza of Rharden Square.

In the dark, it had the feeling of a war camp. The more permanent booths were shut tight with clunky locks on their shuttered fronts, while the colorful tents had their flaps down to hide their interiors. Nothing of any real value would be left around, but some of the venders grew weary of hauling everything in for the night. So, some merchandise remained, locked within chests that were chained to their tent poles. Others hired watchers to sleep in the tents to keep an eye on the wares.

It was how Mouse, before joining the guild, earned a coin now and then and kept out of the rain. But not every night. Competition for the job was steep—the streets of Har Tesera had always been plagued with homeless urchins. Which was why he was so thankful he'd discovered the abandoned bell tower.

At a sort of jogging crouch, he wended through the plaza. A few bored city guards patrolled about to deter thieves, but they were easy enough to avoid. Mouse followed the path he remembered so well until he came to the back side of a bright blue tent. He tugged up the canvas to create a gap and slithered inside on his belly.

It was dark in the apothecary's tent. Lighting a candle would be risky, even with the dark color of the canvas, but he'd been in the tent enough times to find his way about by feel alone. He knew where the locked chest was, and the lock was poor quality and laughably easy to pick. No point in splurging on a quality lock when the risk of someone stealing jars of herbs was low.

The apothecary had unknowingly kept Mouse well supplied for years.

Mouse smelled the contents of the jars to locate what he was looking for and scooped what he needed into a small fabric pouch. Then, carefully, he returned everything as he'd found it and wiggled under the tent's side once again.

The knife in his boot thrummed against his skin as he drew closer to the abandoned clock tower. It did that on occasion, and he had no idea why. Usually, it happened when danger was near. Mouse always told himself it wasn't the knife at all. It was likely his mind warning him, his deep senses picking up something that he wasn't quite aware of on the surface. It was reminding him of the knife by making his muscle tingle.

He came to a stop. A bit of shadowy movement caught his eye. A dark figure leaned one shoulder against a shabby wooden booth. A black cloak obscured the shape of the body, and the hood covered the head—but by the size, Mouse assumed it was a man. A gloved hand lifted to reach under the hood, and a thread of pipe smoke curled out from under it a moment later. Mouse caught the smell of it on the night breeze.

The cloaked figure's position gave him a clear view of the clock tower's door.

Low to the ground, Mouse skirted a few tents, then scaled the back of a booth sturdy enough to hold his weight. He shuffled on his belly across the roof. From his higher vantage point, he scanned more of the plaza around the tower.

As he suspected, another figure was nearby. Similarly cloaked. Watching the door.

His door.

Fuck. Will this night never end? No way to know if it was the same people who'd pursued him near the temple or others who'd decided to keep a close eye on him. His popularity of late was disconcerting.

Few knew of his hiding place. He ticked them off in his mind, building a list of suspects. But there was always the possibility he'd been followed last night and he'd missed it. He'd witnessed the skill of Savir's men himself.

Savir, of course, would want to keep tabs on him after their conversation, and his spy had trailed him in this same square earlier. Stood to reason that someone had seen him enter or depart the bell tower. But, of course, Jardem could be behind the surveillance as well. With his own network of spies everywhere in the city, he could have learned of Mouse's sanctuary. Jardem could have sent them to nab him and drag him back to the guild by his ears.

But with the apparent value of the strange document he'd pilfered for Jardem, who knew if more dangerous parties were getting involved? Ones he didn't yet know.

Where to now, then? Not the guild. Not yet.

He could find an out-of-the-way inn, hole up in a room for a day, but his purse was feeling light. He'd have to scrape up the coin somewhere, and it was too late for any quick options.

The solution was obvious. The private river craft at the docks.

The murdered merchant wasn't going to need it. And

rich merchants always had fine bedchambers on their personal yachts. It might take days to travel from one city to another, and gods forbid they sleep on anything but satin sheets and down mattresses.

His meal at the Golden Flute had given him an appetite for finer things.

Orno said the boat was secured…but any city guard assigned to watch it was likely already asleep on the job or had abandoned their post for a tavern to grab a pint. It was an opportunity Mouse should at least explore. He'd be a fool not to.

He eased himself off the top of the shack and slipped away through the dark plaza unnoticed.

#

The docks were always quiet at night but never vacant. Even at this hour, a few dockhands and ship crew milled about, some stumbling back from the taverns. A few guards were stationed here, like in the plaza, but they were clustered around a crate with cards in their hands. Their role here was to be present, nothing more. They paid no attention to anyone milling about.

Mouse cut across the open area that bordered the river, eyeing each of the crafts moored to the docks. Six in all. Most of them were river barges. Though merchants were known to travel with their cargo, word in the tavern pointed to a personal vessel. One of them was clearly a passenger ship for travel up and down the river to nearby towns. That left one craft at the far dock.

As he made his way down the length of the dock, two deckhands laughed with each other as they pissed into the river. They paid him no heed as Mouse leapt from the dock onto the deck of the vessel. It was a fine craft, as far as Mouse could tell. He knew little about such things. It was smaller than the neighboring barges and had a stubby little cottage positioned closer to the front and a tall mast for a sail astern. The small windows in the cottage were dark. Mouse waited for the deckhands to finish their business and moved on before he circled around the cottage, looking for the door.

The door had been broken in; the lock that once protected it was discarded on the deck. The door barely hung from the hinges still, which squealed in protest as he pushed it open enough to slip through.

A few steps down brought him into the rich merchant's living quarters.

Even in the dark, it was clear that the place had been ransacked. Drawers had been turned out, bedding ripped from the large bed tucked into an alcove in the back.

Mouse ferreted out a candle and then dug out the flint kit he carried in his pouch.

Candle lit, he tugged the heavy curtains closed over each window. No sense in announcing the vessel was occupied. He surveyed the quarters with a frown.

Whoever had ransacked the place had done a thorough job of it. Dockhands? Hearing the rumors of an abandoned river craft, they'd could have come in pilfer any valuables before anyone else swooped in to claim them. From what Mouse could tell, this carcass was thoroughly picked clean of any of the dead owner's belongings. But after being in the space for a minute, something about it felt less random. Less frenetic. Whoever the plunderers were, they were hunting for something specific.

Orno told him the city guard had been by to inspect it, but they wouldn't have done this.

Unless they weren't city guards after all. Only disguised as them. Or paid off. That was a possibility, too.

Mouse bit his lower lip. The scene was disquieting, and he wondered if he should remain—but then, nothing was going to happen here over night. He could decide what to do in the morning. But the situation was curious. What were they looking for? Did they find it? And was it valuable?

He scraped some broken glass aside with the side of his boot. It was part of an ornate decanter and some fine stemware.

That *would* have brought in some coin. More evidence that this damage wasn't about rooting out valuables.

Finding things was Mouse's specialty, and he was better at it than most. The ones that had rolled through here had taken a wild boar approach, which suggested two possibilities: they were short on time or not professionals, like himself. Mouse's strategy for such matters was methodical and procedural. Few would ever know he had ever stepped into a room he'd burgled until they discovered what was missing.

The mess would make his procedure more difficult, but he had plenty of time. He started his search.

Getting everything off the floor was the first step. He dumped everything in the center of one of the bed linens, scooped it up into a pack, and hauled it out to the deck. Now, with a blank slate to work from, he went to work.

After a preliminary sweep, Mouse found the wood in one part of the floor was darker than the rest. He lowered to a squat, held the candle close to it, and tapped it with his fingers. Tacky.

Blood. Someone was murdered here, too. Probably someone hired to keep a watch on the place and protect it from thievery. Mouse traced more dark streaks in the floor to the stairs leading out. The body was dragged outside and probably tossed in the river.

He began his search by checking all the usual places people hide valuables—under the floorboards, under the bed, the panels in the furniture. He even gave the wood-burning stove in the corner a thorough look.

Nothing.

Mouse scratched his chin. Every merchant had a place to hide their coin and valuables while away, so it was here somewhere. That wasn't the question. It was well hidden, so it stood to reason that whoever was in here, they hadn't found it either.

He was missing something. There was a chance, albeit unlikely, that it was somewhere else on the vessel. Obviously, the quarters didn't take up the whole length. The crew would need a place to sleep and eat, too. Could the merchant's hiding place be somewhere around there?

He didn't think so, but it was worth checking out, if only to eliminate it.

Mouse started up the stairs to head onto the deck. One of the steps sounded different than the others.

He froze and frowned down at the step. With the toe of his boot, he pressed down on the middle step. It squeaked more and had a slightly different give than the others. The ship was extremely well-crafted, so a difference like that was noteworthy.

He knelt in front of it and examined the step. The top of the step below the one that squeaked had a slight scrape mark on one side, hardly noticeable. But there was a gap directly underneath the squeaky step that was wider than the gaps under all the other steps. He pulled the dagger from his boot and slid it down the length of the gap. He felt a slight resistance and heard a soft click.

The front of the step popped out like a drawer.

Mouse couldn't help but chuckle to himself. Clever. But not clever enough.

Inside was a metal lock box that filled most of the opening. Mouse wrestled it out. The lock wasn't much of a challenge. The real security was the hiding place.

Taking up most of the box was a finely-crafted leather pouch that jingled promisingly. He peeked in. Travel expenses for a rich merchant, but more coin than he'd see in a year.

Technically, by the rules of the guild, he was required to report it and relinquish their cut, but Jardem hadn't given him his fair share for a year. He would never learn of it, that's for certain. Where to stash it was going to be tricky—his clock tower was clearly compromised.

Underneath the pouch was a stack of neatly folded documents. Mouse pulled them out, sat on the bottom step, and opened them up one by one. Most were related to the merchant's business endeavors. Seems he had his hand in the glass trade and some jewelry, as well. The documents outlined warehouse fees, sale contracts, and the like.

He'd signed his name at the bottom of the documents: Darko Pain.

It wasn't a name Mouse recognized. That wasn't surprising. He didn't run with many rich merchants, and this one wasn't even from Har Tesera.

None of this pointed to a reason why the poor bugger was murdered. Or why his private river craft had been ransacked.

But further down the pile, he discovered what he was looking for. A document with the Night Fingers seal.

Mouse scanned down the parchment, his hand quivering. A coincidence he hadn't seen coming. He held the original contract, signed by both Drako Pain and Jardem, for stealing the king's writ. Interesting that this agreement didn't specify what that writ was. The price Pain had paid the guild made Mouse's eyebrows arch. He hadn't been given a fraction of the gold he was entitled to for the job. Hell, he hadn't been given *any* of it.

The next sheet was an invitation to the Dire Moon, a tavern that had a meeting room for business dealings.

The dockhands were surely right. Drako Pain was dead. Jardem had set him up. He'd invited him to the Dire Moon under the ruse of passing over the document. Instead, he'd had Pain murdered.

12

MORNING LIGHT squeezed in from the sides of the heavy curtains to cast an orangey hue about the cabin. Mouse blinked and pushed himself up onto his elbows.

Well, so much for sleeping light.

He had no memory of the night before after his head hit the cloud-like down pillow. He'd intended on dozing, keeping one ear attuned for sounds of danger. Clearly, that didn't happen. The hazards of a quality bed, apparently. One that was absurdly comfortable. The mattress seemed to devour him, and the bedding was cool and soft against his skin. He had no idea such fabrics even existed—ones that didn't scratch and make his skin raw. Someone could have stomped in and dragged him off before he ever knew anyone was there.

The fact that no one did was a good sign.

The ones who rummaged through the riverboat's cabin had clearly been searching for the box hidden in the steps. Not finding it, they apparently moved on. Despite the sloppy and amateurish search, they must have convinced themselves they'd done a thorough job of it.

Everything pointed toward Jardem being involved. He wanted to get his hands on the documents that bore his name and destroy any ties connecting him to Darko Pain and the signet rod. The city guard that reportedly came by to inspect the craft could have been his men. Armor and livery weren't impossible to come by. The Night Fingers kept its own collection for such occasions.

The amateurish nature of the search also told Mouse that Jardem hadn't used anyone in the guild to do it. Even the most thuggish members would have a basic understanding of how to comb through someone's belongings. No, Jardem had hired from outside. He wouldn't risk anyone in the guild learning of his connection to the murdered merchant.

Theft was one thing, but murder was a different animal in the eyes of the city magistrates. Especially when the victim was rich and powerful. Darko Pain wasn't a noble—but the city would still take it seriously and punish those responsible severely.

Mouse thought about those pursuing him the night before. The Scourge? Would Jardem stoop so low as to hire the sworn enemy of the Night Fingers?

This was getting more complicated by the day.

He shuffled to the edge of the bed and put his elbows on his knees. Outside the warm bed coverings, the air in the cabin was cool, and the smooth wood of the floorboards bit at the soles of his naked feet. Autumn was creeping into the city.

He tapped his foot on the floor while he chewed on his lip. What to do?

Jardem had betrayed his oath to the guild. He'd taken a job and murdered the client for his own gain. This was enough to turn the guild membership against him—but proving that would be tricky, to put it mildly. He had the paperwork, but the connection wasn't enough to prove he was behind the murder. The murder of an out-of-town merchant was nothing new. And there was no proof other than some blood in an empty river craft that he was, in fact, dead.

Frowning, Mouse stood and collected his clothes from the floor. Stepping into trousers and tightening the drawstring, he mapped out his plan for the day.

He gathered what he needed, even taking a bit of coin from the stash he'd found. Despite the chill, he kept his tunic off and stuffed it into his haversack instead. He tucked his father's knife into his boot, rose out of the cabin and stepped into the emergent light of morning.

The docks were in full chaos. Hulking stevedores hauled crates on their naked backs down a wooden gangway that leaned against the deck of a neighboring barge. The gangway was little more than a narrow plank, and it bowed dangerously as each dockhand reached the middle. The crates were stacked on the pier in a haphazard mountain of wood. A barge captain shouted commands at the workers while two merchants haggled over the price of the cargo being unloaded.

Mouse took a moment to appreciate their physique as they paraded back and forth, muscles tight and bulging beneath their sun-bronzed skin, before he leapt nimbly from the deck of the riverboat onto one of the pylons. Shirtless, he fit more with the crowd, though he was too small and too pale to really seem like he belonged. But it was only those out looking for him he needed to fool.

It took little time to locate the pier manager that oversaw the operation. It was their job to be conspicuous, so merchants and sailors alike didn't try to cheat the city of its docking fees. The portly man stood at a desk positioned inconveniently at the base of the pier, looking like he might break out into a speech. His face was weathered and craggy, likely from the years of sun exposure while standing at his location on the pier, and his wiry grey hair was pulled back into a loose tail. He was dressed in a very official looking black coat, which also was weathered and was on the verge of being labeled tattered. The coat was obviously too warm for him in the sun—beads of sweat dotted his hairline.

He had already eyed Mouse as he made his way to the

shore, swerving to avoid the workers that had no interest in avoiding him. The manager's quill hovered over the pages of his open ledger as he watched Mouse approach.

He made no attempt at greeting Mouse but instead waited for Mouse to announce what possible business he had with him. The man had one job. Document the traffic in and out of the docks and acquire the coin for the privilege. That task did not include chatting with the loaders and lumpers.

"Milord," Mouse greeted with a bow.

Silence.

"I was sent to ensure the fees are current on one of the vessels on this pier."

The man pursed his lips and looked down at the ledger. "Name of the craft."

Mouse laughed. "I don't fucking know. I was paid a crown to hoof down here for the errand."

The man sighed without lifting his eyes. "Can you point to it?"

Mouse did.

"Ah." The man eyed Mouse askance. "*The Glad Desire?* The one inspected by the city guard yesterday?"

"A misunderstanding," Mouse replied. "So, I'm told."

The man continued to study him closely. "Rumors about a murder...."

"Well, I spoke to the man just this morning. Master Pain is his name." Mouse tapped a finger on the top of the ledger. "I'm sure your records can confirm that. If you care to look. I can assure you he's very much alive."

The man shooed Mouse's hand away, as if afraid it'd soil his work. The answer seemed to settle him, and he returned his eyes to his ledger, tracing a line across the page with a finger. "Day late on fees. One more and it'd be hauled off and sold at auction."

"Well, then I was sent just in time," Mouse replied. "I've been instructed to pay fees for an advance of five more days. Six then in total?"

The dock manager grunted and scribbled into the ledger. He told him the price and held out his palm without looking up.

Mouse dug out the coin from his pouch and extended his hand, then stopped just before placing the fistful of coin into the palm.

"Oh, I nearly forgot. I'm to ask that you speak nothing of the craft to anyone. Especially with all the undue attention it received yesterday. People may have questions. You understand."

The eyes lifted again. "I collect the fees and monitor the arrivals and departures. Nothing more."

"Of course. But the owner is a private person and would like to conduct his business without interference. So, the less you notice, the better."

He crossed his arms over his ledger and leaned in. "And what exactly am I to not notice?"

"Comings and goings, that sort."

The man was no fool. He had already concluded some illicit activity surrounded the vessel. But like everyone else in the city, he was willing to profit from it. "That attention—or lack of it—will cost extra."

Mouse deposited the coin in the man's hand. Some of it went into the desk. Some went into his own purse.

Without another word, the man went about his business as if Mouse had already left.

Mouse left the pier and thrust himself into the chaos along the shoreline. The area was choked with every manner of person, and the shifting throng swirled like unsettled waters. Supplies loaded onto carts and dollies cut through the crowd like the bows of a ship. Fishmonger tables were set up near the water, loaded with catch, while hordes of people crammed in to buy it up. The smell was pervasive throughout the square, masking the arguably worse smell of the crowd itself.

He located a carpenter's workshop—a ubiquitous element around all docks since ships were always in need of some repair. He paid the carpenter for repairs on the broken door, extra to get it done quickly, then slunk off down an alley.

Toward the guild.

It was time to return.

Jardem blinked a moment at Mouse in the doorway. Surprise turned quickly to fury.

"Where the *fuck* have you been?"

Mouse made an exaggerated limp into the office. "I'm fine. Thanks for asking."

Jardem didn't catch the sarcasm. Standing behind his desk, he punched his knuckles into the desktop and leaned in. "I've been asking for you for days. And you just fucking turn up?"

A few others were in the office with him. There was a bruiser named Korver—a favorite of Jardem's to use when someone needed to be intimidated. He was an ugly bastard with a misshapen skull and tufts of hair that grew in odd patches. He towered over everyone and made Mouse look like a toddler. A woman by the name of Henni had one shoulder to the wall while she picked at her nails. She wasn't part of the thieves' collective, per se, but instead ran reconnaissance in places before a job. The two of them in Jardem's office made for a strange pairing. Didn't make much sense that they would be working on a job together.

Mouse had interrupted some planning meeting.

Jardem's eyes narrowed on Mouse. Something then cut into this anger. The limp, perhaps. Or maybe the scrape Mouse had given himself across the cheekbone or the blood stain on the tunic.

"What the fuck happened to you?"

"Ah, is that concern I hear?"

Jardem's eyes narrowed even more. "I needed you for a job."

"Well, I was a little busy being hogtied and thrown into

a dungeon."

Jardem rolled his eyes. "Another of your fucking pub fights. Tired of your run-ins with the city guard inconveniencing me, Mouse. You're to be here when I call for you." He stabbed at the floor with his finger. "Understand? This guild—"

Mouse scoffed, cutting him off. As if Jardem cared two shits about the guild. Mouse limped closer and felt the curious eyes of Henni and Korver on him. One thought burned into Mouse's mind: getting this traitorous fucker out of this office. Not only for him. But for everyone in the guild.

"No guardhouse cages this time, Jardem." The others winced at the brazen use of his name. Neither of them had guts to use it. Mouse fought a satisfied smirk when Jardem's face darkened from it. "No, I was the special guest in the dark, lower-level accommodations of someone in an organization called the Shadow Elite."

That got Jardem's attention. His eyes shot up and widened. His cheeks blanched.

"You've heard of them, I see." Mouse nodded. "They know of you, as well. Seems they learned of my involvement in the heist at that Agata estate."

"That's impossible!"

"Is it? They had many questions about the document, Jardem."

Jardem winced at the mention of the writ. Mouse watched him carefully, wondering if he might slip and unintentionally give Mouse a hint to where it was hidden, but instead his eyes shifted to Korver and Henni, who watched the exchange with interest.

"Leave!" Jardem snapped. The two made quick bows, as if Jardem was some fucking noble, and hastily left the office and closed the door.

Mouse groaned inwardly but kept his face hard. He was hoping they'd be around longer, hear more of the conversation to come. He wanted rumors. Gossip. It would make it all the more believable when the proof of Jardem's dealings surfaced.

Jardem waited until they were alone. "How do you know it was the Elite?"

"They made it clear enough. They have a seal. And a secret handshake. I can show it to you if you'd like."

"And *you* let them nab you?" Jardem growled, dropping into his chair. "Drunk, I suppose."

"I adore how you hold me in such high esteem," Mouse replied dryly.

He had carefully cultivated this view of him, manufacturing a history of drunkenness and clashes with the city guard. He would never be so rash, of course. But the standing opinion dampened expectations and gave him wiggle room if he needed time. The strategic excuse that he'd been stuck in a cell overnight had benefited him more than once.

"The Shadow Elite clearly pay more than you," Mouse said. "They can afford better thugs."

Jardem grunted. He was buying this ruse…so far.

Mouse leaned his own arms on the opposite side of the desk. "So, who sold me out, Jardem?"

Jardem's face darkened. "I hope you aren't implying—"

"Simply asking a question." Mouse shrugged. "That's all. Because the only way the Elite knew about my involvement was if someone in the guild talked."

That at least was true. Someone *had* leaked it to the Elite. Mouse shouldn't have been surprised, really—the guild had spies all over the city. Logic dictated other factions had their own spies in circulation and had infiltrated the Night Fingers. Other guilds. The city guard. The Shadow Elite. The question was, who was close enough to Jardem to know of Mouse's mission to steal the king's writ?

Jardem stared back at him. Mouse was pushing him into dangerous territory. Anybody else would likely end up at the bottom of the river tied to a rock for speaking to him so. But Jardem wasn't about to sacrifice his best and *cheapest* thief.

"No one in this guild would knowingly—"

Mouse scoffed. "Because we're all family here, right? You honestly think you inspire loyalty, Jardem?"

The muscles of Jardem's jaw tightened, and his cheeks flushed. He moved as if to stand again, but he reconsidered and settled back into his chair. "I could have you publicly flayed for how you speak to me." He let his eyes drift over Mouse as he reached for a crystal chalice filled with an amber liquid. "What you fail to understand, young Mouse, is loyalty comes in a variety of flavors. My particular brand is inspired by fear. Like the fear you have that I'll release what I know to the city magistrate. Fear is the only thing I need to keep our…." He paused and considered his next words with a lift of his eyes and a hint of a smile. "…rather motley family in line."

The glee radiating from his face stunned Mouse into silence.

Jardem took a sip from the chalice. "If what you say is true, I will find who revealed our mission to the Elite." His tone had shifted from the sinister to casual. "And they will pay for their disloyalty. I will put Cassar on it to smoke them out. In this interrogation you suffered, did you reveal anything to them?"

Mouse clucked his tongue. "Of course not."

"And how did you escape this?"

"No cell can hold me for long."

Jardem's mouth pressed in annoyance, but he accepted it. "Considering your ordeal, I'll chalk your flagrant insubordination up to that. But you will check that sharp tongue of yours behind your teeth. I grow tired of it."

Mouse wanted to laugh, but he let it go.

Jardem leaned back and spun the glass to swirl the liquid inside. "So, out with it. What did you learn?"

"Other than the Shadow Elite treat their prisoners no better?" A hint at the conditions of the rich merchant in the cellar. Mouse kept an eye on his face for a change in expression. Nothing broke in his expression.

"Stop wasting my time. You wouldn't have spent that

much time with them and not noticed…something.”

“Not interested in hearing how I made my daring escape?”

“Not even a little bit. Spill it. What did you learn?”

“They know who you are, first of all.”

Jardem chuckled. “No surprise. I’m the guild master. Everyone knows who I am.”

“Well, they have concerns. Seems they think the document never made it into the client’s hands. You did give it over to them already, yes?”

“Of course I did.” Jardem averted his eyes downward. “The day after you handed it over.”

Even if Mouse didn’t already know, his too quick response, laced with invention, would have tipped Mouse off.

“Well, *they* aren’t convinced. I’d add an extra bodyguard to your retinue if I were you.”

Jardem tried to disguise it with a false chuckle, but Mouse could sense a spike in his concern. *Good.* And it was only going to get worse. Mouse was going to make things even more uncomfortable for him in the days ahead.

“What was it I nabbed from Agata, Jardem?”

Jardem scoffed. “Your run in with these Elite is precisely why you aren’t privy to that information. Knowing you, you would have blabbed the first moment they tried to tug on your fingernails with rusty pliers.”

Mouse shrugged. “I chew them to the quick, so they’d never be able to grip them anyway.” He couldn’t argue with Jardem’s assessment of him. The guild—or more accurately, Jardem—hadn’t earned *his* loyalty, and its secrets weren’t worth even the hint of torture.

“What else do they know?” Jardem pressed.

He was fishing. Jardem needed to know if the Elite knew of the prisoner. It was a fair question that Mouse didn’t have the answer to. Savir didn’t mention it, only the document.

“Little else,” Mouse said.

He’d toyed with Jardem enough. He’d successfully

convinced Jardem that his absence had a plausible reason. An important part of him being accepted back into the fold. And he'd stirred Jardem from his arrogant complacency—a bonus, to be sure.

But he had to be careful not to rattle him too much. Not yet, anyway.

"Apparently, I was their only lead in the heist," Mouse continued. "How they learned I was even involved, or how to find me, suggests an inside informant, whether you want to accept it or not. But...it doesn't look like they know much else."

Jardem nodded stiffly. Mouse could tell his mind was whirling on the idea of a spy here. He demanded respect and unwavering loyalty, earned or not. Everyone was supposed to do what he commanded simply because he commanded it. "Good," he said finally. "Report back to me in the morning. I'll have an assignment for you—"

"I need some time. I am hardly in any shape to—"

Jardem lurched forward, elbows on his desk. "That wasn't a suggestion. You again forget I own you, Mouse." His lips were thin, and his cheeks were red. He grew explosive when rattled. The information about the Shadow Elite had him unnerved. "You will do as I command. In the morning, here." He stabbed his forefinger to the desktop.

Mouse opened his mouth as if to argue back, then closed it again. He feigned a note of surrender—not too much to tip his hand, though Jardem was too obtuse and consumed in his own worries to see through his playacting, anyway.

Mouse crafted an elaborate bow. "As you wish," he said with anger lacing the words.

He left the office and gave the door a little slam—for show. Standing in the corridor, he heard something crash from the other side of the door. The fine chalice, presumably. Mouse let out a long breath. As much as he wanted to relish in the tantrum to come, he was too relieved to take any real joy in it. His heart rate betrayed him. He'd been more nervous about this meeting than he'd wanted to admit. But Jardem had fallen for the story, and Mouse had sidestepped the full extent of his rage.

But the worst was yet to come. Mouse had much to do, and if successful, it would only push Jardem further over the edge.

13

THE MAN approached the metal bars with slow, deliberate steps.

"I know you," he said. "You were the one skulking in the shadows before. When the creepy one—"

"Jardem," Mouse put in for him.

"Yes, him. When he was down here."

The prisoner was looking rather tattered and worn after his time in the cell. The fine clothes were soiled and torn, his face smudged with dirt. His somewhat unruly beard gave him the look of a tavern brawler.

How quickly the glow of a fine gem can fade in the mud.

Since Mouse's last visit, the man had unbuttoned his doublet, exposing the linen tunic beneath it. Sweat soaked it, and it clung to his skin, giving Mouse a hint as to the shape of his meaty chest.

"I owe you a bit of thanks for that," Mouse replied. "I might've been spotted had it not been for you."

"Thought you might be here to help me. Then you left." The deep resonance of his voice reverberated off the stone and filled the dark gloom in the cellar like words from the divine.

It made Mouse's toes curl a little.

"Wasn't an opportune time for such an endeavor."

"How about now?" He turned to the guard, now slumped in the chair like an ungainly and misshapen sack of grain. The man's head drooped forward, chin to his chest, and Mouse could hear the rough snores that sounded like he might be choking. "I assume that is your doing."

The tray with the empty bowl was next to the chair. The good little soldier had eaten every drop of his dinner. Mouse had stirred a liberal amount of the apothecary's herb into the meal. More than necessary, but with a man of that size, it was hard to gauge, and Mouse preferred to play it safe. Of course, there was always the danger that Mouse had overdone it. He'd check to make sure he was breathing later.

"Some poor sops can't handle their ale, it seems."

The cage man grunted impatiently. "Are you here to let me out or not?"

"Not sure yet."

His face darkened. "Then why are you here?"

Mouse eased closer to the bars but remained out of the man's reach. Mouse had arrived just in time. Though he tried to disguise it behind a hard countenance and level voice, the caged fop seemed on the cusp of breaking. It was clear he'd believed he'd be out of this place by now, and the reality that he might never see the surface again was soaking in. Gone was the aroma of privilege, replaced by the stench of smoldering dread and uncertainty.

"Let's start with introductions," Mouse replied brightly. "Name's Mouse."

He stared a moment. "I just met you, and yet, that seems oddly fitting."

"And yours?" Mouse pressed.

The man's brow knitted in suspicion. Mouse could see him trying to work this out in his head. Why would this man bother to free him if he didn't even know who he was?

"Tenric," he said finally.

Mouse already knew that much. He'd heard Jardem call him by his name when he snuck down here before. "Your family name, if you would, sir."

Tenric hesitated, clearly uncertain why Mouse would need to know that. "Aval," he said finally. "Aval. My name is Tenric Aval."

"From Har Purdea."

Tenric's brow lifted on one side. "You know of my family?"

Lucky guess. "Your accent gives you away. Welcome to Har Tesera, Tenric Aval." He made a little bow. It was what one did in polite company.

Tenric brought his face up to the gap in the bars, one hand gripping the iron with white knuckles. "Why is it you are here? Have you come solely to torment me? Mock my circumstances and waste my time?"

"I apologize. I can come back when it's more convien—"

"What is it you want?"

Mouse's lips broke into a smile. "Only to talk a minute." He glanced at the unconscious guard. "Perhaps ten. But I wouldn't risk any longer than that."

"More talk!" Tenric turned his back to Mouse and moved to the back of the cell. Looking exhausted, he lowered himself onto the flimsy cot against the wall. "If this is some ruse, arranged by that slimy hood, Jardem, I will tell you what I told him. I don't know anything. So, if it is information you seek, if my freedom hinges on that, you might as well return to the hole you climbed out of."

Mouse's tone turned serious. "I assure you I am not here on account of him."

Tenric didn't seem to catch the shift in tone. "I have coin. Plenty of it. If that is what you're after. If that is what will persuade you to open this door."

"Never opposed to lightening a man's purse, sir," Mouse said with a shrug. He drifted over to the unconscious brute. He made a quick search and discovered the iron ring at his belt, adorned with a single key. Mouse removed the ring with a flourish. He spun the ring on his finger, whirling the key in circles through the air, and approached the bars again. "Though it is not my primary interest. I seek to strike a bargain with you but am yet unsure if you can be trusted."

Eyes on the spinning key, Tenric stood from the cot.

"Me? As if I have reason to trust you! You look every bit the unscrupulous rogue and are likely here for the same reason as the others. To use me for your own gain."

"You wound me with such words, sir," Mouse replied, hand to his heart. "We've only just met and already you're tossing out wild assumptions about my character?" Then he laughed. "Don't be naïve. Of course, I am here to use you. Think I'm here for altruistic reasons? I'm not. At least I'm being honest about it."

"How refreshing!"

"Cooperate, and you'll gain your freedom. Easy as that."

Tenric scoffed and approached the cage again. "Fuck off. I'm done with talk. I'm done with being a pawn in everyone else's game."

Mouse gave him a level stare. "You'll find my game very different, Master Tenric."

Something in Mouse's words or tone hooked into Tenric. He locked his gaze into Mouse's. Feeling the full weight of those blue eyes on him, lit by the lantern light, Mouse's breathing hitched a moment.

He was striking, even disheveled and nearly broken as he was. His body exuded strength and an aura of control, but underneath it, Mouse caught a glimpse of something else. A greenness. An innocence. Someone who found themselves out of their depth. His body was a shield protecting a lost and forsaken boy inside.

"I do work for that slimy hood," Mouse told him, holding his gaze. "But not by choice. I have as much love for him as you. I am not down here working for him, like you suspect. I'm working directly *against* his interests."

Tenric tried to pull away but was drawn right back in. His gaze searched Mouse's face for signs of deception. "So, you say."

Mouse allowed a slight smile to escape as he held up a finger. "I will add that I agree with you on one important manner. Earlier with Jardem, you protested you knew nothing about the whereabouts of the king's signet. Well, I believe you."

Tenric tried to hide his surprise, but his eyes widened a fraction. "The signet was never mentioned in any of our conversations. Jardem was careful to not state it openly in front of any others. How did you know what it was?"

"I keep myself well informed."

Tenric's mouth opened, ready to respond, but it seemed some inner voice coached him into silence, and he shut it again.

Mouse took another step closer to the bars. "I am the thief that stole the document from Agata. I am the one who put it into Jardem's hands."

Tenric chewed on the inside of his cheek. That was enough to pique his curiosity now.

Mouse broke the gaze between them. "How do I know you are ignorant of the signet's whereabouts? A hunch. But a solid one. It makes sense that the document you received from the king would be in your—or your family's—possession when it was stolen, however the king's signet, an item of incredible value, would never leave the possession of the Crown Notary."

Mouse paced in front of the bars like a magistrate at a trial, waving his finger in the air. He paused to take in Tenric's expression, but the young merchant's face was icy and wary.

"It doesn't make much sense that the signet was ever in your family's custody, does it?" Mouse went on. "Both items would have been found and taken. Therefore, the two were nipped from two separate locations by two separate thieves."

Mouse spun to face Tenric with arms extended. "Therefore, you don't know where it is."

Tenric was quiet a moment, staring at Mouse with tight lips and narrow eyes. "Your...*employer* has come to a different conclusion. He seems to think I have knowledge of its whereabouts."

"Well, he's an idiot," Mouse answered, letting his arms drop. "For whatever reason, he thinks you are stringing him along. But your protestations of ignorance will eventually be believed. When that happens, he'd have your throat slit, your body dumped in the river, and he'll move on with his day. Just like he did with your bodyguard."

Tenric's face blanched as his eyes shot open. "My—" He cut himself short and swallowed hard. "He...he said he set him free."

"He lied."

Tenric swallowed again. "Of course he did." His eyes lowered. Mouse could see shame darken his face—shame that he'd allowed himself to believe Jardem. The reality that Jardem would never allow him to walk out of here tightened around him. "And how long before that happens?"

Mouse dropped the cheery routine and affected a more serious tone. "I can tell you his patience is waning. You've not long."

Tenric ran a hand down the length of a bar, then strolled away. He kept his back to Mouse, but Mouse could see in the dim light Tenric's shoulders rise as he took in a long breath.

"If you pegged your hopes on a rescue, Tenric—the city guard, friends in the merchant guild—they do not know you're here. No one is coming for you."

"You've made your point," Tenric said, his back still to Mouse. "This is the time you tell me what it is you want."

"Not your fucking writ, that's for sure." Mouse grumbled. "And not the fucking king's signet."

Tenric spun toward him. "What then?"

"Something far baser. Revenge."

Tenric stiffened, but curiosity seemed to hook its claws into him. He approached the bars again. "Revenge?"

"Yes. Against your fine host. The slimy hood."

Mouse watched as Tenric's eyes widened and took on a light of hope. "And, like you, I want liberation. Something we share, Tenric. The desire for freedom. I think you can help me get both."

"I see no bars around you. You seem free to move about at will."

Mouse sighed. "Prisons come in many forms, friend. There's a different writ that concerns me. One of Indenture. I intend to be free of it forever." There was more fire in his voice than he intended.

Tenric was quiet a moment. "How can I possibly help you?" He was interested now.

"Easy. You'll share with me what you *actually* know—"

"If I didn't say anything to…that thug, what makes you think I'll tell you?"

"Because I'll get you to safety first. Then you'll talk."

Tenric considered that with pressed lips. "Fine words. How do I know I can trust you?"

Mouse shrugged. "You don't have much of a choice. I could just leave you here. Work it out on my own. But it'd be easier with your help. Jardem is eventually going to realize you really don't know anything. When that happens, you're dead. Trust in me, and you have a better chance."

"How do you know I'll cooperate once I'm out?"

"Because you strike me as someone with some decency. That is what I needed to see in you."

"And what if what I know doesn't help you?"

"It will. You know more than you think."

Tenric still seemed reluctant. He folded his arms and stared at the wall.

Mouse shrugged again. "Suit yourself." He tossed the keys into the lap of the sleeping brute and marched back down the corridor.

"Wait!" Tenric called as Mouse reached the corridor beyond.

Mouse made a slow spin on his heel and raised an eyebrow.

"You'll take me at my own word?" Tenric asked. "If I agree to this?"

Mouse took a few steps back into the room. "I am in the business of lies and deception. I will know if you are lying to me."

Tenric took in a long breath through his nose. "Fine. I agree. I wouldn't mind getting a bit of my own revenge on that fucker for his treatment of me in here."

Mouse grinned. He was earnest enough, and Mouse knew he could trust him. Mostly.

"That's the spirit!"

He retrieved the key again from the guard's lap and slipped it into the padlock hanging on the door. It fell to the floor and clanged like a broken bell. Mouse pulled open the door and tossed in a prepared sack he had waiting on the ground by the entrance. It landed at Tenric's feet.

"Put those on. Your dandy attire, even soiled as it is, will be noticed."

Tenric reached into the sack and pulled the garments out one at a time and dropped them on the cot. He started to slip the grubby olive doublet off his thick shoulders.

"I'm going to give you clear instructions on how to walk out of here—"

Tenric's head popped up. "You're not going with me?"

"If you're seen with me, it'll draw unneeded attention and raise questions. I'll be following behind you in case there's trouble, but if you follow my instructions, you'll have no problems."

"Won't it be obvious I don't belong if no one recognizes me?"

"The guild's membership is high. No one knows

everyone. Act like you belong and no one will bother you."

Tenric still looked uncertain, but he nodded. He'd removed his coat and trousers and stood shivering a bit in his smallclothes in the middle of the cell. Mouse took the opportunity to take in his fine shape before Tenric began tugging on the garments Mouse brought him. What he lacked in height—he was taller than Mouse, but then, who wasn't—he gained in a frame that was solid and packed with muscle. He had a broad torso, thick arms and sturdy thighs that supported a deliciously full ass. Mouse caught himself grinning at it until the trousers swooped over their round glory.

Gods, his appetites were thundering of late. Unsatiable. He made a hasty adjustment within his own trousers. Later, when this task was over, he thought he might have to visit Taurin again—then remembered that he was likely already gone from the city. Gone forever. A tiny sadness darkened his already charcoal mood.

He scowled as he pushed the thought aside. "Let's go. We don't have all day."

Tenric slipped arms through the faded velvet jerkin. It was likely once a plush red but was now reduced to a sad ochre. It hugged his shoulders a little too tightly, but no one would take notice. Ill-fitting garments were the norm among the guild. People took what they could get their hands on.

Mouse handed a folded parchment to Aval, who took it suspiciously. He unfolded it and tilted it toward the lantern to read it.

"Direct instructions on how to exit the guild," Mouse told him. "Read it over several times until it is committed to memory. Pull them out only as a last resort. I'll be close behind and catch up with you outside. I drew a little map as to where we'll meet."

"*You* wrote this?"

Mouse rolled his eyes. "Why is it always so entirely shocking that I know my letters?"

"Well…your penmanship is…well quite good, actually.

Not what I would have expected from a…person like you."

Mouse scoffed. "There's more to me than cutting purse strings, I assure you." He pulled out one of the cards he'd lifted from the Golden Flute's dressing room from his waist pouch. Gently, he pulled back the sleeping man's bottom lip and slipped the long edge of the card into his mouth until it ran against his teeth. Hopefully, it would remain in place until he was discovered. "Now. Read it over again. Then recite it to me out loud, so I'm confident you remember the details. Then, we can begin."

14

MOUSE MADE him recite the details back to him three times before he led him back up the stairs toward the door leading to the main floor of the guild complex.

He stood at the door and listened. Nothing. Some distant rumblings of conversation, but there wasn't anything directly on the other side of the door as best as he could tell. But Mouse wasn't one to take chances.

He grabbed the short sword he'd leaned against the wall by the door earlier and slid it through the gap under the door. When nothing happened, he wiggled it around a bit.

Still nothing.

"What are you doing?" Tenric asked.

"Hush," Mouse replied tetchily.

He slid the blade around more aggressively.

An image flashed into his mind—a view of the first floor of the guild on the other side of the door. The vantage point was from the same landing he and Cas had stood on only days before. Now Mouse had a clear view of the door and the surrounding area. He could see the guild members milling about and tending to their business—which mostly was slugging down mugs of ale and throwing dice.

No one's attention was on the door.

"It's safe. Go."

"How can you—"

Mouse grabbed his firm arm and moved him closer to the door. "Go. Now."

Tenric jolted as if startled from sleep. Mouse tugged open the door, but Tenric still hesitated. He reeked of nerves. Mouse shoved him out into the guild's hall.

"I'll be right behind you," Mouse growled in a low voice and closed the door again.

Gods. Working with this green peacock was going to kill him.

It had taken a bit of finagling to get the door unattended for the length of time he needed. First, a strategic suggestion in the ear of the kitchen grunt that his footlocker had been broken into—which it had, of course, by Mouse. The rumor sent him sprinting from the kitchen, leaving it and the guild stores unattended. The grunt was a notorious tinder box, unreasonably protective of his gear and oddly paranoid. After he inventoried his belongings, accusations and the eventual fisticuffs would keep him busy. Then, the hint that a keg of Purdean red was left without a chaperone was conveniently mentioned in the presence of the guard at the cellar door. Mouse knew the brute, originally from Har Purdea, would be unable to resist the opportunity to indulge in the famous wine too costly for him here in Har Tesera. The guard practically sprinted from his post.

It was Jardem's private keg—which only made the ploy sweeter.

Even if the kitchen grunt returned, he'd find the guard guzzling the red, which would only lead to more fighting.

In his mind's eye, with the aid of Cassar, he watched Tenric move through the hall, looking wildly obvious that he didn't belong there. The garments did little to hide that. He moved at a stoop, and his head made furtive jolts at everyone around him. Thankfully, everyone was either too drunk or too involved in something else to notice.

Cassar was likely helping nudge their attention away as well.

It was Mouse's turn to slip out.

Later, when it would be discovered that Tenric had flown his cell, several people would have a vague memory of seeing Mouse elsewhere, thanks to Cassar's ability to gently sway their recollections. He would be free of suspicion. The calling card he'd left in the guard's mouth would do the rest of the work.

The sounds of shouting came from the kitchen. The grunt had returned to find the wine stores being pilfered.

Mouse felt a tinge of guilt. The poor brute would be flogged for not only leaving his post but also guzzling down Jardem's personal stock.

He didn't follow Tenric's path, of course. He needed to be clear of the hall entirely so there were no witnesses of him anywhere near that cellar door. He crossed to the opposite wall and started up the stairs to where Cassar waited for him.

"He make it out? No one noticed?"

Cassar scowled at Mouse as he shook his head. "Still don't know how you talked me into this."

"Because you have no love for Jardem, either."

Cassar couldn't argue against that. He was, if anything, a staunch loyalist to the guild. Or, at least, the ideals of the guild. He had been, like so many, rescued from dire circumstances on the streets of Har Tesera and provided more than he'd ever dreamed. Amazing how a bed and a full belly on a regular basis could cultivate such unwavering fealty. But then, someone like him didn't tend to last long on the street alone. And the sense of camaraderie and shared security certainly added to Cassar's devotion.

But keeping a prisoner down in the cellar—or more to the point, keeping it secret from the membership at large—was against guild protocols. It stank of self-serving machinations.

The same kind of suspect and clandestine behaviors that Jardem performed with increasing regularity. Cas knew in his gut it was wrong.

"You take care of the rest of it?" Mouse asked.

Cassar turned away and leaned on the railing, looking out over the lower floor. "Several people will recall seeing you in the upper levels, heading to your hole in the ceiling. No one should suspect you."

"Excellent," Mouse said with a grin, but the grin faded quickly. There was more going on. "What is it?"

Cassar glanced his way with a cool gaze. "You're not coming back." His eyes narrowed at him. "Are you?"

The proclamation staggered Mouse into silence. He could only look back at him, not knowing what to say.

"You're leaving the guild," Cassar added with cold finality.

Mouse hadn't told anyone his plans—certainly not Cas. Appears he didn't need to. It was as if he was reaching into his thoughts, and the notion made Mouse's insides twist. "Cas," Mouse started, but Cas turned away from him again. Mouse sighed. "I've not made any decisions. I don't know yet what's going to happen."

"I do," Cassar said.

Something in his tone sent chills chasing over his shoulders and arms. What information had his sight made him privy to? Mouse wasn't sure he wanted to know.

Cassar stared down the steps. "You better move along."

Mouse nodded and headed the opposite direction to the upper floors, a sensation tightening his gut that he couldn't explain.

\#

The exchange between the two of them was brief, but still Mouse had lost precious time. Tenric was probably almost out of the guild by now. And Mouse couldn't let what was going on in Cas's head worry him right now—he had to stick to the mission.

From the top of the stairs, he navigated the corridors toward the back of the guild, the river side. He'd swoop through, hopefully get noticed by some who knew him, and slip out through the window over the covered entryway. Cas had done his work, but it wouldn't hurt to have more witnesses placing him as far from the cellar as possible.

He nodded to a few people while he scratched at his belly and raked fingers through his hair in an attempt to look like he'd just woken up. No one would bat an eye that it was late afternoon. A thief's life was a nocturnal one.

He had almost reached the window when someone barked his name from behind. Mouse closed his eyes and froze. He knew that voice without having to look. Ludvic.

He turned on his heels to see Ludvic stomping toward him. "Where you think you're going?"

"Just woke up. Heading out for a pint."

Ludvic chuckled. "No…you're not. Quickblade's asking for you. Wants you in his office. Now."

Mouse's gut sank. "He said the morning." He turned to leave, but Ludvic grabbed his arm and yanked him closer. He leaned over Mouse, still gripping him tight under the bicep, and grinned down at him, flashing the five teeth he proudly still possessed. His breath was putrid, like rotting foliage. It could strip paint.

"He says *now*."

Mouse twisted his arm to break the brute's hold. "Alright, alright. Now it is."

Fuck. He didn't have time for this. But if he was going to cover his tracks on springing Tenric, he didn't have a choice. How long would Tenric wait?

Not long. If he had his chance, he'd bolt, and Mouse would never see him again.

He had to make this quick.

He made to step around him. "On my way."

Ludvic slapped a massive hand on Mouse's chest, stopping him. "Think I'm gonna take the word of a slippery fish like you? No, I'm escorting you right to his door this time."

Forcing a smile, Mouse shrugged. "Fine." He gestured with an upturned palm. "Lead the way."

Ludvic chuckled as if he'd out-smarted Mouse. Perhaps he had, but Mouse was ready to make a quick exit if he allowed it. He gave Mouse a shove to get him moving.

"Easy!" Mouse grumbled. "You forget I'm still recovering from days of interrogation and abuse."

Ludvic laughed a bit harder. "I didn't forget."

He continued to loom over him from behind like a mountain with feet. Mouse kept a hard pace toward Jardem's office. Every second counted. Ludvic waited until Mouse rapped on the door before he sneered and moved off again.

All Mouse could think about was Tenric waiting for him outside at their meeting point. Yet, standing at the door, a new flame of dread came to life in his gut. Why the sudden summons? Had he already learned of Tenric's escape? Unlikely. Jardem's brutes would be combing the building if he knew, and Mouse didn't see any signs of that kind of panic. The guild as a whole wouldn't be alerted—Jardem wouldn't want it known that he'd had an illegal prisoner in the cellar in the first place.

There was another option, though. One that also worried him. Had Jardem discovered somehow that Mouse's capture by the Shadow Elite was fiction? Jardem may be terrible at running the guild, but he was brilliant at mining for information on his enemies.

"Come," came the curt reply.

Mouse pushed his way into the room.

Jardem was behind his desk, rummaging through a stack of scrolls. He spun a quill between his fingertips but didn't appear ready to write anything. "About time," he grumbled. "Took your sweet time, as usual."

"Had to send your ogre after me?" Mouse answered. "You said I'd have the night to recov—"

Jardem's eyes lifted to meet Mouse's. "Said no such thing. You're heading out now." He shook his head as he set aside a few of the documents. "You seem to forget who runs this guild."

"Hardly," Mouse said. "I am aware every waking hour of who sits upon that throne."

Jardem fell against the chair's back, a look of incredulity darkening his face. Mouse had his full attention now. His mouth formed a sneer and his nose crinkled, like the smell from the docks had wafted through his window. He tapped the tip of the quill on the arm of the chair in a steady rhythm.

"Think you could do better? Is that it? You have an eye on this chair?" Jardem waited for a response with a hard stare, and when none came, he scoffed and rolled his eyes. "Should remove your tongue for your ceaseless insolence. But it's your tongue that gets you into doors, isn't it? Quite the conundrum."

Mouse sighed. He grew tired of these vague threats. "Why am I here?"

Jardem seemed annoyed that his intimidation techniques didn't have the effect that he wanted. His mouth pursed as he stared at Mouse. "I need you to collect a payment. For work completed."

"You have goons for that."

"Not in this case. I need it handled delicately."

"Delicately," Mouse repeated. "And you come to me?"

"The client in question is of some influence. But he has not paid the Night Fingers the remaining sum owed."

Mouse shrugged. "Still don't see what this has to do with me."

"It will require a more nuanced touch. The client needs to be found first. He's gone to ground for some reason. No sign of him." Jardem shook his head. "He didn't strike me as the type—"

"Didn't seem the type," Mouse repeated wryly. Fuck. Mouse knew where this was going. "This is the client that hired you about the document, isn't it?"

Jardem hesitated, frowning. "Yes. He has not contacted us."

"You said you delivered the document. You did this without payment?"

"A good-faith gesture, considering his sway in certain circles. Half was paid upfront. I was assured payment would be delivered when we acquired the package. It was not."

Mouse knew exactly what was happening here. Jardem needed to cover his tracks. Based on the interest of the Shadow Elite, Jardem figured that they knew something, perhaps could even pin the murder on him. He needed to establish a believable alibi, deniability. He wanted Mouse to discover that Darko Pain was murdered and that the writ of nobility was nowhere to be found.

Mouse folded his arms and scowled. Going to the city guard and announcing that Darko was found dead would likely put Jardem off the hook as a suspect. It was going to be easy enough to learn the truth. Murder rarely went unnoticed. But if Mouse didn't do it, Jardem certainly had someone waiting who would.

Jardem tented his fingers, elbows on his desk. "Something's not right about it. He scheduled more work from us, so I find it strange that he would stiff us and disappear. The document you took is very dangerous. Someone might be after him, so he was forced into hiding. I need you to find him. Fast."

Mouse sighed. A good story. Pretend he's still alive. Act shocked when he's found murdered. Jardem was setting the stage smoothly. Unfortunately, Mouse already knew the fate of the man he was going to be sent to find.

"I'll need a name."

Jardem nodded. "Pain. Darko Pain. Rich merchant. Very rich."

Mouse nodded as if this was new information. "Better get started then." He turned to leave.

"No dragging your feet, Mouse. The situation is

sensitive. I need this taken care of quickly."

Mouse grunted and left the office, leaving the door open intentionally. Jardem hated that.

Jardem was forcing him to clean up and cover up his own fucking betrayal of the guild. Mouse would have to tread carefully. A delicate balance. Any outright refusal would tip Jardem off. How was he to pretend he was looking for information that would shield Jardem from exposure while at the same time attempting to subvert him?

Precious time had been lost. This conversation with Jardem had put him well behind schedule. Tenric, assuming he made it out of the guildhall, would be alone at the meeting location. Was he wondering where Mouse was? Anxious and uncertain? All recipes for bad decisions.

Mouse quickened his pace through the upper floor of the hall. He crawled out the window at the end of the corridor, shuffled across the roof of the entrance's overhang, and dropped down to the street level. After a quick check to see if anyone had spotted him, he rushed off.

He'd given Tenric directions to a quiet alley that ran between two warehouses, a quick jog from the guild. The narrow gangway bent halfway down before it came to a dead end, providing a secluded hiding spot out of sight from the street.

Confident he wasn't spotted or followed, he set a hard pace down the street. Running would look suspicious. He reached the entrance of the alley and ducked in. Heart pounding, he rounded the corner, hoping to see Tenric sitting on a crate waiting for him.

But no, standing among the piles of garbage and a grated cistern, Mouse was alone.

No Tenric.

Sure enough, the rich fop had scampered off.

15

HAND ON his hips, Mouse puffed out his cheeks.

Fuck.

There was certainly nowhere for Tenric to hide among the abandoned junk that cluttered the area. Mouse would have spotted him easily enough. He'd selected this location because it was not only close to the guild, but the alley was seldom used and safely away from any eyes on the street. Even the warehouse doors at the far end were never used to Mouse's knowledge.

At great personal risk, he'd liberated the comely merchant, and for what? He was no closer to solving the mystery of what Jardem was after. It had always been a calculated risk, but Mouse assumed the danger was more Tenric being spotted during the escape and recaptured.

Now he stood to gain nothing. And if the finger was pointed at him, it would ruin him—and his father.

His only hope was that he'd covered his tracks enough that he was above suspicion in the escape. Jardem's task for him at least gave him the opportunity and excuse to be absent from the guild for a while.

He would have to try and track Tenric down again, but he didn't hold out much hope. Tenric would go to ground—he had the coin and the influence to do it. There would be plenty of his rich brethren willing to protect him and smuggle him out of the city. And Tenric had a significant head start on him. Mouse had little time to lose if he was going to find him.

A squeal of metal on metal came from behind him.

Mouse spun about. The door, hanging on a metal track, rolled to the side. Tenric's face poked out of the opening.

"There you are," he said.

Mouse fought to mask his relief. He wanted to kick himself. Checking if the doors were locked had never entered his head. He'd always assumed they'd be locked from inside—like all doors in the city were. What idiot would leave their warehouse unlocked in this neighborhood?

"Got held up unexpectedly," Mouse said, trying to project a calm control he didn't feel. "Glad to see you made it here. Worried you'd gotten lost."

Tenric pushed the door open wider. The rusty wheels on the track resisted, not turning, but Tenric, arms bulging, forced the wheels to scrape along the track. The door gave way in a series of short jerky movements until he had enough room to slip his thick torso through.

"Your instructions were rather precise." Tenric jumped down from the wooden platform at the door. He dusted off the front of the vest with his palms, which was ridiculous since the garment was faded and tattered and worth nothing. "When you didn't show up right behind me, I wondered if you'd run into trouble. I figured it was best to be out of sight."

"Clever move," Mouse replied. He had to admit he was impressed. The fop had quick instincts.

"Was there trouble?" Tenric asked. "Have they figured out I'm gone?"

"No." Mouse hoped it would be a while, too. At least until the potent herb wore off. "And it was nothing I couldn't handle. But we should be moving."

Tenric looked worriedly at the open door. "I should close it, though, right? I think I might have broken something on the inside when I first pulled it open. The lock maybe?"

Mouse stared in disbelief. *How strong* was *this guy?* "Leave it."

It didn't matter. With a tilt of his head, he gestured for Tenric to follow.

Tenric seemed unsure and looked back at the open door as he fell in behind Mouse.

As Mouse marched back toward the street, he itched to ask Tenric why he'd stayed, why he hadn't taken the logical action and bolted toward the safety of his wealthy peers. But he also didn't want to put the notion into his head.

"This time, stay close to me. We'll avoid the main streets, stick to ones less occupied during the day. Less chance of being noticed. But keep your eyes open."

"For what?"

Mouse grunted. Perhaps he *wasn't* so clever. "Anything that looks like we're being followed...or watched."

"Will it be dangerous?" Tenric had a strange earnestness to his voice. It wasn't fear. More like curiosity.

They were near the mouth of the alley. Mouse turned to him. "No, as long you stay close to me."

Tenric nodded with enthusiasm. "Understood." Now free of the cell, his demeanor had changed. Below, in his cell underground, he'd been guarded, wary of Mouse and his intentions. But now that he was again back onto the street, he had a buoyancy about him, as if he'd been liberated after decades of imprisonment. In the cell, he'd been more worried about his fate than he was letting on.

They strolled out of the mouth of the alley at an easy pace, side by side. Mouse asked him banal questions—age, city, upbringing—to keep up the appearance of a conversation, ensure their movement and mannerisms were casual and relaxed. But Mouse was silently mapping out their route in his head while he nodded along to Tenric's replies.

They didn't have far to go. The guildhall was a stone's throw from the docks and Darko's river craft. Mouse decided on a more circuitous path. If he was spotted by someone, he wanted them to see him heading in a direction that made the docks an unlikely destination.

Mouse guided him into a pocket of small little shops—seamstresses and lacemakers, mostly. The byways cutting through it were wide enough for foot traffic only and were a twisting jumble that made no practical sense. On the opposite side, they were deposited at the edge of the district dominated by warehouses and larger production industries.

The streets here were quiet. Like he'd hoped. A few sweat-drenched workers hung outside a wide barn-sized door. Backs to the wall, they drew on their pipes and chatted among themselves in low grunts and growls. From the fragrant haze that hung around them like a brewing storm cloud, they glanced up as Mouse and Tenric passed but lost interest immediately and returned to their griping.

Mouse had ended the pretense of talk between the two of them. No need here, and Mouse was in no mood for chatter. Tenric seemed content with the silence, too. He had retreated into himself. It was sinking in, Mouse imagined, that his grim and frightening ordeal was over, and he was gauging what to do now. The fop was certainly not accustomed to such ill treatment, and now that it was over, the trauma was taking root.

Since he was distracted, Mouse took the opportunity to assess the man now in the better light.

The clothes Mouse had found for him, although grubby, did more to accentuate the finer points of Tenric's shape than his doublet had. Mouse had muscle, but his overall shape leaned more towards lithe and solid. Tenric had bulk. He was thickset and bearlike, but not in a brutish or barbarian way. His biceps filled out the tunic sleeves, straining the seams. Tenric had pushed the sleeves up to the elbows to expose the forearms—thick logs of knotty muscle.

Perhaps sensing Mouse's eyes on him, Tenric glanced his direction. His blue eyes were soft, gentle. He looked away again, sighed, and swept fingers through the brown curls draping over his brow.

"Thank you," he said. "For getting me out of there."

Mouse chuckled. "Don't thank me yet. You aren't out of danger." He slowed and looked up at Tenric. "I need to be clear. This wasn't a kindness. Nothing about it was…philanthropic. I have use for you."

"I know," Tenric replied softly. "You've made yourself clear. But I'm thankful, nonetheless. Who knows how long I would have been down there if not for you?"

"Not long," Mouse said dryly as he regained his earlier stride.

Tenric nodded and hurried to keep pace. "Suppose you're right." Gloom had elbowed its way into his voice. "Suppose I owe you my life."

"You'll owe me something. But we'll get to that."

They ended up at the riverbank. A boardwalk followed the narrow band between the buildings and the water. Private docks jutted out over water that was deceptively calm. The current was faster than many believed. More people congregated here by the water, as Mouse suspected, but still fewer than would be at the docks at this hour. Most loitered about, wasting time, tossing in fishing lines. Others just milled about the boardwalk, enjoying the warmth of the afternoon.

The clump of their boots on the planks drew no interest or curiosity. No one paid them any mind.

Mouse could hear the activity of the docks before they rounded the bend in the river. As the two of them came around the side of the large warehouse that acted as a wall to the wide-open plaza, the change was jarring. The noise rolled over Mouse in a wave.

"Stay close," Mouse said.

They slipped delicately into the throng, skirting a crowd gathered around a screeching auctioneer. The crowd's attention was fully on the caller, pointing and waving as numbers spilled from his mouth in a mesmerizing stream. Mouse spotted a tantalizing pouch at a belt—red leather, thick like a juicy apple, and its owner captivated by the auction.

Foolish. New to the city, clearly.

He bumped into the man as he walked behind him. Nothing more than a gentle nudge, the kind of jostle one expects, and usually ignores, when in a crowded space.

With practiced ease, he slipped out his dagger and sliced through the thong holding the pouch to the belt. He never understood how his father's dagger remained forever sharp. He'd never had to run it over a whetstone. Not once. But times like this, he appreciated its edge. The bright, plump, leather apple fell into his other hand with nary a jingle. Not that anyone would hear it over the shouting of the auctioneer and the industrious din around them.

"What are you doing?" Tenric demanded in a harsh whisper.

"Staying in practice," Mouse replied, loosening the drawstrings with wiggling fingers. "Though that wasn't really a worthy challenge."

"Now really the time?"

"Take opportunity when it presents itself. First rule of the guild." With the pouch open, Mouse spilled a handful of the man's coin into his palm, then tucked it away into his own, more carefully concealed pouch. He tugged the drawstrings tight again and tapped the man on the shoulder.

"Pardon me. Appears you dropped this." He extended his hand, revealing the red pouch.

"Merciful gods!" the man exclaimed, his eyes widening. "How…"

"Found it right here at your feet," Mouse told him. "It is yours, is it not?" He took the man's hand and placed the pouch in it. "You really should be more careful. Some unscrupulous types about here on the docks."

"I…shall. I shall, indeed. Thank you, lad. I am most

grateful. Appears the famed corruption and vice of this city is exaggerated."

Mouse smiled at him. "I wouldn't go that far."

"Well, clearly there is *some* good here."

Mouse turned to leave, but the man took his arm. "Wait." He fumbled with the drawstring. "Let me at least reward you for your kindness."

"That won't be necessary," Mouse replied. "I couldn't."

"No. I insist." The man put two more coins in Mouse's palm.

Mouse grinned down at the paltry sum. A fraction of what he'd pilfered from the pouch already. It was a wonder the man hadn't noticed the difference in weight. "If you insist, then." Mouse made the effort to bow. "Thank you kindly, master. It always feels good to be rewarded for doing the right thing."

The man's smile broadened. "Indeed, it does."

"Appears the legendary parsimony of you merchant types is equally exaggerated."

The man blinked at Mouse a moment, clearly stunned and unsure what to say. In the awkward silence that followed, he turned stiffly back to the auctioneer without another word. Mouse grabbed Tenric's sleeve, and the two slipped away into the crowd.

"I…I don't understand what just happened," Tenric said behind him.

"Did you not witness the whole event?"

"Why did you give the man's purse back after you went through the effort to swipe it?"

Mouse stopped and turned around to face him. "If the man noticed his pouch was missing, he would have started to scream and call for a guard. He was certainly the type to do that. We didn't need that ruckus."

"Well, you could have just not taken the pouch in the first place."

"Where's the fun in that?"

"What if he caught you?"

Mouse gently tapped Tenric on the cheek with his palm. "Ah, there is so much you have to learn about me. Now come on. We're almost there."

Without waiting to see if Tenric followed, he made a sharp cut to the right and headed down the center pier. As he passed the dock manager, still stationed at his podium, spectacles resting on the very edge of his bulbous nose, he slapped the coins the merchant had slipped him as his reward—plus a few more for good measure—onto the surface of the podium just north of the ledger.

"Anything of interest happening on the dock today?"

The man eyed the coins a moment before his gaze lifted to Mouse. Then he lifted one side of the ledger and the coins disappeared underneath it.

"A quiet day, young master, overall. Just a visit from a craftsman, here to repair a door, apparently."

Mouse nodded. "Then enjoy what remains of this fine day," he said and moved on. Loyalty was expensive. A steady flow of coin would keep this man on his side.

He made a quick scan to confirm no eyes were on them before he leapt onto the river craft's deck. Tenric followed, although with some reluctance.

"This…is your craft?" he asked.

Mouse started down the steps to the cabin below. "Don't be daft." The door was indeed repaired. Crudely, but it was all that Mouse required.

Tenric followed him into the cabin, and Mouse closed the door once he was inside. Tenric scanned the space, clearly unsettled by the state of it. He pointed to the floor. "Is…is that—?"

"Best not think about it," Mouse replied.

"Did you kill—"

"You hold me in the highest regard, I see. If we are not proper merchants or nobles, we must be murderers and thugs."

Tenric looked away sheepishly. "I didn't mean to—"

"I didn't kill anyone. But the owner of this craft was murdered."

Tenric pointed, wide-eyed. "Right there?"

"No," Mouse said. "That was where one of his bodyguards was killed." As if that somehow made it better. "Sit. There on the bed will do."

"Are you certain we're safe here?"

Mouse pulled out the chair tucked under a built-in bureau and sat on it backwards, chest against the back. He rested his forearms on the curved top, then plopped his chin on his wrist. "Safer than anywhere else I'd wager. No one will think to look for you here. And we weren't followed."

He hoped.

"Sit," Mouse repeated, this time more gently. "We have much to discuss."

Tenric obeyed. He sat tentatively on the edge of the mattress, hands in between his thighs, looking like a boy awaiting a reprimand. "Someone ransacked this place."

"They did," Mouse replied.

"Looking for something. And you said it was guarded?" His eyes involuntarily swept to the bloodstain. "Meaning something valuable was here. No coincidence we're here, is it?"

"So, you're not a complete dolt."

"I know what a ransacked place looks like. Firsthand."

"Certain you do."

"Who owns this vessel, Mouse?"

"Owned," Mouse corrected. He hesitated a moment, calculating how much he wanted to reveal. But if he was to get the information he needed out of this young fop, he'd need to open up. "The owner was a merchant from Har Klandu by the name of Darko. That ignite any fires of recognition?"

Tenric frowned. All the confirmation Mouse needed.

Mouse continued. "He was the one who hired the guild to find and steal the document—the king's writ—that at one point belonged to you."

"Darko was a family friend." His eyes turned glumly down to his hands. "Or so I thought."

"There are no friends when power is involved," Mouse grumbled. One of old Surev's sayings. He was right. As usual. He was right about everything. Mouse wished he had listened to him more. "Only temporary allies. But you're from Har Purdea, yes?"

Tenric nodded. "Darko shipped glass out from Har Klandu along river routes and canals. Safer than roads. My father had some business ties with Darko. Not sure what they were. Our main estate was in Har Purdea, yes, but we had a summer home along the river there."

Okay. They were getting somewhere. "So, this is where you tell me what you know."

"Seems you have all the answers already," Tenric replied.

"Maybe I do. So, I'll know when you're lying to me. I freed you from your cage, little bird. Now sing."

Tenric sighed. "Fine. From the beginning then. Mind if I get comfortable first?"

"By all means," Mouse answered with a wave of his hand.

Tenric shrugged out of the jerkin first and tossed it to the floor. He unlaced the boots and kicked them off one at a time. Then he scootched back, pulled up his thick legs, and sat cross-legged on the bed. "Gods, I could use a drink. Anything in here?"

"You're stalling."

"I'm thirsty. And hungry. I've been in a cell for days and not well provided for."

Mouse was willing to grant him that. But he still wasn't going to venture out and hunt him down a bottle of something right now. "Nothing here, I'm afraid. You'll have to suffer for a spell yet. I'll ferret out a meal and some spirits when this business is concluded."

Tenric sighed again. "Very well. Though I'm not even

certain where to start."

Then his stomach growled so loud that Mouse heard it across the cabin. Tenric put a hand to his stomach, and his eyes shot up to meet Mouse's. He winced sheepishly.

"We're not getting anywhere, are we?" Mouse said. He had to admit Tenric was looking rather pale, and dark circles had appeared under his eyes. Despite his apparent strength, the race from the guild had taken more out of him than Mouse had calculated.

"I'm sorry," Tenric said. "You've done so much already. I promise I'll be more clear-headed with something in me."

Mouse slapped his knees and pushed himself to his feet.

"Stay put," he said. He moved to the door but turned about again. "I mean it. It's not going to be safe for you out there."

Tenric nodded, understanding. His eyes were a mix of gratitude and unease. The warning struck home. Mouse didn't expect him to bolt, given this opportunity. He'd had a chance earlier and didn't take it. And the fear of ending up back in that cell, or worse, was likely to have him choose hiding over escaping. And he didn't look like he had the energy to go scampering off anyway, even if he wanted to.

But Mouse was wary, nonetheless. Dandies like this were unpredictable when facing the dangers of the street for the first time.

He ducked out of the cabin and onto the deck. The sun had sunk behind the line of buildings, casting the docks in shadow. The commotion of earlier was beginning to wane as the day slipped into evening. Many of the dock workers had already vacated the area, and tradesmen were packing up their tools and preparing to close their workshops. Still, more than a few milled about. Some merchants were unloading the last of their wares at discounted prices, while others were ferreting out the best deals. Mouse scanned the area in search of signs the craft was being surveyed. From what he could tell, no eyes were on the pier or Darko's river craft.

He thought about asking the dock manager to interfere if Tenric tried to leave, but he knew better. The man wouldn't lift a finger and then cry that he'd tried. No point. So, he nodded to him instead, and dropped another coin on the podium. Maybe then he'd confess which direction Tenric ran off to.

Still nervous, he glanced back at the craft as he crossed into the open plaza of the docks. Nothing. No hunched figure creeping around.

Soon, the river craft was out of sight as he pushed into the thinning crowd. Food venders were on the opposite side. He approached a shop that had a line of steaming vats set into a long counter. Mouse pointed to what looked like a thick beef and turnip stew, and the craggy-faced woman behind the counter nodded and ladled the brown slop into a hardened leather bowl.

"Extra if you're taking the bowl with you," she snarked with her hand out.

Mouse paid her, grabbed a flagon of ale from another nearby vender, and headed back—steaming bowl in one hand and flagon in the other.

The dock manager said nothing as he marched by. Mouse hoped that was a good sign.

Tucking the flagon under his arm, he fumbled with the door and descended into the cabin.

Tenric was still there but passed out on the bed, dead to the world.

16

MOUSE STRUGGLED with how big of a dick he was willing to be.

He slid the bowl unceremoniously on the bureau under the window and dropped into the chair. He made a sound that was half growl, half sigh, then gulped down a hearty portion of ale from the flagon—ale intended for Tenric. His lips pinched, and he drummed his fingers on the chair's arm as he stared at the unconscious fop. He wanted to kick him. Poke him. Jar him awake with a loud noise. But with a grunt, he set the tankard quietly on the bureau next to the stew. No point in waking him. He would let the princess sleep.

Tenric was still fully dressed—save the jerkin and boots, which were on the floor where he'd discarded them. Obviously, as soon as Mouse had left, he'd leaned back to wait for Mouse's return and been swallowed by the mattress, surrendering to its seductive spell. Just as Mouse had done the night before. Tenric's soft snores sounded like the rutting of a pig. He was deep asleep. And possessed by dark dreams, no doubt, after his *harrowing* adventure in the custody of the guild.

A minor inconvenience, more like. A regular cot to sleep in and meals brought to him? Practically treated like royalty.

One leg still dangled over the edge of the bed, his naked foot twitching. It was a nicely shaped foot, Mouse decided. And a good size one.

Not that *that* meant anything.

Resisting the urge to tickle the foot with something, he growled deep in his throat and thrust himself to his feet. The sinister magecraft imbued in the mattress could not be denied. Mouse knew that from his own experience. After days spent in a cold, dank cell on an uncomfortable cot, Tenric wasn't waking any time soon. He'd be out 'til dawn.

If Mouse woke him now, any attempt at conversation was pointless. He needed him cogent to answer specifics, and he'd be in no state to recall important details. Fine. He'd wait. Not ready to call it a night himself, he'd take care of other business in the meantime. He grabbed some coins from the hidden stash in the stairs and climbed out onto the deck.

The dock manager was gone for the night, the pier all but abandoned now. The plaza's crowd had thinned, as well. The shops and stalls were shuttered, and the bands of laborers, their work completed, departed in rowdy wolf packs toward their favorite tavern. The piles of crates that had cluttered the plaza all day like slain wooden giants were now gone, hauled off to their new homes in the surrounding warehouses, leaving a vast empty field of stone.

The city guards had taken their positions under an awning and were too busy throwing dice to notice any of the goings-on in the plaza.

Out of habit, he followed the line of buildings, staying in their thicker shadow, rather than cross the open plaza, which was painted rust by the last remnants of the day. He scanned, eyes alert, as he slunk along. No one from the guild was around, but a few local thugs for hire were stomping about at the opposite end. They looked like they were on a mission to break some knees. Jardem's private goons? Maybe. But he was likely being paranoid. Jardem wasn't behind all the nefarious works in the city. Mouse made sure he stayed clear of them and out of their line of sight, nevertheless.

Tenric's absence would be noted by now. As certain as shit steamed on a cold night, the guildhall would be in chaos right now. Jardem would be having convulsions. He'd be furious—and panicked. He'd have the entire hall on high alert but wouldn't be able to announce why. So he'd lash out at everyone for no apparent reason while at the same time unleashing his outside goons to figure out how Tenric had gotten away.

Mouse was almost sorry he was missing it. The mayhem would be delicious.

The card from the Golden Flute should be enough to throw Jardem off the scent. It was a subtle yet pointed message that he'd gained the attention of the Shadow Elite. Jardem was well-informed enough to know of their connection to the Flute…

But Mouse, after the fact, wondered if the move had been too clumsy and obvious. Jardem may be slimy and ambitious, but he was still clever and wily. Annoyingly skilled at obtaining information. Could he already know of Mouse's clandestine meeting at the Flute?

No. Mouse grunted at himself. He was too much in his own head right now. Jardem had no way to connect him to the card.

The sun was nearly gone. Dark was thickening in the narrow streets as Mouse put the docks behind him. Lamp lighters were on their ladders doing their part to push back the encroaching night. Mouse kept to the quieter, unlit byways.

Night was his home. He felt at ease in the darkness and relished in the soft absence of people. The dark washed away the ugly stains of civilization—the perpetual grime that coated the cobbles, the stone, the walls of every building. Mouse felt his muscles loosen, the constriction in his chest ease. Something about the starkness of the day made him feel exposed. The sun was a constant menace that felt biting and accusatory. But embraced by the night, he could breathe easier, move freer, without the threat of judgment. His mind was sharper.

This was the kind of night he might seek out Taurin if he was free.

His route kept him well clear of the guildhall. He knew where he was heading—in general. The Merchant District. He skirted Rharden Square and his old sanctuary, the bell tower. Too risky. He had to assume it was being watched still. His destination was west of the square in an area where the richer merchants had their homes and offices. Some were without question Shadow Elite.

Even in the dark, Mouse could tell the area was maintained for a different sensibility. His nose told him all he needed to know. No smell of rotting garbage or urine. The neighborhood had been scoured clean of such offending elements.

He stepped out from the dark alleys and took to the main streets. The lamps here were larger and more frequent, basking the cobbles in a warm, almost dawn-like glow. It took a bit of searching, crisscrossing through the neighborhood, before he found what he was looking for.

The Dire Moon.

The tavern was located at the intersection of two angled streets, the building that housed it wedge-shaped. The Dire Moon seemed from the outside a fine establishment. The half-timbered building was well maintained, the plaster freshly painted. The entrance was at the point of the spear, a solid piece of oak, the face of the moon intricately carved into the center of it.

This wasn't the Flute. Still, Mouse likely wasn't dressed properly for the establishment. Not that he cared. Though his appearance might garner some unwanted attention and some pushback from the proprietors. He should have thought to don the foppish coat he'd swiped from the Flute. He'd fit in better.

But he wasn't in the mood to play the part of the privileged tonight. Coin in the palm would remedy any grievances they had.

He pulled open the door and plunged into the tavern.

The hum of conversation and the sweet fragrance of charred meats and pricy herbs greeted him in the short, dark hallway. His stomach was only too happy to remind him that he'd scrounged up a meal for Tenric but not for himself. Easy enough to remedy here. The food would prove better than his normal haunts, and now he had the coin to enjoy it.

He slid through the curtain into the main room of the tavern.

Mouse immediately felt ill at ease. The energy was all wrong. Patrons sat and talked with each other instead of shouting. No one was punching anyone or threatening to do so. The men weren't slobbering and hanging on each other or trying to shout the words of the song the lute player in the corner was strumming. Mouse couldn't even catch the faintest whiff of piss. It was all so very…civil. And Mouse hated it.

How could this even be called a tavern?

As upscale as this was as far as taverns went, it was not The Golden Flute, however. It had a sort of false humility, as if the room was trying to capture the quaint essence of the rank and file. But the tables were too well constructed and didn't wobble when leaned on, the chairs too sturdy to break apart in a fight. And…there was actual art on the walls. Not pinned wanted posters with poorly penned caricatures of mischief-makers.

With a snarl, he crossed the room, meandering through the tables toward the bar at the far end. He bumped into an occupied chair intentionally just to see what would happen. The man seated in it was attempting to take a sip from his chalice, and the wine splashed onto his black doublet.

"I beg your pardon!" the man exclaimed as he grasped for his table linen and dabbed his coat.

Mouse ignored him and kept walking.

186

"How very rude," the man whispered to his companion. After a pause where Mouse could feel himself being evaluated, he added, "This establishment is slipping, it appears. They're letting anyone in these days."

Mouse allowed himself a chuckle. A part of him was now pleased he didn't put on that costume from the Flute. This was more fun.

The barkeep, a tall, severe woman with white hair pulled back in a tight bun and a hard gaze in her dark eyes, was less than amused by his antics. She watched him cross the room and approach her bar, her mouth tight.

"Lost?" she asked.

Mouse smiled back at her. "Ah, your famed courtesy and hospitality. Will my coin not be recognized here?"

"Quality is expensive, lad. And I wager your coppers are few enough to not ever meet each other in that purse."

Mouse sneered at her. "I assure you I can afford a meal and ale. Regardless of your inflated pricing."

"Folks here pay my prices to shield themselves from the likes of you."

He released the knot that secured his purse to his belt and dropped the bulging thing onto the bar counter.

"How much of that is earmarked for your madam at the brothel?" she asked.

Mouse guffawed. "A wicked volley, my lady. I approve greatly." Her expression didn't alter. She continued to glower at him. "Allow me to sully your counter and stool for a spell, and I would make it worth your while."

Her eyes made the slightest lift. "Enough to compensate for the loss of customers when they see I've allowed you to stay?"

Mouse loosened the drawstring, pulled out a full crown, and placed it on the counter. More than enough to cover the cost of a meal and some ale—even at the Moon's bloated prices. The barkeep remained unimpressed, so Mouse added another crown next to it.

"Sit your ass at the end of the counter," she said finally. "Far enough from others that your stench won't offend and fewer might notice you. I have a reputation to maintain, sirrah." Her expression softened for a reason Mouse couldn't explain. Perhaps she'd started to take notice of his charms. Perhaps she saw this as her charitable deed for the day. "I will inform anyone who asks that you are here to repair…something." Without asking, she preemptively dropped a full mug of ale in front of him.

Mouse took a swig of it. Likely from their cheapest keg, but still arguably better than anything he'd get at his more typical haunts. Still, he would have liked the option to choose. But he was grateful she hadn't had her hired brute throw him out on his ear.

A meal arrived—again no choice offered. The plate was filled with a hodgepodge of tubers that were overcooked, some over ripe tomatoes cut into sections, and poultry cuts that were likely left over from the day before. Food that would end up with the pigs. The barkeep saw an opportunity to make a coin or two off food that she would never dare serve to her typical clientele.

He shrugged off the insult. He wasn't here for a fine dinner, and the food in front of him wasn't anything worse than he'd eat normally.

He started in without complaint, tearing meat from the bone with his fingers—if he was going to be treated like a barbarian from the west, he'd ignore the utensils and eat like one. As he popped meat in his mouth and licked his fingers, he felt her eyes on him.

"What is it you want here?" she asked.

"A meal. Some ale."

She scoffed. "You don't fool me. Your kind don't wander in here by chance."

Keeping his eyes steadily locked onto hers, he slid three more crowns across the counter in her direction. "Allow me the honor of providing a round for all your fine patrons this evening. Anonymously, of course."

She stared at the coin as if it were something wicked. He could read her thoughts—where did this street rat get his dirty fingers on five crowns? And was there blood on it?

"I'll ask again. What is it you want here?" A tinge of unease colored her voice now. Her demeanor stiffened.

Mouse kept his voice light. Non-threatening. "Maybe a look around your fine establishment. Call it curiosity. It interests me."

She still didn't touch the coin. "I don't give tours."

"I can peek about on my own, if you don't want to leave your post."

She folded her arms. A seething suspicion was building up strength in her eyes. "All this sudden interest in my facilities."

Sudden?

Mouse frowned. So…someone else had wanted a look around recently.

"What are you playing at?" she asked. Her hackles were up. Something had put her on edge. Mouse knew he was in the right place.

He sighed and gave his voice the sad timbre of coming clean with the truth. "I'm here on behalf of a client. A rather private one. I understand you have a meeting room with a private entrance. So, a party of…say eight, can discretely enter without the notice of your other patrons."

She studied him a moment, but her face remained rigid. He couldn't read her.

"No dark business," Mouse added, palms out. "If that's your worry. Nothing that would gain the attention of the king's guard and taint your immaculate reputation. Just a wealthy bugger wanting a private room to have a few contracts signed."

Her eyes still on Mouse, she used the side of her hand to sweep the coin across the counter and into her cupped hand. Then she stashed them away somewhere under the counter.

"Make it quick."

"Of course," Mouse said. "A turn about the room is all I'll need. Where do I go?"

She pointed to a door to the right. Mouse slid off the stool.

The barkeep made as if to leave but turned back around. She leaned one forearm on the counter and leaned in. "I doubt the room is what you expect," she growled softly. "See yourself out."

Then she stomped to the other end of the counter to speak with the impatient customers flagging her over.

Mouse grabbed the mug of ale and carried it with him toward the door.

Mouse's awareness of the dagger in his boot became heightened. The cold metal seemed to thrum against his skin. Danger? The dagger always seemed to know somehow.

Beyond the door was a narrow corridor, painted in a baroque pattern of rich blue and bright gold. Another door awaited at the far end. Mouse put his hand on the latch, took a breath, and pushed his way inside the meeting room.

Zelianna sat in a chair by the opposite wall, feet up on the long table that dominated the center of the room. Her arms were folded, her chin low. She was deep in thought.

The chamber was cozy and comfortable. Not grotesquely opulent, like many of the rich estates that he'd burgled over the years. Whoever had decorated the room understood restraint. The furnishings were high quality, the wood paneling on the walls warm and inviting, the carpet lush and soft—but none of it was garish. None of it tried to look expensive, but Mouse knew without question that it was.

Zel didn't look up immediately when he entered. She must have assumed that he was just one of the workers there or, perhaps, the warm and hospitable barkeep coming in to check on her. But as Mouse closed the door behind him, the latch made a distinct click, and she looked up. Her expression soured.

"Mouse," she said with disdain.

"Well," he said, with syrup in his tone. "What are the odds?"

Zelianna pulled her feet off the table, and her chair dropped onto four legs. "Why am I not surprised to find you here?"

Mouse took another step into the room, cautiously. "Yet *I* am surprised to find *you* here. What an uncanny coincidence."

"Is it?" she asked. She eyed him with dark suspicion as he eased up to the table. He stood between two high-back chairs cushioned with deep blue fabric. Mouse saw no fear or apprehension in her gaze. Only superiority.

"Appears you dressed for the occasion," he said.

She wore a flowing plum-colored gown, finely embroidered down the top of the sleeves and the neckline. It was laced with yellow ribbon up the breastbone. Mouse had never seen her out of trousers.

"Unlike you," she told him, "I know how to have doors opened for me."

"I can open doors," Mouse said.

Zel chuckled. "Why pick them when you can walk on through?" She stood and strolled around the table closer to Mouse. The draping fabric of the gown flowed luxuriously with each measured step. "How, pray tell, did you convince Tenya to allow you back here?"

"I have my charms," Mouse replied.

Zel scoffed. As she rounded the table and drew closer, her face turned cold and serious. "You better have a good reason for showing up here, Mouse."

Her arrogance sent a surge of anger through him. Her standing in the guild might surpass his own, but she didn't have any authority to dictate his actions.

"I answer to Jardem. Not you."

She blew air through her lips as she turned and leaned her ass against the table. Still watching him, she folded her arms. "Both of us know that's horseshit."

It was an opening, though a strange one. An uncomfortable one. She knew of his disdain for Jardem. She was inviting him to come clean.

He considered her a moment, wondering how much he could trust her. The danger here was like a slick, odorless poison—too easy to graze against it if he wasn't careful how he navigated around it. She was close to Jardem. Had his ear. But her presence here was intriguing. Her obvious suspicion of him weakened his own suspicion of her. It could mean opportunity. He decided to test the waters. "I'm following a lead."

She lifted an eyebrow at him. "A lead?"

He matched her eyebrow for eyebrow. He wasn't about to give up anything. Not yet.

She waited, but when Mouse didn't offer up a response, her mouth pursed. "Curious. Poking around isn't your forte. Not your normal line of work. You wouldn't be working outside the bounds of the guild, would you? Sticky territory if Jardem finds out."

So, she wasn't privy to Jardem's special orders for him. If she knew, that would give him the cover he needed, a reason to be here.

He considered announcing he was here on official guild business, with Jardem's blessing. But for reasons he wasn't certain of, he wasn't ready to let her believe he was working with Jardem currently. "Not something I'm making a habit of," he replied dryly. "I assure you. But your concern for me is touching. And you? This fall within your jurisdiction?"

"Everything exists under my dominion, Mouse. You should know that." She uncrossed her arms and started to stroll around the perimeter of the table again. "A few of my contacts whispered some disturbing rumors in my ear. The kind of talk that makes my spies uneasy should they hear it. I don't like news that makes my clients skittish and consider taking their business elsewhere."

Mouse hitched on her casual mention of spies. He felt a sharp stab of inadequacy. Should he have spies? He knew the guild employed them, but individuals within the guild had their own? That was news.

And how much coin did she bring in if she could afford her own network? Something to ponder over later, he decided.

"Needed to check it out to see if there was any validity to the talk," Zel continued.

She'd opened the door, deciding to trust him. Now he was expected to open it further. But she really hadn't divulged anything, either.

"Did this rumor involve a murder?"

Her eyes lifted and locked on his. "It may have. How did you learn of it?"

"I keep my ear to the ground."

"Well, your ears are closer to it," she muttered. Mouse let the dig about his height slide. "But let's cut the bullshit. Come clean with what you know."

It was an attempt to intimidate, flex her authority in the guild, which Mouse easily ignored. Yet he could use her help in this. She'd be a powerful ally against Jardem—if she was willing to turn on him. She had much to gain if Jardem was brought down—she had to see that. But Mouse wasn't convinced yet that she'd betray him or the guild. The danger that she might run back to inform Jardem of what Mouse knew was too great. She was too cozy with him. He wasn't about to tap open that keg with her just yet.

At the same time, he didn't want her to think he was dragging his feet to avoid cooperating.

"I learned of the murder yesterday. Gossip in a tavern. A little digging revealed the victim had been in contact with Jardem."

Zel pursed her lips at him. "What kind of contact?"

"Vague on that," he lied, and wondered if she could see through it and tell he was keeping things back. "Possible discussions about a contract?" He hesitated, and with a tilt of his head, said, "Aaaaaand references to details associated with my most recent job. Hence my curiosity."

She was quiet a moment as she took that in, then swooped her dark curls from her eyes. "Did your latest job involve something that could lead to murder?"

"They all do…but usually it's me they want to murder."

"I understand the sentiment."

Mouse made a face, then drew serious. "Possibly," he said, answering her question. But he wasn't open to saying more. The question implied she didn't know what he stole, which surprised him. If she was being honest, Jardem had kept it from her.

She strolled to the opposite side of the room again, each footfall of her boots a dull drumbeat on the carpet. Frowning, she leaned on the table with locked elbows. Dark locks fell across her face as she narrowed her black eyes at Mouse.

"You think the guild was involved somehow." It wasn't a question.

He hesitated. "It's why I'm here. To find a few answers."

She continued to stare at Mouse a moment longer. "Same." It was a more honest and forthright response than Mouse expected. "Some folks feel this murder is a bit hard to write off as coincidence. The guild's reputation is at stake, Mouse. Clients don't like feeling they are in danger from the organization *they* hired."

"A knife to the belly would tarnish our stellar list of references," he said. He kept his eyes on her, looking for any glimpse of what was behind her dark eyes.

"Murder is always bad for business." She seemed earnest, even if her motives, in Mouse's view, were dubious. This wasn't some altruistic venture, he knew. She wasn't devotedly protecting the guild's status and reputation. Fewer clients meant a cut in her share of the earnings.

Mouse mused a moment what it might be like to worry about such things. He wasn't privy to such luxuries as a fair cut.

"You've clearly had time to search the place. Find anything that would shed light on this mystery?" he asked.

"No. The room is clean. Too clean. And too new. This furniture has never been used." To emphasize the point, she ran her hand over the smooth and unmarred oak finish of the table.

The barkeep's words echoed in his head. *You won't find anything.*

Mouse bit the inside of his cheek. "They erased all evidence of it."

"Bad for business," she repeated, her voice sharp and judgmental. "The Dire Moon didn't have anything to do with whatever treachery occurred here. That much is clear. They're victims, too."

Mouse agreed with her. "What now?"

She straightened and adjusted the folds of her dress. Preening like a cat, she acted like she'd forgotten Mouse was even there. Then she drifted toward the door. "Stay out of this, Mouse. Jardem has little patience with you already, and he'll not suffer you pursuing any side projects."

Mouse stifled a scoff.

He didn't need her advice on how to handle Jardem. She fell just short of being his lap dog.

"But of course, Zel. I have every confidence you will handle this matter with the heart of the guild in mind."

She stopped and turned an icy gaze to him. The flash of anger in her eyes told him his meaning was clear and understood. He had no intention of abandoning this inquiry to her. He would continue to turn over stones.

She put her hand on the latch. "Learn anything, it comes to me. No one else. Only me. Understood?"

Mouse fashioned a compliant smile. "You have my word."

Zelianna's lips tightened slightly. Then, with a flip of her hair, she marched out the door and was gone.

Mouse was tempted to do a search of his own, but he

knew he'd find nothing. Zel was right. The room was turned over, and all evidence of the brutality that had occurred here was gone. Scrubbed clean, replaced or hidden. So, he left.

He couldn't help but wonder as he put this impromptu thieves' meeting behind him how much Zel knew. Did she know who had been murdered? And did she know about Tenric in the cellar?

\#

It was deep night by the time he returned to the river craft. Moonlight pushed blue through the sole window, casting just enough light for Mouse to find his way around. Tenric was a thick lump at the far side of the bed, still asleep and snoring gently, but since Mouse had been away, he'd found his way under a blanket. The bowl on the side table was empty, and a basin of grey water was on the floor next to a pile of his clothes. He'd woken up at some point, ate his meal, cleaned himself up a bit, and passed out again.

A second opportunity for Tenric to slip away. Again, not taken.

A bit of ale remained in the flagon. Tenric had graciously left him a few swallows. Mouse gulped it down. Subpar from the ale he'd had earlier at The Dire Moon.

He stripped down naked and tossed the clothes over the chair. He didn't want them soiling the fine linens of the bed and wanted nothing between him and their soft touch.

Fatigue hit him then, as if at that moment the fuel no longer reached his wick, and he stifled a yawn with the back of his hand.

He sat on the edge of the bed. The linen felt cool and supple against his ass.

Maybe he should sleep on the floor, he thought. There was danger in getting too accustomed to these finer things. The fine ales, the expensive linens and soft mattress, the exquisite meals that the wealthy took for granted every day. Food was supposed to be functional. Not an experience. Ales should make someone wince a little when choked down. Taste wasn't why you drank it. And he would have to be able to sleep anywhere when the time called for it.

He sighed and gave in to the hedonic call of the bed. One more night, he told himself. He stole some of the blanket from Tenric and slipped under. Tenric's body had created a lush pocket of warmth. Mouse kept a gap between them, rolling onto his side with his back to the rich fop. Already the mattress was spinning its magecraft on him. His eyes were drooping.

This bed probably means nothing to Tenric, Mouse thought as he drifted off. He might even think it was uncomfortable. Mouse hoped he'd never get to a point like that in his life.

Sometime before dawn, Mouse woke to find that Tenric had rolled over and his meaty leg had draped over Mouse's calf. Mouse noted in his half-dozing state, before he drifted off again, that the man's skin was even softer than the linens and blanket.

When Mouse finally did wake up, bright morning sun filled the cabin of the craft.

Tenric was gone.

17

FUCK!

"Fuck, fuck, fuck!" he said out loud. He leapt out of the bed and scrambled for his clothes. He grabbed his trousers, tugged one leg through, and while he hopped on one foot trying to get his other leg in, he noticed his drawstring pouch on the table, loosened, a few coins on the counter next to it— as if a handful had been hastily removed from the pouch.

Fuck.

Curse his idiocy. Tenric hadn't made his escape before because he didn't have any means to survive the city. Mouse had foolishly provided it by leaving out his stash for Tenric to take. Most of the coins Mouse had found were still safely hidden away in the step, but there was enough in the pouch to give Tenric the chance to get somewhere he considered safe.

And curse that fucking bed. How had Tenric climbed over him to get out without him even waking? That was it— from now on he was sleeping on the floor.

Searching for Tenric again would be a futile effort, he knew. The fop would be long gone by now. He could easily disappear into the city and, considering his status, would have access to places to hide that Mouse would not easily gain entry.

As he pulled his tunic over his head, he heard a noise. Boards creaking outside. On the deck of the river craft.

Mouse froze. The latch on the door clicked open.

He suppressed a groan. What the fuck now? Had Jardem's goons returned for another look about the cabin? Had Jardem or the Shadow Elite tracked him down already?

As the door swung open, Mouse lunged for his dagger—thankfully still there. If Tenric had stolen that too, Mouse would have no choice but to track him down at any cost. The thought of how close he'd come to losing it made his stomach twist.

Tenric ducked into the cabin holding a loose weave sack in one hand and a red earthenware jug in the other. He had on a floppy and oversized muffin cap on his head. "Oh good, you're up," he said with a reserved lightness. "I procured a meal for us. For you, really, my intrepid rescuer."

Mouse dropped into the chair and let his head fall back. "Fuck. Would you stop doing that to me?!"

Tenric's head tilted to the side. "Doing what?"

Mouse grunted and pinched the bridge of his nose. "Never mind." He wanted to scream.

Tenric set the jug and sack on the table. "Hot tea and some fresh pastries. Best I could find in the vicinity. I asked around and most swear by this baker."

Mouse sighed, letting his hands drop to either side of the chair. The smell of the pastries reached his nose. They smelled warm.

"Hope you don't mind. I took some of your coin to buy it," Tenric continued. He returned a small handful of coin to the pouch and tightened the drawstring. "I'll replace what I spent…when I can."

"You shouldn't have gone out alone. You could have been spotted."

Tenric looked confused and a little wounded by Mouse's

tone. "I found this cap," he said, pulling it off his head. He shook out his wild dark curls with his fingers. "Figured it was enough to keep me from being recognized. And I never left the plaza. The boat was always in sight."

Of course, he was probably right, but Mouse didn't like him taking chances. He was naïve, almost childlike when it came to the streets. Mouse reined in his irritation.

Tenric pulled the stopper from the jug and poured the steaming liquid into two mugs. He handed one to Mouse. "You were sleeping so soundly I didn't want to wake you." He held the mug with two hands and brought it to his lips. He made a soft cooing sound as he sipped.

Mouse sighed. The sweet innocence disarmed him—and he caught himself irritated with himself for falling for it. He wasn't typically around someone considerate. Anyone at the guild—and most in the city—would have kicked him in the head *and* stole his entire purse on the way out.

"Just…oh, never mind," he said, softening his tone. He nearly launched into a lecture about the dangers of the street, and an offer to do the legwork from now on was right behind his teeth.

Thankfully, he held off on promising something he would regret later. Where was this compulsion to protect him coming from?

Tenric wouldn't be his problem soon enough. Mouse would have the information he needed, and the beefy toff could be on his way.

He gave into the aromas coming from the sack. With a grunt of surrender, he reached in and snagged one. The bread was buttery and flaky and filled with something sweet and nutty. Mouse closed his eyes as he chewed. Each bite sent warm waves of delight through his mouth. Three bites later, he noticed Tenric staring at him.

"What?" he demanded with a full mouth.

"Er…no one is going to take it away from you, you know. And there are more."

Mouse scowled. "Should I get out the fucking china and utensils? Eat with my pinkies out?" Bits of flaky bread rained out of as mouth as he spoke.

Tenric lifted out a palm in capitulation. He grabbed a spirally bun for himself and climbed up on the bed. Legs hanging over the side, he wedged the mug between his thick thighs, then tore the bun in half and took a bite.

"I'll eat how I want. You eat how you want," Mouse grumbled. But he made sure he'd swallowed it all down before he took another bite.

"Of course," Tenric replied and took another demure bite. He took a long drink from the mug and sat quietly, looking glum.

Mouse finished the roll and fought the urge to grab another. Instead, he licked his fingers, then brushed the crumbs from his tunic. Again, more foods Mouse would never have picked for himself. A hard day-old roll from a second-rate bakery was his typical morning meal. Sometimes, if he felt he had the coin, he'd splurge on a spoonful of butter or currant jam. He had to quit with these extravagances. It would spoil him. Didn't matter if he had the coin. How does one go back to stale bread after eating something so…delicious?

In his world, food was survival. Not something to be enjoyed. He had to remember that.

Tenric broke the long silence between them. "I wasn't sure I could trust you." He wiped the crumbs from his lap distractedly. "Even after you rescued me."

It certainly wasn't the first thing Mouse expected him to say. "Trust is over-rated." His tone was colder than he intended. "Distrust can mean survival."

"Are you saying I cannot trust you?"

"I'm saying I'd think you're a fool if you did."

Tenric continued to look down at his lap. "Then perhaps I'm a fool. You left me alone. I could have just…left if I wanted to."

"And why didn't you?" A simmering pot of anger

churned beneath the surface. He was irritated with himself for his own foolishness. Tenric *should* have scampered off. And it was right that Mouse should suffer for that blunder.

Tenric shrugged. "Considered it. But you did go through the effort to free me. Figured I owed you…something. The answers you seek, at least."

Mouse bit his lip. "You owe me nothing. I didn't rescue you for you."

"I know. But you are the only one in this city that can probably help me. Is *willing* to help me. And keep me safe."

Mouse grunted. "Let's not get ahead of ourselves. I made no such commitment. Besides, any number of rich families here can provide you better safe harbor in their estates than I can. You're one of them," he added with a note of disdain.

Tenric was quiet a moment. "Not as easy as that."

"Hmmmm," Mouse replied, stroking the tightly cropped beard on his chin with a knuckle.

Tenric lifted his eyes and pulled his lower lip into his mouth. "I'm going to be honest, Mouse. I've nowhere to go."

Mouse made a non-committal grunt and made a point of not meeting his eyes. He didn't like being cornered. "You could leave Har Tesera. Head home."

"Again. Not that easy."

He was tired of riddles and half statements. "Well, you're here. With me. Safe for now. Time for *you* to keep up your end of our bargain."

Tenric nodded. His demeanor shifted, a darkness encircling his eyes as he looked to Mouse.

"Can I stay?"

"What? Here? I'm no bodyguard, Tenric. If that's what it is you're asking."

"You got me this far."

Mouse groaned inwardly. He hated where this was going. He could feel it careening towards him, like a runaway carriage with a spooked horse, and he felt powerless to stop it. He dared not look into Tenric's eyes. They were dangerous.

"Tenric…" he began, then paused. He took in a long breath. "Protection is not what I do. I am good at one thing. Thievery."

Tenric didn't reply. He looked down at his hands holding the mug. The silence between them grew dense.

Mouse made a grunting sigh. He'd wanted the information from Tenric—nothing more. Tenric was supposed to spill what he knew and then leave. Be on his way back to his happy, little, privileged life. Mouse wouldn't need him anymore. He wanted answers, not… a *charge*. "I cannot promise how safe you'll be with me. Especially since I have no idea of the danger you're in," he added under his breath. "Or its cause."

"Safer than on my own, I suspect."

Mouse forgot himself and, without thinking, glanced Tenric's direction, catching his eyes. The sharp blue cut into Mouse like cold daggers. He tugged his gaze away and exhaled.

Fuck.

Tenric wasn't wrong. He wouldn't last a day on the street. And he wasn't going to talk until Mouse agreed. "Fine. Accord struck. Now talk."

Tenric pulled in a breath. "Where to even begin." He closed his eyes, and his face took on an expression Mouse knew all too well—because he bore it himself enough times. He was fighting back a wave of anguish and sorrow that threatened to overtake him.

Mouse closed his eyes and prayed to any god that might be eavesdropping on this. *No fucking tears.* He wasn't about to be a shoulder to cry on for some sobbing toff.

But to Mouse's intense relief, Tenric rallied and swallowed down the emotion that had darkened his face a moment ago. He lifted his chin.

"My father was murdered."

"Ah," Mouse found himself replying. Not what he'd expected would be the first words of this tale.

"About two fortnights ago. Found him in his study. Knifed in the back. I fled here, to Har Tesera, fearing I was next."

Tenric paused and Mouse waited. Then Tenric chuckled softly.

It wasn't a warm sound. It was cold and humorless.

"He was a foul bastard." His eyes unfocused as they lifted to the ceiling of the boat. "A loathsome and spiteful dog. I hate myself daily for shedding any tears for the loathsome maggot. But my tears…well, they weren't for him, I suppose. More for the situation he thrust upon me, alone and ill-prepared."

"You…didn't get on, then."

The same cold chuckle. "No."

"And he wasn't murdered because of these fine qualities you describe? Enemies are made in the running of a business, I'm told."

"Again, no." He seemed to remember the tea and took a drink from the mug. "Should have gotten something stronger."

He was slipping into his own thoughts. Mouse didn't have time for long meditative pauses.

"Why Har Tesera?" he prodded.

"Friends. My family has ties with the merchant guild here. I thought my presence here would be kept secret, like I asked. Apparently, these friends were not as trustworthy as I'd believed."

"Not necessarily," Mouse replied with a weak shrug. "There are any number of ways that the information could have leaked. Servants. Carriage drivers. Others that visited their estate. Spies are everywhere." He gave Tenric a pointed stare. "You'll do well to remember that. Consider that your first lesson in life on the streets here."

Tenric looked sad as he nodded in agreement. "I shall certainly bear it in mind, always. A lesson my father should have offered me. But then I suppose he felt he didn't need to."

"Because of this mysterious writ from the king."

Tenric nodded.

"Which was the reason he was murdered."

Another nod.

Fuck, this was taking too long. "Time to come clean, merchant boy. Out with it. What is this document everyone is after?"

Tenric lifted the mug to his lips again.

"I won't protect you if I don't have all the information." A lie, but Mouse needed to move things along.

Tenric nodded slowly and began his tale. "In my father's youth, he happened on some communications, missives. A series of letters. They were in a haversack forgotten in his shop. This was in the early days of his business when he ran the shop himself. My father, more high-minded in those days, apparently, read the letters in the hope of finding out who owned the abandoned bag. The man I knew would have tossed the haversack in a rubbish heap or the fire and been done with it. Wasn't one to get involved, my father. But…men change, I suppose." He took in a breath. "One of the letters hinted at a plot against the king. A plan to assassinate him and the entire royal family."

That got Mouse's attention. "There was a plot to kill King Harus?"

"No, no…this was decades ago. Before I was born. The plot was against King Haden."

"Wait." Mouse leaned forward, elbows on knees. "You're referring to the Black Massacre? *Your* father happened across documents about *that*?"

Mouse had heard dozens of bards sing tales of that dark night. Each bard fabricated the details of what happened since no one knew what really took place. Or why. But the essence of the story was always the same: the Black Guard fought against the onslaught but failed to protect the royal family. All were slaughtered, save one. One Black Guard managed to flee with the then-prince Harus and saved the bloodline.

"Yes," Tenric confirmed. "This was only months before

the attack took place."

"What did your father do?"

Mouse's insides churned. Even though it had happened before he was born, the slaughter of the royal family was something everyone knew about and still, to this day, debated and argued about.

Tenric's smile was tainted with bitter sorrow. "Expecting some reward, no doubt, my father traveled to Dar Arendia with the letters and tried to seek an audience with the king himself."

Mouse could guess where this was going. "He was denied."

"Not entirely. He did speak to a few clerks within the palace. And a few noble-born willing to hear his story. He gave them the letters and was promised that the information would be passed on to the king. But clearly that never happened. The assault on the palace took place soon after."

Mouse felt chills slither down his arms. "So, the palace was warned of the attack and did nothing."

"Father believed that the letters were intercepted and destroyed. They never made it to anyone in the court that would have the king's ear. More likely, the palace just didn't take the threat seriously. Threats against the powerful are commonplace. My father used to get threats fairly regularly."

Mouse wasn't sure that was the same. Threats are one thing. A plan is something different entirely. But he didn't challenge it. He felt slightly ill. This information felt too big for him.

Tenric continued. "The next part of this is somewhat unclear. Details of what my father attempted to do somehow surfaced. How, I have no idea. But the attempt reached the ears of King Harus. Apparently, when the king learned of what my father had tried to do all those years earlier, he was moved by it. He decided to reward my father with a special dispensation."

"The writ that somehow ended up at the Agata estate."

"Yes. That."

"And? What is it? What did the king reward your father with?"

"A writ of nobility," Tenric said.

Words failed. His breath locked in his chest. Mouse could only stare back, stunned.

"It grants the bearer complete and unfettered noble status. It comes with an allotment of land and a stipend. From the moment that writ is signed and sealed, all within the family are henceforth considered noble-born."

Icy chills raced down Mouse's arms. He had held that in his hands. *Yes, definitely worth killing over*, he thought.

"That—that does not occur every day, I imagine," he said. Never would he have imagined such a thing was even possible.

"No. It is a rare honor indeed." Tenric shrugged. "Many at court were apparently surprised by the gesture, arguing it went too far. Maybe it was a political move to encourage people to come forward with similar intelligence. Who knows?"

Mouse pinched the fingers of one hand in the fist of the other to stop the trembling that commandeered them both. The details were crashing together in Mouse's head like rough waves trapped in a rocky alcove. Quickly. Too quickly. But he forced his expression to remain neutral and stoic.

"So, what went wrong?"

Tenric fell quiet. He stared at the empty mug of tea clenched in his tight fingers. "Well...everything. Once my father received the notification of the king's intent, he shared it with some people he trusted. Obviously, a mistake. He even showed the writ to a few when it arrived by courier."

Mouse frowned. "Not the wisest course."

"No. Made worse by the fact that the writ didn't yet have the king's seal."

"That seems a strange decision."

"The document is delivered so a magistrate can go over

all the details of the arrangement. Mostly so the recipient fully understands the parameters of the king's decree before it is signed. But also to give time for any special requests or changes to be approved by the king."

Mouse chuckled dourly. Who would do *that*?

"The document is signed and sealed during a special ceremony. We had a scheduled appointment for the event to take place at the magistrate's office. The Crown Notary would arrive and handle the rest. But father was murdered a short time later, before the ceremony could take place."

"Someone your father spoke to decided they wanted it for themselves, then," Mouse put in, nodding.

"I thought so too…at first," Tenric said slowly. "But I don't believe that to be the case. The reason father was murdered was because they felt no one should have it."

Surprise broke through Mouse's tight control of his countenance. His brow lifted.

"Father was growing more powerful and more influential. And had a new influx of equally powerful friends now. He never admitted it, but I long suspected he'd joined in with the Shadow Elite."

Them again.

"I think the Shadow Elite was concerned about a shift in power," Tenric continued. "Father would not give up his business, and as a noble, he was exempt from practices that commoners are not. As much as it galls them, the merchant class—including the Shadow Elite—are still commoners in the eyes of the king and are not granted the same privileges. He would have unfair advantages in his business dealings, pay few taxes. He'd acquire political influences and connections denied all other merchants."

"Making your family richer than anyone could imagine," Mouse said softly.

"Exactly that. Something the Elite was loath to allow. But even beyond that, the Shadow Elite has been a stone in the king's shoe for a very long time. Father knew intimately the members of that organization and all their unscrupulous practices. Imagine that information in the hands of the nobility…." He trailed off, shaking his head. "Clearly a danger they weren't willing to risk."

It was a compelling theory. "So, they assassinated him and took the writ."

"Surprisingly…no. They tore my father's office apart searching for it—but at the time, it was in my custody. The Elite didn't realize that he wasn't going to sign the writ himself. Instead, he wanted *me* to sign it. I was to be the first noble. To show his loyalty to the other merchants, he told me. A sign of solidarity." Tenric made a dramatic waving of his arms. "He didn't want to create a conflict of interest."

Mouse narrowed his eyes at him. "But you weren't convinced."

Tenric's jaw tightened slightly, and he remained quiet. Pensive.

"Father was many things," he said after a time, "but considerate wasn't one of them. I knew what it all meant. It was an act to appease those in the Shadow Elite. Calm their fears and assuage suspicion. But he thought, with my help, he could straddle both worlds and win at both. Use me and the influence the nobility awarded me while he remained in the inner circle of the Shadow Elite. Fool," he spat, and tossed the empty mug across the cabin. "As if the Elite wouldn't see right through that plan. It's possible, I suppose, they found out about the writ before he had a chance to tell them his plan, but in all likelihood, he told them, and they didn't fall for it. Not willing to risk it."

"Hence the fears for your own life."

Tenric was naïve perhaps, sheltered certainly, but he wasn't stupid. That much was evident. He understood more than his father the futility of the plan to not only hold power but grasp for even more.

Tenric nodded.

Mouse leaned back in the chair and crossed his arms.

Telling his tale had left Tenric looking drained and lost. Strange that a man of his size could look so boyish and vulnerable.

Mouse knew that look. He'd seen it on the faces of some of the other urchins he'd run with on the streets. The ones that had abandoned their homes because life on the streets was more tolerable. He'd seen it on the faces of some of the workers at the brothel when he'd visit Taurin.

Tenric had faced trauma at the hands of his own father. He'd put a mask on his pain, but he was tired, worn down by his confinement in the guild cellar, and uncertain of his future. The mask was slipping.

Mouse's heart went out to him.

He caught himself staring longer than intended. Gods, Tenric was well formed. His shape was different from Taurin's—a body that Mouse knew intimately—but no less striking. Tenric was thicker, stronger. Had more pronounced curves. Shirtless, he would fit in comfortably with the dockhands were it not for the manicured nails and pale skin.

Tenric, likely curious about the silence filling the room, lifted his eyes and caught Mouse appreciating the size of his thighs and how they filled his trousers. Mouse quickly dropped his gaze and felt his face redden.

"So, you had possession of the document," Mouse said quickly to mask his embarrassment. "Obvious why. Your father suspected an attempt to steal it. How did Agata get his hands on it?"

"I'm not sure. I hardly knew the man. It may have changed hands before he acquired it. I fled Har Purdea after...." His voice hitched. "After the attack. Went to our home in Har Klandu, thinking I'd be safer there. Someone must have figured I had it with me there."

"You're lucky to have escaped the same fate as your father."

Tenric nodded. "I was out for the evening when it happened, thankfully."

"Is Agata part of the Shadow Elite?"

"Not that I know of. Could be, I suppose."

"And when was it taken from you?"

Tenric's mouth twisted. His eyes lifted, filled with sudden fire. "Why do I feel like I'm being interrogated? This feels like your leader's hand behind these questions—"

Mouse leaned in fast, elbows on his knees, his eyes slits. "Suggest that again and you can face those chasing you on your own."

Tenric averted his eyes from Mouse's hard gaze, then continued.

"I kept the appointment with the magistrate to go forward with signing the writ of nobility. I traveled back to Har Purdea and arrived at the magistrate's office at dawn and waited. The Crown Notary never arrived. The magistrate told me to go home, and he would investigate the matter and reschedule. I returned to Har Klandu, and the writ was stolen a few days later."

"Did you ever learn why the Crown Notary didn't arrive?"

"Not from the magistrate. But there were rumors."

"That the Crown Notary's caravan was attacked on the road?"

Tenric looked up, surprised. "Yes." For a moment he stared at Mouse, baffled by how he could possibly have learned of it. But he recovered, and his expression softened. "But other rumors circulated too. That I was in league with the Shadow Elite, that this was somehow their plan all along. To get their hands on a king's signet."

That might explain Savir's insistence that Mouse steal the writ and put it in their hands. Mouse never believed the nonsense that he wanted it destroyed. If they had the signet in their possession, they could select anyone they wanted to be part of the nobility.

Or Savir might just want that honor for himself.

Mouse paced the small cabin, tugging the hair of his chin

with his forefinger and thumb, thinking. "Jardem clearly thinks there's some stock in that rumor." He narrowed his eyes at Tenric over his shoulder. "Did you tell anyone of your meeting with the magistrate?"

"Of course not."

Mouse made a low grunt. "Doesn't mean the magistrate didn't. Or someone in his office. Let's outline what we know for certain." He turned about and leaned on the back of the chair. "If the persons involved in the signet heist on the road and the burgling of your estate were one and the same, the document would have been signed and sealed. So obviously, two separate parties."

Tenric lifted his eyebrow. "So, just a coincidence?"

"Appears so."

Tenric nodded.

Mouse wasn't convinced this was everything. For some reason, Jardem believed Tenric had possession of the signet—or knew who did. Jardem wasn't a fool. And if anything, he was thorough.

What was he missing?

"I find it staggering that anyone could sign that document," Mouse asked.

"With the king's seal on it, it is done," Tenric said. "It would be added to the imperial records, no questions asked. I doubt anyone one would bother the king with it. No one person knows all the things the king promises."

Would the king, with an entire country to manage, even remember who the recipient of his gift was? Mouse couldn't help but wonder if the king was ever actually told the rod was missing.

All this explained why Jardem wanted this document for himself. In his ambition-soaked brain, becoming a noble was, of course, the logical trajectory for him. It explained why he didn't care about the welfare of the guild anymore. He was moving on to greater heights.

It made his insides roil with anger.

Nobility was not in Jardem's future. If Mouse had any say, the opposite was going to happen to that fucker. He would find a way to bring him low.

"Jardem wants you, obviously. Who else?"

"The Elite," Tenric replied as if it was obvious.

"But you don't have the writ anymore. Why would they care?"

Tenric rolled his eyes, looking a little exasperated. "I came to Har Tesera to hide, yes. But it was also one stop on my way to the palace. I planned to petition the court to redraft the document and have it stamped with the king's seal there, directly in court."

"Will they do that?"

Tenric shrugged. "Wouldn't hurt to ask."

Mouse stopped his pacing to rub his eyes. "And the Elite would do anything to stop that from happening. You would be a real problem for them as a noble."

"So it would appear."

"I'm not convinced this is all to prevent your ascension. This isn't entirely about any balance of power."

For a moment, Tenric looked wounded. But it was a fact he couldn't deny. "Then why?"

Mouse narrowed his eyes at him. "Someone wants it for themselves. And you need to be dead so you can't talk. That sole document would change the trajectory of a family for generations. Every single one of them would stop at nothing to get it."

"I…I fear I'm putting you in too much danger, Mouse."

"I'm already deep into this. The Elite already knows I'm the sucker that stole it—and they want me to steal it again. Which would be madness for a whole slew of reasons. By liberating you, I put myself in even deeper."

Tenric's expression turned uneasy.

"Look," Mouse continued. "I told you. Rescuing you was no altruistic act. I'm in this for my own reasons. By helping you, you're helping me."

"What are you getting out of it?"

"I told you," Mouse murmured. "My own liberty."

Mouse could tell Tenric had questions—questions about him, questions Mouse wouldn't want to answer. Thankfully, Tenric didn't push.

"So, what now?" Tenric asked.

What now, indeed? Mouse thought. His mouth had gone dry. A bead of sweat trickled from his neck down the center of his back. "I go out and check on a few things—"

"I'll come with—"

"No," Mouse said firmly. "You'll just get in my way."

More of the wounded look. "You can't expect me to stay cooped up in here forever. How is this any better than that prison?" he said gloomily.

"Sunlight. No bars. Better food. A very comfortable bed. And you are choosing to remain. In Jardem's care, you didn't have that luxury."

Tenric looked deflated. "Fair point."

"I'll be back before too long," Mouse added. "With food. And something strong to drink. Remain patient."

"What if they come here? What if they figure out where I am?"

"They won't."

Mouse picked up the pouch of coin and weighed it in his palm. Enough for his needs right now. He thought about opening the stair to grab more but was reluctant to show Tenric the stash. He'd make do.

As he pulled open the door, Tenric leapt from the bed and put a hand on Mouse's shoulder.

"Mouse, how long are they going to be after me?"

Hand still on the latch, Mouse glanced over his shoulder and frowned. Tenric's eyes, steeped with anxiety, clung to him.

Mouse wouldn't lie to him. "Your best hope now is to become the noble you're supposed to be. The penalty for murdering a noble-born is severe." Something Mouse understood too well. "It may be enough of a deterrent to protect you. But I can't promise even that will be enough."

Living daily with risk and danger was Mouse's world, not Tenric's. He had never had to contend with the reality that each day he faced death. That any sunrise might be his last. Until he had found his father murdered, that is.

Mouse had had years to grow accustomed to a life resting on the blade of a knife. Tenric had had a few fortnights, perhaps.

"We'll figure this out," he said, his eyes downcast to the floor. He couldn't look at him. His heart thumped as if he was running for his life. Perhaps he was. "You…you can trust me."

He almost wanted to laugh as the words left his lips. They felt bitter on his tongue, like a fiction, a meaningless platitude, but a part of him needed Tenric to believe them. Did he mean it? He honestly couldn't tell if the words were genuine…or just more of the cack he spilled out to hide behind. He had been compelled to say something—though he didn't understand why. Something that would help put Tenric at some ease.

"In the meantime," he added, "stay fucking put this time."

18

ALONE ON the river craft's deck, hands on hips, eyes closed, Mouse pulled in long breaths.

The blue sky from earlier had been overtaken by a swift moving ceiling of gray. A sharp, chill wind cut over the wide river, like war hounds racing the lengths of the docks and onto the plaza. Mouse could feel the whispers of rain on the wind as it nipped at his face.

It suited his mood.

Now free of the cabin, he could breathe again. He'd escaped the crushing weight of the conspiracies and machinations of the most powerful and the inevitable task that loomed ahead of him. The cabin had coiled tighter around him as Tenric unveiled more of his story. The truth of it lodged in his throat, choking him. Toward the end, he had been desperate to get out. He needed air. Needed to clear his head.

His neck and shoulders were tight, the muscles quivering like tight bow strings under the skin. He had maintained a performance of calm while listening to Tenric, but his insides were anything but. They roiled and tossed like a cauldron of hot pitch. This was beyond anything he'd imagined. Or feared.

He was a petty thief now embroiled in schemes involving the most powerful of men. *Abandon this*, his instincts screamed at him. *Run. Go back to the guild and pretend you weren't involved in any of it. Let it ride itself out.*

That voice had kept him alive all these years. Survival was all that mattered in the end. But now, Mouse wasn't sure he trusted that voice anymore. It spoke folly. It spoke lies.

He couldn't run from this. He knew that. Not now. He'd bought time with Savir, but his request wasn't the kind Mouse could ignore. That had been clear enough. Already, the sands of that hourglass were slipping quickly through his fingers. Savir would expect an answer soon. It was only a matter of time before the Elite became more…insistent.

Even if he found a way to bypass Savir's request, he could never return to the guild and go on like before. It meant returning to chains. He'd be back groveling at the feet of Jardem, who was happy to destroy the guild for his own gain.

And then what? Jardem wouldn't release him from his indenture even if the guild collapsed around them. Mouse was his prisoner for life.

As much as it loathed him to admit it, he was caught in the current and had no choice but to see where it took him.

And…making matters even worse, now he was shackled with a naïve merchant's son who knew nothing about survival and was very likely going to end up dead regardless of what Mouse did to protect him.

Mouse the protector. Laughable. It took the better part of each day to keep himself alive. Now he'd promised to keep Tenric's head where it belonged.

So, what now? he mused.

The writ of nobility seemed to have changed hands a few times now—everyone's plan was obviously to sit on it until the signet rod showed up. Seemed this document was common knowledge among the right circles. But so far, no clues had emerged as to who'd attacked the Crown Rotary's entourage and where the rod was located now.

That, in and of itself, was odd.

People talk. If something was stolen, and a lot of effort and coin was spent to make that happen, someone tended to talk. Bragging rights. Frustration. Trying to find someone to buy the thing you stole. There were myriad reasons why someone would say something about the object they had stolen.

Not to mention the people involved in the actual theft of the thing. There were those that had paid for the deed and those that had executed it. This wasn't a small endeavor—it would require dozens of men. Were any of them talking? So far, no one had even hinted of where it might be....

Granted, the theft hadn't taken place here in Har Tesera. He had his ear to the ground in the wrong city. Tenric's home was the city of Har Purdea, but he also had roots in Har Klandu, upriver to the north. A smaller but somewhat wealthier city than Har Tesera. A strong and powerful merchant guild resided there.

It would take Mouse a full day to get there. Another one to come home. He wasn't about to spend that time traveling. And he would have to either leave Tenric alone the whole time—an option he wasn't keen on—or bring him with. Another terrible option.

He'd have to find another way.

Yet his number one priority was getting his hands on the document. He had to figure out where Jardem was keeping it and get it from him. Mouse was certain Savir's offer to steal it for him was not an exclusive one. Others were in on it—others hungry to get good with the Elite. Mouse had to get it in his hands before any of these others figured out where it was.

The sky was starting its first volley of rain, but it was a flimsy and pathetic attempt, at best. It felt vaguely like being spit on by a wet talker. The clouds weren't even trying. Yet, soon enough, the cobbles were darker, painted with a glossy sheen. With one swoop of his hand, he flipped the hood of his cloak up onto his head and stepped off the deck and onto the pier.

He cut through the industrial sector again along the river, keeping clear of the more populated areas for as long as he could. Eyes were still out there searching for him. How many, he couldn't even wager a guess. He wasn't about to make it easy on them and promenade right through an open plaza. When it came time to cut away from the river's edge and slip among the tightly packed buildings, he considered crossing the city by roof instead. But the fresh layer of wet would make the tiles slick, like ice. He wasn't desperate enough to take on that risk. Not yet, anyway.

At least the threat of rain provided the excuse to keep his hood up and his cloak pulled tight around him. The streets, too, were thinning as people hurried indoors to escape it when it came, and shopkeepers hustled to bring in their wares from outdoor displays. Only those that were up to something seemed to not even notice the rain.

Mouse recognized a few. Brutes from the Scourge were lingering about, making themselves as obvious as a horse on a roof. They lumbered about, scratching at their balls, grumbling to each other. Something was afoot with them—otherwise they would be out of the rain, drinking and throwing dice. They did nothing without being paid for it. Even bathe, apparently.

Whatever they were up to, Mouse stayed clear of them—they were a tetchy lot and sworn enemies of the Night Fingers. If the Night Fingers were finely crafted tools for delicate work, the Scourge were hammers. Of course, the guild used blunt force tactics when necessary, but that wasn't their standard mode of operation. The Scourge relished in the violence. And their brutal practices usually just got in the way of legitimate business and made everything worse for everyone.

The eyes of one of them landed on him as Mouse made his way up the opposite side of the street. The brute's gaze narrowed. Mouse's insides twitched, and a part of him wondered if he was the target of their surveillance.

He was being skittish and paranoid, he told himself. Sure, Jardem or Savir could have hired the Scourge to keep tabs on him, but they had no reason to be combing this specific sector of the city for him. This part of the city wasn't one of his usual haunts. And they both had better, less conspicuous spies on payroll to do the job of hunting him down.

Mouse marched on and kept his eyes forward and did his best to ignore the stare. The goon lost interest, and his attention reverted to the street at large.

One street over, Mouse passed into the region simply and affectionately called The Cage.

This strange quarter was tiny by city standards. A few blocks, no more. It was a tightly compact region that consisted almost exclusively of gambling rooms, bookmaker offices, and coin lenders. A few brothels were peppered among them, of course. They knew well what men did when they discovered they were suddenly flush with coin. This quarter was unique from all other quarters in this city in the sense that it did not discriminate by how extravagant one's attire was or how much coin was held in their purse. All were welcome here.

The proprietors of the establishments that filled this little quarter hired their own security to monitor activity in the streets. Violence was bad for business, and a murdered nobleborn could get the area shut down, so the streets were well-monitored. And these men and women were the epitome of respectability and professionalism.

The Scourge was never allowed within the perimeter of the Cage. The hired muscle made certain of that. Which explained their presence a block over—they were waiting for someone to leave.

The thrum of music wafted down the street. Once night came, these streets would be teeming, and lines would form outside the various houses as patrons waited for a seat to open at a table. But even at this afternoon hour, there were people about. The dreary day had given many a flimsy reason to drift here and take up a hand.

It was easy to determine where the Cage's territory began. The cobbles here were scrubbed clean of any shit or piss—human or otherwise. And none were missing, though carriages on these streets were frowned upon. The well-maintained buildings were festooned with bunting and streamers year-round. Encouraged by the duke and his council, no doubt. Out-of-town dignitaries looking for a night of decadent entertainment were frequently escorted here, and the duke, of course, wanted it to impress. The quarter had just the right amount of depravity to thrill out-of-town guests without making them uncomfortable.

Mouse let his ears direct him to one of the larger gambling halls. He was recognized at the door, but not because he was a frequent patron. Mouse was of the view that coin was not a plaything. It was so infrequent a visitor to his own purse, he would not insult it by tossing it away for fun. But his work brought him here enough to be a familiar face. These chambers were the best place to mine for information.

He wended through the tables, most of them empty. A bar wench, looking tired and irritated, offered a curt nod as she slid past him with two foaming tankards in one hand. The musicians set up on a low stage in the center of the room stopped their set for a break. No one was listening, anyway.

Mirna was where she always was. In the back, near the door to the kitchens. She had her chair tipped back on two legs, her feet on an empty barrel. Spectacles rested on the end of her nose as she focused on the stitched fabric in front of her. Carefully, again and again, she slipped a needle through the linen and pulled it through until it was taut.

She heard Mouse's footfalls as he approached. Her eyes lifted to take him in, and a moment later, they narrowed.

"Well, now," she said, letting her hands and the linen fall into her lap. "Look who crawled out of his hole."

With her graying hair and deepening crow's feet around her dark eyes, Mirna could be perceived as on the edge of matronly. At times, she radiated kindness and caring, as if she was ready to bring you warm bread from her hearth with fresh butter she'd churned herself. But Mouse understood the calculating and brilliant woman that resided underneath the kindly persona. When Mouse looked at her, he saw only masterful control of everyone around her.

She dictated everyone's moves, and they all loved her for it.

"A good day to you, Mirna," Mouse replied, adding a bit of counterfeit cheeriness to his tone.

She made a sound that might have been a chuckle. Or not. She studied him a moment over the top of the glasses before she lifted her stitching again and resumed. "Surprised to see you around. Today, especially."

His shoulders stiffened. "And why is that?"

Her eyes lifted again as she pulled the thread. "Word about town is the guild's in a bit of a kerfuffle today. Any chance it has something to do with you?"

Mouse forced a laugh. "And why would you think that?"

She made that sound again. "Odds are my business, my boy. And I know how to read cards."

"Sorry to disappoint you, Mirna. Whatever you're hearing doesn't involve me."

Her eyes made it very clear she could tell he was lying.

"I've not been to the guild today," he added. "What's the gossip?"

"Hardly gossip. I don't deal in idle speculation, boy. You know that."

"Then I'm certain you'll share with me what the turmoil is all about?"

She pursed her lips, looking thoughtful. "No one seems to know, oddly enough. But your leader is in quite the state, I'm told. Accusing just about everyone of being a traitor to the guild. I have it on good authority an ugly scene has ensued."

Mouse forced himself not to smirk. She was watching him, though she tried to disguise it by turning her stitching to

222

the light.

"Good authority," Mouse repeated. "Your spies have the measure of the situation, do they?"

Mirna shrugged. "May be wise you don't check in with the guild for a spell," she added.

"Don't intend to," Mouse added. There was a measure of spice to his voice he couldn't mask. She was being notably forthcoming in her information. Mouse was on his guard.

"What brings you here then, boy?"

He took a breath. "I need information."

She tugged on the thread to tighten it, then broke it off with her teeth. "Boy, don't waste my time. Do you think I haven't figured that much out already? As much as I enjoy your visits, it's the only reason why you come to me. You're fortunate I don't take offense easily. Out with the specifics, boy."

For Mama Mirna, table talk was the pickaxe, and information was the ore. With all types circling through this establishment, from every strata of society, all manner of conversations were overheard. And documented. The gossip was carefully collected, sifted and refined into shiny nuggets worth shameful amounts of coin in the right hands. At any moment, Mirna had a perspective of the city's activities like none other.

"The information I seek isn't local. There are things I need to find out from Har Klandu."

That seemed to change her demeanor. For the moment, the stitching in her lap was forgotten. She pulled her legs from the barrel and let the chair drop, then set the linen on the barrel.

"Har Klandu doesn't fall under my sphere. I have little knowledge of the goings on there."

"You have people—either there or here—that can find what I'm looking for."

She studied him intently. "Which will be costly. You aren't known to be blessed with an abundance of coin, Mouse."

"I've come into an inheritance of a sort."

Her brow twitched. He had her interest. And her wariness. This wasn't something she'd seen coming, and Mirna was no fan of surprises.

"How quickly do you need this information?" she asked.

Mouse closed his eyes to consider this. "Quickly. Time is an issue here."

"Well," she said after a time. "There's the rub. Har Klandu is more than a day's ride from here."

"I'm aware. Can you still do it?"

She chuckled. "Of course, I can do it. I have my ways." Which Mouse knew to mean magecraft. It shouldn't surprise him that she had mages on her payroll.

"That particular requirement means it's likely too rich for your blood, Mouse. Even with this newly found wealth. What you are suggesting is an endeavor typically reserved to noble-born. And the Elite."

"A trade then," he said. "Part coin payment. Part...I owe you."

Her eyes narrowed. "As in, a favor? A job of my choosing?"

"Yes."

"Strictly against guild policy. I don't have to tell you that."

"Leave the guild rules for me to deal with."

"Punishment is death."

Mouse stayed silent. He let his eyes convince her of his conviction and earnestness.

Mirna set her hands into her lap. She considered him with a deepening frown. "Oh, my dear little Mouse. What have you gotten yourself into now?"

Mouse's expression hardened. Mirna had always treated him kindly. He'd known her since before his days with the guild, when he was a street rat fighting to stay alive. In those days, she would pass on word of odd jobs. A kindness he never forgot. Even now, she was willing to pass on what she knew on occasion with no expectation of payment. But Mirna always put her business first. Mouse respected that.

"You know me, Mirna. I never do anything the easy way." He put on his business face. "So, do we have a deal? My coin—and my favor?"

She considered that a moment. "You trust me enough to break with your guild rules? You are aware that the Cage and the Night Fingers currently have a binding pact?"

He wasn't aware. "You made an alliance with Jardem?"

"A loose one."

"You've given him access to your network?"

Mirna scoffed. "Don't be dull, boy. I'll always keep my cards close to my breast. But we have shared resources against a common adversary."

"The Shadow Elite."

She smiled coolly, which was neither a confirmation nor denial. "I am cautious about what information I share with Quickblade, or whatever he calls himself nowadays. But he is not without his ability to root out information. He's a wily one. And has ways of finding out what he needs."

"I'm aware."

"And yet you are willing to proceed?"

Mouse shrugged. "Perhaps I am a fool. But I doubt you would warn me if you intended to go to him with this."

"And if he finds out on his own?" Mirna asked.

"I'm counting on it that it won't matter."

The corner of Mirna's mouth broke and lifted a fraction. She picked up her needlework again and, without looking at him, asked, "What kind of information are you looking to acquire?"

Mouse laid out the basics of the assault on the king's caravan and the theft of the signet rod. He was careful not to reveal any other details about the writ of nobility or Tenric and his family. Mirna's face, while she pulled the thread through the fabric with steady intent, was stoic and unreadable.

Once he'd finished, she proceeded with her needlework

as if he wasn't there. Mouse could tell she knew he'd held back details. For a moment, he thought she was going to reject him outright.

Then, she made a sound low in her throat and formed her lips into a tight hole. A sharp, high-pitched whistle blasted from her mouth.

Moments later, a lithe man with rust-colored hair emerged from behind the heavy velvet curtain. He was dressed in a loose beige tunic and trousers, sleeves pushed up to his elbows. His hands were dirty, and a muddy smudge streaked across his cheekbone.

All in all, he was rather ordinary. Outside of the red hair, nothing about him would make him stand out in a crowd. He wasn't particularly comely—though he wasn't ugly, either. He didn't appear rich or sinister. Nothing about him would draw one's attention. He was simply ordinary.

"What is it now?" he asked in an impatient tone.

Mirna smiled up at him warmly. "Take a break from that. I want you to meet a friend."

His eyes shifted to Mouse suspiciously.

Mirna gestured to the man. "Mouse, I'd like you to meet my nephew. Rylo, this is Mouse."

"Mouse?"

"Don't interrupt," Mirna told Rylo. Her attention turned to Mouse, her eyes narrow. "Rylo has an uncanny nose for this sort of thing. Cover-ups. Scandals. If anyone can dig up what you're looking for, it's him."

"Where am I going?" asked Rylo.

"Har Klandu."

Rylo rolled his eyes back. "*That* snake pit?"

Mirna smirked and gestured with her hand. "Have a seat at a table. Give Rylo the details he'll need. I'll send over an ale. On me."

Mouse turned to follow Rylo but stopped. "What about payment?"

"Hold your coin for now," Mirna replied. "The favor

may be all I require from you. But you must be ready to accept when I call on you to collect. No questions asked." Her eyes tightened at him. "Are we agreed?"

"We are," Mouse replied.

Mirna's smile was tinged with something close to sadness. "You be careful, boy. I smell trouble on you like a dog that rolled in shit."

Mouse laughed it off. "I can take care of myself. You know that."

Mirna's eyes made her look weary. "I know you believe that."

The words sent ripples of ice down Mouse's arms, but he disguised it by straightening his back and marching to the table to join Rylo.

19

MOUSE FED as many details of the theft of the king's signet as he dared to Rylo, who stared back impassively at him.

"I trust you are getting all this?" Mouse asked dryly.

Rylo moved his head as if shaking himself from a dream. He lifted a single brow. "How old are you? No, really. Twelve?"

"Excuse me?" Mouse exclaimed. He looked young—he was used to comments about that. Rylo was just being rude. Mouse pointed a stiff finger at his own face. "I have a beard."

Rylo nodded as if that was a compelling argument. "That part did perplex me." He pushed the chair back and made as if to stand. "I think I have all I need."

Mouse stared incredulously. "Do you? Were you even listening?"

Rylo made a grunting laugh as he pushed the chair back under the table.

Mouse closed his eyes and shook his head. "This is a mystery that has confounded the king's guard. Yet you've asked me no questions—"

"I've heard enough, Mouse."

Mouse felt his ire flare. He was taking an enormous risk with the deal. His life depended on its success. "Are you even remotely equipped—"

Rylo braced his hands on the back of the chair and leaned in. "This unscheduled assignment conflicts with time promised to a particularly amorous woman. So instead of getting my cock wet, I'll be traveling to a shit hole. I have no interest in making you feel at ease about my abilities."

Mouse's teeth clenched. "I just need to know if I can trust—"

"Who do I work for?" Rylo interrupted sharply. "You or Mama?"

Mouse's eyes narrowed. There was no need to answer that.

"Then that should answer all other questions about my ability to accomplish this, yes?"

Mouse had to admit it did.

Rylo pushed off from the chair. "If we are done, and gods, I hope we are, I'll be on my way. Should I have need of you, I'll be in contact." He left without a look back.

Feeling less than confident in the arrangement he'd made, Mouse stood and made to leave the gambling hall and hit the streets again. But someone approached—another of Mirna's minions.

Mouse had seen him drifting around. He was easy to spot, dressed in a fine coat of black with silver brocade and a high hat resting on his brow. Mouse thought he was some rich merchant who'd arrived early for the night's activity. But he moved about Mirna's space with too much familiarity.

The man smiled at Mouse as if they were old friends. The cane gripped loosely in his hand made loud, intentional claps on the floor as he drew closer.

"Now this is an assignment I fully endorse." There was a lascivious lilt to his tone as he dragged his bright eyes over Mouse from foot to head.

"Excuse me?" Mouse said.

"Name's Daru. Mama has charged me to keep you informed of Rylo's progress. I will let you know as soon as any information is known"

"How soon should I check in?"

"That won't be necessary."

Mouse tilted his head, confused. "You will not find me at the guild, and I cannot guarantee my location."

Daru chuckled. "Darling, I could find you in the darkest night. Your many charms are like a beacon of light."

Mouse fought to not roll his eyes. "My charms are few, I promise you."

"A man who doesn't recognize his own appeal is as refreshing as a spring rain," Daru replied.

"You act as if you know me. Have we met before?"

Daru's smile widened. "You may not have noticed me during your past visits here, Master Mouse, but I have indeed noticed you." He put a hand to his heart. "And admired you from afar."

Mouse felt his insides tighten. He wasn't keen on the idea of being watched so closely and not being aware of it. His work depended on keeping out of people's notice, not being their focus.

"I think I would have noticed you."

"I tend to blend in when the room is full. Why would you pay attention to yet another entitled peacock?"

"Fair point," Mouse said.

"So, now that we are officially acquainted, keep an eye out for me. I will arrive unannounced, and when you see me, you should slink off somewhere so we can have our chat. Somewhere *intimate*, I hope."

"Fine. I look forward to hearing what Rylo discovers."

"As do I," Daru said with a turn of the shoulder. He circled around Mouse, close enough to whisper into his ear. "Until our next encounter."

Mouse didn't turn around as Daru walked away behind him. He waited until the *tap tap tap* of his cane had faded, then he left the Cage.

The day remained gloomy, though the clouds seemed to have given up on any attempt to rain properly. Instead, they'd turned to bluster. Heavy gusts raced through the streets, swiping hats and hoods off heads and making the signs above shop doors creak and swing. Mouse pulled his cloak in tight.

He lowered his head as he marched on against the wind, his stomach grinding, his mind a whirlwind. *The deal is done*, he told himself. No sense in fretting on it now, but his head wouldn't stop churning out all the scenarios where everything could go horribly wrong. Yet the die was cast, as they say. He'd taken the gamble—and now he could not fail, or he'd face doom.

He knew what he needed to do now. His feet knew where to go, so he let them guide him without argument. He would have to visit with Othmar soon, who would likely know best about the details of the writ. But for now, that would have to wait.

He was about to do something bolder than even he would have imagined.

Some time ago, Jardem had made the rare mistake of letting slip where he lived. Not a precise location—but he'd given Mouse a vicinity to track him down.

He mentioned in passing he would leave his home, grab some apple tansies from the "best bakery in Har Tesera," and eat them on his way to the guild. A deliberate brag, since most couldn't afford such luxury at all, let alone regularly. Bakeries were aplenty in the city, but most dealt in breads and little else. Apple tansies were popular treats, but only select bakeries carried them.

Jardem took a carriage to and from the guild, of course. But on pleasant mornings, he opted to walk—with a thug contingent in tow to keep him safe from harm, of course. This meant the bakery—and his flat—were a walkable distance from the guild. Mouse knew Jardem well enough to know the prim coxcomb wasn't about to risk a blister with a long, exhausting hike.

Mouse swung back east toward the warehouse district, close to where the guild was located, but still keeping his distance. Fighting the wind, he gripped the top of his hood to prevent it from being snagged and yanked it back. This close to the guild, he had to be vigilant. His eyes were on a constant search for a recognizable face from the guild.

He kept more to the north, closer to the boundary of the Merchant District. Too far north and it would be too expensive, even for Jardem. But this bakery would not be found closer to the docks. There was a narrow quarter that seemed his best bet.

He knew these streets, but bakeries serving high end pastries wasn't part of his normal routine. Yet, there couldn't be many. The Warehouse District wasn't known for its elegant array of cuisine. A hard loaf and a bowl of thin stew was the typical height of refinement there. Mouse combed the streets, back and forth, inspecting each bakery he encountered. Most, as he suspected, didn't serve pastries. Those that did seemed to miss the mark somehow. Knowing Jardem, he wouldn't frequent just any bakery. He had sophisticated tastes, and the establishments Mouse discovered all fell shy of what Jardem would condescend to patronize—especially on a near-daily basis.

He skirted a plaza with a pathetic fountain at the center that squirted water from the spout in intermittent bursts, like an old man attempting to piss in the middle of the night.

As soon as he laid eyes on it, he knew it was the place.

The placard hanging from curls of wrought iron proudly read "For Butter or Worse."

He groaned and wanted to punch himself in the face, wishing he'd never laid eyes on it. It was a quaint little place, sitting demurely on a quiet little corner like a young noble ingénue that had lost her way in a sketchy neighborhood. It seemed so glaringly out of place, so arrogant and lofty, that Mouse wondered how the neighborhood tolerated it.

It sang of Jardem. He'd probably chosen this location for his flat based on the bakery alone.

The building had three floors, likely made up of several flats each—one of them was bound to be Jardem's. The first two levels were stone, the third above that was wattle and daub with diagonal beams.

He loitered about the fountain for a while until the sad splattering of water made him want to piss as well. So, he aimlessly drifted around the plaza and the connecting streets looking bored and forlorn but gaining a feel for access into the bakery's building. For Butter or Worse rested between streets that spun out from the plaza like the spokes of a wheel. Behind the building, threading together the two streets, was a dark and narrow alleyway, not wide enough for a cart to pass through.

Mouse slipped into the alley and surveyed it.

A few doors were at street level. Locked, of course. Clay drainpipes clung to the building and disappeared inside a dark stone circle at the far end. A cistern, collecting rainwater. A few windows faced the alley side, a floor or two up—one of them slightly ajar.

Cracking his knuckles, Mouse eyed the open window. And trailed his eyes down the side of the building, calculating his path. Easy. The stone was slick from the spitting rain, but it wasn't anything he couldn't handle. The old wall was craggy, the mortar cleft and fissured. He slipped out of his cloak and rolled his shoulders to loosen them up.

He avoided the drainpipes. Old clay could fracture with the sudden weight. That would be riskier than the slick wall. Bracing his foot on a protrusion, he lifted himself up against the wall and gripped his fingers against the cold stone.

His fingers were conditioned for such work. He'd scaled more difficult walls for sport. And his small size made the risk of fracturing masonry less likely. He shimmied up at a fair clip, finding handholds and places for his feet easily. And in a manner of moments, he was at the window and wiggling his way through.

Crouched on the floor, he scanned around. The flat was empty except for a couple of orange cats who pranced over to check out their visitor, straight tails up. He let them smell his fingers, and he scratched the tops of their heads a moment. They lost interest when he was clearly empty handed and wandered off.

This wasn't Jardem's. Too cluttered. The occupant had an affinity for hearty, leather-bound tomes, it seemed. They were stacked on every surface and on the floor near the hearth next to a well-worn chair. Jardem didn't strike Mouse as the literary type, nor one to sit by a fire and read. Mouse lifted a book from a table and fanned through the yellowed pages. Old. Very old. The script was off, unlike anything he'd seen. Were these borrowed? Stolen? This many books were rarely seen outside of the university or a rich noble's library.

The flat was little more than one room. Mouse peeked out the front door and into the dark hallway. One other door and a staircase down.

He crept out and put his ear to the other door. Nothing. Then he removed the small case of tools he kept inside his belt pouch and set to work on the lock. When he heard the satisfying click of the release, he let himself in. This one was an orderly place, well maintained. But a quick inspection inside revealed a wardrobe of shifts and dresses. Mouse slipped out and locked the door again.

He descended the stairs, sticking close to the wall out of habit to avoid creaking. As he neared the bottom and gained his first view of the corridor, he spotted a lump of a man on a stool, arms folded over his chest, back to the wall. He was parked outside a flat.

He may have been asleep. Mouse wasn't sure, and he wasn't about to linger about long enough to find out. He backed his way up the stairs.

Only one reason to post a thug outside a door.

Mouse didn't recognize him from the guild. Scourge? Was Jardem hiring meat from the enemy? Mouse grit his teeth.

Could he loathe the man any more deeply?

He had to get into that flat. No question. But this guard stationed outside the door complicated matters. It likely meant there were others about, too.

Fuck.

At least, Mouse thought wryly, his instincts had served him. He knew Jardem wasn't going to keep something as valuable as the writ of nobility in his guild office—in a building crawling with the most talented thieves in the city. Unless he stayed in that office day and night, he wouldn't risk leaving it there. He would have it somewhere guarded.

Mouse had planted the seed that the Shadow Elite were looking for it in earnest, but surely Jardem had already arrived at that conclusion. It was stolen from powerful people—where else would they look to retrieve it than the thieves' guild?

Mouse returned to the flat with the books and the cats, who came by to visit again as Mouse contemplated his options.

Jardem was certainly still at the guildhall, wreaking chaos over the loss of his prisoner that no one knew about. He'd be occupied there indefinitely. Mouse had the time to slip in unnoticed, conduct his search, and disappear.

He walked around and considered the tenement's layout. Jardem's flat was on the opposite side of the hall, which meant his window faced the street, not the alley.

He crossed over to the other, tidier flat and stuck his head out the window. The masonry on the street side was better maintained, leaving far fewer grips. And it was drizzling again, leaving the wall slick with a fresh sheen of wet. Scaling it would be a tricky business, and he'd be plainly visible from the street below.

And knowing Jardem, he wouldn't leave the flat's only window vulnerable. It would be locked and barred from the inside. He'd not get in that way, anyway.

He would have to do this the hard way.

He had to take the brute out.

This had the potential of turning into a catastrophe. If the

Scourge got enough of a look at him, even an estimation of his size, it would be easy enough for Jardem to tease out who'd attacked. And if Jardem knew Mouse betrayed him…

Then what would he do?

He dug through the wardrobe and pilfered an understated brown dress. The fit was tight, especially in the shoulders, but he managed to wiggle his frame into it. No one was going to have the time to inspect him that closely. He looped a dark-colored sash about his head and draped it in front of his mouth like a maiden's veil to disguise the tightly cropped beard along his jawline. A floppy hat with a wide brim completed the look.

With no mirror about, he had to take it on faith that he looked enough of the part to fool the brute for a few moments. The grim light of the windowless corridor would help. He grabbed a tall silver candlestick from the mantle and stepped into the hall. At the top of the stairs, he took in a long breath. He had one go at this.

Hoisting the front of the dress, he descended at a natural pace. This time, he made no effort to disguise his footfalls.

The brute lifted his chin at Mouse's approach, a lazy gaze following him. The expression was curious, but not alarmed. Mouse kept his own eyes forward as he swished past. He held the candlestick against his side, tucked in the folds of the brown fabric.

The dagger in his boot thrummed against his calf.

One stride past the brute, he lunged. He spun about and whirled the candlestick about in a wide, sweeping arc.

The brute saw it coming—his reaction time quicker than Mouse would have predicted. He twisted his torso forward and ducked his head sideways. The base of the candlestick careered over him, missing his skull by two fingers. It crashed into the wall, putting a deep divot in the plaster.

Fuck! Mouse screamed in his head. This was going to be bad.

The guard recovered too soon and lurched off the stool. Mouse had to react quickly before the brute noted any specific details about him. He leapt and threw himself onto the massive back.

On his feet, the brute clawed at Mouse over his shoulder. Mouse whisked the sash from around his head with one hand while gripping where the leather armor looped behind the man's neck with the other. He wrapped his legs around the man's middle and locked his ankles. While the man thrashed about, trying to buck him off, the wide-brimmed hat lifted from his head and drifted to the floor. Mouse's face was fully exposed.

If the man got a look at him, it was over.

Mouse strung the sash under the chin, crossed the ends, and pulled it taut against the throat. He groaned through clenched teeth as he tugged harder, tightening the silk against the windpipe.

The brute tried to pull in a breath. In vain, he soon learned. Mouse's grip against his raw throat was firm. He figured out quickly that his only hope was to dislodge Mouse from his back.

The man flailed about the corridor. He turned his back to the wall and lunged backward. Mouse was slammed against the wall, plaster and wood cracking under him. Pinned between the man's thick back and the wall, all the air left his lungs in a whoosh. His vision whirled and lights flickered. It took all his willpower not to cry out. His vision darkened around the edges.

He held on, wrapped the silk another time around his hands and pulled the fabric tighter still.

The man pulled away from the wall and lunged back again. Pain exploded throughout Mouse's entire torso—one rib was broken, at least. He let out a cry—but managed to make it high pitched. Mouse felt his consciousness slipping from him. More black closed in around his vision. All he could see was a small circle in front of him.

Still, he held the sash firm.

The man staggered forward again, drunkenly. The two

were in a race for who would black out first.

The brute thrust back again. Weaker this time, but with bones likely already broken, it was still excruciating for Mouse. He wouldn't be able to hold out much longer.

The brute peeled from the wall once again, swaying. Slower still. His arms made desperate flaps around him. He positioned his legs to kick back one more time.

New tactic, thought Mouse, *or I'll end up dead*. He let his legs swing free from around the man's waist and braced them against the wall behind him. Before the man could push back once more, Mouse thrust his own legs outward.

Nearly unconscious, his balance compromised, the brute toppled forward like a meat landslide. He flew across the width of the corridor. His arms were too slow to brace himself, and his face struck the wall with surprising force. Mouse and the brute collapsed to the floor in a twisted heap, but Mouse held the fabric taut until he was certain the man was truly unconscious.

A conspicuous dark stain was on the wall. The impact had shattered the man's nose.

When the flailing stopped, Mouse released the sash. Before he shuffled away, he checked to make sure he'd started breathing again.

It took him time to regain his feet, and he needed the help of the stool and the wall to do it. Everything hurt. His whole torso would be one solid bruise later. Front and back.

He stood in the new stark silence of the corridor, panting, waiting to see if their battle brought anyone running up the stairs. So far, nothing.

His head still swam about, and his vision blurred as he manipulated the picks in the lock. His hands quaked, so it took longer than it should have. Once unlocked, he shuffled inside and shoved the door closed behind him.

He had to hurry. Find what he needed and get out.

The interior was exactly what he'd expect of Jardem. Furnishing too luxuriant for a space of that size. The rooms were trying too hard to be something they weren't. Mouse couldn't help but wonder where it all came from. Stolen, most likely. He knew Jardem well enough to know he wouldn't shell out any of the coin for it. The walls were painted a lush burgundy, and a variety of paintings—also stolen, certainly—hung on them in gold-leafed frames. Intricately carved crown molding capped the walls of every room. None of the other tenements had that detail—Jardem had had it installed himself.

Limping through the flat, bleeding on the lush carpets, he circled through the three rooms to get a feel for Jardem's life inside these walls. If the writ was here, Mouse had to understand Jardem enough to glean where he'd hide it.

The question was, how paranoid was he? Was he worried that someone would search the place? Or did he feel his little sanctuary here was safe? He was arrogant enough to believe that he had everyone fooled. Jardem's past as a spy gave him insight into secrets and scandals, but he wasn't a thief. No, he didn't *think* like a thief. Mouse understood there was a reason behind where valuables were hidden. Nothing was chosen at random. Everything was part of a larger story…

Mouse just needed to understand it.

He gave the more obvious places a perfunctory look to rule them out. He looked for false bottoms in the wardrobe and holes behind the paintings. He checked there wasn't a chest under the bed or a tucked in the ashes of the hearth or the flue. He didn't expect to, but he found nothing. Jardem wasn't that lazy or so pedestrian.

Eliminate the obvious. Focus on the unseen.

A true master of the concealed compelled someone to see only the mundane. The truth was glossed over by most, unseen. But the answer, Mouse knew, was here. In plain sight, if one had the eyes to see it.

He circled about the flat, looking for anything that didn't fit, didn't make sense. His eyes constantly scanning, searching. His fingers ran across surfaces, testing for changes. His ears listened for any distinctive sounds as he walked.

A work desk drew him closer. It was a small, delicately carved table, a tad understated compared to the rest of the room. A cushioned high-back chair was tucked under it. The rest of the furniture in the flat had a staged quality about it—a hollow notion of status, an interpretation of affluence. Mouse burgled enough prosperous homes to recognize the real thing when he saw it. This wasn't it. It rang of fiction. But the desk—it was the only piece that spoke of any authenticity.

It had the patina of age about it. Subtle nicks and scratches, areas worn to glass-like smoothness, told the story of years of use. A personal piece. An heirloom perhaps. Yet, it wasn't the same ostentatious style as the rest of the room. Well made, yes, but not designed to compete for attention. This, Mouse realized, was something from Jardem's past.

He approached with something akin to reverence. An item of personal importance to Jardem seemed to require it. He valued *this*, Mouse's instinct told him. The notion that he would value anything beyond its worth in hard coin was something he wouldn't have considered possible. But this desk had *meaning.*

Gently, with eyes and fingertips, he inspected the surface. Black splotches were visible over the caramel-colored wood. Ink stains. This wasn't decorative. Jardem indeed used this as a desk. So, this wasn't just a hideaway from guild business. He did work here, too.

But no papers. No leather-bound journals. No ink supplies or quills.

They'd be hidden close by. He looked under the table and tried pulling up the cushion of the chair. Nothing.

Then something else caught his eyes. Scrapes on one edge of the tabletop. The stain had been worn clean, exposing the blonde of fresh wood like bone underneath a wound. He inspected it more closely, running his fingers over it. It was more than just a casual scratch. The wood had been worn down. They were scuff marks, made from a boot.

Mouse lifted his eyes directly above the marks on the

table.

Nothing was on the walls. No paintings. No shelving. Mouse trailed his eyes slowly and deliberately up to the crown molding at the ceiling. Molding that Jardem had installed. Then, he saw the very thin, almost undetectable, hairline seams in the wood.

"Fucking sneaky bastard," he mumbled.

Jardem was taller than him. Even standing on the desk, Mouse knew he'd not reach it. With some effort, sore from being battered against the wall, he hoisted the chair up onto the table. Then he worked his way onto the chair—which wobbled a bit on the desk's slightly warped surface. He used his dagger to pry open the tiny door hidden in the molding, which hinged upward.

He reached in and dragged everything out with one hand and tossed it to the rug below.

Cross-legged on the floor, legs buried underneath the fabric of the dress, he spread it out in front of him and attempted to make sense of it. Jardem had a pouch of coin tucked there—a goodly amount in it, too. Mouse put that aside. Might take it out of spite—back payment for the services he'd done for the guild. There was a journal tied with a leather thong and a cluster of loose parchment documents.

He started with the loose documents, weeding through them with a quick scan of each. There was no telling when the body in the hall would be discovered. He had to be mindful of time.

He was tempted to scoop them up and take them all with him, but he wasn't sure he wanted Jardem to know they'd been discovered. At least not yet.

Many were letters from various prominent members from around the city. Mouse recognized a few of the names. The notes were requests for jobs, mostly. Strange that Jardem would keep them here and not at the guild, but nothing stood out as dodgy or, worse, at odds with the guild. A swath of them were responses to what must have been letters of extortion.

Some angry. Some pleading. Seemed Mouse wasn't the only one Jardem was blackmailing.

Mouse grunted. That should have been obvious to him. Why should Mouse be special? This was a game Jardem was well practiced at.

The revelation gave him a cold, unsettled feeling in his gut. If any of these others decided to take their revenge out on Jardem and put a knife in his back, Mouse—and his father— would suffer for it.

He didn't relish the notion of some stranger having any sway over his own fate. All the more reason to get out from under Jardem's heel now. It was only a matter of time before some idiot poked at Jardem's failsafe.

He shuffled through the papers again. All of them. Twice. The writ wasn't there.

He pulled several long breaths to keep himself calm. If not here, where? There had to be some clue he wasn't seeing. Jardem had it somewhere, a place no one would connect to him.

Mouse pushed everything else aside and set the leather-bound journal in front of him.

He pulled back the cover and thumbed through the first few pages.

Neatly organized columns, written in careful script. Notes, numbers, dates.

A ledger.

Curious. Why keep a ledger hidden here? The answer came to him immediately. Jardem was up to more than running the guild. Mouse flipped through more of it, page by page, tracking the numbers. Slowly, a story emerged. Mouse wasn't an expert on finances. He stole expensive things, and could recognize their value, but the intricacies of a merchant's business made as much sense to him as magecraft. Bu, he was still able to piece together a fairly cogent idea of Jardem's secret dealings.

Many of the items were regular earnings from his various

blackmailed clients. Those were easy enough to discern. But the trickier elements to tease out related to Jardem apparently siphoning guild money and funneling it through a business here in Har Tesera. It took time to figure out the business, but once he did, Mouse sat back on his heels and puffed out his cheeks.

Jardem's little side operation was apparently fabricating elaborate forgeries of Volfric artifacts that were being sold around the city.

Were this operation explicitly tied to Jardem, the ledger would be enough to launch an action against him. He'd be removed from his seat and thrown from the guild. Even though Mouse recognized his hand in the script, nowhere in the ledger was Jardem ever mentioned. Jardem would deny he ever saw it and claim he was being framed. Mouse would need to scrounge up more evidence that the journal, in fact, belonged to him.

Mouse bit his lower lip in thought. He would have to tread carefully here. He couldn't be the one to bring the journal forward in any case. Someone else would have to do that. Even in his fall—well, especially in his fall—Jardem could exact his revenge on Mouse.

He'd have to leave the ledger behind, he knew. Taking it would tip Jardem off that someone was on to him. But he knew where it was.

And now he knew where to find the writ of nobility as well.

He climbed up on the chair again and began placing everything back into the hidden compartment.

His hands were shaking. This new information whirled about in his head like a bird caught in the house. It changed things. Sort of. He had a new way to bring down Jardem. Yet, as damning as this secret illegal shop was, he still needed to locate the writ of nobility. He wasn't about to allow Jardem to benefit from it. Or Savir, for that matter. He'd return it to its rightful owner. Failing that, he'd destroy it.

Mouse heard a thump out in the corridor. The sound of someone punching a wall. It was followed by a very loud, very primal scream.

Jardem was home.

20

MOUSE'S HEAD fell back, and he let out a frustrated groan.
Fuck!

"Cover the door," Jardem commanded from the hallway. He wasn't alone. "Search the area outside. You, with me."

They were coming in.

He slammed the section of molding down—too loudly. He winced and brought his shoulders to his ears. They'd heard that, certainly. He leapt down, then hoisted the chair from the desktop and returned it to its original position under the table.

The door latch clicked, followed by the screech of old hinges.

Slowly. They were readying for a potential ambush. The creak of the floorboards let Mouse know they were inside the tenement. Then silence as their boots hit the rug in the main room.

Mouse dug into his pouch again and pulled another of the cards he'd stolen from The Golden Flute and placed it strategically in the center of the desk. Anything to throw Jardem off his scent.

He flipped the latch on the shutters, threw them open,

and leapt out. Dangling from one hand on the window ledge, he eased the shutter closed with the other.

Rain was coming down more enthusiastically now. The water was quickly soaking into the fabric of his dress, adding to its weight. It clung and wrapped around his legs as he dangled and tried to find a place to land his footing.

Directly below him, thugs were canvasing the street, searching. All they needed to do was look up, and they'd see him hanging from the outside of the sill.

He couldn't drop down. He'd be spotted immediately. His only option was up.

As predicted, the mortar on the street side of the building was far better than that in the alley. He started his ascent, using the framing around the window to give him a solid boost upwards. Progress was slow. The dress tangled with his legs. He fought to get his boot on brick and not cloth. Climbing in boots was a challenge enough—he preferred scaling walls barefoot. But the added encumbrance and weight of the wet dress and the walls made slick from rain made the trek upward nearly impossible.

He was directly above the window when the shutters flew open again.

Jardem's head thrust out the window.

Mouse held his breath and hung against the wet wall as still as he could. His fingers struggled to hold on with the added weight.

"They escaped this way," Jardem told whoever was inside the tenement. "The shutter was unlatched. Whoever was here leapt down to the street."

"Did they find anything?" came a voice from within.

Jardem ducked back inside. "Let's find out," he answered with a snarl. A moment later, "Fuck!"

He'd found the card on the desk.

Mouse suppressed a chuckle. He wasn't out of this yet. He could still be spotted by any of Jardem's hired thugs canvasing the streets for him. And he needed to climb up this well-maintained wall in the rain…and in a gown.

Why hadn't he taken it off when he had the chance?

Slowly, he worked his way up the slick wall. His body felt broken. Every time he reached up, the muscles of his back and sides ignited in agony. And he was reliant on his fingers more than his feet. The dress kept getting in the way, tangling around his boots, and even when the boots found purchase, they felt clunky and awkward—like he was swimming in them. He couldn't feel the wall. Several times he thought he landed his boot onto a secure ledge only to have it slip off, leaving him at the mercy of his grip strength.

And fuck, this dress was getting heavy.

The thugs below called off to each other. No one spotted him.

Because no one bothered to look up.

Mouse reached the next floor and the next window. Here, on the street-facing side, the third floor was wattle and daub construction, wood beams crisscrossing the face. The plaster provided no hands holds and the wet wood, although thicker, was still slick and harder to grip at the sharp angles. And there was nowhere to brace his feet. His boots were pressed against the plaster, leaving the entirety of his weight on his fingers. He'd never make it to the roof. Not unless he could shed the fucking dress.

He checked the shutter. Latched from the inside, of course. Just as Jardem's had been. Mouse cursed to himself that he hadn't thought to unlatch it as a precaution. He could force his way through it, but that would cause enough noise to draw attention. The thugs were directly below him. His only option was to keep climbing.

"Well?" a voice asked from the tenement below.

"You worry about the intruder, dammit," Jardem snapped. Mouse envisioned him rifling through all the documents that were stashed behind the molding, looking for anything missing. He could hear the raw panic in Jardem's voice.

Good.

This uncertainty would rattle him. And uncertainty would cause mistakes in judgment.

He kept climbing, shifting gingerly up the angled wood. Rivulets of rainwater rolled into his sleeves and down his legs.

Fuck, the dress was heavy.

One boot slipped. Fragments of broken plaster tinkled down like rain and hit the ground a single pace behind one of the thugs. Mouse dangled for a moment, the strength of his hands the only thing preventing him from plummeting.

The thug didn't notice and continued his sweep of the area around the bakery.

Mouse paused at a relatively safe location with his boot resting on the top of the window's frame and his fingers wedged into a crack in the diagonal beam. He eased under the heavy folds of the sopping dress to reach his boot and slipped out the dagger. Positioning himself carefully, he stabbed at the place the beam met the plaster and wedged the blade in deep. Surprisingly, it held his weight, and he eased up along the diagonal. He wiggled it free with his right hand, then wedged it in again with the left.

His fingers were cramping—scaling this in wet clothes was taxing even for his grip. The sharp pain in his side wasn't helping matters either. Bit by bit, he eased along the crossbeam until he came in reach of the roofline and the overhanging eaves. Mouse hauled himself up over the edge and onto the clay tiles of the steeply raked roof.

The base of the roof met with that of the next building, forming a sort of red clay gully. Rainwater ran in a little stream along its length to the edge and tumbled to the street below.

Panting and scrunching his tight fingers into a fist, he flopped his back on the roof, ignoring the water streaming over the tiles and onto his clothes. He gave himself a moment, now that he was out of sight, to catch his breath and allow his muscles to relax. He clenched his fists a few times, then bent his fingers back, one by one.

Then he tugged the sodden dress over his head and tossed it aside.

Once his heart rate slowed and his breathing was regulated again, he stood and peered over the edge of the roofline. No sign of the thugs. But Mouse wasn't about to take any chances. He scurried over a number of rooftops until he calculated he was well outside their search parameters, then used a building with multiple balconies to lower himself back to ground level. Much easier without the weight of a waterlogged dress.

Still keeping his eyes open for Jardem's thugs, he cut a hasty path through the streets, cutting through any alleys or narrow byways he could. He didn't relax until he was well out of the warehouse district.

His mind still whirled. As more evidence of Jardem's self-serving corruption surfaced, he still needed a vector to reveal it. The acolyte Etar had the right of it. Someone other than him needed to bring Jardem's behavior into the sunlight. Someone that had clout within the guild. Someone not being blackmailed by Jardem.

Mouse just needed to convince them this was best for them—and for the guild.

He knew exactly where to go.

\#

He entered a small merchant plaza, mostly abandoned. The new bout of rain had driven afternoon shoppers inside. He grabbed a bowl of stew from a bored vendor and sat on a stool under a tent and out of the rain. The patter on the canvas drummed into his thoughts as he ate, bowl in one hand, wooden spoon in the other. He was wet and cold, and the greater share of his body was bruised and aching. And the stew had been sitting in the kettle too long. It was pasty and dry, and he could taste what was burnt and stuck to the bottom.

Damn. His palate was already changing. A few days ago, he wouldn't have cared what it tasted like. He would have eaten it without complaint.

His mind cycled through everything he had learnt. He had been lucky to get away. He knew that. Luckily, he hadn't fallen and broken anything else, something serious, nor had he been spotted hanging from the wall.

He prodded lightly against his side with his fingertips and immediately sucked in through his teeth. That was going to be tender for a while.

Perhaps some divine influence was at play, after all. He thought about his conversation with Etar again and about the gigantic naked statue of their deity, Inir. Were he to discover religion, that at least was a deity he could get behind. Or under. He might have to revisit that temple again, just to check. Then, he chuckled to himself at the thought of him in clerical robes, devoting his life to a maybe, an unknowable truth, and spending his days passively at a temple.

The meal gave him some strength back. The ale helped cut the edge of his soreness and helped boost his courage for what was to come. Perhaps a prayer to Inir wouldn't hurt any…but then he wasn't prepared to promise anything in return to an entity he wasn't even convinced existed.

A black carriage pulled by two black horses rolled conspicuously into the plaza. Everyone stopped whatever they were doing to stare at it as it circled about, Mouse included, and a small lump of dread materialized in his stomach.

This was not the neighborhood for such deliberate swank.

The carriage didn't belong to a noble-born—it would have had the house insignia proudly displayed for everyone to see. This particular carriage carried no such badges of authority and privilege. But it was still unapologetically lavish. It had enough gold accents to purchase a small manor estate.

It came without a protective detail. No hired retinue of bodyguards to follow and deter any trouble. Very strange. On the road between cities, highwayman would have it stripped down in minutes and then be off to enjoy retirement. Gods, even a few blocks over, and the Scourge would have their way with it.

Of course, it rolled to a stop outside the tent where Mouse enjoyed his lunch.

A footman stepped off the back and circle around to the door. A small stool was placed beneath it before the door was unlatched and swung wide. The black opening within remained quiet.

People on the street were eyeing the carriage with interest. Mouse didn't care for this kind of attention. Rich carriages showing up sullied his carefully sculpted reputation as a reprobate.

Mouse knew the drill. He was expected to step into the carriage and have a conversation with the occupant. The footman looked anxious, eyeing Mouse with a confused expression, unsure why Mouse wasn't behaving the proper way. Mouse raised his mug to him and took another swig.

Eventually, as Mouse expected, someone stirred from inside the carriage.

With an exasperated sigh, Savir poked his head from the open carriage door and glared up at the raining sky as if this was a new phenomenon for him. Perhaps it was. He was dressed this time in a stunning doublet of grey with blue stitchwork down the center line and blue velvet epaulets at the shoulders. Humidity and rain dampened the jaunty curls atop his head.

He crinkled his nose as he stepped from the carriage and ducked under the tent with Mouse.

"So," Mouse began, suppressing a laugh. He allowed himself a moment to gloat at this ridiculous victory. He'd made the fop leave the comfort of his carriage to join him outside. Petty and dangerous, he knew. This was not someone Mouse should fuck with. "Come to join me for a meal at one of *my* haunts this time?"

Savir looked around to see what eyes and ears were around before his gaze narrowed down at Mouse. Other than the vender behind his counter, who was suddenly very busy cutting onions, they were essentially alone.

"Hardly," Savir replied. His tone was tight. He was *not* happy.

"Brave of you to venture this far into the perils of the Merchant District without an escort."

Savir sneered. "Charming that you seem to feel I'm unprotected." He took another step closer. "You did not arrive for our scheduled appointment, Master Mouse."

"Ah yes. Apologies. Something unforeseen interrupted my schedule," Mouse replied. "It was unavoidable."

"Disappointing," Savir said.

"I would have sent a courier to inform you, but you see, I don't have any coin and don't know where you live." He lifted a brow. "Unlike you, who seems to know where I am at any given moment."

Savir's creepy, cold smile sent a wave of duck flesh over his shoulders and down his arms.

Mouse tried not to think about it. He *himself* didn't even know he was going to be here at this plaza an hour ago—but Savir had located him without effort. Disconcerting, certainly, but Mouse didn't want to wrestle with that notion just now.

"You should try the food here. If you want to experience true disappointment." Mouse saw the vender flinch behind the counter, but he kept his tongue. "You are welcome to take a stool."

"I will stand, thank you. Our business here will be brief."

Mouse shrugged. "Suit yourself." He took another spoonful of stew. Fuck, it was terrible. Realizing that was all this bastard's fault, he said, "How'd you find me?"

"We have eyes all over the city, Master Mouse."

Gods, he hated being called that. And thank the gods he had been spotted by one of their spies here and not at the docks. He would have to be careful heading back. They'd trail him for sure now that they had eyes on him.

"I have come—"

"Save me your speech, Savir, about how saddened and

disheartened you are. I know why you're here. Get to it."

Savir's lips tightened. "I would have thought you wiser than that, Master Mouse. I suggest you mind how you speak to me. We can be a powerful enemy."

"Is that meant to frighten me, Savir?" He lifted his eyes to lock onto Savir's. "You're a commoner. Like me. Your blood is no more special than my own." He returned his attention to his bowl. "You'll get no reverence from me."

He was pushing his luck. Savir's fury was rising.

"Keep in mind, Savir," he added, scraping the last of the gruel from the bottom. "I am called Mouse for a reason. You may catch sight of me for an instant. But then I'm gone."

"Yet here you are. Foolish enough to be cornered again by a cleverer cat."

"If I didn't want you to find me, you wouldn't have." Mouse tried to sound convincing, but he heard the doubt in his own voice. His insides were still shaking. He gave up on the stew. He dropped the spoon in the bowl and tossed the bowl on a table. "I have not decided whether I am going to take you up on your generous offer."

"'Offer' was perhaps a generous term. People are unlikely to turn us down."

Mouse smiled at him, to show he didn't fear him or his implied threat. "May be time to grow accustomed to disappointment. I am bound by my pledge to the guild, sir. You nor any of your…cadre can compel me to break it."

Savir returned the grin—it was even more chilling than before. "Such a principled response…for a thief, low in the pecking order of things." He pivoted and put his back to Mouse. Under the edge of the tent, inside just enough to protect himself from the rain, he looked out at the wet and empty plaza. "Boundaries, Master Mouse, are arbitrary and plastic. Given the right amount of influence or coin, they can become quite fluid, in fact."

"Enough to purchase, say, a king's pardon?"

Savir laughed openly as he turned back around, then

stopped short when he saw Mouse's hardened face. "You're actually serious."

Mouse didn't respond.

"Very curious. Why would you, at your young age, require such a document?"

"Long story." Mouse was already bored with this conversation. He'd made his point that he wasn't in this arrogant prick's pocket. It was now time to get rid of him. "Look, truth is, I'm already working on it."

Savir's expression tightened. "Is that so? Then why not settle the arrangement with me as planned?"

Mouse put his elbows on his knees and held his hard gaze on Savir. "Because that's not how I work. If I can retrieve it, and that is currently an open-ended question, I will decide on the market value of it at that time. No contracts. When it's in my hands, we'll see then how badly you want it."

Savir's cheeks darkened. He didn't like that. He was functioning under the belief that Mouse didn't know what it was or its value. Learning what it was would inflate the price. He hoped to get it passed over at a discount. "That is not how *we* do business."

"Take it or leave it."

Savir broke eye contact and paced around the tent a moment. "What did you mean, '*if* you can?' I was informed you could steal the tail off a cat."

"I can't steal it if I don't know where it is. Jardem moved it. I'm tracking it down."

Savir's patience was nearing its limit. "Perhaps we should hire someone more…open to our terms."

Mouse lifted from the stool, trying to not look like every bone in his body protested the move. He grimaced at Savir and shrugged. "You can certainly try." As he walked out of the tent, he added over his shoulder just before he pulled up his cloak, "If I locate it, I'll be in touch."

#

Mouse could feel Savir's eyes stabbing at him as he

strutted across the plaza. In truth, his legs were wobbly and ready to give out at any moment, but he wasn't about to give Savir—or anyone—the impression he was afraid. In time, he heard the carriage door close and the carriage grind into motion as the team of black horses carried it away.

He risked a quick look over his shoulder as the carriage disappeared around a cobbler's workshop. He let out a long sigh. He fought the urge to drop hands to his knees and wait until his heart rate recovered.

The disturbing question remained, and it nagged at him as he reached the opposite side of the plaza. How had Savir been able to locate him so quickly? Shadow Elite spies were clearly everywhere, but this was spooky.

Was it luck? Unlikely. And dangerous to assume that.

He'd bought himself more time with Savir—not much, but some. He had to move things along, or he'd end up at the bottom of the river.

And he still needed to talk to Othmar, but his office was across the city. By the time he arrived there, business hours would have concluded, and Othmar would have likely left for the day. He could try to meet up with him at the Hallows' Ball again, but Taurin was clear that his schedule for attendance was a regular occurrence—and tonight was not his night.

That would have to wait.

He stood in front of the three-story tenement building that faced the plaza. From the outside, it seemed maintained well-enough, but what did he know about such things? He called the rafters of an old warehouse home. Staring at the front door like it might do something, he took in a long, calming breath. If this was the wrong decision, things could turn south very quickly for him.

The door was unlocked at street level. He let himself in and closed the door behind him. Zel's little sanctuary was on the third floor.

He'd been here only once before. Zelianna had invited him over to discuss the layout of a manor he'd already cased and burgled. She had barely let him inside her space—they had spoken mostly in the open doorway, but Mouse could see enough of the place to get a sense of it. It had seemed fitting for her. Comfortable without it screaming it belonged to a woman.

Mouse trudged up the stairs. He grunted with each step, his bruised and likely broken body struggling to lift himself upward. The cold wet against his skin made his muscles knot up as if his blood was congealed meat fat. He made no attempt at stealth. No need here.

Up two dark flights, he slogged and rounded the corner to the corridor. Her door was at the far end.

He hadn't really thought about what he'd do if she wasn't here. With all the chaos at the guild, she might have been called back. Or off doing whatever it was she did during the day. He really didn't know. But if she wasn't home—he'd leave a note. A meeting time and place.

Would she even come, he wondered?

He approached the door, prepared to knock. But his fist froze in the air. The door was open.

His throat tightened. She would never leave herself or her belongings unprotected.

He lowered and removed the dagger from his boot.

Gently, he placed his palm on the door and eased it open. The hinges squealed a little, but there was enough of a gap now for him to pass through. Holding his breath, he listened but heard nothing other than the muffled sound of the street outside.

He turned his torso and slipped in.

The tenement was encased in darkness. Some light filtered through the joints of the closed shutters, but with the day's gloom, only the faintest tint of grey was cast about the room. Not enough to see by. Mouse stood in the quiet dark long enough for his eyes to make out rough shapes in the room, but he saw nothing move. He strained his ears for the slightest sound of breathing or for a creak in the floorboards as someone shifted their weight.

Nothing. Only silence.

He eased toward the window. Dagger ready, he drew the shutter open to allow in the day's pale light.

The scene was grisly. The battle that had occurred here had been intense and violent. A small bedside table was smashed into kindling, objects were tossed about the room as if a twister had landed in the center. A crumpled body lay on the floor next to the simple bed large enough for one. Mouse didn't need to examine it to know it was Zelianna.

She had been brought down by numerous stab wounds. Blood was everywhere—the walls, the linens on the bed, but mostly she had bled out on the floor, leaving a sticky dark residue of her life on the wooden planks.

The fight had been brutal. The movement of blood and her shattered belongings told a story of how she had fought against her attackers, even though she herself had been gravely injured. And when she had finally succumbed, collapsing next to her bed, her assailant had finished her off by slicing her throat. Zel's head was tilted back, her eyes open, and the wound stared back at him like a gruesome carmine smile.

Raw and unbridled fury surged up in a torrent of heat and red, unlike anything Mouse had ever known. His fists clenched until they were white. He stumbled and turned his back to her, eyes wrenched shut to block out the grisly image of her.

Jardem. The name burned through his mind like hot iron. Zel had gotten too close to the truth. Perhaps she had confronted him, challenged him about what she'd learned about the murder of the merchant. And he had silenced her.

It began as a simple quaking of his hands, but the impact of the scene soon had his entire body shaking with rage. This time, Jardem had gone too far.

Zelianna hadn't been a friend—she was barely tolerant of him. But gods, she didn't deserve *this*. She was talented. Of that, there was no question. And principled. She had stood with the guild, always. And as much as he was loath to admit it, even to himself, he had…admired her. Not as one would a mentor. But as a symbol. She had embodied the status and respect he might one day claim. Like him, she had started with nothing.

He closed his eyes. Fuck, he *respected* her.

And she deserved better than to be slaughtered in her own space and left here, forgotten.

This could have easily been him—his throat slashed, his broken body left to bleed out.

A voice from within, small at first, cut through the thick layer of red anger and reached the surface of his consciousness. This battle would have been loud. Someone would have heard it. Even from the street. Someone was probably running off to find the nearest guard post and leading them back to investigate.

He couldn't be discovered here, or he'd be blamed for it. He had to flee. Now.

The window was out of the question. The outside wall was old plaster that would crumble under his weight if he tried to scale it. The only option was the way he had come in.

He couldn't bring himself to gaze upon her lifeless form again as he circled back to the door. Out of respect, he should close her empty eyes at the least, but he couldn't bring himself to do it. His instinct to escape this trap was too great. The dagger seemed to buzz in his hand, sting his skin. He shoved it into his boot.

Out of the apartment, he bolted for the stairs and scurried down, leaping two at a time. He made it to the second floor and was about the descend the remaining stairs when he heard a voice call out from below.

"This way, m'lords."

Mouse used the corner of the wall to bring himself to a sudden halt and yet still nearly tumbled forward down the steps.

Fuck! Seriously? Again?

His timing was decidedly an issue today.

He launched back up again and darted for the nearest door, scrambling for his tools.

He could hear the footfalls on the steps as he thrust the picks in and fumbled with the lock. His hands shook, and he struggled to keep the pick and hook steady. He recognized the work, knew the locksmith that constructed the lock. This should be easy for him. This wasn't like him.

The clumping and unhurried footfalls on the wooden stairs, which moaned and creaked under the weight of at least three men, fractured his concentration. He couldn't focus on the sounds inside the lock.

They were nearing the top of the stairs.

He closed his eyes and tried to tune out the sound of them approaching. In seconds, he'd have to abandon this lock and sprint back to the third floor and try another door up there. Working by feel alone, he maneuvered the inner workings of the lock, easing back the tumblers. He felt more than heard the mechanism inside shift. He gasped in relief as he lunged inside and flung the door shut again just as he heard the first boots on the floor of the corridor.

"I'll go up with him and check it out," a gruff voice said. He sounded bored, as if this was a waste of time. "You two ask around. Find out if anyone heard or saw anything."

Mouse snuck through the dark room, navigating around the bed and other furniture toward the closed shutters at the back. Unlatched, which surprised him. When he gingerly pulled them open, letting in the grim light, he discovered why. Metal bars blocked access to the outside. No alley. The window faced a single-story building with a pyramid shaped roof sitting behind it. A shop of some kind. It was clear why the bars had been installed. Anyone with access to the smaller building's roof had easy access to the flat.

He was trapped inside.

A knock came at the door.

He held his breath. If he remained quiet, the guard outside would assume the place was unoccupied. The knock came again.

"Open up," the knocker called from the other side. "I know someone's in there."

A bluff? Likely. But he couldn't risk the idiot getting aggressive and kicking in the door for fun.

Mouse whipped a dirty blanket from the bed and tossed it over his head. Then he opened the door a fraction.

"Is there a problem, good sir?"

All city guards in their uniforms looked the same to Mouse, with some variation in size and hair color. This one was no different. Gruff and weathered, with an unkempt beard and shaggy hair sticking out from under the ill-fitting helm. Both likely weevil infested. He was dressed in the standard brown leather jerkin that bore the city's insignia on the breast. His dark eyes narrowed at Mouse. "You live here?"

"I do."

"Hear or see anything recently?"

"Only just got home myself. Wasn't around to hear anything. Is anything amiss? Am I in danger?"

The guard scowled. "Just answer my questions. Where were you if not here?"

"At my master's shop, like I am most days."

"And where's that?"

"In Dungrel's Plaza, the tannery. I'm Master Endelor's journeyman, good sir."

"Hmm," grunted the guard.

"If you need repairs to that armor of yours, I'd be happy to accommodate you. A fair discount for our city's brave protectors."

He grunted again. "Stay put. Don't leave. I may have more questions."

Mouse closed and locked the door again as the guard moved on. Moments later, he heard him knocking on the next door. Terrific.

Not what he needed. City guardsmen were more interested in getting back to their dice games, so they would drag anyone in and call the matter closed. He needed to find a way out of here before he was chosen as a convenient scapegoat.

He went to the window again and one at a time, tried each of the bars. First three were solid and didn't budge. The fourth had a wiggle at the low end. The spikes driven into the wattle had loosened over time.

He gripped the bar with two hands, and with a low grunt, shoved. It took several attempts for the play in its movement to increase. The spikes squealed as they were ripped from the wall. With more play, Mouse started building momentum, back and forth, back and forth, and eventually, the bar popped out of the wall.

The space between the window frame and the next bar was narrow, but his body was tight and small. It'd be a squeeze but perhaps enough for him to wiggle through.

More voices from out in the hall. The guard was talking to a woman. The neighbor would likely rat him out as not the one who lived here.

Mouse grunted. The guard would be back, and Mouse would be dragged to the guardhouse. He had no choice but to try to slip through the opening.

He hoisted himself up on the sill, gripping one of the bars. He started with his legs—those would fit through, he knew—and he stepped through the gap.

He didn't run into trouble until he reached his torso. He wiggled and squirmed but couldn't get any farther than his chest. His legs dangled on one side of the window; his arms dangled on the other. He pulled himself out again.

A knock came at the door. An aggressive one.

Fuck!

He squirmed about trying to force movement, any movement. The bar pressed painfully against his breastbone, and the wood frame scraped against his back. His already sore muscles and bruised ribs from earlier cried out in agony from the pressure.

The knock came again. Louder this time. "Hey you! Open up in there."

The last thing he needed was to be wedged in the window when the guard and his friends broke through the door.

He wiggled out again and dropped onto the floorboards. "Anon, good sir," He called out. "Patience. I'm coming."

"Open this door," came the replied.

Hands on hip, Mouse scanned the room. He spotted what he needed. A lantern.

He unclasped his cloak and, hissing through his teeth, managed to tug his jerkin and tunic over his head. After wadding them into a tight ball, he tossed all three garments out the window and onto the roof of the building. He grabbed the lantern and shook it. Good—it wasn't empty. He tugged free the stopper to the reservoir and poured the oil into his hands, then rubbed the oil over his chest.

"Last warning," the guard growled.

"Coming now!" called Mouse, pouring more of the oil over his shoulder and down his back.

He dashed to the window, leapt up again, and thrust his legs through the opening.

A crash came from the door. The wood popped and cracked from the force. The guard was shouldering his way in. The old doorframe wouldn't last long.

Mouse was quickly back where he was before, unmoving and wedged in.

He took in as full a breath as he could manage, then exhaled it all until his lungs were emptied. Bracing a foot against the side of the building, he pushed with his leg and wormed his torso about. Movement. But only a little. He felt the wood was stripping the skin of his back like old paint.

Another crash. The guard would be in the room too soon.

Mouse repeated the same actions. Breathe in. Breathe out. Push.

The edge of the door splintered apart as the lock was pulled from the frame. One more, and the door would open.

Like a cork from a bottle, Mouse jettisoned from the opening. He flew backward and landed hard on his back. He groaned out in pain as he tried to roll onto all fours. His head swam dizzily. Blackness swirled in eddies at the edge of his vision.

Frantic movement from inside the tenement. They were searching for him. They hadn't noticed the window yet. He had mere moments.

He snagged his garments and scrambled on all fours up over the peak of the pyramid roof. On the other side, he lost his grip on the wet wooden shingles and started to slide. Unable to stop, he picked up speed and flew over the edge. With a grunt of pain, he hit the street below.

He could only lay there in a heap, face in the mud. Surely, he'd broken something. But he knew he couldn't stay there. He had to move. The guards would figure out where he'd gone quickly enough and come around the building looking for him.

Groaning, he lifted himself off the wet cobbles and to all fours again. Everything moved the way it was supposed to, at least. His entire body ached but nothing *too* excruciating. Nothing broken. A few people were about, staring. "I'm all right," he said with a lift of his hand. "Nothing to see. Go about your business."

He used the aid of a lantern pole to hoist himself back onto his feet. And forcing his legs into motion, he headed down the street at a graceless, limping jog. Those on the street gawked at him as he shuffled past. He must look as bad as he felt. Although his body screamed at him to stop, he didn't quit until he was well away from that quarter and satisfied he wasn't followed.

He ducked into an alley and, with difficulty, managed to pull his clothes back on. The wet fabric stung the deep abrasions on his back. He could only imagine how bad the damage was.

Evening was deepening, and the alley was fast becoming

choked in cold shadow. He sat on the ground, shoulder to the wall, and tried to get his breathing and heart rate under control again.

Then he started to cry.

He wasn't sure why, really. Exhaustion? Frustration, perhaps? Pain?

Or was it the death of Zel? His thoughts drifted to their last conversation at the tavern. Something was different, then. He'd felt it. She had been almost kind to him. In her own way. Maybe something had been changing between them.

Now she was gone.

It started slowly, with a burning in the back of his nose, but picked up steady momentum until he was curled into himself and convulsing into his knees in wave after wave.

He let it run its course. No point in fighting it. No one was around, and he didn't think he had the strength in reserve to stop it, anyway.

Eventually, the sobs tapered off, leaving his eyes puffy and his throat burning. He swabbed his eyes with the wet cloak and wiped his leaky nose on it. It smelled of mildew, sweat, and blood. He climbed back to his feet and limped weakly out of the alley.

With the comfort of rising darkness embracing him, he circled back through the empty streets toward the docks.

21

"THANK THE gods!" Tenric exclaimed as Mouse stepped through the cabin door. He swung his feet over the edge of the bed, eyes wide with worry. He tossed a small book aside and leaned forward in earnest. "I was ready to head out and see if I could find you."

He wore only his trousers. The skin of his naked torso was the color of linen, smooth like butter in the sun, unmarred. His meaty arms showed no division of color where the sun would have deepened the complexion. He would never be able to pass as a laborer, Mouse thought absently. The only variation in color was the ruddy-brown hair that rested high on his full chest, around his dark nipples and the trail that ran down the center of his abdomen to the navel. The toes of his bare feet hovered just above the floorboards.

"That would have been foolish," Mouse replied dryly. He looked down at the box he was carrying. "Brought you food. A roasted chicken, turnips, some—"

"Mouse, what happened?" He launched off the bed and was at Mouse's side. He took the box and set it on the table. "You…you look terrible."

"Then, I look better than I feel," Mouse said. He tried to

shrug out of the cloak, but pain flared in his shoulder. He winced and sucked air through his teeth.

"Wait. Let me." Tenric gently removed the cloak from Mouse's shoulders, tossed it aside, and helped him get his arms out of the jerkin. "This tunic's done for, I'm afraid."

Mouse reluctantly agreed. It was torn in a dozen places and covered in dirt and blood.

"Instead of trying to pull it up over your head," Tenric said. "I'm going to cut it off."

Mouse sighed and hesitated. As much as he hated to admit it, he liked that option better than suffering the effort to lift his arms.

Tenric retrieved a knife from somewhere and sliced through the fabric. The tunic was old, threadbare. It took little coaxing to come apart. In moments, it was a soiled rag on the floor.

Mouse heard Tenric gasp when he saw the extent of the bruising and abrasions that Mouse knew covered his back.

"Gods!" Tenric whispered.

"The price one must be willing to pay for information."

"You need to have this treated, Mouse."

Mouse shook his head as he lowered to the edge of the chair. "No time for that." He could see the protest forming on Tenric's lips. "Just…just need some clean water to wash up a bit. There's a public fountain on the other side of the docks, near the southern entrance. Perhaps…"

"Understood," Tenric replied with a quick nod.

He must have been eager for a task to get him out of the cabin, for he was quick to pull on his tunic and step into his boots. Before he ducked out through the door, he remembered the floppy hat. He smashed it onto his head and left without another word. Mouse heard his boots jog across the river craft's deck and fade on the pier.

Mouse sighed. He shouldn't have sent him off. Reckless. He wasn't thinking clearly. Tenric was safer here.

He uncinched his belt and let it drop to the floor, then

loosened the ties of his trousers. He had a sudden urgency to be out of them, too. He was tired of being wet and cold. His legs had taken less damage than his top half, so getting out of them was easier to some degree. Once he peeled them past his hips, they dropped around his ankles, and he stepped out of them. He kicked them aside as if angry at them.

He wrapped himself in a blanket and sat on the bed.

Then his eyes sprang open at the sound of the door.

Without realizing it, he'd dropped to his side and fallen asleep. Groggy, his eyes blurry, he pushed himself back into a sitting position. It felt like only moments had passed since he'd sat down, but some part of him knew it was longer.

Tenric shuffled in, wielding a bucket in one hand and a canvas sack in the other. He looked up to meet Mouse's eyes, then kicked the door shut with his foot as he set the bucket down on the floor.

"Now, don't be cross with me…"

Mouse groaned. "What did you do now?"

"I knew you wouldn't agree to getting help. So, I sought some out—"

Mouse's back straightened. "Fuck, please tell me you didn't bring anyone here!"

Tenric waved a hand about. "No, no, no. Nothing like that. I promise. A friend of the family. They own an apothecary here in town. I paid a visit—"

"Tenric, we talked about this! It's too dangerous for you." *And by extension, me*, he thought gruffly. If it came to another fight tonight, he'd be defenseless.

Annoyance flashed on Tenric's face. "I'm allowed to assume risk if I choose to."

Mouse pinched the bridge of his nose. "But I know what the risks are. I agreed to keep you safe. I can't if you keep doing things that could get you recognized." He gestured to his discolored torso with a wave of his hand. "This is what happens when you underestimate the risks involved. This…or worse."

That seemed to penetrate. Tenric's eyes shifted away, and his mouth pinched. "I could learn, you know."

"Learn what?"

"How to survive. Like you."

A bubble of laughter entered his throat, and too late, he fought to disguise it as a cough.

Tenric's eyes burned angrily at him.

"I'm sorry," Mouse said, shaking his head. "You'd be dead on the first day."

"Not if someone guided me," Tenric said coolly. He waited for Mouse to reply, and when he didn't, Tenric grunted and looked away. "Gods, you sound like my father."

Mouse sighed. "Tenric, this is what life on the streets of Har Tesera looks like. It's not suffering through a boring party or having your grouse over-cooked."

"Is that what you think my life is like?" His eyes were wide. "Those are the extents of my daily struggles? Dry poultry?"

"You forget what I do. I infiltrate your plush lives and steal from you every day. I *see* your lives."

"Do you?" Tenric asked. "Do you see anything past the gilt and the glamor?" He was seething now and started to pace. He spun on Mouse, his jaw tight. "Father called me weak. Pretty much on the daily. Said I lacked the necessary instinct. Called me unworthy of the empire he constructed and saw the only way forward for me was the nobility. Then I might be taken care of and not risk losing the family's wealth. Yet he never took a moment to show me how anything in his self-built empire was run. Never thought to put me to a task and see how I might do."

He took a step closer to Mouse. His fists were clenched. "During my imprisonment, and my time here, I have had nothing but time alone with myself. Time to *really* look at who I am. I am *tired* of feeling like a leaf on a stream. No control of my own fate. Being swept along in a storm of forces I don't understand. Well, no more. Yes, I said I wanted you to protect me. But I will no longer sit back and let others do something I am capable of doing for myself. I need to learn how to stand on my own feet, and I need you to help me."

"Life is hard, Tenric," Mouse said quietly. "Harder than you know. I'm not sure you understand that."

"But I want to."

"Words you may regret."

Tenric scoffed. "I've come to realize, if I'm to survive any of this, it's not going to be because someone shielded me from all the danger. And all the risk."

Mouse frowned and looked down at his hands. "I propose a trade then."

Tenric's brow lifted. "I'm listening."

"I, too, could use some tutelage. I need to know how to blend in with *your* kind. I can play the servant, the attendant, even a fucking scullery, but I want to know how to *act* like one of you. My attempts so far have been…clumsy."

Tenric's expression cooled before he replied. "I've been a study of that my whole life. Been born, you might say, in the enemy camp and had to learn how to fit in myself."

"The perfect mentor, then. Are we agreed?"

Tenric chuckled dourly. "Why do you insist everything hinge on a pact or a contract?"

Mouse narrowed his eyes at him. "Lesson one. Nothing is ever free. Not really. Know the details up front of what you're getting involved in. Deals and contracts are your protection. Without them, you'll be stripped naked in no time. Never underestimate anyone's ability to take advantage of you."

Tenric retreated into his own thoughts a moment. "Very well. I agree."

"Good," Mouse replied. "Lesson two, then. Don't fucking go visiting people you know that can turn you over to the Shadow Elite. You didn't buy that off a shelf. The apothecary's shop couldn't have been open at this hour."

Tenric, realizing the bag was still in his clenched fist, set it down on the table next to the box of uneaten food. "No. It wasn't. I went to her manor."

Of course, he did. "Her?" Mouse repeated.

"Yes. Daughter of the shop owner. Not just any shop, mind you. An exclusive one, catering to nobility. She has taken over the business since her father grew ill. She was one of the women father urged me to betroth myself to. They were in talks regarding a dowry before he was murdered."

"None of this suggests she is someone you can trust. She could be speaking with Savir right now for all you know."

"I didn't give away any information about here, Mouse." Tenric said. "I'm not *that* naïve. Plus, I may have hinted that as a newly appointed lord, I will need to marry soon."

Mouse stared for a moment in surprise, then threw back his head and laughed. "Well, fuck. Maybe I underestimated you, after all. Perhaps you *do* have some street instincts about you."

"Thanks," he replied tetchily. "She had the supplies on hand at her manor. Only too happy to share them with me." One by one, he started to pull items from the sack and set them on the table. "Her personal stock, I imagine. When I explained the injuries…." He lifted out a black ceramic vat the size of a fist. "She generously offered this."

Mouse's eyes narrowed with suspicion. "Which is?"

"Your lucky day. This comes at a very steep price and is extremely hard to come by. Mistress Dalphane must be very keen to take on the title of Lady if she was willing to surrender this so eagerly. Time for you to be treated as the nobility are treated."

That made Mouse's stomach tighten. He wasn't sure about this.

Tenric moved the bucket to the floor by the chair. "First, we clean it all out."

Mouse held out his palms. "This really isn't necessary—
"

"It is. And I didn't do all this for nothing. You helped

me. Now I help you. Come here."

He directed Mouse to sit backwards on the chair. Mouse reluctantly complied. He eased off the mattress and slid the blanket from his shoulders. Then, he positioned himself on the chair, back facing outward. Tenric lit a couple of candles to see better and arranged the bucket directly under Mouse.

"Lean forward a bit." Tenric soaked a clean cloth in the water and wrung it out.

The cool water both stung and brought relief. Every time the cloth dabbed against the skin, Mouse hissed. While Tenric worked, little rivulets of water ran down the center of his back and trickled into the crack of his ass.

"Stop squirming," Tenric said. His voice was soft. Patient.

Mouse grunted and dropped his forehead against the top of the chair's back. He lingered at the precipice of leaping to his feet and calling it done. Tenric worked slowly and deliberately, taking time to limit the pain, but Mouse just wanted it finished. He felt awkward, uncomfortable. Closed in. Trapped.

The people in Mouse's life didn't act like this.

But for some reason, he stayed, and he let Tenric work.

"All right," Tenric said after a time. "That should be enough, I think." He dropped the cloth back in the water and slid the bucket aside with his foot. Mouse caught a glimpse of the cloth floating on the water. Once cream colored, it was now blackish-crimson.

"This jar first," Tenric announced, holding it up. "This will prevent festering and accelerate healing."

Mouse looked over his shoulder. "Such a concoction exists?" he asked, genuinely surprised.

"For those with the coin to buy it, yes. I suspect this isn't strictly herbalism either."

Mouse chuckled. "What? You're telling me this is magecrafted?"

"Such things exist, Mouse. For those who can afford it,

there are far more options."

Something about this made his insides squirm like a sack full of nest beetles. Maybe he should instead heal naturally and sell these mysterious inventions. But who would believe him that they were brewed with magecraft? He shifted to lift himself, but a strong hand rested on his shoulder.

"Relax," Tenric said.

Mouse puffed out his cheeks but complied. "And she simply handed this over to you."

"As I said, the gesture was designed to advance her chances of being my wife."

"And how are her chances?"

Tenric paused a moment before answering. "She is not my type."

With two gentle fingers, Tenric applied the grey goop to the wounds on his back. It was cool at first, and moments later, he felt it tingle beneath the outer layer of his skin. It seemed to reach into his muscle.

Mouse shook his head. "What very different worlds we're from, Tenric," Mouse said softly.

Tenric was quiet a moment. "I suppose that's true. But strangely, I wonder if yours is the better one."

Mouse couldn't help but chuckle. "You are either being disingenuous or wildly naive."

"It is your view of my world that is naïve. Do you think people are not attacked or tortured or murdered in my world?"

"No," Mouse replied. "Because they hire people like me to do their deeds for them to save on laundering the bloodstains from their crisp white tunics."

"The amount of cruelty, brutality, and corruption among those in my circles would alarm you, I think."

An image of Zelianna's lifeless form thrust itself into Mouse's head, unbidden. "We have all of those things too, Tenric." His voice was smaller than he expected.

"Borne out of necessity. Out of survival. My father, in contrast, didn't need to lean on tactics of barbarism to build his business, but instead, he relished in it. Celebrated it, in fact." A pensive silence followed. Mouse could almost feel Tenric's sad smile against his back. "Those with considerable means feel they are not only more deserving of it but entitled to even more. They won't be bound by the morals and ethics of others. They are above the moralities thrust upon the common citizen."

Mouse grunted. "I caution you. Do not romanticize my life. One night with an empty belly or a knife at your throat would cure you of that ridiculous notion."

"I doubt it. Cruelty exists in my world. Evil exists in my world. I would argue to a greater degree. Because evil begets evil when there is no fear of consequence. No one admits it. No one faces it or challenges it. The knives at my throat are simply of a different nature. With a different intent."

Mouse had robbed enough manors, encountered enough of the people he ran with, to know that at least some of it was true.

"So, how did all this happen?" Tenric asked.

"I was caught snooping around where I wasn't welcome." He wasn't in the mood to elaborate, so he added nothing more.

Tenric seemed to accept that. He fell silent then and didn't ask any more questions.

It didn't take long for him to apply it to all the wounds. He even had Mouse turn around, and he slathered it on the chest abrasion where the metal bar removed a layer of skin, too. Once finished, he set the jar aside and rinsed his hand in the bucket.

The pain was ebbing away, like retreating tide waters. Slowly, gradually, but noticeably. The strange tingling seemed to penetrate deeper and infect his muscles. They felt warm. Loose. He rolled his shoulders a bit to test it. He felt the tug of the wounds as he moved, but the pain was distant, a fraction of what he'd felt earlier.

"Now we need to wait until it dries," Tenric announced.

They spent the time then taking apart the cold chicken with their fingers. It was seasoned poorly, but neither Mouse nor Tenric complained. They ate in silence until only bones remained.

Tenric licked his fingertips and wiped them clean on his trousers. "Enough time, I think." He poked at Mouse's wounds with his forefingers. Mouse felt only a hint of dull pain and the pressure of his finger against the skin. Tenric held up the dark grey jar this time and showed Mouse. "Now, this next ointment is for your muscles. It will relieve you of your soreness and eliminate the discoloring of your skin."

Mouse looked down at his flank, now entirely awash with purples, reds and ochres. It had the look of an oil sheen in a puddle of water. "It may have met its match tonight."

"I am told it will make you drowsy, so best to apply it with you already on the bed, I think."

"Drowsy?" His first thought was the danger of being too groggy or muddled if were they discovered here.

"You need sleep, Mouse. This will help. Get on the bed, face down."

With a sigh, Mouse did as he was told. He rose from the chair and crawled up onto the mattress, then plopped his belly in the center of it.

Tenric crawled up and kneeled next to him. Mouse closed his eyes as the soothing ointment was rubbed all over his back, shoulders, and down the length of his arms. It warmed like campfire heat when massaged into the skin, and Mouse could imagine it seeping right to the muscle underneath. The effect was swift and strong. He felt the knots in his shoulders untangle. Soon after, the room was spinning a little, and Mouse found it difficult to keep his eyes open and caught himself drifting off. At one point, he thought Tenric was massaging the paste over his calves and thighs. He wondered if that was real—he didn't recall any bruising on his legs—or if he had drifted off and was fantasizing what he wanted Tenric to do.

274

Half dozed, Tenric's voice broke the almost unnatural serenity of the cabin. "I hope you don't mind, Mouse. I prefer to sleep nude."

"Same," Mouse replied. His voice was muffled by the mattress. It wasn't at all true. Mouse never slept nude. He wasn't even sure why he said that. And as Tenric settled in next to him, he promptly fell asleep.

\#

He woke sometime deep in the night. His head was murky with lingering sleep, and he had the vague sense of strange yet potent dreams that already had disintegrated like pipe smoke on the wind. In his sleep, he'd rolled over onto his back, and onto the fresh wounds. He felt some discomfort, but not pain. The tingling of the skin had faded, and he was only aware of a dull ache.

Tenric, sleeping along next to him, had rolled over in his sleep and now lay onto his stomach. In doing so, one hand had landed on Mouse's upper arm, and Tenric's meaty thigh, bent at the knee, had slid over the top of his own bare leg.

Bare leg. Mouse didn't have his pants on either. When did that happen?

An innocent enough occurrence—but Mouse couldn't help but wonder. Whether the contact was intentional or not, the sensation of skin against skin sent pulses of desire through Mouse's body. He felt his breathing quicken. His body reacted on impulse, and his cock swelled. It pivoted and landed on his belly like the swing of a trebuchet.

Since Taurin had left the city, Mouse hadn't laid with anyone. Not that he'd had the time or opportunity. He'd spent time with Othmar, of course, but that wasn't the same. Taurin's departure had left something of a hole in Mouse. One deeper than he would have imagined.

It wasn't the memory of their intimate times together that ached in him. Not really. Taurin was someone he could talk with. Someone who understood him and still wouldn't judge him. At least not harshly. The hours after their bedding, when they had dozed and chatted lazily until near dawn, was what he pined for again.

He hadn't realized how much he depended on that. Hadn't realized how much it shored him up and protected him from collapse. Until now, when it was gone forever.

He reached down and let his hand curl around himself and felt his cock lurch under his own touch. The skin of the head flared with desire as his hand cupped the end and squeezed. Sticky juices leaked against his palm.

Fuck. He ached to give in to the craving. And with Tenric already touching him, the invitation was there. It would be so easy to roll over and wrap his own body around his.

He rolled his head toward Tenric, who snored softly in his sleep. Enough moonlight filtered in through the window to glaze the meaty roundness of his shoulder. Gods, he was exquisitely made. His skin was unmarred by pox or by the sun. His body radiated both strength and beauty, but his boyish face was flush with this maddening, untarnished innocence.

He was aggravating, to be sure. Unlike anyone he'd met before. His unwavering kindness and warm gentleness were almost unsettling. Aspects of humanity Mouse didn't experience that often. If ever. To find them neatly packaged in a foppish merchant boy seemed preposterous. How could it possibly be real? Mouse wanted to reject it as a weakness, as a failing—but try as he might, he couldn't.

Tenric was right, in a way; Mouse didn't understand his world like he pretended. Tenric existed in a foreign kingdom. Something alien. Mouse only understood what he gleaned by peering through their windows. Their lives were an enigma to him.

But what difference did that make? Did they not feel the same desires he felt?

It would be so easy to kiss his neck until he came awake.

But Mouse couldn't bring himself to act.

He'd made that assumption once before, assumed someone had shared his attraction and desire. It had ended in catastrophe and changed his life forever. He was still paying the price for that foolishness, for reading those signals wrong. He wouldn't make that mistake again.

He shifted away and rolled onto his side. Tenric's leg dropped off him and onto the mattress. Their silky connection was severed. Tenric groaned in his sleep and rolled over, putting his back to Mouse.

And Mouse's heart constricted as he tried to find sleep again.

22

BY DAWN, the pain was nearly gone.

Mouse rolled over and climbed from the bed. He tested his muscles by reaching his arms over his head and then crossing them over his chest. He felt some stiffness, and a hint of soreness, but nothing more of his injuries. He'd sidestepped a week of recovery in a single night.

How had he never heard of this miracle? He needed to get his fingers on more of that ointment.

He'd never be able to afford it, of course. And the laws around magecrafted items were strict. Nearly as strict as murder. Stealing something crafted by mages came with stiff penalties. If he were caught, of course.

Tenric was still asleep. His legs were tangled in the blankets, like he was halfway spinning a cocoon for himself, and a thick arm draped over his face to shield him from the dawn sunlight pushing through the window. The rain had moved on, and now warm sunlight streamed in like an assault. He still snored softly. Mouse allowed himself a moment to drink in the shape of him. Then he forced his eyes away.

He'd made his choice. He'd live with it. No point in

torturing himself over it.

Mouse tugged on his trousers but didn't bother with the rest. Then he opened the cabin door and climbed out onto the deck. The wood was chill and wet with a layer of dew against the soles of his feet as he stepped across the craft's decking and seated himself on the edge, feet dangling over. The wind rolling off the river toward the shore had a bite to it and made his skin prickle, but the warm sun breaking the trees across the river felt soothing on his shoulders.

He faced the docks and the early bustle of dockworkers starting their day. A new day, and everything proceeded with a predictable normalcy. Mouse found it disquieting, in a way. After everything that happened yesterday, watching people going about their normal business seemed oddly obscene to him. Did they not *feel* that his entire world was breaking apart? Zelianna was dead. The guild was in chaos. The Shadow Elite had put him in their focus. *Him*, of all people. Which meant he'd more than likely end up dead.

And with the pain of his injuries now absent, too, the events from the day before seemed erased, forgotten. As if they'd never happened.

A new river barge had docked opposite them, and a group of lumpers was hard at work unloading the crates stacked atop the deck. The bare-chested team streamed back and forth, hoisting crates on their shoulders and carrying them off to the shore.

They were a rugged bunch. Weatherworn and brackish. The opposite of Tenric and his silken complexion. Still, Mouse caught himself assessing the physique of each of them as they paraded in front of him.

Gods! What was wrong with him? Maybe he needed to hunt down a quiet hole. Give the basher a quick yank. The release would help him reclaim his focus.

Frustrated, he stood and descended back into the cabin.

Tenric was sitting on the edge of the bed, rubbing his eyes. He'd untangled himself from the blanket and now sat naked in front of Mouse and made no attempt at covering himself. Mouse tried to divert his eyes—he really tried—but he couldn't pull his eyes away. His gaze instead stared at Tenric's torso and raked down every curve he had on full display. His throat constricted when he sighted Tenric's cock, which was currently experiencing a typical morning stiffness.

Mouse was both shocked and somewhat in awe. Tenric was fully comfortable in his nudity. Even partially erect, he made no effort to conceal himself.

With a form like that, it was a small wonder.

Tenric wove his fingers together and extended arms into the air in a full stretch that flexed his chest and biceps gloriously. He let out an extended groan that sounded disturbingly like an orgasm.

Mouse groaned inwardly as he turned around and shut his eyes. Gods, he had made his choice! Tenric could stop making it fucking harder already. Mouse waited for it to be over.

He heard Tenric's feet hit the floor. "Morning," he said.

Mouse grunted something incoherent.

"You're in grand health this morning," Tenric added, clearly unaware of Mouse's current torment. "Moving about adequately. The ointment did the trick, it appears."

"I feel…" He paused to pick up his tunic, intentionally keeping his back to Tenric so he wouldn't clock his own stiffened cock through his loose trousers. He made a quick adjustment to point it upward so the protrusion wasn't as obvious. "I feel unnaturally normal."

"That is the point of it," Tenric replied.

Mouse pulled on his tunic to avoid responding. It was unsettling, knowing he was altered by powers incomprehensible to him. Powers beyond his understanding. What was the unknown effect such mysteries would have on him in the long run? He didn't trust mages. He never would.

"The back looks good," Tenric added. "Some redness, but the wounds are closed up."

By the time Mouse turned around again, Tenric had pulled on his trousers and tunic and sat back on the bed. Mouse was relieved and disappointed in equal measure.

"Looks like we're even, now," Mouse said.

"Hardly think that's the case," Tenric replied. He leaned forward, elbows on knees, and stared at his bare feet. "I was thinking." He paused a moment, looking pensive. "You have the information you need now. I think I should hide out in an inn or something. Under an alias. Wait there for my opportunity to get out of the city."

"We covered this. You are safer here."

"What happened to you yesterday—"

"Was entirely my doing and had nothing to do with you," Mouse said flatly. He tried to read his expression, tease out where this was coming from. "I thought you wanted me to help you learn how to be more like me."

Tenric closed his eyes and sighed. "I do. But I also don't want to see you get hurt because of me." Mouse chuckled, and Tenric's eyes flashed up. "If I'm here, you're at risk. Asking you to protect me was selfish. I was reacting to fear. Asking you to teach me how to survive was…folly."

"You are under no obligation to stay, of course," Mouse said. "You satisfied our bargain. I wouldn't advise it, though."

Tenric nodded.

Yesterday, Mouse would have rushed him off. He had all the information he needed from him—Tenric was just in the way. But today felt different.

"I was thinking too," he said. "About how you said you were tired of sitting back and letting things happen to you. Well, if you're interested, I could use you today."

Tenric lifted his head and then his eyebrows. "For?"

"A mission."

"Dangerous?"

Mouse shrugged. "More for me than you."

Tenric held his gaze for a moment, his eyes narrowing in interest. "What's this plan?"

Mouse smirked at him. "I know where your writ of nobility is hidden. I want you to help me liberate it."

Mouse fully expected Tenric to back out, to have an excuse why he couldn't or shouldn't join in. It was one thing to feel powerless. Quite another to get your hands dirty.

Tenric's mouth pursed. He appeared to think on it a moment, chewing on the inside of his cheek. Then he leapt to his feet and reached for his tunic and boots. "I'm in."

TENRIC'S IMPATIENCE was palpable. Every few moments he'd release a sigh or goose his neck out from their shadowy cover to scan the street or look up toward the sun, as if the entire day was slipping by and the wait was pointless.

"How much longer?" he asked again.

"I told you, these things take time," Mouse replied. "And I had to be extra careful."

They were sheltered in a shadowy alcove, out of sight of most people on the street. Mouse wasn't keen on being spotted again. He'd taken every precaution, used every trick to get him to this point unnoticed. He wasn't about to spoil it now while they waited.

"You could be back in that cabin," he reminded Tenric with a cool stare.

"Fair enough," Tenric grumbled.

Mouse spotted a lanky hooded figure heading up the street. The size and shape were right, but he watched until he was certain he recognized the gait.

He elbowed Tenric. "Stay put."

Tenric's eyes widened with sudden vigilance and looked about the crowded street corner as if he'd spot anything.

Mouse stepped out into the direct sunlight. Made no gesture or sign, just waited to be seen.

The hooded figure slowed a moment, then approached.

"Was starting to wonder if you didn't get my message," Mouse said.

Cassar tossed the hood back, exposing the chaos of white-blonde hair. "You're lucky I received it at all. Even luckier I answered it."

Mouse put a hand to his breastbone. "Is there a problem—"

"Save it, Mouse," Cas cut in. "You have no idea the chaos you've caused with this business."

"That bad?" He fought down a smile. He couldn't help but feel a wellspring of glee over the news but could tell Cas wasn't in the mood to appreciate the gloat.

"Just getting clear of the guild was an ordeal. He wants to know everyone's whereabouts at all times."

Mouse didn't need to ask whom he referenced.

"You didn't—"

"Don't be daft, Mouse. No one saw me leave; no one knows where I am."

Mouse allowed himself a sigh.

"He's gone mad with rage and paranoia," Cas continued, massaging the back of his own neck. "Or close to it. He's had me using my sight to search rooms and eavesdrop on conversations. He's convinced there's a coup being planned."

"Is there?" That would solve things for him.

"More the opposite. Everyone is terrified of him right now. He's made a few examples of those who aren't fully compliant with his demands. His cruelty lately has everyone chewing their fingernails." Cas's eyes narrowed at him. "How have you, of all people, managed to escape his wrath?"

Mouse lifted his eyes. "He believes I'm looking into the matter for him."

Cassar shook his head. "The one he should be watching the closest."

Mouse shrugged innocently and smirked. "Delicious irony. No sweeter vintage."

Tenric stepped out of the shadows and joined Mouse at his side.

Cassar's eyes raked Tenric, his expression curious. "And

here is the little bird you sprang from Jardem's cage. The cause of all our current troubles." Mouse never told him he was behind Tenric's escape, but Cas was quick enough to draw the conclusion. It wasn't that big a leap, Mouse conceded.

Tenric's face darkened. "I was the victim, you'll recall. I did nothing to cause any of what happened at your guild."

"No, that was your rescuer's doing. Surprised to find you still in town. I would have exited the closest city gate if I were you."

"He's most generously offered his aid," Mouse said. He left it at that. He wasn't in the mood to explain all the nuances of what was happening. "Considering I did save him from certain death."

Cas tilted his head. "And your plan is to hide him in plain sight…as the rich fop that he is?"

Tenric was dressed in a long black doublet, hose, and boots. New purchases from a small clothier specializing in quality garments not custom-tailored. Inventory was limited and finding one that fit Tenric was tricky—most rich elites weren't shaped like him. The doublet they settled on, adorned with beads and satin ribbons, was out of season and more an evening garment than daytime. Mouse didn't care. It didn't matter if it was fashionable. It simply had to look expensive. The new garments, along with an hour at the baths—springing extra coin for a private chamber *and* a trim of both hair and beard—cut farther into his reserve of coin than he wanted, but Mouse wouldn't worry about that now.

Tenric had to look the part.

Mouse was astonished by the ease of the transformation. In the privacy of the room at the baths, Tenric dressed in the new attire. By the time he was latching the doublet across his full chest, the change in him was profound. He stood differently, spoke differently. It wasn't merely the garments on the man. It went deeper. It was instinctual. Innate.

Tenric's claim he had to be taught to fit with his crowd in was evidently hogwash. He took to it with the ease of a bird taking flight.

"The scheme requires the involvement of a very wealthy merchant," Mouse told Cassar. "Tenric will be stepping into that role today."

Cassar's eyes flicked at Tenric a moment, then returned to Mouse. "Seems some new gear for you is part of the scheme as well. Where did you get the coin for all this, Mouse?"

Mouse glanced down at his own new tunic. A necessity since the old one was shredded and bloody. It shone embarrassingly bright in the sunlight and didn't smell like him yet. He was tempted to roll around in the street to sully it up. "Never mind that. Not important."

Cas scowled at that. He spent his days procuring information and grew cranky when it was denied him. "I hate this already," he said, with a shake of his head. "I should have listened to my gut and stayed well away from here. Your *schemes* mean disaster."

"Oh, don't get yourself all peevish. I haven't even gotten to the best part yet. You get in on the opportunity to spoil Jardem's day a tiny bit further."

Mouse caught a glint of surprise in his eyes. "So…still at that, are we?"

He gave him a hard look. "We are."

"Stealing his prisoner out from under his nose wasn't enough?"

"You know the answer to that."

Cassar cast his eyes about the small plaza, biting his lip. Mouse could tell he was intrigued but working it out in his head. Mouse waited it out—which wasn't long.

"Not committing to anything. What mayhem do you plan to cause today?" Cas asked, eyes curious.

"Nothing too terrible. A simple heist."

Cas looked skeptical. "Nothing is simple with you."

Mouse chuckled but held his eyes firmly on Cas's. "Need your help with this, Cas."

Cas grunted. "Still not a yes. But it will have to be quick.

I can't be dragged into some big ordeal, Mouse. My absence will be noted."

"No need to fret. You'll be right back in that chaos before you know it." Mouse pulled his hood up and started walking. "Come. I'll explain more when we arrive. It's not far." Tenric stepped in beside him. They must have looked like the oddest pairing.

Cas held back. "Strange," he called to Mouse's back. "I recall specifically saying I hadn't agreed to anything yet."

Mouse ignored the complaint. As he predicted, Cas sighed loudly and followed too.

Mouse stopped on a corner outside a small vegetable market. He gestured with his chin toward the rundown workshop diagonally across the intersection.

"Tenric is going to do a little shopping in there." Tenric, to his credit, seemed solid to a casual observer, but Mouse spotted his fingers drumming against his thigh. Now that they were getting closer, his nerves were starting to fray.

Cassar narrowed his eyes at him. "For what?"

"Art. That little shop makes convincing forgeries that sell for good coin. Which is why Tenric needs to be his rich young merchant self today. He's in the market for a special item."

Cassar stared at the building for a time. Mouse wondered if he was somehow scrying inside. "What do you want with forged art?"

"Not the art. But something else is hidden in there that I need."

Cassar folded his arms as he considered the shop across the way. "This is what's going to put a stone in Quickblade's shoe?"

"Do you really want me to answer—"

Cas held up his hand, his expression hard. "Enough, Mouse. Enough. I just need to know what I'm sticking my neck out for this time." He stepped closer and spoke low. "He's looking for heads to roll. Whatever it is you're up to…if

286

you get caught—I need to know I'm not getting dragged into it, too."

Mouse was silent for a dozen heartbeats, his lips pressed. "You were never here."

Cassar stared down at him. "What are you after?"

Images of Zelianna's body bobbed to the surface. He fought down a fresh wave of fury.

Mouse had to be careful how he worded this. Cas's talents could often pick up deception. Mouse needed to be honest without giving too much away. "The document. The one from the job the other night."

Cassar frowned. He'd been eavesdropping on that conversation with Jardem, had witnessed Jardem's behavior. His eyes shifted toward the building. "This belongs to the client?"

"No," Mouse replied flatly.

He could almost read Cassar's thoughts. *Then what was that document doing here?*

"So, your plan is to steal it back." Cas closed his eyes. "I'm afraid to ask. But why?"

Mouse gestured to Tenric with a wave of his hand. "It belongs to him. I'm returning it to its rightful owner."

"How charitable of you," Cas replied dryly. His eyes shifted between the two of them.

"You know me. Compassionate and selfless. To a fault."

Cassar looked at Tenric. "So, that's how you fit into all this. What's the document?"

Mouse jumped in before Tenric could answer. "He'd rather not say. It's a sensitive family matter."

Hands on hips, Cassar spun his back to them and grunted low in his throat. "I hate you sometimes, Mouse."

"No, you don't. Which is why you're going to help us out. Tenric is going in to look around. I need to hear and see what he's experiencing."

Cassar's head rolled as he turned to face Mouse again. "Both will require a lot of concentration. I'll be drained. If I'm needed later—"

"Take a nap," Mouse replied.

"Are you comfortable with this plan?" Cas asked Tenric with one raised brow.

Tenric made a halfhearted shrug. "Mouse said the danger for me will be minimal."

"And you believed him? More fool you. Mouse is a lodestone for trouble."

Mouse's jaw tightened. He didn't need Cas spooking Tenric into backing out. "Hardly fair, Cas. We are merely casing the place so I can find my way about in there later tonight. Just as we've done one hundred times before. I've coached Tenric extensively on what to say and do."

Cas's expression softened…some. Mouse knew he had him. "Fine."

Mouse forced his face to remain neutral and not break a smile.

Cassar returned his attention to Tenric. "What did he tell you about me?"

"Only that you were required for this to work. Should I be concerned?"

Cassar's eyes shifted to Mouse. "Not about me. But the company you keep should certainly worry you."

"On with it," Mouse growled.

"I will be in your head, accessing your senses."

"In my head," Tenric repeated.

"Yes. And I will project what you see and hear into Mouse. You won't know either of us are there unless I want you to know. Are you comfortable with that? You need to agree."

Tenric looked to Mouse for reassurance, then back to Cassar. "You…won't be rummaging around in there or anything, will you?"

Cas rolled his eyes. "That's not how it works. Your secrets are safe, merchant. Scrying doesn't access thoughts or memories. Mouse and I have done this more times than I care to count. If I was exposed to the dark shit that is mucking about in that skull, I would likely never attempt it again."

Mouse wanted to protest, but he knew Cassar wasn't wrong.

Tenric looked uncertain, but he eventually offered a slow and less than convincing nod. "All right. I agree to it."

"Very well," Cas said. "Let's get this over and done with."

Mouse gripped Tenric by the shoulder. "Relax. We've gone over this. You know what to say. What questions to ask. I just need you to look around as much as you can."

"So, you've done this?"

"Many times."

Tenric swallowed.

"It will be over before you know it," Mouse told him, turning him about to face the building. "Once inside, don't move your head about too much." Scrying was disorienting and unnerving. Being at the mercy of someone else's attention often made Mouse nauseous. "If something looks interesting or important, stare at it for a few moments to make sure I got a solid look at it."

Tenric nodded.

"Through Cas, I will be with you the entire time," Mouse added. "You won't know, though. If you want me to know something, and it's safe, whisper it, and I'll hear it."

He nodded again.

"Off then." Mouse gave him a gentle nudge forward.

Tenric strolled across the intersection with purpose. He was so focused on the task ahead, he almost got struck by a passing carriage. Tenric leapt back as the driver hollered at him and called him an idiot.

"Going to work at this range?" Mouse asked.

"It'll do. But you don't expect me to scry here on the street, do you? We'll both be blind and deaf to our surroundings."

"Up here," Mouse said.

He led Cas around the corner and climbed up a flower-covered trellis attached to the outside wall of the fruit market and onto the roof. Cassar followed with an annoyed huff. They took seats on the leeward side of the roof, out of view from the street. Cassar took a cross-legged position, which looked awkward and uncomfortable with the angle of the roof. Mouse sat down next to him and loosely hugged his knees.

He'd barely gotten himself situated comfortably before his vision faded as if he were blacking out.

"Some warning would have been nice," he grumbled.

If there was a reply, he didn't hear it. He was already in Tenric's head.

He could still feel the hard clay roof tile underneath him and the wind on his face, but his hearing was gone, along with sight. He took in a full breath. He hated this part—an irrational corner of his mind always worried it would be permanent somehow.

Sounds came first. It was the easier of the senses for Cassar to collect and then transfer. For Mouse, it started as a distant roar that steadily grew until it was a cacophony of indistinguishable noise. It was overwhelming, and it took a few heartbeats for his practiced mind to untangle it all, like a loose clump of colored twine. One by one, he separated out each sound. Voices. A cart rolling by. The crunch of boots on the street. Tenric's breathing.

"Stay calm," Mouse muttered, even though he knew Tenric wouldn't hear. Cas's conduit was one direction.

Sight returned, blurry and distorted at first, as if breaking the surface of water. Once the connection was established, everything snapped into sharp focus.

Tenric was standing outside the door to the warehouse, certainly drumming up the courage to pull open the door. "I hope you are in there," he said. "Or all of this is for nothing."

He pulled open the door and walked through it.

Inside was a relatively small customer space for a woodworker's wood shop. An innocuous collection of furniture pieces was on display on either side, creating a center aisle that led to a counter at the back of the shop. None of it wildly creative or artful. A few fireplace mantels, a barrel filled with balusters for a staircase railing, a few chairs. These pieces were not designed to sell or drum up new business. Mouse knew the real merchandise was available in back and only shown by special request.

Tenric picked up a wide-based wooden candlestick and turned it over in his hand to examine it.

Not important, Mouse wanted to yell at him. But, of course, he wouldn't be able to hear it.

"Can I help you?" came a voice.

Tenric, clearly startled, put down the candlestick rather clumsily, nearly knocking a similar one over in the process. He swung his gaze toward the counter at the far end of the room.

After an uncomfortable pause, Tenric remembered his role. "Ah, good day, sirrah." As instructed, he took on a haughty and superior tone. He would channel his father, Tenric had said. Mouse had to admit he had the voice down rather well.

Tenric strolled toward the counter at a casual gait.

Mouse didn't recognize the man. He had no affiliation with the Night Fingers, certainly, but that didn't mean he didn't belong to one of the other criminal enterprises in the city. There were too many to monitor.

He was older, his long hair streaked with gray and pulled back into a tight and fastidious ponytail. His warm skin was creased at the eyes and at the corners of his mouth. His garb was unassuming, but neat—a tan coat with a stiff ban collar, brass buttons and light embroidery at the sleeves. He rested his hands in front of him on the countertop and intertwined his long, bony fingers.

"Is there something I can help you find? We aren't taking on any commissions at this time, I'm afraid, if that is your interest."

The tone was cool. Mouse had heard more inviting greetings from the city guard.

Tenric took his time to reach the counter.

"This shoddy trash? Do you think I'm furnishing a tavern by the docks? No, sirrah. That is not what brought me into your shop today."

The vender behind the counter attempted a smile. It was a ghastly thing that made Mouse want to punch him. "Then, pray tell what we can do for you? We are rather busy today, I'm afraid. Most of our business is by appointment only, you understand. And I am unaware of any appointments on our calendar today."

"I see," said Tenric. "I was led to believe that you had some special merchandise I might be interested in. Apparently, I was misinformed. Good day, sirrah."

Tenric turned on his heel and started for the door.

"Special merchandise, you say?" asked the shopkeeper. His tone warmed a fraction, like a candle in a wintry cabin.

Tenric made a slow turnabout. Thankfully. Quick spins made Mouse dizzy. "Indeed. I am visiting from Har Purdea, conducting some business. I was hoping to return with some unique gifts for my associates."

The shopkeeper was tentative in his response. "Unique how, Master....?"

"Azul," Tenric replied.

"Master Azul," the man repeated with a bow of his head. "Call me Zardoon. What items did you have in mind?"

"Well, seeing we are relatively close to the barbarian border, I really had my heart set on some ritual artifacts from the Volfric Wastes."

The man listened and nodded.

"But, Gods, they are pricy things, aren't they?" Tenric added.

"First and foremost, the king has decreed it is illegal to carry such items. That tends to drive the price up. Furthermore, acquiring these items and smuggling them out of the barbarian lands is challenging. Those that do such work are understandably loath to give such items away."

"Yes, yes, I understand that," said Tenric. "But your particular shop happened to spring up in a conversation with an associate of mine. He said you might be the solution I'm looking for." Mouse could hear a flutter of nerves escape Tenric's tone. Likely not enough to make Zardoon suspicious. Tenric was here to deal in contraband, so a fit of anxiety would be believable.

"Is that so?"

"I hope I was not misled or deceived. He said you carry a wonderful assortment of coveted merchandise at a far cheaper price than most of the other dealers in the city."

"And who, pray tell, is this associate of yours that was kind enough to recommend us to you?" Zardoon's tight smile could cut glass.

"Master Gebhard Basia. Do you know of him?"

It was one of the names that Mouse had seen in on an invoice in the ledger. One he remembered.

Zardoon's smile warmed. "I do, indeed. How fares dear Geb?"

"Famously," Tenric replied. Mouse could almost hear his fake smile. "I would very much like to gaze upon your merchandise, sirrah. If you are willing. I have plenty of coin on hand." Mouse heard the jingle of coin. Tenric was shaking his belt pouch.

Zardoon tilted his head in consideration. "I suppose one unscheduled tour of our stocks can be allowed today."

"Excellent!" Tenric exclaimed.

Mouse had to admit, he had taken to the role rather effortlessly. Once the initial anticipatory nerves had relaxed, Tenric had settled into the performance and even seemed to be having fun with it. A grand adventure for him. A relatively safe peek into the underworld he had no idea even existed.

Zardoon gestured for Tenric to follow and headed toward the door at the back of the shop. Tenric followed him through the threshold—

Mouse's vision suddenly went black. At the same moment, Cassar cried out in sudden pain next to him.

Blindly, Mouse reached out for him. Cas was thrashing about, arching his back. Mouse gripped him, crying out, "What is it? What happened?"

The sight eased back. Cassar's face had gone sickly with pain, but his eyes were open. He lay on his side, panting.

"Cas, what happened?" Mouse demanded.

"Gods burn you, Mouse! The back room of the shop was warded."

"Warded?"

"Protected! With magecraft runes. They cut me off."

"Fuck!" That meant Tenric was alone in there. And had no idea that Mouse wasn't watching over him.

Cas grabbed the front of Mouse's new tunic. "It's worse than you know, Mouse. They know. They know someone was trying to scry into their shop. Tenric is in some real shit now!"

23

MOUSE SCRAMPLED over the roof and leapt down to ground level. Ignoring the jarring pain in his ankles, he sprinted across the street, dodging around a cart and leaping over a dog that wandered into his path. Someone shouted at him as they dodged clear of him. He barely heard them.

He couldn't just barge into the shop—that was clear. He had no idea what dangers he'd be hurtling himself into. And his sudden appearance would make it worse for Tenric—and himself—if those inside thought they were being attacked. But he had to find a way in. And fast. He'd talked Tenric into this operation, convinced him it'd be safe. He wouldn't allow anything to happen to him.

Wards? Fuck—that meant mages were involved with the operation somehow. How much coin did this operation bring in? Mages didn't come cheap.

Beneath the panicked concern for Tenric, anger surged in his blood. He despised those strange and reclusive cultists with their black robes and face tattoos. He'd only had the barest encounters with them, but those times left him with duck skin and the inexplicable need for a steaming bath.

Something about them that felt…wrong. And Mouse hated the idea of unseen powers he couldn't combat. It didn't seem fair.

Frantically, he circled the outside, getting a sense of it. He spied a few windows near the roofline, but they'd had been boarded up—a telltale sign that they didn't want witnesses. The place was sealed up like a tomb. He circled around the row of buildings to hunt down access to the back of the warehouse. Along the parallel street, he came across a junk-filled alley—one he hoped would lead him to some form of opening. He jogged down its length at a crouch, ears straining for signs that Tenric was being tortured—or worse.

Tenric, gripped by fear or pain, might say anything to save himself. Mouse didn't have much faith in Tenric's fortitude to withstand torture. But if he even mentioned Mouse by name, it could mean disaster.

The alley intercepted another perpendicular one that ran behind the buildings from the other street. It was lined with various wide doors for loading and unloading supplies and merchandise. None of the buildings had windows, either. He jogged up the length of it, searching. From here, in this narrow tunnel of brick and stone, it was tricky to even gauge which warehouse was the one he sought.

He tried a few of the doors—all locked from within. Not even an external lock to pick.

Time was ticking for Tenric. He had to figure this out!

The sound of rushing water reached underneath his panic and registered in his ears. Coming aware of it, hope surged, and he searched for the source of the sound. Dragging away a few broken and rotting crates, he located a rectangular metal grate. The grate had a rusted lock on it, but that was quick work for Mouse, and within a few moments he was dragging the cover away from the hole.

Mouse wasted no time. He put his hands on the side of the opening and dropped inside.

He landed in thigh deep water that smelled of mold, piss, and decay. Familiar smells and not at all unexpected. This wasn't the first time he'd traveled through these brick-lined drainage canals.

They webbed through the city just beneath the streets. Mouse had used them as a hiding place or even a quick escape a time or two. But they were not without their dangers.

During heavy storms, the canals rushed water from the surface out to the river to prevent flooding. Getting caught in one during a heavy rain would most certainly mean drowning as one's body was whisked violently through the network and eventually out to the river.

But they had another use. Industry needed water—or needed to dispose of wastes. This network was more extensive in manufacturing districts, often cutting directly under the workshops and foundries, providing access to water or a convenient way to dispose of unwanted byproducts of their manufacturing. That waste sometimes took the form of toxins or scalding water—either of which could strip his skin off.

He ducked his head to enter the canal. The space was cramped, even for him. Anyone larger than Mouse would never fit through. Daylight fell in through the hole and played on the surface of the water enough to allow him to see where he was going. The current shoved against him, bullying him to move. It was much stronger closer to the river.

Blending with the roar of the moving water, Mouse caught the sound of voices echoing off the brick and water. Stooped, he shuffled through the water as fast as he dared toward the sound. He took an even narrower tributary on his right.

"I promise you, I don't have the slightest idea what you are talking about."

Tenric. He was still speaking with the elitist air he'd affected from the start. Mouse could hear some anxiety in his voice, but he had to hand it to him for having the wherewithal to not break character.

Mouse heard a grumbled response from someone but couldn't make out the words. Then he heard the loud clap of skin against skin.

"Ow," Tenric responded. "That hurt very much, I'll have you know. My father will not be at all pleased to hear how I'm being treated. I shall be reporting you all to the magistrate the moment I walk out of here."

Don't overplay it, Mouse warned silently in his head. He pushed through the water, getting closer to the source. Ahead of him, gold light rolled on the surface of the water in the shape of many little squares. Another grate.

There were a few chuckles in the room. "He thinks that hurt. Wait 'til he feels this in his ribs."

Someone had a weapon, clearly. A dagger. Or some torture implement. Mouse heard Tenric gasp. "Now, that isn't necessary at all. How do I impart on you three good sirs that I know nothing of what you speak?" Desperation was rising in Tenric's voice. But was he intentionally letting Mouse know how many were in the room? He wouldn't have expected that amount of composure from Tenric. The situation was dire— he had to know that. Or was the cosseted merchant boy really that naïve?

"I'll not ask again," came the reply in a low growl. Mouse moved under the grate. He could hear the nuances of the exchange much clearer now. "Who was scrying on us?"

"I don't even know what that is—" Tenric's voice was cut short with a quick expulsion of air. Mouse knew that sound. Someone had punched him in the gut. A second loud slap followed.

Mouse then heard Tenric spit.

Time was running out. Tenric's interrogators were growing impatient. It wouldn't be long before they kept good on their threat to use the weapon they brandished in front of him.

"Enough lies." Mouse recognized that voice. Zardoon. "I felt the ward trigger. It is quite unmistakable."

"If that's even true, surrah, someone did so without my knowledge or consent."

The argument was a valid one—if they knew anything about how scrying went. And Mouse could tell by the silence that followed they considered the idea. But Tenric had already made the mistake of telling them that he would go to the magistrate. He would not leave the warehouse alive now.

Mouse put his hand to the grate and pushed. It resisted at first, then popped up with a small grinding squeak of metal. The thing was heavy, and Mouse resisted the urge to grunt as he used the strength of his legs to elevate himself and it. He pushed his face into the opening and peered out.

The drainage grate was to the back of the warehouse—typical from what he knew about such things. Crates and equipment blocked a visual of where they held Tenric. The smell of freshly cut wood and oils wafted down and cut through the smell of the conduit. Holding his breath, he hoisted the iron grate up higher with one hand and wiggled his way through the opening and onto the floor. Then he lowered it again back into its recess. It made a slight clank as it fell into place. Mouse winced and held his breath, waiting for an indication they'd heard it.

Around him, workbenches were cluttered with tools and paint supplies and half completed barbarian "artifacts." Others were hanging on wooden racks to dry. Masks. Jewelry. Statuary and idols.

Tenric was coughing and sputtering. "This…this violent behavior is unnecessary." Mouse could hear the desperation in his voice surging. He clung to the affected accent, likely thinking he'd committed to it, and it would be worse if he dropped it. It would only confirm that he was a fraud and a liar. "I implore you. I know nothing of what you speak."

Mouse was honestly amazed—and more than a little impressed—that he hadn't confessed his role and spilled Mouse's plan to save himself.

He was dripping water onto the flagstone floor. Little rivulets followed the seams between the stones and dribbled back through the grate. He rose enough to put his head over the top of a workbench. Tenric was tied to a chair, slumped forward. One eye was swollen shut, his lip was puffy and bloody, and crimson trickled from a nostril. Mouse could see the blood on the collar of his tunic, but the black doublet hid what was likely a lot more.

His interrogators formed a half-circle around him. Zardoon stood more to the side, observing while the other two did the ugly business of trying to make Tenric talk. One was lanky and pale, like a birch tree with arms; the other was stocky and cloddish. Mouse was positioned behind them.

Three of them—just as Tenric said. Not good. How was he going to get Tenric out of here and not be seen?

"We are getting nowhere with this…fool," Zardoon said with an extended exhale. "Either he is irrationally faithful to his accomplice, or he doesn't actually know anything. Either way, he is useless. Finish him."

Tenric's eyes popped open with sudden alarm.

The lanky one spun a dagger about in his hand. "About time." He stepped closer to Tenric, still playing with the blade. Even though the man's back was to him, Mouse could *feel* his toothless grin like ice walking down his spine. "I loathe your kind, you know. Fucking coxcombs like you, strutting about, ordering good folk like us about like we're vermin. Hate the whole fucking lot of you."

In his boot, Mouse's dagger buzzed against the skin of his calf.

"Your anger is misplaced, surrah," Tenric answered. There was calm strength in his voice. Resistance. Even facing death. "I've done nothing to you."

"Arrogant and entitled to the end," the man replied. "I will enjoy this and make it last. Scream all you like, but promise not to die too quickly."

The man brought the knife toward Tenric's throat.

Mouse acted on pure instinct. In one fluid motion, Mouse had his dagger in his hand, rounded his arm over his shoulder, and flung it across the workshop.

His intent was to strike the shoulder or arm—just prevent him from putting the blade into Tenric. But instead, the dagger struck the base of the neck.

The lanky man gasped as the blade sunk in, and his arms flung up in the air. The knife fell from his hands and onto the floor. He staggered back, hands flailing over his shoulders to reach the dagger, but he didn't have the dexterity to clasp it.

The two others whirled their attention toward where the blade had come from.

But Mouse was already in a crouch and on the move, slipping behind another workbench and a stack of crates.

"The accomplice," Zardoon hissed, as he turned about. "Come to make a daring rescue."

"How'd he get in here?" the other growled.

"Find him, idiot!" Zardoon snapped and shoved him.

The pale, lanky man, now collapsed to the ground, spasmed and then went still. Zardoon and his lumpy partner separated and eased toward Mouse's last known location from two different directions.

Mouse was panting, on the verge of panic. He tried to gain control of his breathing so he wouldn't be heard. The man was dead.

He'd committed murder. Again.

He hadn't intended for it to happen. He'd only wanted to stop him from killing Tenric. He was protecting an innocent life—that had to account for something. But would the city guard and the magistrate see it that way?

If he was caught, it didn't matter what information Jardem had on him. He'd be executed. And if they learned who his father was, he would be too.

His instincts told him to run. To simply flee and not be seen. If they never saw him, he couldn't be connected to this murder.

Except his dagger—his father's dagger—was in the man's neck. Could that be traced to his father somehow?

Fuck!

Fuck! Fuck! Fuck!

And he couldn't leave Tenric. It was his fault that Tenric was in this mess.

"Ah," came Zardoon's voice from across the room. Intentionally loud enough for Mouse to hear. He chuckled in a way as if he'd already won. Mouse could tell he'd discovered the wet spot where'd he come out of the drainage canal.

His wet clothes were going to lead them right to him. He might as well shout and wave his hands about. He grunted inwardly, realizing he had no choice. From the shelter of the crates, he quickly stripped down to his skin. Boots, trousers, tunic and jerkin—all of it was deposited on the floor in a soaking heap and Mouse padded off on bare feet to a new hiding place.

Terrific plan, he thought. *No weapon, and now completely naked.*

He forced his breathing under control, though his heart still pounded. Panic wouldn't solve anything, he chided himself. And would only lead to mistakes. Free Tenric, retrieve the dagger, get out—then no one would be able to pin the murder to him.

Murder. He wanted to vomit.

Mouse heard an unhappy grunt, followed by a sloshing sound. Zardoon had reached where Mouse had abandoned his clothes—perhaps picked them up and tossed them back down again. From his current cover, he didn't have eyes on either of them, but from the silence that followed, he knew they were signaling each other, mapping out a plan to sweep the room. It wouldn't be long before they cornered him. The workshop wasn't that big…

Focus, he growled at himself. First, free Tenric. Cut his bindings and get him out. Once he'd ensured Tenric was safe, he'd deal with the other two. Yet getting to him would be tricky. His back was to the wall.

"Mouse? Is that you?" Tenric yelled out tentatively.

Gods burn you, don't use my name, you dolt, Mouse

screamed in his head. Now they didn't have to see him to identify him.

He circled around from the side of the workbench to the end as he heard the soft scuff of a boot getting nearer. Stealth wasn't the stocky one's strength, thankfully. Mouse could follow his movements as easily as watching him.

Behind him, a few strides back and encased in shadow—a door, partly open. He'd almost missed it.

Slowly, he reached up onto the workbench and curled his fingers around the first item that met his palm. A block of wood. Careful to not be seen, he lobbed the chunk across the workshop to the far corner. It made a gentle clunk against something else that was wooden when it landed.

As soon as Mouse heard the quick gasp of surprise and a scrape of a boot pivoting on the stone, he broke for the door.

He stayed low, turned sideways, and slipped through the opening. His back nudged the door, and it swung open further, making the slightest mouse-like squeak. He ducked behind the door and held his breath—and waited.

"You have nowhere to go, whoever you are," Zardoon called out. It came from the other side of the workshop. They hadn't spotted him.

The long, narrow room was overcrowded for its size. Wooden desks, piled with leather-bound books and scrolls, lined one wall, and a shelf cluttered with things that Mouse couldn't identify in the dark lined another. Instinct told him immediately this was the room he was looking for. The writ of nobility would be here.

But to his surprise, the room was not unoccupied. Seated on the floor were two figures, huddled close and gripping each other with fear. From the shape, Mouse discerned one male, one female.

Fuck, this was growing ever more complicated.

Even in the dim light, Mouse could see their wide eyes staring at him. He couldn't blame them. A small naked man had just barged into their hiding place.

These were not the people assigned to protect the place, clearly. It took only a moment for Mouse to discern how they fit in here. The two of them were here to do the labor. They were the artists creating the fakes.

He lifted a finger to his lips and narrowed his eyes at them sternly.

They both hesitated a moment, then nodded.

"We will find you," Zardoon called out again.

"And make you pay for what you did to Jah!" The other one was closer. *Much* closer. Mouse strained his hearing to locate him.

"But in the meantime," Zardoon added, his tone shifting from irritated to something more gleeful. "We can finish the work on your accomplice. Then we come for you."

Mouse closed his eyes and took in a deep breath. He could hear the footfalls crossing the workshop.

"And I will slice him apart with your own dagger," Zardoon added.

"Mouse?" Tenric called out to the room. The affect in his voice was gone. All that remained was mounting terror.

"Come out, and you might still save your friend."

"Don't do it," Tenric cried. "They'll only kill us both. Get out of here!"

Mouse's heart pounded in his ears. Sweat trickled down the spine of his naked back. As much as he wanted to listen to Tenric, to escape and not look back, he couldn't. He couldn't let the fucker gut Tenric. And wouldn't allow his father's blade to end up in Zardoon's possession. He'd rather die than let that happen.

There was nothing left for him to do.

Lifting to his feet, he pulled the door open and stepped out. He'd figure something out. He always did.

As soon as he stepped out of the door, the lumpy man lunged and grabbed him by the throat with his meaty hand. He yanked him close and thrust his face right into Mouse's. "Thought you were clever, huh?"

Fighting to get air into his lungs through tight fingers around his neck, Mouse gagged on the rancid breath.

"This little thing is what was causing all this trouble, Master?"

Zardoon chuckled. "Bring him here so he can watch his friend die. Then, he'll be next."

Mouse struggled against the arm and fist clutching him as he was dragged across the room, but he was helpless against the man's strength. His feet barely scraped on the floor as he was brought closer to Tenric and Zardoon.

His back was to them. He couldn't see what was happening, but he could hear Tenric's frightened grunts and the scraping of the chair on the floor.

"I have no taste for vengeance and don't view killing as sport," Zardoon said. "And I've grown bored with the two of you and the time you've wasted. So, I will make this quick."

The man swung Mouse about so he could see as Zardoon approach Tenric. He already had his father's dagger in hand, and he was examining it, his expression curious. He turned toward Mouse. "Why do you use such an unwieldy thing? The balance of this blade is terrible. No matter," he added with a shrug. "It'll do the job at hand. And it'll get tossed in the river along with your body."

Zardoon stood over Tenric, who stared back up at him, ashen, his mouth open like a dead fish. He brought the dagger to his throat.

No, Mouse cried silently. He couldn't let this happen. Gasping, he fought against the man's grip, but he couldn't break free. He felt like a rabbit struggling feebly in a rope trap.

Zardoon suddenly cried out in anguish. The dagger fumbled from his grip as he staggered back. His hands slammed against his eyes as his screams intensified into a high pitch shrill.

The man at Mouse's throat lost focus in his surprise. The arm lowered; the grip lessened.

Mouse had no idea what was happening, but he wasn't

about to waste the opportunity. As soon as his feet settled on the floor, he shoved off and sprang up. He lifted his leg and brought a foot against a workbench and shoved off again, arching his back.

He flipped, legs spiraling through the air, twisting the man's wrist along with him. The man cried out in surprise and pain, and he released his hand on Mouse's throat.

Mouse landed inelegantly but managed to keep his feet. While the lumpy creature staggered a bit and tried to recover, Mouse snatched the closest thing to him. An unfinished wooden statue of some unknown Volfric god.

He gripped it by the head and wielded it like a club. He whirled it backwards over his head, and then upwards at terrible speed—just as the man was coming for him again. Mouse's aim was precise. The corner of the square base slammed neatly between the oaf's legs. The man tried to scream, but nothing came out. He choked and sputtered, and his eyes rolled back.

Mouse didn't hesitate. He spun it about over his head and smashed the base into the man's temple. Blood gushed outward like a wineskin rupture. Mouse could feel the skull disintegrate under the impact. The statue cracked in half, and the free end flew across the workshop.

The man teetered and collapsed. He struck the workbench on his way down, bounced, rolled, and hit the ground like a felled tree.

Mouse tossed the fragment of the statue aside and stumbled toward Tenric, whose attention was now on the motionless form of Zardoon.

"What happened to him?" Mouse asked.

Tenric looked up, his eyes alight with adrenaline. "Mouse! You're a happy sight, I can tell you. No idea. He just started to convulse and—uh, you're naked!"

"I'm aware," Mouse replied dryly. He picked up his dagger from next to Zardoon and moved behind Tenric.

"Why are you naked?"

Mouse sawed through the rope that bound Tenric's wrists together. "Not important. Are you alright?"

Tenric shrugged as he massaged his wrists. "Hope there's some of that mage cream left." He made a sad, forced chuckle. "That could have gone better, I think."

"Yeah," Mouse said. "Could have gone better."

Tenric bolted from the chair as if it was on fire and stumbled in a circle around Zardoon's body. "Gods! I thought we were both done for. In my head, I was planning what I'd say to the guardians of the veil when I arrived." Without warning, Tenric lunged for Mouse and wrapped his thick arms around him. Unprepared for the assault, Mouse lost the air in his lungs as Tenric squeezed. "You came for me!" he all but shouted in Mouse's ear. "I can't believe you came for me!"

Mouse couldn't think what to say. He was more distracted by how Tenric was pressed hard against his naked body, arms enveloping him.

Tenric leaned back, and his eyes locked onto Mouse's. "Thank you," he said, and before Mouse could react, Tenric came in again. He pressed his mouth against Mouse's own. Tenric's lips were soft and full, like pillows made of bunnies.

Mouse's knees started to buckle as he was drawn into the kiss. *Fatigue*, he told himself. But with the strong grip against his back and the succulent lips pressed against his own, he felt himself stir. He didn't need to look down to know he was swelling. The head of his cock pushed against the brocade fabric of Tenric's coat.

"Well, this is heartwarming," came a voice.

Mouse sprang back, exploding from Tenric's embrace. He dropped his hands to cover his groin.

"Fuck, Cas!" Mouse snapped. "How long have you been there?"

Cassar was leaning against the door frame, smirking. "Long enough. Sorry it took so long for me to get in. They'd locked the door."

"This is your doing, then?" Mouse asked, tilting his head

toward Zardoon. He wasn't ready to remove his hands yet.

Cas shrugged. "I had to get inside the ward before I could do anything. Why *are* you naked?"

"Doesn't matter. What did you do to him?"

"I didn't kill him, if that's what you're wondering." Cas strolled closer. "I whisked his mind up a bit. That's all."

"You…you can do that? How did I not know you can do that?"

Cas scowled, glancing over his shoulder at Mouse. He squatted next to Zardoon, took his chin, and turned his head. "There's plenty you do not know about me."

"Apparently." Mouse stared back in shock. A part of him felt betrayed. Another part was worried. What else was he hiding?

"I didn't want you looking at me like everyone else does. Like how you're looking at me now. I knew this would be beyond your tolerance."

Yeah, he thought. *It was.* He might never let Cas in his head again.

"He's not dead?" Mouse asked.

"No."

"A drooling idiot?"

Cassar rose to his feet and made a fleeting glance toward him. "Always a danger. But no. The worst he'll experience is a terrible headache and won't remember anything that happened for the last day."

That was a relief. Zardoon wouldn't remember the name Tenric shouted out. "How long will he be out?"

"Hard to say. Hours certainly. You're fortunate I like you, Mouse," Cassar added with a glare. "Gods, help me understand why I do!"

"Thank you," Tenric said. "You saved our lives."

"I had it under control," Mouse grumbled. "I was almost ready to make my move."

Both Tenric and Cas narrowed their eyes at him but didn't say anything.

"I'm getting dressed," Mouse said.

"Please," Cas said.

Mouse marched across the workshop with his shoulders back. The clothes were still there, left in a wet heap. He wrung out the trousers before he tugged them over his legs. The fabric was icy against his skin.

"By the way, two more are in that office, hiding," he told them as he returned.

Cas and Tenric both stiffened, heads spinning toward the door.

"Relax," Mouse added. "They're the artists. Forced into the work. I think they're Volfrian." Mouse was confident they wouldn't share what they'd witnessed here. They'd be happy to be free of the place. After tonight, they'd disappear.

"Barbarians? Here?" Tenric asked, alarmed. Amazing how the word so quickly struck fear in people.

"Slaves," Mouse countered. "Likely smuggled out of the Volfric Wastes. They're the ones creating the fakes."

"Are they fakes, then?" Cas asked with a lifted brow. "They're technically Volfric, aren't they?"

Interesting point. "Not authentic relics, at any rate. They're not from any Volfric tribe. And certainly not sacred."

He wrung out the tunic and shook it out in front of him— it was still damp and cold. With a grunt, he tossed it onto a workbench. He wasn't about to pull on any more wet clothes.

"Might I suggest you locate that document you're convinced is in here?" Cas said. "Others might be notified of the triggered ward and be en route."

A fair point.

"Head back to the guild before Jardem notices you're missing," Mouse said. He grabbed a lantern hanging from a hook on the wall. "You've done enough here. More than enough."

Cas held his hard gaze on him a moment. Mouse could tell he wanted to stick around, that curiosity was poking at him and he was on the verge of offering to help the search. Cas was itching to know what this document was and what Mouse was up to, and it nettled him that Mouse was keeping quiet. But he also knew Mouse was right. He'd been gone too long already.

"Right," Cas said. With clear reluctance, he left the workshop.

Tenric watched him leave, then hurried across the room to join Mouse. His energy was still elevated, but he kept his tongue as he followed Mouse into the small office space. The lantern spilled light into the room, and the two figures were still huddled on the floor. Mouse remained near the doorway so as not to alarm them. Tenric, at Mouse's back, stared over his shoulder at them as if they were exotic beasts in a circus tent.

"Do you speak our language?" Mouse asked.

They glanced at each other. "I do," said the woman. "Some."

Her accent was thick. Mouse never heard someone from the Volfric Wastes speak. The pronunciation was harsh and guttural. If he had any doubts about where they were from, their speech settled it.

"Your employer is…." He considered words they would understand. "Asleep for a long time."

They stared back at him.

"It is safe for you to leave. No one will stop you."

Still, nothing but cold stares.

"Do you understand me?" Mouse asked.

"Are they dead?" she asked.

"Some are. One is asleep but no danger to you. They will not pursue you, I promise. Do you have somewhere to go in the city? Somewhere safe?"

Again, they exchanged glances. "We know not where to go."

Mouse exhaled. Volfric people, stolen from their tribe, here in Har Tesera. He worried what would happen to them. If any suspected they were from the Wastes, they would not survive.

He reached into his belt pouch and pulled out several coins and set them on the desk closest to him. "Use this to buy food. And clothes so you can look like you belong here. Wait until dark. Then head out of the city. West gate. Can you find that?"

They nodded.

"If anyone asks, you are from Har Rusara and returning home." A city close to the desert reaches to the west. The people there had similar skin tones as these two. In fact, some came out of the Volfric wastes to trade with the people there. Perhaps some remained longer. "Can you remember that? Har Rusara?"

Again, they nodded, but made no effort to move.

They felt trapped, Mouse realized. He gestured to Tenric to step out of the room again. They cleared the doorway and waited. In time, the two emerged.

They lingered in the doorway as if this wasn't possibly real, as if they couldn't believe their freedom had been truly gained again. The man clutched a carpet bag at his midsection. Either they'd grabbed a few of their belongings or helped themselves to things sitting around the office. Mouse didn't care. They could take whatever they wanted as far as he was concerned.

"Thank you," the man said with a low bow. They were skittish. Like rabbits caught in the middle of a field with the scent of a fox nearby.

Mouse grunted. Their thanks made him uneasy. He hadn't done anything worthy of it. They were simply beneficiaries of a mission that had gone terribly wrong. Nothing more. "Go out the back and avoid busy streets. Once you are out of the city, travel quickly. Trust no one."

"We will remember." And they shuffled off.

"Good luck," Mouse said more to himself, as they unlatched the door at the back of the workshop and disappeared. It was a long way back to the Wastes. Mouse couldn't help but wonder if they'd make it back to their home.

For a time, he stared at the open doorway.

"Mouse?" Tenric put a hand on his shoulder.

Mouse had drifted off in thought, and the touch made him flinch.

"You alright?" Tenric asked.

Mouse made a quick, dismissive nod. "We'll need to inform the city guard about this."

Tenric's eyes flitted to the bodies on the floor. "Is that wise?"

Two dead. Both by his hand. The first time he'd killed since…

His stomach felt like it was lugging around wet cement. "I want this shut down. For good. No chance of it resurfacing somewhere else." He gestured with his chin at Zardoon. "I want *him* to pay dearly."

Logically, he had nothing to fear. The city guard would not connect him to these murders—if they, for example, received an anonymous tip or someone from the neighborhood reported it.

But something ugly clung to his skin now. Something indelible. Guilt, maybe, but that wasn't entirely accurate either. He'd done what he had to do to protect Tenric. And himself. No, it felt like he had passed through an unseen door, and it had tainted him somehow. There was no returning from it.

This time, these deaths, the blood on his hands, were no accident. The first he was intending to harm but not kill, arguably. But the second…Mouse knew exactly what he was doing.

The assertion it was justified—arguing they would have killed him without hesitation or remorse—meant nothing. He'd taken a life and hated how it made him feel.

Or, rather, what he didn't feel.

"Let's get what we came for and get out," he said.

Lantern still in hand, he returned to the office. He first swept his eyes over the room, gauging it, deciphering how it was used. Unlike Jardem's flat, this space wasn't intended for ego stroking. It existed for one purpose only—industry and commerce—and used by Zardoon. Almost exclusively, Mouse would guess. Jardem likely spent little time here himself.

He would put the document where he could find it among the clutter, in a space that was his own.

Mouse could feel Tenric behind him, could feel the weight of his eyes on his back. He was still drunk on the reality he was somehow alive. His blood was pumping with the rush that came from dancing so close to certain death and escaping it. Mouse could feel it radiating off him.

"Are you certain it's here?" Tenric asked.

"Positive. But it may take some time."

He turned around to face him. Tenric's bright, eager face and lightly parted lips reminded him of the kiss they'd shared. People acted funny when they survive such an ordeal. But he wouldn't have expected that from him.

He didn't have the time or mental energy to figure out what any of that meant. Right now, he had to focus on what was next.

"Tenric, I want you to go to the city guard. Tell them some tale about how you entered the shop and found a gruesome scene."

"Now?"

"Yes, I can handle it from here."

"But…" Mouse could see questions and conflicts circling behind Tenric's eyes. "Will that be enough time for you?"

"I'll be done before they gather up their forces and make it here. The closest post is a ten-minute walk. Gives me enough time."

Tenric still looked worried. "Will they want to interrogate me? Get a statement of some sort?"

"Dressed as you are, they won't push you too hard. Act firm and important, and they'll leave you be. Tell them they can find you at some inn if they have questions. When you're done there and safely away, go back to the riverboat."

"Mouse, I could help…"

"No." The response came too quick. Too harsh. "No," he repeated. Softer this time. "This is a job for me. I'm on the lookout for other things, too. I'll need to concentrate."

His mood was dark, and it butted against Tenric's rush of exhilaration.

"I understand," Tenric said. His voice had lost some of its zest.

Mouse gave him directions to the guard post. As a thief, it was a requirement you know the location of each one intimately. "I'll meet you at the river craft. Promise. I may be late."

Tenric made a sad little smile, then nodded. He looked like he wanted to say more, but he turned on his heel and left, giving the bodies a wide berth before exiting the door.

In the fresh silence of his absence, Mouse sighed. A part of him wanted to change his mind. He wanted to go after him again, keep him around instead, even though he knew it was the wrong idea. Damn him. That kiss had muddled his brain.

He let him go, ignoring the hollowness in his stomach. He had a job to do, and he needed it to get it done.

With a frustrated grunt, he turned his attention to the office.

Nothing was really hidden here. The entire place itself was believed to be protected, and very few supposedly knew of Jardem's involvement in the operation. But he still needed to sift through the chaos. Zardoon was not as meticulous when it came to paperwork and managing an office as his wardrobe would suggest. Perhaps someone else managed the paperwork. Someone that wasn't currently in the office.

The danger that someone else might investigate when the ward was triggered was still a real danger. He had to finish this up quickly.

His search was fruitful, despite the disorder. As he'd hoped, he found the documents he'd suspected were here. He set them aside, and he continued his search for the main prize.

In one little corner of the office, near the top of a cluttered bookshelf, was one tidy shelf. It stood out from the rest of the room by its starkness. As if that one shelf was used by someone else. Mouse had to stand on a chair to access it. On it was a leather portfolio and, pushed toward the back, out of sight from floor level, a lockbox.

The portfolio contained more enticing documents. He selected a few of them but kept most in there since they would be noticed if missing. He had enough of what he needed already.

The lockbox was nothing fancy and easy enough to pick. Almost disappointing, really. Anticlimactic. But Jardem didn't expect anyone nosing around this office. Mouse opened it up. Only one thing was inside.

Mouse lifted the folded parchment gingerly by the corner as if it were delicate glass. Knowing what it was now, his heart thumped in his ears. It made his insides feel strange. The wax seal looked like a splotch of dried blood. Fitting, Mouse thought, since enough people had died so Jardem could acquire it. The wax had delicate cracks running through it— probably from when Mouse had shoved it into his boot. He squinted and looked closely at the emblem of the king embossed in its center.

Puffing out his cheeks, he added the writ of nobility to the other documents he'd gathered. Not how he'd envisioned this day going, but he'd gained what he needed nonetheless. He worried about Tenric. Once the rush of the day's events left him, he might be in a very different state when Mouse returned. At the very least, it had likely cured him of any romanticism of his life on the streets.

He locked the box again and returned it to the shelf where he'd found it. Everything he'd assembled went into a leather satchel he found tucked underneath the desk.

Jardem would soon learn of the attack on his business. Then things would spiral very quickly.

He had to be ready.

He finished dressing, pulling on his somewhat less wet tunic and boots, then slipped out the back of the workshop into the alley. Just in time, it appeared. He could hear shouts from the city guard as they gathered outside the front of the building.

From his pouch, Mouse pulled out the scrap of paper Othmar had given him. Mouse needed to pay the scribe a visit. There were questions he needed answered about this writ from the king.

24

WITH THE haversack stuffed with documents, Mouse arrived at the docks in the small hours of the night. The hired security was cloistered under a shadowy tent, drinking and throwing dice. They paid him no heed as he stepped onto the pier. The clomp of his boots on the wood planks punctuated the stillness of the river.

Fatigue had settled into his bones like an affliction. Never had he felt so frail. His legs managed to carry him the length of the pier, but all he could think about was the comfort of the cabin's bed. The burden of the last several days was taking its toll on him, and as a result, it darkened his mood. His mind was a storm cloud of every dark emotion—rage, gloom, sorrow. Guilt, too, was mixed in there, though he was irritated with himself for it. All of it was melded together in some caustic alloy that ate at his insides.

The good achieved didn't seem enough to offset the tide of darkness and anger that churned inside him.

He descended the steps and knocked. "It's me," he said. A moment later came the sound of the bolt being released.

Mouse stepped in through the cabin door as it opened.

Warm candlelight basked the inside. Tenric, a book in his hand, stood in his tunic only, the front hem dipping to his naked thighs. His chest rose and fell. It was clear he'd just leapt off the bed when Mouse knocked. He'd cleaned the blood from his face, leaving yellow bruises around his temple and eye and rough scabs where the punches had broken the skin. A little white residue from the ointment was visible, too. He'd tried to clean the blood from the tunic without much success. The rest of the ridiculous garb was folded neatly on the chair.

A fine banquet of foods was arranged on the table, as was a small wine keg and some wooden chalices.

"I took the liberty," Tenric said a little sheepishly, as if he'd broken some rule.

Mouse sighed. "Thank you, Tenric," he said softly. And meant it. He hadn't eaten. And the smell of the meats made his stomach realize how empty it was.

Tenric tossed the book onto the bed. "Well, did you find it?" Holding a chalice under the spigot, he allowed a stream of red to fill it, then handed it over to Mouse. Then he refilled his own. Mouse wondered how much of the keg had already been emptied.

Mouse lifted the haversack up as evidence. "All in here."

Tenric nodded in relief. "It's so late. I was starting to worry you'd been captured."

Mouse scoffed as if such a notion was ridiculous. "I had a friend to visit first. He helped me organize what's in those documents and answered some important questions for me."

"About?"

"About how things work in your world." He was being intentionally evasive but was too tired to care. He set the haversack on the floor and dropped in the chair with a grunt, then took a long draught from the goblet. Of course, it didn't burn or hitch in his throat when he swallowed. This vintage didn't come cheap—and Tenric had splurged on an entire keg. "Tomorrow, you can leave the city with the writ and take it to

Har Purdea. Or the capital. Whatever you prefer."

Tenric stared, his face a mix of reactions Mouse couldn't read. "You don't need it? For your own designs on Jardem?"

"Not any longer. I have what I need. I'll arrange for the river transport for you in the morning."

Tenric's mouth pressed, and he took a drink from his goblet. "May not leave just yet. I've grown to like it here in Har Tesera." He looked down at his bare feet as he spoke.

"It would be better if the writ was out of the city."

"It's worthless without the seal, Mouse."

"Not everyone agrees. And you said yourself you can take it directly to the capital and have it authenticated by a Crown Notary. You should leave tomorrow."

A fresh hardness settled in his eyes. "That's for me to decide."

"Tenric, it's too dangerous for you here. Things will get—"

He lifted his gaze at Mouse. "I'm not afraid."

You should be, he thought, but held his tongue.

Tenric leaned against the wall opposite Mouse. "You don't understand. Today was..." He lifted his eyes to the ceiling, seeming to search for the word. "Exhilarating."

Mouse frowned up at him. "This isn't a game, Tenric. We were both almost killed."

Tenric's expression darkened. He looked down at the goblet in his hand. "I've been dead most of my life." He grunted mirthlessly. "Well, not alive, at any rate. Numb. Going through day after day without direction or purpose. But today...." He shook his head and closed his eyes. "Today was the first time I felt alive. Truly *alive*."

Mouse didn't know what to say to that. Every day he faced the prospect of death or injury. Or a dungeon cell. None of it was exciting. Or exhilarating. It was survival.

Tenric put a hand to his breast. "I felt my heart pounding today. With fear yes, but also with actual purpose. I was part of something. And was actually *trusted* with a task." He shook his head. "Funny, isn't it? It took facing almost certain death to realize that living is better."

Mouse remembered how he never intentionally gave him up during the ordeal.

Tenric took another drink and chuckled. "There was a moment I was fighting not to shit my trousers. The pain was…terrible. Like nothing I'd ever felt. I could feel blood pouring down my face, and I could taste it in my mouth. I was so terrified and was certain I was going to die. Well…until I figured out you were there. But…I didn't break, did I? I didn't snivel or beg for my life. I wasn't *weak*." He struck the last word as if it were a nail.

Mouse stared up at him, and when he spoke, his voice was soft. "No. You were stronger than I would have believed."

Tenric broke a smile at that. "Shows you don't know how you're going to respond to a situation until you're right there in it. That whole time, Mouse…know what I was thinking? What would my father think of me now?" His eyes lifted to take in Mouse. "And I hated that the answer mattered to me."

Mouse thought of his own father, then. What his father must think of him now? The thought was like a knife in his gut. It mattered to Mouse what his father thought—and there would be no way he could ever change that.

Tenric was quiet a moment. He drained the contents of the chalice. "I don't know what Jardem did to you. I'm certain it's far worse. But he put me in a cage for days. And now I almost died because of him. I'm invested in this. I want to stay, and I want to help you if I can."

Mouse took that in with a slow nod. "And this decision…." He paused, wondering if he should continue. He had no idea where it would lead. "Is it at all influenced by what happened…after?"

Tenric paused. His expression turned curious. "You mean when I kissed you?"

Mouse's heart was racing. That moment had cycled in

his head over and over all day. "Yeah. That."

Tenric's eyes dropped. "I'm sorry. Appears I got caught up in the excitement of it all. Swept up in the elation of…not dying. I apologize if I crossed a line."

Mouse frowned and looked at his feet. "Is that something you do often?"

Tenric made a small shrug. "Well, it's not every day I look death in the eye."

He was avoiding a straight answer.

And even now, Mouse wasn't certain of how he wanted the conversation to go. Tenric could easily dismiss the occurrence as an anomaly, a one-time event, never to be repeated. But he didn't. And Mouse stood on the precipice, still unsure if he should take one step forward or step away from the edge entirely. He'd given into his attractions once with disastrous consequences.

His sexual encounters never really troubled him. They served a purpose. For him…or for someone else. Sex was a tool. A means to an end. Those that wanted to get naked with him typically wanted something from him, too. He enjoyed the experience, but attachments didn't play any part in it.

But his thoughts turned to Taurin.

The time Mouse shared with him was somehow different from the other encounters. Taurin *himself* was different. He occupied a different place in his head. Their romps were something comfortable and reliable. Guaranteed. He knew what to expect from the experience, and it came without ties or complications. He'd take care of that need, then go on about his life.

It took Taurin leaving for Mouse to realize there was more to it. A camaraderie between them, a shared misery in their circumstances that was both unspoken and consoling. Taurin understood Mouse, and he him.

Too late, he realized what Taurin meant to him. He would never have the opportunity to tell him, either.

Mouse sighed. Tenric didn't know him. Didn't know his

life, his circumstances, his history, like Taurin did. Then why did Tenric make his insides squishy? Why did Tenric stir uncertainty in him and make him want to instead run away?

A part of Mouse needed Tenric to leave, to be out of this river craft and out of Har Tesera. His being here made things complicated. Mouse hated when things were complicated. He hated when he didn't understand his own thoughts.

Tenric's eyes were on Mouse. He could feel the weight of his expectant gaze. Tenric must have gleaned something from Mouse's sigh, for he made a low noise in his throat. He went to take a drink from the chalice, realized it was empty, then moved to the keg again. The silence between them filled the tiny cabin like a dense cloud as Tenric filled his goblet again.

"It felt like a celebratory moment," he said after a time. His voice had changed. It had a decisive quality to it, as if in that moment a conclusion had been drawn. "It was improper of me. I understand that it's… not your way."

Mouse bit the inside of his lip. Why was his heart fluttering like a mad bird in a cage? And why was a rock lodged in his throat? "I…I didn't say that it wasn't."

Tenric lifted his eyes again. His head tilted a fraction, and his mouth pursed. "Hold on. Are you telling me you enjoyed it?"

"Well…'enjoyed' is a bit of a reach. It wasn't much of a kiss."

Tenric's brow arched. "Excuse me?"

"It was forced on me rather unexpectedly," Mouse added defensively. "And we were interrupted. It was all too quick for me to gauge it properly."

Tenric gave him a level stare. "So, what I'm hearing is you need a larger sample size to accurately appraise the quality of my…osculation."

Mouse stared at him. "I…I don't know what that means."

"Kiss, Mouse. It means kiss."

"Oh. Well, more information would be helpful," Mouse

replied, lifting his eyes to the ceiling. "If you want to know how well you—"

Before Mouse could finish, Tenric swallowed the distance between them with one step. One strong hand scooped behind the base of Mouse's skull, fingers raking through his hair, and Tenric's full, soft lips were against his own. The other arm snaked around the small of his back and tugged him in tighter.

For a heartbeat, he considered fighting against it, pushing Tenric away. But the sensual ripple that surged through him chased that notion aside like an annoying, buzzing insect. Tenric's head tilted, his lips parted. Mouse inhaled Tenric's breath as he did the same. With a slow undulating wave of motion, Tenric's mouth gently kneaded Mouse's lips. His thick tongue penetrated and dominated Mouse's throat. His own tongue was powerless against it.

Tenric's hard body was tight against him. His arms enveloped him. And his tunic was not equipped to hide or restrain the quick rise below his waist. Mouse felt the cock swell between them.

His arms tightened their grip around Mouse in an almost crushing grip, and Mouse's feet left the floor. Tenric's mouth pressed harder. He bit at Mouse's lower lip, then dropped to chew on the side of his neck, sucking the skin into his teeth. Mouse gasped for breath and exhaled a groan, born somewhere between pleasure and mounting hunger as he swept his legs around Tenric's middle and locked his ankles.

Tenric chuckled into his neck while his tongue and lips sank lower and followed the taut muscles leading to his shoulders. He spun around, and before Mouse could prepare, Tenric peeled him off his body and tossed him onto the bed like a rag doll.

Mouse laughed as he bounced and landed in a befuddled heap. Tenric grinned at him with narrow, hungry eyes as he stepped closer. He snagged Mouse's boot by the heel.

"All the hints and signals I sent you," he said with a slow

shake of his head. "You were playing me."

"I wasn't!" Mouse protested.

Tenric had transformed. He was no longer the unsure, entitled merchant brat trying to navigate life beyond the tall fence of his manor's property. His confidence was palpable. It radiated off him like a musk. He was in an element he knew intimately and thrived in.

The change made Mouse quiver. This wasn't how things were with Taurin. This was new. This was…unpredictable. Uncharted. Mouse had no idea what was about to happen, and to his surprise, the prospect thrilled him.

With a single tug, the boot was off. Tenric tossed it to the floor behind him as if he were annoyed with it.

"You rejected my advances," Tenric said.

"I didn't. I…was simply unsure. I—oh fuck."

Tenric's tongue dragged up the arch of Mouse's foot, causing him to throw his shoulders back. Tenric put his nose against the bottom of Mouse's toes and inhaled deep—and groaned low in his throat as if he'd just smelled a great wine. Then, his mouth engulfed Mouse's big toe and sucked. His tongue tickled between the toes.

Mouse tossed his head against the mattress and arched his back. "Gods, Tenric!"

Tenric chuckled again. He was enjoying making Mouse squirm.

Everything drifted away behind some translucent veil. The fight at the workshop. The deaths of the two men. Jardem. Zel. Savir. All of it was out of reach. He was only aware of the four walls of the cabin, the mattress, and Tenric's tongue on his skin.

Tenric popped his mouth off the toe and grabbed the other boot. As Tenric threw that one aside too, the dagger fell out and clanged to the floor.

Mouse stiffened.

"Relax," Tenric commanded. And he moved his nostrils up the length of Mouse's foot as he drew in a long, full breath.

Mouse's own cock was pressing against his trousers, uncomfortably confined. He reached down to undo the laces, but Tenric snagged his wrist. "No. That duty belongs to me."

Mouse wasn't one to relinquish control, but he complied and removed his hand from the drawstrings of the trousers.

"Good boy," Tenric said. "Now, I reward you for saving my ass."

His hand slipped up the length of Mouse's calf, under the bottom of his trousers. Mouse closed his eyes and swallowed. He felt the touch everywhere, but the skin under his palm screamed with tingling power. Tenric hooked fingers under the crisscrossing trousers' drawstrings and tugged to loosen them. He gripped the waistline on either side of Mouse's flank.

"Lift that ass."

Mouse obeyed, thrusting his hip. And Tenric ripped the trousers off him—none too gently. His cock sprang out and smacked against his belly.

Tenric shook his head in wonderment. "The beauty of that cannot be overstated." His hands caressed the inside of Mouse's thighs but kept his distance from Mouse's cock. Mouse ached for him to take it into his grip. He moved his hand to embrace it himself, but Tenric guided the hand away.

"Now, now," Tenric chastised gently, with a sinister grin. "I'm in charge this time. And you'll get your satisfaction when I decide it's time."

Mouse acquiesced, though his cock burned to be touched. He had no idea why he gave in. This was so different from anything he'd experienced. He wasn't in control. He didn't get to decide anything. And there was something wildly exhilarating about that. Tenric had the power here—and strangely, Mouse trusted him with it. It was liberating, in a way. He had to do nothing.

Never had he been with someone so entirely focused and committed to *his* pleasure. Tenric's desire was to please Mouse.

To have someone dedicated to pleasing him

was…surreal. It was a luxury beyond anything he could have imagined.

With the grace of a brothel veil dancer, Mouse's jerkin and tunic were removed, as well, and discarded onto the floor like unwanted refuse. Mouse was now entirely naked with Tenric standing over him, shaking his head as if he was admiring art hanging on the wall.

"Gods!" he whispered. And he slipped out of the tunic and tossed that aside, too. "Has anyone told you how glorious your body is?"

"Well, not today—"

Tenric ignored him. He put his hands under Mouse's knees and hauled him closer in one swift tug. With a push, Mouse's ass was lifted into the air. A moment later, he felt Tenric's tongue run the entire length between Mouse's cheeks. Mouse spasmed with unexpected desire. No one had done that before. Ever.

The tongue lingered around his hole, and Mouse squirmed with the sensation. His body trembled from the waves of hot pleasure that roiled through him. Tenric buried his face in the space between his ballsack and the leg. He breathed in as he licked the length of it.

"Fuck, Mouse. Your smell." He lifted his head.

Mouse wasn't sure how he was supposed to take that. "I could jump in the river. Clean up a bit—"

"Don't you fucking dare," Tenric growled. "You're intoxicating. It reaches right into my brain and makes it swim. All the rich boys smell so…clean. You smell…like you're supposed to. Raw. I could keep my face here all night. In fact, I might." He took another long inhale under Mouse's sack.

Mouse wouldn't argue. The sensation of Tenric's tongue exploring areas he'd never had explored made his entire body spasm. His skin was charged like a lit fuse. He wanted more than anything to grip his cock, but he abided by Tenric's rules. So instead, he threw his hands up over his head and arched his back.

"Gods, your ass is delicious," Tenric whispered.

Mouse's heart continued to flutter. He had no idea what was happening. This…this had never happened before.

When Tenric buried his face in the crack of Mouse's ass and felt the strong tongue probe around, Mouse gasped—both from shock and ecstasy. His hole tingled as Tenric pushed in deeper; his head swam as if soaked in spirits. Some sober part of his brain felt he should be repulsed—but it thrilled him beyond measure. He had never experienced anything like it, and as his hips squirmed in delight, he wished it would never end.

But Tenric lowered him down again, and his face came back into view, Tenric was grinning like a boy who'd eaten his first berry tart.

"I could do that all day," Tenric said.

"Please do," Mouse said, panting. His front hairline was wet with sweat.

"Oh, but we have so many other things to explore today."

Tenric noticed the sticky mess Mouse's cock had left on his belly. He scooped it up with a finger and lapped it up with his tongue. He then encircled Mouse's cock at the base with his hand and wiggled it about. He shook his head. "This is…unexpected. Not exactly proportional to the rest of you."

"So I'm told."

Tenric used his other hand to run his knuckles under Mouse's balls and gently probe his ass with a finger. He continued to stare at Mouse with an evil grin.

"Fuck," Mouse said. "If you don't do something quick, I cannot be held responsible…"

And Tenric's mouth descended on Mouse's cock. With one smooth, fluid motion, it disappeared. All of it. Tenric lips were at the base, his nose buried in Mouse's thick bush of hair. Tenric worked the shaft from inside with his tongue. Mouse snapped his head against the mattress and arched his back as pleasure exploded through him.

Low purrs of delight rolled from Tenric's throat as he

slowly eased up and down the cock. Each time Mouse felt himself shove into the back of Tenric's throat, he reverted into a groaning idiot, unable to form any words. Tenric's hand gently cupped Mouse's tightening sack.

Time blurred as Mouse thrashed his head about, eyes closed. He hitched briefly as he felt a finger probe and gently ease into his spit-wet hole—but the burst of new pleasure squashed his initial instinct to protest. The combination of Tenric's throat and finger overwhelmed his brain, and he was lost inside the sensation.

Tenric pulled off with a pop of his lips. Smiling, his tongue licked the tip, and his fingers pinched and tugged on the skin of the tight ballsack. "Ah…not yet, my friend," Tenric said. "I'm not ready for you to finish just yet."

Mouse stared at up at him dizzily through slits. How had he known Mouse was on the verge?

Tenric crawled up onto the bed over Mouse, propping up his torso with his thick solid arms. He hovered over Mouse, smiling down at him for a moment, then dipped down to lick Mouse's nipples and the line of hair from his navel to his sternum.

The candlelight behind him traced his beautiful shape and made the skin glow golden. Mouse raked fingers through Tenric's hair, gripping a clump of it as Tenric's tongue circled his navel. Mouse ran his hand over Tenric's shoulder and the powerful muscles of his upper back. The skin was like satin against his callused palms.

"But first," Tenric added as he lifted himself, "you're going to fuck me." He grabbed something at Mouse's side and set it on Mouse's chest.

The jar of ointment.

Mouse blinked in surprise. He did not expect *that*.

"Isn't this for…"

"Trust me," Tenric replied with a snicker.

Mouse scooted himself up onto his elbows. Their faces were almost touching. "You are full of surprises tonight, merchant boy.”

Tenric chuckled. “I’ll let you in on a little secret. Growing up posh is dreadfully boring. We fucked to entertain ourselves because there is little else to do. With anyone willing. And in doing so—” His eyes held an impish twinkle. “We experimented.”

“So, is that what this is?” Mouse asked. “Are you bored?”

Tenric’s expression turned serious as he lifted himself on one elbow to face Mouse. His thick hand laid gently against Mouse’s temple. “The opposite, Mouse. I told you. I’ve never felt more alive than at this moment.”

Their eyes connect for a hot moment, and Mouse felt his thoughts scramble like eggs on a steaming griddle.

Tenric broke the gaze with a lascivious grin. “Enough talk. Get inside me.”

He climbed further onto the bed and plopped onto his belly next to Mouse, who stared at the perfection of his two round cheeks, flexing and relaxing. The thick thighs were parted in an inviting fleshy partition. Propped up on his elbows, Tenric looked back over his shoulder, and his eyes bore down onto Mouse with an intensity that locked Mouse’s breath in his chest. Though passion coursed through him with the heat of a kiln, something unlatched in his head and a dark something escaped. A worry. A concern. An alarm. A part of him urged him to retreat from this as if danger awaited him if he went further, and he didn’t understand why.

Perhaps it was Tenric’s sexual ease. It was unnerving. Outside of Taurin, most of Mouse’s encounters were clandestine affairs or felt somehow wicked. They’d always served a purpose, though. They took place in alleys or backrooms. Sometimes at an inn. But it was never his room, and he never stayed the night.

Tenric was unapologetic about what he wanted. Mouse was unsure if this was a refreshing change…or something unsettling.

To cover his tentativeness, he focused on the ointment. He picked it up, tugged the cork stopper from the wide hole, and swirled two fingers into the jar. He avoided Tenric's gaze as he applied it to himself first. Gods, the silky concoction made his cock throb with anticipation. Then, he reached between the meaty cheeks and eased his fingers inside Tenric, who moaned and gyrated his hips into the mattress.

Almost immediately, Mouse felt a tingle on the skin. It began in his shaft and spread steadily into his legs, his tightening scrotum, and abdomen. His face flushed.

Mouse moved into position between his thighs. All he heard was Tenric's heavy breathing as he lifted his hips higher. Mouse leaned forward, braced himself with one arm, and gripped his cock by the base with his free hand. He guided his cock in slowly.

Mouse's head swam as the skin of Tenric's ass met with Mouse's groin. The skin-to-skin contact sent a wave of pleasure through him.

He gently pushed his hips forward. There was a momentary resistance, then Mouse burst inside with a sudden and luscious jolt. Tenric cried out as his head dropped to the mattress. He pushed his hips back to drive Mouse in deeper.

Mouse groaned as he lowered his torso to bring his chest against Tenric's hard back. He slipped a hand under to feel the curve of his pecs while he rocked his hips forward, again and again. With each thrust, he bore himself deeper into Tenric.

He licked the center line of Tenric's back, the salty taste of sweat lighting his tongue.

The enchantment in the white balm had taken its effect now. It surged through his body and infected his mind like a brushfire. His vision twisted in a euphoric distortion.

With Tenric's moans driving him onward, Mouse rode him steadily harder. The cries that escaped Tenric were at times whimpers, but at other times, they bordered on sobs. He pulled himself out completely, then sank himself in again. Distantly, he heard his own groans as his hunger and desire continued to mount.

Lubricated by their combined sweat, Mouse slid up and down Tenric's muscled back. His hips rolled in a quickening cadence. With each thrust, he tried to drive himself ever deeper inside. The sensation within him was mounting—he could feel it edging closer to the surface. Each time he plunged his cock inside, he was closer still.

And then Mouse was beyond the threshold of control. His face flushed with sudden heat. He groaned, eyes shut, his body seizing in preparation for the release. In a surge of clenching power, it rose in his body—an unstoppable tide of raw pleasure. Tenric must have sensed his nearing, for he tightened his cheeks around Mouse's cock.

"Now," Tenric breathed into the mattress. The linens were tangled into knots around his hands. "Do it now."

And with his release, Mouse cried out like he'd never done before.

He felt the gush enter Tenric. His back arched, and his legs shook from the strain. Wave after wave of fierce contractions rolled through him. It kept on going—making his entire body shake—as his cock pulsated again and again.

When it finally ceased, it left Mouse bereft of everything. He collapsed against Tenric's back, breathing like he'd been chased down by the city guard. They lay there for a moment. Tenric was chuckling softly.

Mouse found himself laughing, too. Hands to either side of Tenric, he pushed himself up, ready to ease himself out again.

But the sensation wasn't over. His cock was still hard, and the movement stirred more in him. He felt the tightening beneath his balls again.

Gods burn him! He wasn't finished. Another surge erupted to the surface, and Mouse unloaded into Tenric a second time.

"Twice?" Mouse said between gasps.

Tenric continued to laugh. "Thank the mages."

Mouse crawled off him and dropped onto the bed, still panting. Tenric rolled onto his side to face him, evidence of his own ejaculate covering his belly and the bedcovering. He had finished, too.

They grinned at each other for a few minutes, but already Mouse's eyes were beginning to droop.

He didn't remember much after. Like before, the power of the ointment settled in his head, and with the added effect of having fired his arrow—*twice*—the draw toward sleep was irresistible. His eyes closed, the world around him clouded, but he was dimly aware of Tenric's chest spooning up against his back and an arm roping around him.

\#

Mouse woke sometime later.

He felt the night's chill on him. Tenric was no longer against him, keeping him warm. He rolled over and opened his eyes.

Moonlight fell into the cabin from the port window and spilled on the floor like a thin blue rug. Tenric was in the chair, naked, elbows on knees. The light whispered on the contours of his skin.

At his feet was Mouse's haversack, the flap opened. Mouse didn't need to be told what was in his hand.

The writ of nobility.

Mouse watched, afraid to breathe. He didn't want to alert Tenric that he was awake. Tenric stared at the carefully folded parchment, but his face was in shadow. Mouse couldn't read the expression. Tenric slapped it softly against the fingers of his other hand.

Mouse waited for him to start gathering up his clothes. He would take the writ and sneak off into the night. Head home. Mouse would never see him again.

But instead, Tenric slipped the document back into the haversack and closed the flap. With a long sigh that puffed out his cheeks, he pushed off his knees and rose from the chair. Mouse shut his eyes again and pretended to sleep as Tenric crawled in back into the bed. He rolled over with his back to Mouse and was still.

25

MOUSE WOKE before Tenric, who was twisted onto his belly with one leg extended, the other bent. The position pronounced the meatiness of his ass cheeks. It was inviting—and Mouse was tempted to crawl on top of him again and wake him…

Instead, he eased out of the bed.

He grabbed more coins from the hidden compartment in the stairs. Then, he gathered up his clothes from where they were discarded on the floor and dressed and slipped quietly out of the river craft.

It was early still. The sun hadn't yet broken the tree line on the other side of the river, and the night's chill still lingered. Some people were milling about the plaza, setting up their booths or tents, but the real industry of the docks hadn't started yet. Standing on the deck, he relieved himself into the river. Looking down at his dick in his hand brought flashes of memories from the night before. The ointment left him a bit groggy, but the details lingered in crisp detail.

How had that happened? The intensity of their night together almost made it seem like a dream, something not possibly real. Mouse had never experienced anything like it—doubted he ever would again. It was beyond what he thought possible.

The things Tenric had done to him…

He would have to remember those tricks for future encounters. He'd been rendered powerless—definitely a weapon he'd have to store in his own arsenal.

He shook himself dry, tucked himself back into his trousers and headed for the docks, unsure where he was heading. Didn't matter. He needed to walk about. Too much was in his head.

Gods burn him, Tenric was a distraction he didn't need right now. He had to keep his focus on Jardem, on getting free from under his thumb—not keeping some entitled dandy alive, one that decided his posh life was boring and wanted to embrace an adventure instead. Tenric was in enough danger. He didn't need to court more by running around with him. Mouse had what he needed. The idiot should be on a river craft heading back to Har Purdea.

The night's frolic had layered a fresh coat of bright paint over the dark events from earlier, but they still lingered under his skin at a low burn. His insides ached. The success of finding the writ at the workshop was tempered by the deaths of two men by his own hand. He was no longer the thief who didn't kill, a title few could claim. That trophy had been ripped from him. He felt forever changed.

Would time come, like with so many others, he would no longer feel the impact of such a thing?

He felt a little sick. And strangely guilty. As if enjoying last night was somehow wrong. The gods should have punished him for what happened at the workshop, not rewarded him.

He circled well clear of the guild, but still kept his eyes on the darkened alleys and recesses of the building. Guild members were numerous and were trained to see what common folk missed. And if Jardem was calling for him, any of them would rat him out without the slightest hesitation. A part of him was aching to know what was going on in the hall. He hated feeling blind to what was happening there, and the not knowing made his skin itch. After both the break-in at Jardem's apartment and now the assault on his side business, Jardem would be in a froth for sure. Enough to weaken his grip on the guild?

Not likely. That would be too much to ask. Jardem knew how to keep his people in line. These events would only cause everyone more misery.

He wondered if he should feel guilty about *that* and landed rather quickly on a decisive "no." None of them ever took an interest in his strife. Most relished in it. They could suffer Jardem. Most deserved him.

Mouse spotted a couple of the heavies that kept watch on the guild's territory from beneath shadowy overhangs. Backs to the wall, they scanned the street, arms crossed. Their heads were tilted toward each other.

Talking about guild matters? Or were they were heading to soak their brains after their shift? He was tempted to swing closer to find out the topic of their conspiratorial whispers. But it wasn't worth the time or risk. These two were not likely sharp enough to understand what was happening or to do anything but do what they were told. They would believe anything Jardem told them.

Mouse easily slipped by unseen.

Fast-moving clouds rolled in from the north, and a cutting wind raced through the narrow streets. The day wouldn't lose its chill by the looks of it. Thoughts of Tenric's warm, naked body back in the bed wormed its way back into his head.

What the fuck was he doing? Why was he so unsettled by someone who offered themselves to him without any expected recompense or favor? He could be back there now, enjoying the fruits Tenric enthusiastically provided. Instead, he was off in the streets again, sulking and lurking. And taunting the fates by risking being spotted.

Several streets over, well outside the Night Finger's immediate sphere, he eyed Chelka attempting to look nonchalant behind a wagon. Her mark was easy enough to spot. From their garb, they were clearly out-of-towners. They fingered fine fabrics on display outside a weaver's shop. Their pouches dangled heavily like temple bells.

Mouse hurried around the opposite side of the wagon as Chelka was moving into a crouch, preparing to ease closer for the take. He clasped her small shoulder from behind. She flinched and let out a gasp as she spun about, knife in her hand. Mouse had her wrist in his grip before the blade came anywhere close to harming him.

Her eyes widened with recognition, then narrowed again. "Gods, Mouse! That was my quota, for sure!"

Mouse spun her about and pointed over her shoulder. A man was not far off casually watching the shoppers while picking at his teeth.

"Bodyguard," he said. "You could've been spotted and chased down. And that one's no slouch. City guardsmen are just down the street, too."

Chelka was quiet a moment as she processed how close she'd come to possible disaster. She might have escaped. More likely, she would have ended up in a cell for the night. Then maybe sent off to a workhouse if the guild didn't catch wind of the nick and send the necessary coin in time. Guards often alert the guild and pocket the release coin. But not always.

"Thanks, Mouse," she replied sheepishly. "How'd you know?"

"Folks that rich and that at ease in a strange city have protection with them. It's only a matter of locating who's with them."

Chelka's expression turned glum.

"Don't let it worry you," Mouse told her. "An easy mistake."

"One you wouldn't make."

Mouse chuckled. "I've made more than my share. Believe me," he added with a lift of his eyes. He tried not to think about all the scraps he'd found himself in. "If not for Surev's guidance, and more bribe coin than I care to admit, I'd still be in a work camp." He narrowed his eyes down at her. "Chelka, you running short on today's take?"

She sneered and looked away. "Slow morning. Some lousy mage-fucker followed me across half the city."

It was a common assumption that the city guards were in league with the city mages up in the Academy District. An understandable mistake, considering the number of guardsmen the district employed. But the Academy guards functioned separately from the rest of the city and were not even under the purview of the magistrate. Much to his chagrin, Mouse imagined. The mages wielded enough power and influence to warrant their own elite patrol.

Mouse dug out coins from his pouch and put it in her hand. "This should help."

Her eyes widened. "Mouse—"

"Stick to easier prey today." He closed her hand around the coins. "Whet your edge. One thousand light purses lead to liberating that one heavy one. Remember that."

She nodded, but she still made a pining glance toward the shoppers who were now moving to the next block. They were easy words to say. But Mouse knew Jardem's cruelty. Miss your quota, and all your take goes to the guild. None for you. And Jardem had been steadily increasing the quota amount, making it harder, if not impossible, to make it every day.

Mouse guided her attention back to him with a finger on her chin. "Listen to me. Don't relinquish your full take. Set some aside for those hard days where purses are light."

She paled. "If Quickblade found out—"

"He won't. Jardem has more to worry about than the few coins you squirreled away." Guild rules were firm about pocketing coin, and the punishment harsh for it. She reported to Ludvic, who was likely too dim to pick up on it. "Be smart about it, and no one will catch on." He lifted a finger. "Just…don't stash it at the guild. Find a safe rock to put it under."

He could tell the suggestion made her anxious. Which was the reaction Jardem wanted. Fear made his young cutpurses toe the line.

"You're not pocketing more than your share," he added. "You're redistributing it. Spreading it out. *And* protecting what's your due."

Chelka grimaced. "I suppose." She wasn't convinced. But a few days of losing everything would tip the scales and inspire her to work smarter.

"Been back at the guild?" he asked. "What's happening?"

"Quickblade's—"

"Gods! Would everyone please stop calling him that?!"

"—been asking for you. He's real angry about something, Mouse."

He had no doubts about that.

"He's not angry at you, Mouse, is he?"

"Now why would you think that?" Mouse replied with a grin. "I'm his favorite."

Mouse expected at least a chuckle, but she squirmed uncomfortably. "Well, some at the guild—"

"Ignore that talk, Chelka." His expression turned more serious. "Look, I need you to do me a service. It's important."

"Anything, Mouse. You know that."

Mouse smiled and nodded. "Go to Jardem. In the state he's in, he won't want to bother with you, but let him know I sent you. Tell him I'm still working on the assignment. Tell him…there's been new developments. I'm making progress but need more time. Got all that?"

Chelka repeated it back to him.

"Good." The cryptic message should be enough to keep Jardem wondering. If Mouse's loyalty was in even mild question—if Jardem suspected he might be somehow involved in the downward turn of his business venture—this should further muddy the waters. Jardem's arrogance had him never question whether Mouse was in his pocket—never realizing the pocket had a hole. "And tell him I'll report soon. Expect a message."

"Good."

"Should I go to him now?"

"No need. Head back to the hall when you normally report. Don't change your routine. But make sure you seek him out as soon as you're there."

"Sure thing, Mouse. You can count on me."

He shoved her shoulder. "I know," he replied with a wink.

26

BY THE time Mouse returned, the sky had lowered into a dull grey ceiling, blotting out the sun, but the mercantile chaos at the docks told him it was sometime past noon. He wove his way through the crowds and dodged a parade of stevedores hauling in fresh crates off the dock. When the path was finally cleared, he lifted his chin in greeting to the portly dock manager as he marched down the length of the pier.

He'd been gone longer than he intended. Tenric would be losing his mind at this point, wondering where'd run off to. Some part of him needled at him that he should have woken Tenric before he left, but he bristled at that notion. He was used to coming and going as he pleased. Even Jardem wasn't ever given the curtesy of his schedule. Mouse wasn't about to be accountable to someone now.

The dock manager cleared his throat as Mouse passed him at his wooden podium.

Mouse stopped and turned on his heel.

"M'lord?" Mouse inquired with a raised brow.

"Seems your four days have passed, sirrah," the manager said.

"I paid you for five, you'll remember," Mouse said, stepping closer.

"I am quite positive it was four. I have it documented right in here." He patted the large leather-bound ledger splayed out on his podium. "Would you care for me to show you?"

Mouse sighed. It didn't matter—the man had certainly entered four in his ledger and pocketed the fifth day for himself. Mouse had no recourse but to pay up.

He opened the pouch at his hip and scooped out the coins. "Two more nights," he said as he dropped them into the extended palm. "Perhaps I should acquire a receipt this time. If only to prevent this sort of confusion from happening again."

"Won't be necessary. You can depend on me to keep track of these details." He tucked the coins away in his desk under the ledger.

Mouse turned to leave, but the dock manager cleared his throat again.

Mouse grunted audibly this time and turned about again. He made no attempt to hide his irritation. "Was there something else?"

The pier manager's expression turned serious. His lips pressed together, and his eyes squinted into thin slits, making the lines at the corner of his eyes deepen. He crossed his arms on his podium and leaned closer. "Your friend is not alone."

Mouse's stomach lunged into his throat. The pier manager forgotten, he made for the river craft at a cautious jog, keeping to the edge of the pier where the planks would creak less.

Mist rolled off the river, obscuring the water. The boats moored to the docks looked like they were floating on clouds. He stepped off the pier and onto the deck of the *Glad Desire* and edged closer to the window.

Voices.

Too soft to be discerned. The curtain covered the glass. He couldn't tell where anyone was inside the cabin.

Mouse pulled his blade from its sheath inside his boot. He remained at a crouch and crept around closer toward the doorway. Tenric said something. His voice was easier to identify. The tone was somewhat elevated, but he didn't sound like he was in danger. He sounded more irritated.

Someone responded. It appeared only one other person was with him, but the voices weren't loud enough to tell him anything.

Mouse eased down the steps. He was mildly surprised the door was unlocked when he triggered the latch and launched his way in.

The two figures in the cabin jolted as Mouse bounded in.

Tenric was one of them—which Mouse expected. He stared at Mouse with wide-eyed fright. The second occupant caught Mouse by surprise.

"Cas?" he said.

"Finally!" Tenric exclaimed, throwing up his hands. Frustration was evident in his voice.

"Cas, what are you doing here?" Mouse asked, shutting the door behind him.

Cassar sighed, and his shoulders slumped. "Looking for you, obviously."

"Obviously," Mouse repeated.

"Your new friend wouldn't tell me where you were."

Mouse glanced at Tenric. His lips were tight, his face flushed. "He didn't know. I didn't tell him."

Tenric raked his fingers through his hair. "That's what I've been trying to explain to him, Mouse. He wouldn't listen."

"How did you know I was here?"

Cas looked sheepishly at the floor. "Mouse…I've been worried. Ever since that catastrophe at the warehouse. About this whole Qu—"

"Don't," Mouse said, his inflection rising in warning. "If you are about to tell me that you scried on me—"

"No. Of course not." Cassar sighed again. "I promised I wouldn't, and I hold to that. I scried on him." He gestured with a tilt of his head toward Tenric. "After the…incident, I um… I traced him. Once I had the connection, I could stay with him easy enough. He led me here."

Mouse felt his face flush. He shifted his eyes to Tenric and saw the same anger reflected in his eyes.

"You had no right to do that!" Tenric spat.

Cassar responded with a cool gaze in Tenric's direction. Tenric didn't matter to him. "Perhaps. But I wanted to know where you were in case I needed to contact you." Cas took a step closer. "And thank the gods I did, Mouse. I wouldn't have come if it wasn't urgent. But I'm in serious danger."

"What? From who?"

Cassar took in a long breath. "Qui—" He stopped and reconsidered. He must have sensed Mouse ready to cut him off. "Jardem. Mouse, he knows I was involved."

Mouse scoffed. "That's impossible, Cas. You're imagining things."

"I thought so too. But Mouse, you know him. He finds a way to learn everything. And he knows I had something to do with it." His voice was rising.

Mouse held out his palms. "Calm down a moment. How do you know?"

"I can't get into that right now, Mouse. But you have to trust me. He knows. And he's going to see me dead."

Mouse let his head fall back. "You don't know that—"

"I do. And he's going to come after me. Unless I make this right."

Mouse paused to think. "We'll find a place for you to hide. Jardem doesn't know about this riverboat. You can stay here until we—"

Cassar closed the distance between the two of them and grabbed the sleeve of his tunic. "There is only one way, Mouse. You have to give me the document so I can return it to Jardem."

Mouse was momentarily left speechless. He stared up at Cas as if he was a stranger. He grabbed Cas by the wrist and

344

pulled his hand from his tunic. "I can't do that, Cas. I won't do that. You know that."

"You are condemning me to death, Mouse. You know Jardem won't tolerate this—I'll end up at the bottom of that river. And you cannot hide me. Not forever. Giving the document back is the only way. Then maybe he'll forgive me. And if *I* give it back, he will never know of *your* involvement. See? I'll be protecting you. And your rich merchant." The last word spilled like poison from his tongue.

Mouse chuckled low in his throat, though the pain in his heart was nearly unbearable. "You were right about one thing, Cas. Your lies are pathetically transparent." He could feel Tenric's wide eyes on him.

Cassar started to protest, but Mouse swung, and the back of his hand struck Cas in the cheekbone. Cas cried out as he collapsed to the floor.

Cas lifted himself to all fours, spitting bloody splotch onto the floor. "Mouse, what are doing? I'm your friend, and I need your help."

"Get out before I kill you," Mouse growled.

Tenric was at his side. "Mouse? What if he's telling the truth?"

Mouse didn't remove his eyes from Cas, who made no attempt to return to his feet. Fury and betrayal engulfed him like he was trapped in a burning building. His vision had gone black at the edges.

Cas's head dropped. "I told you he wouldn't fall for it." There was a profound sadness in his voice, but Mouse didn't care. Cas was lucky Mouse didn't slit his throat right there.

Mouse's teeth clenched as he heard the boots on the deck of the craft. Several men. Cas had been scrying the entire exchange to someone, and whoever it was descended the steps toward the cabin with a slow, intentional gait.

"You might as well come in now," Mouse said loud enough to make sure he was heard.

The door opened.

Savir stepped into the cabin liked he owned it.

He was, as he always seemed to be, dressed in white. Or ivory, in this case. The three-quarter length doublet had elaborately embroidered wings at each shoulder, gold clasps down the center, and was lined with a striking emerald green silk. He used his cane to push the door open further to give himself enough room to step into the cabin. He had to duck his head to get through, and standing at his full height, his head almost brushed the ceiling.

It was suddenly very crowded in the cabin.

"Get up," Savir snarled at Cas.

Cas obeyed and regained his feet, albeit somewhat wobbly.

"Now get out. Wait at my carriage. We'll discuss your failure later."

Cas nodded and scurried out of the cabin. He held his cheek where Mouse had struck him, but his eyes never looked at Mouse again.

"So, Cassar is your pet," Mouse growled.

"Does it surprise you that spies creep among the Night Fingers?" Savir said.

It didn't. But it stung more than he cared to admit that Cassar was one of them. He'd always been loyal to Surev and the guild. Or at least Mouse thought he had. Something had persuaded him to instead spy for the Elite.

"What do you have over him?"

Savir chuckled coldly. "So banal. Always a sinister reason. Never occurring to you that your friend willingly works for me."

Mouse searched his memory for signs of betrayal, indications Cas would turn his back on the guild. He hated Jardem like everyone else, but enough to work against the guild itself? Mouse couldn't allow himself to believe that.

"Fidelity is a fickle mistress, isn't it?" Savir continued. "So easily swayed by just the right influences."

Mouse's mind was whirling. How much had Cas to

revealed to him? How much did Savir know?

Likely everything.

"You know why I'm here," Savir said, stepping closer. "The king's writ, if you please."

Mouse stood firm as Savir towered over him. "Does the rest of the Shadow Elite know you're after it for yourself?"

Savir smiled. "The operations of the Elite are no concern of yours, thief. We are simply ensuring that someone unworthy does not become elevated to a station that doesn't suit them…or the citizens of Davenia."

"How altruistic," Mouse replied. "Thinking only of the common good."

"See? Someone of your station could never grasp or appreciate the broader view."

"I grasp horseshit when I hear it. You hope to rise above your brethren hiding in the shadows and wield some real power. Openly. Legally."

Savir chuckled and stepped closer until he stood over Mouse. He ran a knuckle down Mouse's cheek. "Ah, young Mouse, you truly believe you understand how the world works, don't you?"

He'd had his fill of the haughty prick's arrogance. "I understand enough." Dagger still tightly gripped in his fist, he thrust upward, aiming it for under the ribs.

But Savir's reactions were fast. Faster than Mouse would have anticipated. He felt a vice-like grip around his wrist, and his arm was twisted around.

Savir's smile broadened. "So predictable. Typical street rat, not smart enough to come up with anything original. I suggest you build your skills before you take up arms against me."

Mouse seethed. His face burned hot. "I suggest you don't underestimate me."

"Underestimate you?" He grunted a laugh. "You are most certainly *over*-valued at your guild. Even I'm surprised how easily I outsmarted you." He twisted Mouse's hand about until he was forced to drop the knife to the floor. "Now, my patience grows thin. The writ," he added with force.

"And why should I just hand it over?" Mouse growled.

"Because you won't leave this boat alive otherwise. I have a dozen men waiting for me outside. I say the word, and you and the young Master Tenric are both dead. As simple as that."

Savir stepped away and moved to stand by the door. "A signal from me, and the boat will the riddled with flaming arrows."

"Mouse—" Tenric started but stopped when Mouse threw up his palm to silence him.

"You lost, street rat. You had an opportunity to profit nicely had you cooperated with me. But you chose this path instead. So, I will leave with the king's writ, and you will receive nothing."

Mouse sighed. He pulled up the flap of the haversack on his hip and reached inside. He hesitated, taking several breaths, then pulled out the folded parchment, the red wax seal blazing the front of it.

Without a word, he extended his hand to Savir.

Savir paused a moment, as if unsure, then plucked the document from Mouse's hand. Then, with a laugh, he marched up the steps onto the deck.

Tenric launched himself to Mouse's side. "Mouse, are you alright?"

"Fine," Mouse growled.

"I'm sorry, I—"

"Not now," Mouse cut him off. "We don't have much time."

"What do you mean?"

"They're going to try and kill us." He was already in motion. First, he pulled the drawer out from under the steps and grabbed everything inside and dumped it unceremoniously into the haversack.

"Kill us? Why? We gave him what he came for?"

"He doesn't want anyone to know he was after the writ himself. That's why he sent Cassar first."

"So?"

"So, he won't let us live. We know he has it."

"Who would we tell?"

"Anyone in the Shadow Elite. And you know some of them personally. Think, Tenric! What happened to your father when they learned he had it?"

That gave Tenric pause. "What do we do?"

"Can you swim?" Mouse asked as he picked up his dagger from the floor.

"Well enough," Tenric replied.

"Good."

Mouse looked around the cabin for ideas. He considered the mattress but rejected that idea immediately. It'd be consumed in flames within seconds after one fire arrow. Instead, he settled on the cabin door. He stabbed the point of the dagger under the top hinge and wiggled it deeper. Bracing his foot on the jamb, he tugged on the dagger's grip and pried the nails from the wood. They groaned and squeaked. "Help me. Pull."

Tenric grabbed the top of the door and pulled. His raw strength was all Mouse needed. The hinge was stripped from the wall. Mouse started on the bottom hinge.

Mouse heard shouts from the open doorway. Yellow lights flickered through the window. They'd already fired a volley of arrows and set the deck ablaze.

Mouse wondered what was happening in the open plaza. The attack had likely set off a stampede as everyone dodged for cover. The guards covering the plaza had either been distracted, restrained, or paid off to make themselves scarce. By the time more city guards arrived, the attackers would be gone, and the river craft would be a dangerous conflagration, threatening the other crafts on the pier. All effort would be spent to stop the spread—the archers that caused it would be forgotten.

Tenric cried out in rage as he pulled and twisted the door. The wood and nails were no match for his strength and anger.

Holding the door in his hands, he looked to Mouse, panting. "Now what?"

"We get the fuck out." A part of him was sad. The boat had become something of a home the last several days. It was lovely while it lasted, but it was time for him to return to the life he should be living. This was too posh an existence for him. "Hold the door out in front of you as we go up the stairs. I'll be right behind you."

Tenric nodded. Anger trumped his fear, which was good.

The door wasn't a standard size, but it was still about the size of a tower shield. Tenric hoisted it up by the sides, his arms and shoulders bulging from the effort. He negotiated it through the opening and into the short stairwell to the deck. He held it out in front of him as they emerged above deck. Mouse put a hand on Tenric's lower back and stayed close, rising step by step.

As the door breached the surface of the deck, Mouse heard the repeated thump of arrows slamming into the wood. Heat pressed in around them. The entire deck was already consumed by flames, and they were growing quickly. The boat would be fully consumed within moments. The fuckers had thrown casks of oil onto the deck to accelerate the flames.

"Keep facing the docks!" Mouse shouted over the roar and crackle of the flames. An arrow struck the deck right by Mouse's foot. Another archer, thinking he was clever, jumped onto the deck of a barge moored parallel to the riverboat. He was trying to get around the door.

"Now what?" Tenric shouted back.

"We run. Throw the door on three. We head to the water."

"But the flames." The deck between them and the water was a blazing wall of orange and yellow.

"Run fast! They won't harm you. One—" Even if they did catch fire, they'd be in the water a moment later.

More arrows thumped against the door and the deck around them in a steady rhythm like a deadly rain. The archers were spreading out, working for a better angle. The door was no longer enough cover.

"There are too many of them, Mouse! We won't make it."

Mouse had to dodge out of the way of more arrows that struck the deck behind him. Other archers had taken up the idea of jumping on the barge.

"Do we have a choice?"

Tenric glared over his shoulder. "Guess not. Stay with me."

And he started running. Still holding the door aloft, he launched into an impressive sprint.

Mouse had to vault himself into motion to keep with him. He hung close to his back. "It was supposed to be on three!" he shouted.

But Tenric didn't hear him—a great bellowing battle cry rose from his throat as he ran straight into the flames.

Mouse held his breath.

The archers were shouting, but their cries were drowned out as they entered the roaring chaos. The heat closed in around Mouse like he'd stepped into a kiln. Smoke stung his eyes. He was blind, running on faith. Tenric must have been near to him, but Mouse couldn't see or hear him anymore.

Pain raged on the exposed skin of his hands and face.

Then, nothing was under him.

They shot out of the flames and sailed over the water. Tenric released the door as they plummeted. They landed in the water at the same time with an ungraceful flop, and the river engulfed them with a soothing cool.

It was hard to see in the dark water, but the light from the burning boat provided enough light for Mouse to find Tenric. He was swimming back up.

Mouse seized his wrist and tugged on it. The archers would be waiting for them to break the surface. Proving him right, several arrows pierced into the dark water around them.

Tenric understood. He followed Mouse as he swam away from the burning boat. He let the current do most of the work for him and headed downstream.

"NOW WHAT?" Tenric asked. He sat with his forearms on his knees and his brow resting on his arm.

They had dragged themselves ashore well past the cluster of manufacturing buildings, south of the docks. Dripping wet, they dropped on a patch of grass behind a tanner's workshop. Racks of drying hides, positioned to catch the sun, gave them cover from the river and any of Savir's thugs out searching.

Already, Mouse spotted one boat drifting by silently in the water.

Mouse tugged off his boots and turned them upside down to drain them. Then he stripped off his clothes and added them to the tanning rack. The wind off the river nipped at his skin. Tenric had removed his tunic but left his soaking trousers on.

Mouse forced himself to not look at his finely sculpted torso.

They assessed their injuries. Tenric had a burn on the side of his face, and one eyebrow and part of his beard were singed off. Mouse's tunic sleeve was mostly gone, and the skin of his shoulder and arm stung. The new tunic had lasted just over a day. It must have caught on fire just before they jumped into the river.

"Now, you go into hiding for a few days," Mouse told him. "Until I figure out how to smuggle you safely out of the city."

Tenric's head lifted, his brow raised. "Smuggle me?"

"Things weren't safe for you before, but now…you really need to get out of Har Tesera."

Tenric scoffed and pouted. One heel dug a trench in the soft earth.

Mouse sighed. "You've had more experience with the Shadow Elite than I have, Tenric. And they terrify me. They should terrify you. Savir will use every available resource to find you, and he should not be underestimated." His voice dropped to a growl. "Especially with Cassar providing him aid in the search." His heart clenched. It would take time for the sting of that betrayal to subside.

"I shouldn't even matter anymore," he grumbled. "He has the writ now."

As if to emphasize the point, another small boat came into view on the river. Mouse hissed for Tenric to stay low. Two men. One paddled almost silently down the water while the other leaned out over the water and searched the shoreline. They waited until the boat had drifted farther downstream.

Mouse wanted to slap Tenric for being naïve. "You are a witness, Tenric. A loose end that needs tidying up. He knows if you went to the capital now…" There was more he wanted to say, more he planned to say before any of this had happened, but he decided to hold off. Bringing it up now wouldn't change what was to come.

Tenric sighed. "Mouse, let's just leave together. Leave Har Tesera. Right now, before they organize—"

Mouse grunted deep in his throat. "As if it were all that simple."

"It can be."

"No, Tenric. It can't be that simple. I can't leave the guild. Not yet."

"And why not?"

Mouse struggled with how much to say. He turned his eyes away from Tenric's gaze and stared at the ground. "It…it's complicated."

"Jardem?"

Mouse remained silent.

"You know, I have resources of my own, Mouse." Tenric's voice hardened into uncharacteristic confidence. "I can ensure we're protected."

Mouse was quiet a moment. "I'm certain your father felt the same way."

He felt more than saw Tenric's recoil. It was an unfortunate truth Tenric wasn't ready to hear.

"I want to help you," Tenric said softly. "Like you helped me. I think we should stay together."

Again, Mouse didn't respond. Instead, he rose to his feet and stood naked, watching the water.

Tenric seemed to understand. He nodded. "What are you planning?"

"To put an end to this. What else? For me. For you." He turned, putting his back to Tenric. "If I manage it, well…then I can leave Har Tesera with you."

Tenric was quiet. "And if you can't?" he said after a time.

Mouse still wouldn't look at him. "I need you to go to ground. There's a place that will keep you safe. It's a brothel, named Emele's House of Midnight. They know me there. You are going to ask for a man named Taurin." *Gods, please have him still be in the city*, he thought. Even if Taurin had already departed Har Tesera, the mention of his name should carry enough influence to allow Tenric to stay there a few days until Mouse could fetch him. Tenric had the coin; all Mouse needed from them was discretion.

And discretion was a brothel's wheelhouse.

He pulled the lid up off the waterlogged haversack and drew out the dripping sack of coins. He was thankful he'd had the wherewithal to stash away everything he'd need before he arrived at the *Glad Desire*. They'd be useless to him now. He dropped it on the ground between them. "That should cover the expenses at The House of Midnight. With some to spare. We may need what's left to arrange our way out of the city, so don't overpay."

Tenric glanced at him with pitiful eyes before looking back at the ground again.

"You wanted adventure," Mouse told him. "You wanted

to know what my life was like. Well, this is it."

"No," Tenric replied after a time. "I just wanted to spend more time with you."

Mouse's heart twisted—followed by a surge of hot irritation. Why did he allow Tenric to affect him so? Mouse always believed he was made of something more solid. His emotions shouldn't be so easily swayed. It riled him that he yearned to lay a comforting hand on Tenric's bare torso. He longed to feel that satiny skin against his own again. Instead, he looked out at the river. It was quiet out over the water now. No boats. Hopefully, Savir had given up the search.

Leaving the city with Tenric seemed an extravagant fantasy he dared not entertain. It was an absurdity. Tenric would forget about him the moment he was back in his fine estate, surrounded by his own.

He grabbed the wet clothes from the tanner's rack and started to pull them on. The cold clung to his skin like a layer of ice. He forced his feet into the stiff waterlogged boots.

"If I don't return for you—"

"What does that mean—"

"Tenric, it's an outcome you need to consider." He was losing patience. Tenric needed to listen to him and stop acting like an entitled fop. He stole a glance. Tenric looked like a boy whose puppy had run away. "If I don't return in…four days, ask Madam Diamond to arrange a way out of Har Tesera."

Tenric remained silent.

"Four days. I need you to agree to this, Tenric."

Still nothing.

"Say it, Tenric. Agree to it."

Silence followed for a time. "I will do as you ask," Tenric replied finally.

Relieved, Mouse nodded. But Tenric didn't have his eyes on him anymore. He stared at the ground, crestfallen.

Mouse ducked his head under the strapp of the haversack and positioned it onto his hip. It felt heavier than normal.

Tenric looked out over the river.

Mouse wondered if there was more to say and decided there wasn't. He slipped away and trudged back into the city.

27

MOUSE WAS beginning to wonder if Jardem would show after all.

Seated in a high-back chair he'd positioned on the dais, he felt rather like a sad king holding court in an empty chamber. Bored, he stabbed at the arm of the chair with his dagger.

Dusk had come and gone. The gaping hole in the old temple's roof had gone from azure to red-orange to indigo…to finally black. And Jardem still hadn't shown himself.

Perhaps the message had never reached him. He was beginning to feel a little foolish for the elaborate setup he'd created.

He'd arranged lanterns throughout the ruins in a dramatic display of lighting. They cast warm light around the ancient temple and created histrionic shadows among the broken stone and wood cluttering the temple's center, material that had come from the collapsed roof. A few statues that once stood in alcoves along the walls had been pulled down, and their broken pieces added to the rubble.

He'd chosen the location carefully—an abandoned

temple in the Hollows. The deity it once honored was lost to time. It was neutral territory, and Mouse felt he had an advantage here. He doubted Jardem spent much time here in the Hollows. The temple had the added advantage of having only one entrance at the opposite side of the dais. There was no way anyone could enter without him knowing it.

If Jardem ever arrived.

Mouse had given him instructions to come alone. Jardem would know he wasn't in physical danger from Mouse. If something happened to him, the information about Mouse's real name and where his father was located would be released automatically. But still, it was likely a fantasy to think he would abide by that. Jardem did what he wanted. But if he did bring others, Mouse would know.

A new light appeared in the corridor beyond, and the crunch of boots on stones and grit signaled someone's approach. The light pushed its way into the opening first, followed by a figure.

Then a second.

Mouse growled inwardly. "I asked you to come alone."

Jardem stepped further into the long chamber. Holding the lantern aloft, he stepped over sections of the collapsed roof, scowling. He was dressed in an auburn doublet. A fine one, by the look of it. As if he had stopped by on his way to some well-heeled event.

Ludvic was close behind him.

"As if I would ever take direction from you," Jardem replied.

"We have important matters to discuss, Jardem. Matters that you may not want others to hear."

"So you said in that missive," Jardem said, sounding bored. "Your boldness is staggering, Mouse. Even for you, this is beyond anything I would have expected." He stopped in the middle of the chamber, apparently not wanting to step over a larger portion of the roof that was blocking his direct path. "I nearly didn't come. Felt the wiser choice would be to leave you here to reconsider whatever foolishness you dreamt up. But…." He shrugged, hands out. "Curiosity got the better of me. A weakness of mine. I like to know all the answers. And I very much wanted to know what would possess you to make such a dangerous ploy as this." He dusted off the front of his doublet as if the room was collecting on him. "Now, let's get this over with. I have important clients to entertain this evening."

Mouse glanced at Ludvic, who glared back at him.

He leaned forward in his chair, elbows on knees. "I would like to propose a deal, Jardem. A deal that will secure my liberation from the Night Fingers. Forever."

Jardem threw his head back and laughed. "Oh, isn't this rich!" Grinning, he glanced back at Ludvic. "Hear that? He has a *proposal*. Glad I came after all. This is bound to be entertaining." His eyes narrowed back at Mouse, one side of his mouth lifted in a sneer. "Dear Mouse, you belong to me forever. Nothing short of your death—or your father's death, I suppose—will put an end to that arrangement."

"We shall see," Mouse replied. "This conversation will go one of two ways. To your benefit…or your ruin."

Jardem chuckled. "You intend to kill me?" He looked at Ludvic again, who shrugged back at him. "You know what that would mean, yes?"

"I have not forgotten. And killing you, as pleasing as that would be, is not my intention here. Is that why you brought Ludvic? You feared that I would strike you down?"

Jardem stared back at Mouse. "There is nothing I fear less than you, little Mouse."

Mouse allowed a smile to break his lips but said nothing.

Jardem threw up his hands. "By the gods, get to it, man. I haven't all night, you know. Speak your proposal so I can reject it and get back to the day-to-day pleasure of controlling your every move."

Mouse sat back and leaned against one arm of the chair. "It may behoove you to take this parley with more gravity. Do you think I called you here on a whim?"

"No, Mouse. I do not." A darkness took Jardem's eyes. "But I also know you are arrogant and reckless, and that will always be won out by cleverness and meticulousness."

Mouse chuckled. *He* was the arrogant one?

Mouse reached to his side and picked up the rock that was on the seat next to him. It was wrapped in parchment and tied with twine. He tossed it straight up into the air a couple of times before he lobbed it across the room. It landed two strides in front of the two of them.

Jardem frowned at it, then gestured with his head to Ludvic to retrieve it.

Ludvic stepped closer and fished it out of the debris. He pulled out a dagger, cut the twine, and unwrapped the parchment from around the rock. Dropping the rock, he opened it to its full size.

"What am I looking at?" Ludvic asked, his brow askew.

Jardem snatched it from him and scanned it himself. There was too much distance between them and not enough light to tell for certain, but it looked as if the color had drained from his face.

"Ludvic, leave us," Jardem spat.

Ludvic glanced up at Mouse, a curious expression on his face. "I think you were right, Quickblade. It may be best if I stay."

Jardem's face turned crimson, but he didn't respond.

"You have already surmised, Jardem," Mouse said, "that this is an invoice from your secret workshop."

Eyes filled with fire shot up from the parchment. "*You!*"

"Yes, I discovered your secret project, Jardem. And put an end to it."

Ludvic's attention shifted from Mouse to Jardem. "What secret project?" His voice was thick with fresh suspicion.

Jardem rounded on him. "*Quiet!*"

"I will tell you, Ludvic, since Jardem was insistent you come. I tried to protect him, but you know how he is. He doesn't take direction from me." Mouse waited for those words to land. He fought the urge to grin like a drunkard and kept his face neutral. Jardem looked like his head might explode. "Our guild master had a side business of creating barbarian forgeries to sell to rich merchants and nobles craving pieces stolen from the wastelands. He was using guild money to fund the operation but keeping profits for himself."

Ludvic's expression turned cold.

Jardem's hands were shaking. "Idiot. You know how foolish this is? You sealed your fate, as well as your father's."

"Ludvic," Mouse continued. "I don't need to tell you that such an operation is a direct violation of the rules of the guild, established centuries ago."

"No, you do not," Ludvic growled.

"You have any idea how much coin you wasted?" Jardem hissed through clenched teeth. "Good coin that could be spent on guild improvements. That operation benefited everyone in the Night Fingers." It was a lie, of course. Mouse had enough documentation to prove that. "You will pay for this. I promise you. Come, we're leaving."

Mouse stood from the chair. "Leave, and all the documents I stole from the workshop will be handed over and made public. Not only to the guild, but to the city magistrate."

Jardem froze. "You think blackmail is going to free you? If the guild is taken from me, you will suffer along with me. I will see to it."

Mouse knew this wasn't enough to persuade Jardem to turn him loose. His pride was too great for that. He needed both the leverage and a reward so he could salvage this as a win for himself.

Jardem turned to leave again.

"Which is why I have another solution," Mouse called to him. "One that you would be keen to hear."

Jardem kept his back to him. "You best not be wasting my time."

"I know you want the writ of nobility for yourself,"

Mouse said.

Jardem turned about slowly. "And why would you think that?"

"Tenric, kept in a cage in the cellar underneath the guild. You were attempting to locate the lost king's seal."

"So that was you as well," Jardem growled.

Mouse smiled down at him. "Guilty. Easy enough to steal him right from under your nose."

"No point. Despite what I'd been told, the fool didn't know anything about the location of the seal."

"That is where you are wrong. A rarity, I grant you."

Jardem's gaze narrowed.

"I know where to find the seal," Mouse said. "The writ and seal can be reunited."

Jardem reached into his doublet and pulled out a folded document. Mouse caught a glimpse of the red wax seal. "I keep it with me now," he said softly. "After the raid on the workshop, I did not trust it out of my sight."

"Allow me to leave the guild," Mouse said, "and I will tell you the location of the seal and return all the incriminating documents I took from the workshop. I think that is a fair trade, Jardem. You become a noble, and no one learns of the business at your workshop."

"A tempting offer," Jardem said. "But the powerful client who hired me may take issue with the betrayal. I'd be dead in days." His eyes narrowed at Mouse. "And that would be very bad for you."

"Let's not pretend further, Jardem. We both know the client is dead."

Jardem chuckled. "Dead? Don't be ridiculous."

"Don't play the innocent fool, Jardem. I know you had him murdered."

Jardem regarded him a moment, blinking as if trying to solve a puzzle. Then he spun about, throwing up his hands. "Idiot. So that's what your message meant." He turned back around again to face Mouse, eyes alight with contempt. "I sent you off to discover what happened to him. Why would I do that if I was the one who killed him?"

"To cover your trail! Make it look like you had nothing to do with it."

"By sending *you*?" Jardem exclaimed, then his head fell back as he laughed. "What an imbecile! Gods, I forget how witless and naïve you can be, even now. Mouse, you'd be the last person I'd send if I needed some truth concealed."

Mouse's head whirled. Was that a compliment?

"You believe me to be that reckless?" Jardem continued with a shake of his head. "Thought I'd kill a member of the Shadow Elite?"

"To gain the writ for yourself."

"Me, a noble. Can you imagine?" Jardem threw a grin at Ludvic. "Lord Quickblade." He laughed and turned his gaze back to Mouse. "Alas, the notion never occurred to me, I promise you. I didn't have Darko Paine murdered, Mouse. However…now that he *is* no longer around to collect the prize…" His eyes shifted to take in the writ in his hand.

"I don't need a confession," Mouse said smartly, losing patience. "Doesn't matter. I only need you to agree to the deal. Though I would cheerfully kill you for what you did to Zel."

Jardem looked to retort, but he froze, whatever words he intended to say lodged in his throat. His voice dropped to nearly a whisper. "Zel?"

Anger flared and Mouse had no control of it. "Don't, Jardem!" he shouted. "Don't insult me. I discovered your handiwork myself." Remembering the scene brought new, hot tears to his eyes.

Jardem made a clumsy step backward. "What are you saying?" When Mouse didn't reply, his eyes widened with sudden rage. "*Tell me*!"

"You act innocent, even now?"

"No," Jardem choked. "That's not possible. I thought…She said she was looking into a matter and would not be…" He trailed off.

"She must have learned what you did with Paine. Maybe she confronted you, so you killed her."

Something in Jardem's eyes spoke of true horror. His face blanched of all color. "I would never…" He swayed and looked as if he might collapse at the news.

The truth of it was etched into Jardem's eyes, and it struck Mouse with a flash of lightning clarity. What had Zel said to him? *He knows precisely what he has with me.*

Jardem loved her.

Mouse could only stare in disbelief. Was he telling the truth? Did he not kill Pain? Or Zel? Then who?

Jardem took a step forward—then suddenly gasped, eyes wide. He arched his back, and his arms flew into the air. He spasmed again just before the blade pushed through the front of the doublet in a geyser of crimson. Ludvic gripped him by the shoulder as he shoved the blade in further. He yanked the sword free again as Jardem collapsed.

"*No!*" screamed Mouse as Jardem hit the floor. He rushed to the edge of the platform. "No, no, no."

Jardem landed in a heap on the floor. He panted, eyes wide as his life spilled from him, then he was still.

It was over. Once Jardem's death was learned of, the information about Mouse and the location of his father would be handed over to the magistrate.

28

MOUSE'S HEART pounded in his ears. It was over. His father's life was now forfeit.

"Ah, that felt good," Ludvic said. He stood over Jardem and grinned down at the body a moment, then bent down and cleaned the blade of its gore on Jardem's garments. Straightening his back, he said, "I only wish the memory of that feeling, the feeling of my blade running him through, could remain with me for eternity." He stepped over him and spit on him as he did.

"Ludvic," he panted. "Why…Why would you do that?"

"A thousand thanks, young Mouse. You provided the opportunity I'd been waiting for."

Mouse staggered forward, nearly stepping off the raised dais.

Ludvic stooped to grab things from among the plaster and wood on the floor. He stood again with the writ and the sheets of parchment, now scattered about. He grinned as he looked them over, then, with sword still in his tight grip, he stepped over more debris to close the distance between them. "I think everyone would agree that this illegal workshop you discovered qualifies for a leadership change. Don't you? Gods, I've been waiting so long for a reason to run that insufferable peacock through. Never thought the opportunity would come from you, though." His eyes took on a sinister glint as he drew closer. "I will need the rest of the documents you lifted from that workshop."

The shock cleared from Mouse's head as he realized the danger he was in now. Ludvic was a skilled and ruthless fighter, and as the distance between them shrank, Mouse was nearly cornered.

"And," Ludvic continued, "now that you told him Darko Pain was dead, it was only a matter of time until he figured out I was the one who killed him."

Mouse took a slow, cautious step backward. The cover up for Pain's murder wasn't to hide Jardem's plot to steal the writ for himself, as he had thought, but to hide it from Jardem himself. "So, you. You've been the one seeking the writ for himself."

"Not for me. I've no interest in being some fancy lord. Seizing the Night Fingers as my own little kingdom is more my style. But there are plenty of very wealthy merchants out there that would do anything to be granted nobility. And they will pay me enough coin for this to be as rich as one." He stepped closer still, slowly, and with intention, as if he expected Mouse to make some furtive move. "Imagine how much they'll pay when I have the seal in my possession as well."

"Zel," Mouse growled. "You murdered her, too."

"She came to me. Foolishly. She'd discovered I had something to do with Darko Pain, but believed I was following Jardem's orders when I carried it out. She thought, as you did, that Jardem was behind it. But I couldn't let her go to Jardem with what she knew."

Mouse clenched his fists into white spheres. His face burned with rising rage. "You'll pay for that, Ludvic. I promise you."

Ludvic laughed. "What do you care, Mouse? She never liked you, that's certain enough. Why all this indignant outrage over her?"

He was close to the platform now. Mouse eased his way further from the edge. The chair was nearly behind him.

"She was talented," Mouse replied. "I respected that. And she was faithful to the guild. Unlike you. She didn't deserve that."

Ludvic shook his head, smiling. "Deserve," he repeated low in his throat. "Maybe if she was sucking on my cock and not Jardem's, things might have turned out differently. But here we are. I did you a favor, Mouse. I don't know what Jardem had over you. Frankly, never cared. But his shackles around your ankles are gone."

Ludvic had no idea that he had made everything monumentally worse. Maybe there was a way for him to send a message to his father before the king's guard found him. But he had to survive this night first.

"Simply do as I ask, and you are free, unchained," Ludvic continued. "You can go off and do as you will, no longer under Jardem's thumb. I don't want you in *my* guild." His brow tightened. "I never liked you, either."

"All those kind words you said to me over the years?" Mouse replied dryly. "More of your lies? I'm devastated."

"Accept the truth of it. Night Fingers is now mine. And you are handing over the documents from the workshop and the location of the king's seal."

"Why would I do that, Ludvic?"

"I am offering you your freedom, Mouse." He twisted his torso and gestured toward the door.

Mouse wasn't so foolish as to believe that for a moment. Ludvic planned to kill him the moment he handed over the location of the seal.

He tapped a finger against his lower lip while he eased backward another step. "I will need some assurance—"

Ludvic stepped up on the dais. "You are hardly in any

position to negotiate, Mouse. You have no choice."

Mouse continued his slow creep away from him. He stepped aside the chair and was nearly at the wall. It would come to blades, he knew. Ludvic with a sword, and Mouse armed only with his father's dagger. He cursed himself for not thinking of bringing a more sizable weapon.

Not that it mattered. Ludvic's skill with a blade was renowned. Mouse knew everything depended on his own wits.

"Keep silent any longer," Ludvic warned, "and you will not leave this place alive."

"You will find none of it without me."

"I doubt that," Ludvic replied. "*You* found it. How hard can it be?" He lifted the hand with the writ pinched in his fingers. "And…if I have to settle for this alone, it will still bring in plenty of coin."

"*Unfortunately*," a new voice broke in from the far end of the room, "*it isn't worth the paper it's inked on.*"

Mouse's gaze, locked on Ludvic, shot up and past him, to the far door. Ludvic, too, spun about, dropping into a defensive stance, sword up.

Savir stepped into the chamber, resplendent in his beaded ivory doublet. He, too, held up a parchment in his fingers, red seal on its front.

"It's a fake," he boomed. His resonant voice echoed off the stone wall of the empty temple. To emphasize his point, he tore the parchment in half and tossed it to the floor. "I had it inspected. A convincing forgery—but a forgery, nonetheless. I wager the one in your hand is no different."

Othmar's work was indeed high quality if it took that close of an inspection for Savir to learn it was a fake.

Ludvic rounded on Mouse. "Is that true? This is a forgery?" He waved the fake writ in the air in front of him.

Mouse shrugged. "I replaced the one Jardem had with the fake, yes. The real one is safely hidden."

Ludvic seethed to the point of shaking.

"I didn't want Jardem to notice it was missing." He

looked over at Savir and spoke louder. "And I expected you'd try something, so I kept an extra copy on hand…just in case." He was thankful he'd never told Tenric about the fakes. With Cassar's scrying, Savir might have learned of it.

"Then I have…" Ludvic trailed off. The realization was settling in.

"Nothing," Mouse said. "The word you're looking for is nothing. You don't have the writ to sell. And you don't have enough proof of Jardem's treachery to justify killing him and taking the guild."

Ludvic roared and lunged. But the three arrows that thumped into the platform between them brought him to a hasty stop. Archers were on the roof and had fired through the wide hole. No way to know how many.

Panting with rage, Ludvic spun about to face Savir, who was strolling closer. "The writ and seal are to be mine!" He leapt off the platform and started stomping toward Savir.

Mouse sighed. He was never very bright.

Savir needed only to lift his eyes to the hole in the roof to signal the archers. Ludvic was brought down by no less than eight. His riddled body collapsed onto the debris covered floor only a few strides from where he had slain Jardem.

"Well, that has to be the shortest reign over the Night Fingers in history," Mouse mumbled. He had to be very careful now. Or he would be another body added to the middle of the floor.

Savir strolled farther into the chamber. "I will take the real writ of nobility from you now. And do not insult me by saying it is somewhere else. Your intent was to give it up tonight for your freedom. Furthermore, to ensure that we are finished playing games…" He extended his hand toward the door and snapped his fingers.

More figures pressed in through the opening.

Two armored thugs dragged Tenric by his arms, which were tied behind his back.

Mouse stared in disbelief. How could they possibly have

found him?

Savir laughed at his shock. "You are more predictable than you believe yourself to be, Mouse. Your friend Cassar is intimately familiar with all your haunts. It was simply a matter of shaking each bush to see what fruit fell out. Sadly, your contact at the House of Midnight had already departed the city. The others are far less devoted to you and were easily swayed to give him up."

"What makes you think I care enough about him to give up the writ?"

"Very well," Savir said.

A blade was immediately at Tenric's throat. Tenric gasped, eyes wide with panic.

"Wait. Wait. Wait," Mouse exclaimed. "Let's not be so quick to murder any more people tonight." It was worth a try. He didn't really expect it to work.

Savir scowled. "I have no more patience with you, boy. This has gone on quite long enough. Now produce the *writ*."

To make their point, those holding Tenric brought the blade harder against his throat.

Mouse sighed. "Alright," he said, then again in a quiet, defeated voice. "Alright."

He reached into his jerkin and grabbed the folded parchment tucked in there. Most of the red wax that once sealed it shut had broken free and was gone. A necessary outcome if Othmar was to make the forgeries.

"It is here," he called out, holding up the parchment. "Now let Tenric go."

"Not until I've had some confirmation that this is, in fact, the authentic item," Savir said. His eyes shifted for the door again as a new figure emerged. This one was shrouded in black. "You're clever, I'll grant you, but I've grown weary of your tricks, boy. I'll not take chances with you again."

Mouse felt his stomach sink as the cloaked figured glided eerily into the room to stand next to Savir. The hood was up, face concealed. Mouse could tell nothing about the figure except it stood a foot shorter than Savir.

"Retrieve that for me," Savir told the cloaked figure.

The head of the cloaked figure lowered in a simple nod, and the hands rose. The document hummed between Mouse's fingers and began to glow. A quivering violet aura encased it. It tugged like a frightened bird trying to escape his grasp.

A mage? A fucking mage? Savir had a mage in his employ?

Clearly, Savir was no trifling fool. Mages were not available to just anyone—they required significant coin. If he had a mage working for him, he was even more powerful than Mouse estimated.

Unfamiliar with the dangers of resisting such magecraft, Mouse panicked and released it. The document hovered a moment and began a slow trek across the room. Mouse watched with an unsettled stomach. He'd never witnessed such powers firsthand before. The mage held out a gloved hand, finger and thumb extended, and as the folded parchment drew close enough, it was pinched from the air.

Tenric struggled against those that restrained him. "That isn't yours to take."

Mouse closed his eyes. *Quiet, you idiot, or you'll end up like Ludvic*, he shouted in his head. This was not the time to proclaim injustice.

Savir smirked. "Good Master Aval, have you not learned properly from your own father? For those with power, everything is ours if we desire it."

The dark figure pulled the parchment under the hood as if to smell it. After a moment, the figure leaned over to speak. Mouse heard none of it. The writ was handed over to Savir, who plucked it from the gloved hand like he was accepting a rose from a lover.

"Seems you chose wisely," Savir said, just loud enough for Mouse to hear. He tucked the parchment into his doublet.

"Now let Tenric go," Mouse spat at him. "As we agreed."

"Agreed? This was no arrangement. No contract. I am in control, and I decide when I release your new companion. And I am not yet satisfied."

He took several steps closer. "This could have been so much more pleasant for all involved if you had taken the offer I provided. Now, you will leave here with nothing."

"What now?"

"Still, coy. After you know I heard your conversation with…with them." He gestured to the bodies on the floor. "You know of the location of the seal. Tell me, and I might let the two of you live."

Mouse hesitated. His mind was whirling.

Tenric was kicked behind the knees, and he dropped to the floor. One captor pulled up his chin while the other held the sword to his throat.

"It grows late, and my patience is waning. The location. I won't ask again."

Mouse held out a hand. "Fine. It's yours." He reached around his waist to where his hard leather pouch hung on his belt. He reached under the flap and dug inside. When he pulled his hand out again, he held a cylinder.

He held it up for Savir to see.

Savir beamed. "Clever, clever boy."

Tenric's eyes widened with what Mouse would categorize as a mix between shock and panic. "Mouse," he shouted. "No! How did you—"

One of the captors struck him on the head to silence him.

"I must know," Savir said. There was a trace of skepticism in his tone. "The greatest minds of the kingdom were searching for this, yet you were able to find it. How?"

"Tenric had it the entire time. The rumors that he knew something were always true. He was behind the attack on the royal notary's entourage. He stole it and hid it away."

Savir turned his attention to Tenric with an expression that might have been admiration.

Tenric hung his head down. Mouse had betrayed him.

"Why would he go through all that effort to do that?"

Mouse sighed. "He never wanted to become a noble. That was his father's wish. Not his. And he saw what happened to his father because of it and believed it was only a matter of time before the Shadow Elite murdered him as well."

Tenric was silent. His eyes bore into Mouse from across the room. The look of betrayal in his eyes cut into Mouse with an edge sharper than any blade.

"I had it retrieved from Tenric's manor," Mouse continued. He walked to the edge of the elevated dais and sat down on the edge of it. He examined the cylinder in his hand. "Beautifully carved, really." He narrowed his eyes on it as he turned it about, his mouth scrunched on one side. "Not sure what all these symbols mean."

Savir was huffing impatiently. He turned to the mage. "Retrieve it."

Mouse held up a finger. "Ah, ah…not just yet."

"Boy—"

"You see this? The king's seal, here at the end. It isn't ivory. It's a separate piece. Copper, I believe. Whenever there's a new king, and the seal is altered, they replace the disk at the end, so they don't have to re-carve a new piece of ivory. These," he said, indicating the ivory cylinder, "are centuries old." Mouse reached over and slid a broken rock fragment from the ceiling closer to him. "Copper," he said, turning a narrow gaze on Savir. "Easily bent."

He lifted his arm and held the metal end over the rock.

Savir took a quick step forward. "There will be a half a dozen arrows in you before you make your move."

"I will be able to get at least one good slam upon the rock, I think. Ruining it forever."

"And you will both be dead," Savir growled. To emphasize the point, one of the men holding Tenric pulled his head back by his hair to expose his throat again.

"Do you think I'm a dolt, Savir? You tried and failed to kill us before. You'll try again. Those archers weren't meant for Ludvic. They are for us. You never intended for us to leave here alive."

Savir fell quiet, but his face was fiery, his eyes dark. Mouse could see the spiraling ideas behind his eyes as he searched for a solution. He dared not risk losing the seal. Without it, all his plans would crumble.

"Release Tenric," Mouse said, louder this time.

No one moved.

He lifted his hand higher. "It is my turn to lose patience," he shouted. His voice reverberated around the old temple. Birds took flight from what remained of the rafters.

Savir released a petulant sigh. With a scowl, he turned to the men holding Tenric and made a gesture with his head. The men hesitated, unsure if they understood it correctly.

"Release him!" Savir spat at his men.

One of the two sliced the rope binding his hands. Tenric climbed to his feet and shoved them away.

"Mouse—"

"Tenric, leave. Get out of here."

"I won't leave you to them, Mouse!"

"Get out!" Mouse shouted. "While you still can!"

Tenric remained rooted in place, staring back at Mouse with wide-eyed horror. "I won't." His voice was nearly a whisper.

Mouse growled low in his throat. *Damn that fool!* They had a chance for at least one of them to survive this.

Savir chuckled at Tenric, then turned his attention back to Mouse. "Appears we are at an impasse. You move away from that rock, my archers will kill you."

"I could take the rock with me."

"And still inflict enough force on the seal to dent it while you're carrying it? Doubtful. I would take my chances and shoot you down."

Mouse knew he was right. It was a safe bet.

He sat there, hand elevated over the chunk of rock, his mind whirling, searching for a solution out of this. He was tempted to smash the thing, get it over with. Deal with the flight of arrows that would rain down on him. He was fast. Maybe he'd avoid most of them.

Most of them?

Being shot with one arrow could be enough to end him.

"As for how this ends, boy, I will save you the suspense," Savir said. "You aren't leaving with that alive. You might as well hand it over and save yourself the grief. And the pain. And the suffering."

"Tenric, leave," Mouse pleaded.

But the dolt stood there, frozen, not knowing what to do.

Mouse's vision shifted, turning entirely black. His heart launched into his throat. He was blind. What the fuck was happening now…

No…not blind. He realized his vision was not entirely black. Lights. In the distant. Lights of the city. He was high in the air.

His vision adjusted, corrected. He was viewing the roof of the temple. And he watched as the archers, one by one, were plucked from behind. Arrows notched, their focus was on him, down below, and not on what creeped in from behind. Massive hands slapped over their mouths as they were hauled away from the hole's edge. They struggled, limbs flailing, but the fight was short-lived, and one by one, the unconscious bodies were dragged to the edge and tossed over.

Cassar.

His heart swelled with relief. He was out there, close by. Of course, Mouse was still furious with him for his betrayal. But Cas hadn't abandoned him. Not fully. That accounted for something. Maybe.

It was too dark to recognize any of the brutes who attacked Savir's men on the roof, but Mouse had a strong idea who had sent them, nonetheless.

"Alright, Cas," he mouthed under his breath. "Understood. Now give me back my own sight." But his vision remained on the roof.

"You have run out of options, it appears," Savir said. "You have managed to stall this process, but it is becoming painfully clear this will only end one way. So, hand over the seal."

It seemed an eternity that his vision was elsewhere. His heart thumped, not knowing what Savir was doing down below in the temple, paces from him. His vision moved with the eyes of whomever he occupied, but he forced his own head to remain still, pretending to still see, keeping his eyes pointing at where he hoped Savir was still.

He heard the crunch of boots as Savir drew closer. He could only guess how close he was. He could only hope his eyes remained looking forward at Savir.

The light in the room, low as it was, flashed against his eyes as his vision returned. He winced as his eyes stung with the sudden change. One moment he was gazing at the night from the roof above, the next he was staring at Savir as he took steps closer. He was now only a few strides away from the platform where Mouse sat, his grin cutting, his face inflated with imminent victory.

Mouse scowled up at Savir. Everything he loathed was encapsulated in this one man. Arrogance. Pomposity. Entitlement. The sense of being so bloated with power that no one else mattered. He took what he wanted with impunity. Crushing people beneath his heel, ruining lives—it all meant nothing to him. It was a game. And all that mattered was he won it.

"No," Mouse said, more calmly than he would have expected. "I have a different plan."

In one fluid movement, he reached down and plucked the dagger from his boot and flicked his wrist to flip the blade about. He pinched the tip between his finger and thumb, then circled his arm over his head. The dagger sailed across the room.

The real threat, he knew, was the mage. He didn't need that creature's mysterious power bending the advantage in the fight to come. He was already outnumbered. As soon as the dagger left his hand, he felt it—a mystic sense of precision. A knowingness of perfection. The dagger seemed to know where he wanted it to go. He watched it spin through the air with grace and beauty—if such a thing were possible. It struck true, disappearing under the hood. The mage spasmed and fell backwards. By the time the body hit the ground, Mouse knew the mage was dead.

His heart hitched a moment, skipping a beat. He never expected it to be that easy. Wounding the mage was really the plan, keeping magecraft out of the fight. Death wasn't the intention. But it was as if the dagger had had a plan of its own and guided his arm and the release of his fingers.

Another death. Three in only a few days. His stomach turned at the thought, but he pushed that from his mind. He had more important issues to worry him. He'd deal with the consequences of it later.

He sprang to his feet, ready to confront what came next.

Savir stared in disbelief at the heap of black on the floor. One gnarled hand extended from a sleeve, fingers curled as if holding a ball. It was the first time Mouse had witnessed a break in his cool countenance, a splintering of the hard armor of control he collected about himself. He was thrown. Confused.

Mouse drank in each delicious moment of it. He wanted to laugh, but he was not even close to being out of danger.

Savir turned a furious gaze to the broken opening of the roof. The hole was empty, with nothing to see but night sky. When no rain of arrows came down, he made the growl of an animal and spun on his thugs at the opening of the temple.

"Find out what's happened," Savir snarled. "And end it."

The thugs guarding the entrance sprang through the doorway and disappeared into the darkness.

Then Savir turned his white-hot rage toward Mouse.

Mouse inadvertently took a step back. Savir's face was plum, as if he'd forgotten to breathe, his hands white, shaking fists. Mouse could see whirling madness behind his eyes as he tried to make sense of what had happened, how he'd lost control. This was something that didn't happen. Not to him.

The two that had released Tenric moved to apprehend him again, but Tenric snagged a fractured board from the floor and fended them off with crude swings. Swords drawn, they pressed at him. They kept out of the range of the swinging board but drove Tenric backwards toward a corner of the temple.

The battle overhead was far from over. Mouse could hear shouting and the clang of steel. Dust and chunks of stone broke loose and dropped to the floor around Mouse and Savir.

"I'll grant you, boy," Savir grunted. His breathing came in hard bursts like a bull. "It is not every day that someone can surprise me. I may have underestimated you, and you got in a few lucky strikes against me. But no more. It ends here."

Mouse stared in awe at the elegance of the sword, but this was no ornamental weapon. It did not require an expert's eyes to recognize the impeccable quality.

"I believe you're going to have to take this from my corpse," Mouse spat back.

A ridiculous thing to say, he knew, seeing as he had thrown his only weapon away. He had no way to defend himself.

Tenric was being driven back further. His defense with an awkward length of wood was no match for two men well trained at swordplay. He was nearly at the wall.

"Well, on that we agree," Savir said.

Shouts from above told Mouse the fighting on the roof had picked up in earnest. More of Savir's men must have joined the fray. Stone and wood at the edges of the collapsed section sagged and bounced as the melee intensified. More sections broke free and plummeted like a squall of rock, cracking on the floor around Mouse.

"I might have shown you mercy earlier," Savir said. He stepped up onto the platform. He cut the air with his blade several times as he eased closer. "But a fool who thinks he can take on the Shadow Elite deserves no mercy. You were always in over your head. Pity you never realized it."

Mouse too was nearly at the wall. His eyes frantically searched for anything he could use as a weapon. Nothing. All he could hope to do was avoid the attacks. And how long could that last?

Tenric, too, was now pressed against the wall with nowhere to go.

"You could have done well, boy," Savir continued, his breathing heavy. "Had you decided to work for me. You would have had a long career. But instead, you chose…this."

"I would rather be dead than work for you," Mouse answered coolly.

"Then I shall grant you your wish. By my own hand. Hand over the seal and I'll make your end quick."

"Never," Mouse snarled back. "I have more surprises in me yet."

Savir chuckled. He was nearly in range to use his sword. He was holding back, edging in slowly as if he expected some trick. A compliment, in a way. Even now, he still thought Mouse could pull something off.

But Mouse had nothing.

From the corner of his eye, he watched Tenric attempt to deflect a thrust with the sword. The old wood plank fractured apart, and the blade pierced the shoulder. Tenric threw his head back and cried out in pain.

Savir grinned at the sound.

Tenric was defenseless. One more thrust and it was over for him.

A crack from above sounded like the felling of a tree. Shouts rose in sudden alarm. Mouse drew his eyes upwards. A large section of the remaining roof bowed downward—directly over the dais.

Savir was singularly focused. His eyes were locked on Mouse and the cylinder in his clenched in his fist. He slashed the empty air in front of him.

The thugs standing over Tenric, however, froze and stared up, eyes wide and Tenric forgotten.

Time seemed to slow. Mouse watched as the weakened portion of the roof continued to bend inward, snapping beams and cracking stone. It was an odd distortion and seemed somehow unreal. Like an illusion. The first loosened fragments that rained down into the open temple convinced him. It was real—and imminent.

He was either going to be run through or crushed to death.

Neither option appealed to him.

"Last chance," Savir growled as he took one more step closer.

He wasn't wrong, Mouse thought.

Mouse didn't want to stare upwards, and in effect, warn Savir of the danger. He was forced to depend on what he could hear and feel—and his instinct. A rumble began under his feet, and a terrific low groan, like a snoring giant, reverberated through the open temple. It was starting. He lifted his eyes to witness three massive sections twist themselves apart, oddly slow at first.

Mouse locked his air in his lungs. Time to act. As the pieces broke themselves loose and picked up speed, he shifted his weight and lunged backward. With a quick spring, he launched himself off the wall behind him. His trajectory lifted him into the air as he tucked into a roll. He came out of it, extending his legs as his feet led the drop.

His feet landed square in Savir's chest.

Savir was caught off his guard. He attempted to bring up his sword in defense, but his balance was lost. He cried out and stumbled backward from the impact and stepped off the platform. Flailing, he tumbled to the floor to land on the broken stone and wood.

He looked up and saw his fate.

Mouse landed on the platform hard on his side. His

shoulder and arm exploded in pain, but he forced himself into motion. He scrambled back toward the wall before the roof struck the ground. Covering his head, he tried to merge with the wall. He heard Savir's sudden cry of terror and its quick end as the crushing impact thundered around him. He felt it in his bones. With his eyes squeezed shut, the world quaked around him. He was pelted by debris, and dust choked his throat and lungs.

When at long last the world quieted again, and he was relieved to discover he wasn't crushed to death, Mouse dared to open his eyes.

29

MOUSE PEELED himself from the wall.

Everything hurt. Like he'd been punched a thousand times. He groaned as he unfurled himself and tried to stand. The first attempt didn't fare well. Waves of nausea and dizziness swept through him as he fought to get his feet under him. So, he opted to visit the floor again. His second attempt fared better, and he managed to gain his feet, albeit wobbily. He braced a shoulder against the wall and waited for the sick in his stomach and the spinning in his head to wane. He tried to pull in a breath—but only dragged in a lungful of dust, which launched him into a painful coughing fit. It felt like daggers in his throat.

The attack subsided. As did the lightheadedness. Slowly. He rolled from his shoulder against the wall to his back and took his first look at the carnage.

Billowing clouds of dust blanketed the lower half of the long chamber like fog rolling off the river. Mouse couldn't see to the far end of the room. He could barely see to the edge of the dais. A slow and steady drizzle of rock sounded around him as pieces continued to break loose and fall to the floor.

He could not pull in a full breath without triggering more coughing. He slid his arms out of his jerkin, bunched it into a ball, and held it to his mouth and nose. His eyes stung and filled with tears. He wiped them clean with his sleeve, then shuffled half-blind through the rubble.

The largest section of roof had clipped the edge of the dais. Mouse had avoided a direct hit, but the impact had still pummeled him with the flying debris. He'd be one massive bruise tomorrow, for certain. The collapse had created a fresh berm of material at the foot of the dais, a twisted pile of broken stone and wood beams. A few bodies, dusted in grey like the undead of stories, lay in unnatural positions on top of the mess. Unfortunates that were still on the roof when it caved in. From their current state, there was no way to tell whether they were Savir's men or part of the force that had come to his aid.

Mouse saw no sign of Savir. His remains would have to be dug out from under the rubble.

As his mind cleared, he remembered Tenric. He half stumbled, half fell off the dais and circled around the bulk of the debris where travel was easier. Dust was still thick and swirling, but light from the remaining undamaged lanterns pressed through the fog now. It was thinning, settling.

Voices reached him. Shouting. From the ground and from the roof. Mouse found it astounding that anyone would remain up there after a good third of it had plummeted to the ground. Little remained of it—most of what Mouse could see above him was black sky. The outer perimeter of the roof remained intact.

He had no idea who the survivors were. Savir's men? He'd find out soon enough, he thought. If it was Savir's goons, without someone to fill their purses, they'd lose interest in this fight quickly. Too bad a leg or something didn't stick out from the pile—something he could point to as proof.

He'd worry about them later. He had to find Tenric.

His muscles were uncooperative. They fought his movement with every step. And his balance was off. He had to concentrate to negotiate the uneven floor. He headed toward the back corner of the temple, the last place he'd seen Tenric. Through the slowly dissipating haze, he spotted a hulking figure, back to the wall. Mouse's heart raced. In the swirling dust, it was impossible to know who it was.

Mouse passed other bodies on his way. These were Savir's men. One had a sharp spear-like section of wood piercing his neck.

As Mouse finally limped close enough to recognize him, Tenric looked up. His eyes were unfocused and bloodshot from the dust, but they centered on Mouse's approach. Mouse came to a clumsy stop and took in a long breath of relief, then stepped toward him.

"I should have known I'd not be rid of you yet," Mouse said.

"Sorry to disappoint," Tenric replied dryly.

Mouse shrugged. "I've come to expect disappointment these days."

"You look terrible."

"As do you," Mouse answered. "Can you stand?" He extended his hand down to him.

Tenric glanced at the bloody shoulder and shrugged with the opposite one. "Think I'll stay here a bit longer if you don't mind."

Mouse nodded. "Suppose I don't feel like standing myself." Using the wall for support, he lowered himself down next to Tenric.

"Surprised Savir's men left you breathing, to be honest," Mouse added softly.

"Me, too," Tenric replied with a lift of his eyes. They were rimmed with red. "The cave-in was well timed. They prudently decided to head for safer ground. I suppose they thought the roof would do me in for them."

"Very well could have," Mouse said, looking at how close some of the debris had landed to him.

Tenric nodded soberly.

"I suppose I will have to have an uncomfortable but necessary conversation with the House of Midnight tomorrow," he said in a low voice.

"They don't appear to have much love for you. They were quick to turn me over."

Mouse grunted, trying to not be offended. Plenty had good reason to hate him, but he had no idea what he could have done to piss off those in the brothel. To mask the barb he felt poking at his pride, he leaned over to inspect the wound in Tenric's shoulder. "How are you feeling?" The bleeding was heavy and had saturated the entire shoulder and the side of his doublet, but as far as Mouse could tell, no major artery had severed so not currently life threatening. Not yet.

"Like I need more of that ointment."

Mouse had no idea where to even start tracking more down. But he'd need it. Festering would be a concern in the days ahead.

Tenric's expression darkened. "I think I can say I am done with adventuring for the time being. I officially miss my quiet life."

"Took you long enough," Mouse answered with a lift of his eyes.

Tenric made a feeble attempt to brush off the dust from his doublet. His eyes drifted to the fresh pile of rubble in the middle of the floor. The dust had finally dissipated to a thin haze, enough to see across the entire temple. "I suppose we'll have to dig Savir out. Locate the writ."

"No need," Mouse said. He gave Tenric a sinister smile as he reached down and pulled out yet another folded parchment from his boot. He handed it to Tenric, who stared at it in disbelief.

"Yes," Mouse said. "That is the authentic one."

Tenric stared at it a moment, nonplussed. "You gave Savir yet *another* forgery?"

Mouse shrugged.

"But the mage? It was accepted as authentic."

"Had my scribe use official parchment from the capital. He stole it from the magistrate's office. It would have the watermark of the palace in the paper. Plus, I had the seal carefully removed from the original and re-melted onto the forgery."

"I didn't know that was even possible!"

Mouse didn't either. Othmar was a clever minx, to be sure.

Tenric shook his head. "Mouse, how did you afford all these forgeries? Scribes don't come cheap."

Mouse averted his eyes. "A barter system of sorts. I've agreed to pay in…installments."

"This burden shouldn't be on you—"

Mouse lifted a hand to stop him. "No need for you to concern yourself. It's under control." Though…Othmar wouldn't object to Tenric doing his part. He forced himself to not smile at the possibility.

Tenric looked confused but didn't press the issue. His temperament shifted. His eyes dropped in a look that might be shame, might be anger. "Mouse, about the seal—"

Mouse waved him off. He wasn't interested in breeching that subject quite yet. "A conversation for another time, I think. We have visitors."

The crunch of boots on the broken stone drew his attention upward. A figure approached, grey mist swirling about him.

"Master Daru," Mouse greeted with a bow of his head. He drew a knee closer and rested his forearm on it in a casual pose.

Daru crossed the ruined temple, sidestepping debris, with the grace and dignity of an emissary welcomed into an audience chamber. His garments were, of course, free of dust, telling Mouse he'd observed the events from a safe distance. The smirk he wore was one of satisfaction and triumph. "I'm flattered you remembered."

"Hardly. You are someone I am unlikely to forget.

Appears I have you and Momma Mirna to thank for your aid."

The smirk widened. "Momma takes her investments seriously. Her newest acquisition to the family, who was an immense help tonight, by the way, decided not to remain and greet you."

Cassar. "Wise of him."

Daru lifted an eyebrow. "You're acquainted, I understand."

Mouse spoke through clenched teeth. "We are."

Daru pretended not to notice. His aloof gaze took in the pile of rubble. "His former employer's untimely accident provided him the new opportunity. He offered his unique services to Momma, who will put them to very good use."

"I'm quite sure of that."

"He did wish to pass on a message to you."

Mouse grunted. "A veritable torrent of regrets and apologies, no doubt."

"Essentially, yes. Add in a plea of ignorance that any harm would come to you."

"Well," Mouse replied gruffly. "You can save the speech. I'll not hear it."

Daru's lips pressed. "Very well."

"I will warn you against this alliance. I have it on good authority he cannot be trusted."

"Ah, you but forget the power of Momma's guiding influence," Daru replied. "He'll be properly molded under her wing."

Mouse wasn't so certain. "Daru, what is Mirna's interest here? Truthfully. Why the aid tonight? Is she interested in the writ herself too?"

Daru chuckled. "Nothing so corrupt, Mouse. She has no interest in it. It would only complicate matters and bring unwanted attention to her finely run and well-established business. She is content with her own petite kingdom for now. The truth is, she sees something in you, it seems. As I said. An investment."

Mouse felt a cold wave chew into his insides. "Well, I'm free of the guild now. I will honor my agreement with her—"

"She is well aware of all of this, Mouse. You needn't worry. In fact, she feels she is in a unique position here. Direct access to an unheard-of resource—a freelance thief." He lifted a finger. "One with some accrued debts to be covered."

"Understood," Mouse said. The balance on his debt to her had increased this night, for certain.

"Once your agreement with Momma is satisfied, Master Mouse, there likely will be other opportunities laid in your path. Paid ones. A novelty for you, as I understand it."

That would be an acceptable change of pace, Mouse thought.

"Momma's operations are closely scrutinized by city officials and the Shadow Elite, as you can imagine," Daru continued. "Having someone she trusts outside of the organization and, therefore, unconnected to her dealings, will be a most valuable asset to her." Daru gave Mouse a level look, making sure he understood. "Now…shall we quit this dreadful place before more of it collapses about our ears? Our boys will see you and Master Tenric safely escorted to a place where you can recover in peace. Yes, before you ask, a healer will be summoned for Master Tenric. I'm not blind." He glanced Tenric's direction with a sour expression and a shiver. "Expect a visit in the days ahead."

He turned on his heel and marched back out of the temple

When Mouse looked down, Tenric's eyes were on him. "Mouse—"

"Don't say it, Tenric," Mouse warned. He did not need to hear a lesson from him on how to manage a betrayal. "This is my world, not yours. I know what I'm doing."

Tenric sighed. "As if there are no snakes in my world."

"You can't be serious. You think I can trust him ever again?"

Tenric made a sad little laugh. "Trust? No. But allies with such gifts are hard to come by, Mouse. He may be of use to you. Don't toss it aside so quickly."

Mouse frowned. "I won't be able to pretend to forgive him."

"Says the man whose entire existence depends on deceit."

Mouse made an ungainly climb to his feet. Every muscle in his body was seizing up on him. With a sigh, he extended his hand down to Tenric. It was time to leave. "Come on. Let's get you out of here."

30

CHELKA WAS waiting for Mouse at the end of the hall by the solitary door.

Mouse paused at the top of the stairs. He took in a full breath before he committed to finishing this. He marched the length of the hall to stand next to Chelka, but his attention was on the door. "You're certain this time?" Mouse said.

Chelka lifted her eyes. "He asked where you were. Fairly clear sign he's awake."

Mouse nodded. "Maybe you should head back to the guild. Before your absence is noted."

"No one will notice," she replied dryly. "Not now. Not for a while. I'll check in when this storm passes."

Probably the wiser choice, he conceded. How many other members had taken to ground while this upheaval righted itself?

A part of him wondered if this meant the end of the Night Fingers. But no, someone would rise up and take the reins. Blood would be shed, certainly. With the top leadership now dead and no clear successor to the office, the war for control would be an ugly one. But *someone* would rise to the occasion.

He rested his thumb on the latch but stood there taking several breaths. Something fought him from entering the chamber. He wasn't sure what. Why now?

He didn't bother knocking; instead, he depressed the latch and pushed inside. If he'd fallen back to sleep, well, then, a knock would put an end to it. And that would delay what was to come.

The chamber was lit by a sole oil lantern hanging from a nail by the cold fireplace. It cast a weak but comforting glow about the room, dusting the wood furniture in soft gold. The four-poster canopy bed at the far end was mostly encased in shadow, as was the lump within its center.

Floorboards creaked under him as he stepped further into the room, and he goose-necked to get a better view of the surface of the bed.

"Yes, I'm awake," came a voice, muffled by bedcoverings and pillows.

Mouse straightened from his crouch. "About time. People were beginning to say that you were milking this whole wounded act."

"How long was I out?"

"The day," Mouse replied. "As in, the whole day." By the window, he pulled back the heavy drapery to reveal the darkened window. "Already night again."

A head with matted hair lifted from under the coverings, turned to the window and dropped again. "You let me sleep an entire day?" Tenric groaned.

"Not my decision," Mouse grumbled. "I would have turned your ass out hours ago. This bed doesn't come cheap." He grabbed one of the posts at the corner of the bed and gave it a hearty shake. It barely budged. "So, this is what it's like to live the life of a fancy, rich merchant? Beds the size of an entire tenement?"

Bedcoverings flew aside to expose Tenric's face. It was hard to tell in the dim light, but his color seemed better. "I feel fine. You could have wakened me."

"Following orders. The healers were quite insistent."

"Since when do you follow orders?"

Mouse shrugged. "Well, I was told to not be in here, so...."

Tenric rolled onto his back and let his thick bare arm flop across the bedding. He stared up at the canopy. Bandages still circled around the shoulder and arm.

"Your very first battle wound," Mouse said. "How does it feel?" He hoisted himself up on the high bed and sat on the edge, one knee bent, the other hanging off.

"Stiff. Sore. But better."

"Good. You'll be swinging logs at enemies again in no time. Though I do recommend investing in a blade next time."

"I'll take that into consideration." Hissing slightly through his teeth, Tenric shifted his body backward to put his back against the headboard. His head rolled a bit, and he pushed the heel of his hand against his eyes. "That is, if I can shake this fog in my head."

"The ointment," Mouse said. "A rather strong concentration was used on you. No mere flesh wound, that. The sword pierced all the way through. Festering was a concern. I'm told the bill will be sent to your estate."

Tenric grunted. "Well, I'm better now. Fetch me my clothes."

"I prefer you out of them," Mouse replied with a sneer.

"Mouse—"

Mouse sighed. "Give it until morning. There's nothing that needs to be done tonight."

"What has happened since I've been out?"

"Not much. Savir appears to have indeed been working alone. As I suspected," he added pointedly. "This wasn't some effort to stop someone undeserving from acquiring nobility, like he claimed. He wanted the writ and the seal for himself. Being a member of the Shadow Elite wasn't quite enough for him. He longed for power he could flaunt publicly."

Tenric's mouth pursed. "So, no other members have

crawled out from their shadows to make contact? Any others coming for the writ and seal?"

"Not yet. But your location is being kept hush-hush."

Tenric looked around at the room. "Even from me, apparently. I have no memory of this place."

"Our new friends have connections. The accommodations aren't cheap. I'd promised them you have the coin to cover it."

Tenric made a grunt of a laugh. "Of course."

"Many questions out there about who's in possession of the writ. I'm letting them wonder."

"And the guild?"

"In chaos, apparently. It'll be some time before a new leader rises from the ruins."

Tenric fell quiet a moment. "You should consider it. It would be a good move for you."

"Run the guild?" Mouse threw back his head and laughed. "I know you will find it hard to imagine, but I am not taken in high esteem among its membership."

"Jardem wasn't particularly liked."

Mouse dismissed that with a wave. "I work alone. You should know that by now."

"We functioned well together, I think," Tenric said. Mouse could hear the sadness in his voice.

"A rare exception," Mouse answered quietly.

"Look, Mouse…" Tenric began. "About the seal…"

Mouse's expression hardened. "You mean about the business that you had possession of it the entire time, hidden away at your family's manor, and never mentioned that?"

Tenric shifted his eyes from Mouse's to the wall. "Yes. About that. I'm sorry. It's not that I didn't trust you—"

"No," Mouse cut in. "Of course not." The reply was sardonic, not severe. Not angry. If there was anything Mouse understood, it was secrets and why people kept them.

He climbed off the bed again. On a side table across the room, he'd spotted a carafe on a tray surrounded by crystal goblets. This part of the conversation required wine.

"How long have you known?" Tenric asked.

In the dim light of one sole lantern, the wine looked black as he poured it into the goblet. He took a whiff of it, like he'd seen the wealthy do. From the heady fragrance that filled his nostrils, he could tell it was an expensive vintage. It was going to be increasingly more difficult to drink the swill he'd have to go back to eventually.

"Suspected more than knew," he said. "Jardem had you captured for a reason. And he was someone who always had good intelligence. If he believed you knew something, you probably did."

He turned on a heel and faced Tenric in the bed again.

"The whole story about the ambush always seemed odd to me. I know little about the royal notary, but their movements about the kingdom are kept highly secret for obvious reasons. For someone to pull off such an ambush, they would have had to have inside information as to when the notary's carriage was to arrive. And since no one lost their life in the attempt..." Mouse extended his arms in a wide shrug. Some of the wine splashed out. "Well, that screams amateurs."

Mouse approached the bed again, eyes carefully studying Tenric's expression.

"My contact in Har Purdea confirmed what I suspected."

Something that might have been anger flashed across Tenric's face. "He found the seal?"

"Wasn't that hard, I understand. You're not as clever as you think you are."

Tenric scowled. "Thanks a lot."

Mouse shrugged.

"How did your contact get it here so quickly?"

"He didn't," Mouse replied, and smirked at Tenric's confusion. He pulled the rod from his belt pouch and held it up for Tenric to see. "There's a scrimshaw at the docks. Had him carve me one up quick. He put some official-looking squiggles and shit around it. No one knows what one actually looks like, so it was a safe gamble. Fooled Savir, at any rate. Attached a coin at the end, here."

Tenric shook his head. "Gods, you're frightfully clever. Where's the real one?" he asked with sudden alarm in his eyes.

"Relax. In safe hands."

Tenric looked down at his hands in lap. He picked at his thumbnail. "You must think terribly of me. At the very least, a coward."

Mouse made a humorless chuckle. "Because you didn't want to end up dead like your father?"

"It wasn't that," Tenric answered weakly. "Well, not only that. It was all just too much and happening too quickly. My life would be entirely different from that moment. I needed time to consider it, think it over. I felt overwhelmed. An imposter. I couldn't manage the business. So how could I possibly think I'd manage as a noble?"

"Being a noble is easy," Mouse said. "It's not much more than ordering people about, having parties, and getting fat."

"I'm confident that's not at all true," Tenric snarled. "There are responsibilities, ones I know nothing about."

"As a new noble, you would be granted modest holdings, not the city of Har Tesera. You would manage fine." Mouse climbed back up on the edge of the bed. He took a long sip from the wine and closed his eyes as he swallowed down the velvety liquid.

"Tell me," Mouse continued. "Why did you not simply destroy the writ? Throw it into the fire? That would have put an end to all this."

Shame blanketed Tenric's expression. "I...I needed time. Time to consider that option. I wasn't ready to yet to take on that mantle. But that didn't mean I would never be ready. So, I hid the writ away. But I knew the royal notary was scheduled to come. So, I had to delay that, too. I suppose I panicked. I used my father's contacts to arrange for the ambush."

Mouse shook his head. "I'm amazed they pulled it off.

More amazed they were never captured."

Tenric fell very quiet. "They were. Soon after. And they remained loyal to my family…and to me. 'Til the day they lost their heads."

That kind of loyalty didn't come cheap.

It was Mouse's turn to fall quiet. It explained the lack of intelligence about it. They died with their secret. Or mostly. Someone must have known a little something. That was how Jardem had figured Tenric knew something.

Amazing that the palace was able to locate the thieves but not the signet itself.

"And the writ?"

Tenric grunted. "Stolen. Right from my own chamber in Har Purdea. Thankfully, I had the wherewithal to hide the signet elsewhere, otherwise they would have acquired both, and this would have been over long ago. I tried to keep tabs on it. I understand it changed several hands before it ended up in Agata's personal collection."

He looked down at his hands. Mouse could sense it was a way to avoid his gaze.

"You must think I'm a pitiful mooncalf. But when all this began, there was so much I didn't understand. I was…naïve. Ignorant. Afraid. There are so many things I would do differently now."

Mouse understood. Considering those early days on the street, it was astonishing he'd survived. But that life forced him to grow up quickly. Learn quickly. Tenric had been sheltered and protected from the reality of his father's life. The murder thrust him into new uncharted territories, and he was ill-equipped to navigate them.

Mouse grunted and leaned back on his elbows. He was very close to Tenric's thick legs. "For what it's worth, I believe you are not the same timid son you once were."

Tenric lifted his eyes. "I'm relieved you think so."

"You've more mettle than I would have wagered, to be honest. There's a fire in you, one that wasn't there when I discovered you in that cage."

Tenric frowned. "Perhaps."

"As I see it, you have two choices. Take up your father's mantle and run his company. As part of the Shadow Elite or not. That is your choice to make. But I suspect you cannot ignore them entirely. Your father's business was likely deeply entwined with their interests."

Tenric rolled his eyes up to the canopy. "Or become the nobleman as my father intended."

Mouse nodded. "And a chance to do some good, I suspect. You have had ample time to make your choice, Tenric. The seal is on its way here to Har Tesera. Should be here in two days."

Tenric sat up straighter in the bed. "It's coming here?"

"Two days," Mouse repeated.

"What…what if it is intercepted?"

"No one knows it's in transit. It will arrive here as promised. Tenric, you can turn the seal over to the magistrate here in Har Tesera if you choose to. Say you hired the best to hunt it down and recovered it. Return it to the king's hand, and you will be greatly rewarded, I'm sure. Likely have the king's favor, as well. No one need know you were behind stealing it in the first place."

Tenric was quiet, considering all this.

"Should you choose to remain a commoner, return the writ to them and say you reject the offer, the danger to you is over. You are no longer a threat to the Elite. Should you choose the path of the nobleman, I suspect there is no law that decrees you must give up any business interests. Hire someone to manage them."

"And the threat of the Shadow Elite?"

"Easily handled. A lesson I learned from Jardem. Upon your untimely death, all their names and all incriminating documents will be passed onto the magistrate. That will keep you safe from their retaliation."

Tenric stared. "I could kiss you."

"There is no one here to stop you."

Tenric slid a hand behind Mouse's neck and pulled him in. Their lips met. The fire from before, the thrill Mouse felt in that riverboat, ignited again inside him.

Tenric broke the connection and breathed heavily against his neck. "You could…you could come with me, Mouse."

"Come with you?" Mouse replied with his brow raised. "And?" he added teasingly.

"I don't know. Be my bodyguard. Spy for me. You could live with me in my manor and be off these streets forever. Never know want again."

Something in Mouse hitched. His bodyguard. Spy. Nothing more.

He choked down an angry scoff and looked away. Of course, nothing more. The truth of it slammed into Mouse with a stinging clarity. Despite everything, he was still only a street rat. Something to be rescued from a life of strife and poverty. A thing to lift out of the gutter and save.

And to fuck when the mood struck him.

But not an equal. Not a partner. Not someone to share in his success. But someone who can look up at him and admire the success from afar. Tangential to it, but not share in it.

How eternally grateful he expected Mouse to be.

Mouse slid off the bed.

Tenric, still leaning in, looked confused. "What is it?"

"Nothing," Mouse said.

Tenric watched him. "I've said something wrong." His face was dark with concern. Of course, he didn't understand. In his world, showering people with gifts and coin is how things got done.

Mouse scoffed. "No. I…I'm worried where this is heading. That's all. Any longer and we'd not stop ourselves. And I shouldn't over-exert you."

"I think I'm well enough for a little exertion," Tenric replied with a wicked smile that only made Mouse withdraw further.

"I've had strict instructions from the healers, you know, and they are not to be trifled with."

The smile faded. His eyes told Mouse he didn't believe him.

"You should rest," Mouse told him. On impulse, he stepped closer and kissed Tenric on the forehead. "I'll be here. But you should get some more sleep."

"Lay with me then." His voice had a slight pleading quality. He could sense something was off, that something had changed.

"No, I'm going to drink this fine wine out on the balcony. It's a perfect night. When do I get a chance to do that? Sleep."

"Alright," Tenric said, still eyeing him with suspicion. "As long as you stay."

"Not going anywhere," Mouse replied, lifting the glass. Once Tenric had settled in again and closed his eyes, he took the chalice with him out to the balcony. He leaned his elbows on the balustrade, chalice gripped loosely in both hands, and he looked out at the street below.

The city was quiet here. It had rained earlier, and the cobbles glittered in the lantern light like polished hematite. A few people wandered the street, but the rain had chased most in for the evening. A cart rolled by slowly, and the clomps of the horse's hooves echoed off the surrounding buildings.

A block away, hiding in the thick shadows, Mouse spotted a small someone eyeing the street. A young pickpocket waiting for his chance.

Mouse chuckled, remembering.

What would the life Tenric promised actually be like? He wondered. Better clothes, certainly. Decent meals. A place to sleep.

Freedom to do what he wanted? Unlikely.

He wouldn't be seen publicly with Tenric. No social events or dinner parties. Because Mouse was beneath him. A toy. Even after everything they'd been through, Tenric belonged in the clouds, and Mouse did not.

Would such a life be that terrible? He'd have more than he ever dreamed of having.

At the cost of any self-worth.

The knife twisting in his gut wasn't Tenric's fault, really. He was what he was. It was Mouse who had convinced himself that he was somehow not the same privileged fop as the rest of them. The mistake was on him.

Fuck. How could I have been such a fool?

And the truth of it was, he didn't hate his current life. Not really. He hated the guild, not what he did. Thieving brought him a level of satisfaction he couldn't really explain. And now that Jardem was gone, all things had the potential to blossom into something significantly better. Where he went from here was up to him.

A rousing storm rose in him from some deep well. He'd been played and hadn't even realized it. He'd allowed himself to cave to Tenric's charms and believe that he was somehow the exception. That he was not like all the other rich bastards of the world that believed they could take whatever they desired. But no, Tenric was no different. The world was his buffet, and he could fill his plate to the brim with whatever tasty morsel he desired.

Gods, Tenric would make a perfect noble after all.

How long before he bored with Mouse anyway and moved on to something else? Then where would Mouse be? Trapped. Like he'd been in the guild.

Mouse tilted his hand and let the fine wine pour down to the street below in a thin stream. Then he let the chalice go and watched with fascination as it fell. It shattered on the stone into countless pieces with an almost musical crash.

He'd had his fill of nice things.

He climbed over the railing and dropped to street level. With an unexpected lightness to his stride, he marched down the center of the street. Time to put this posh neighborhood behind him and find a grittier place to spend the night. He'd sleep in an alley tonight, he told himself. On the ground.

He wanted to feel the city tonight. The hard, unforgiving beast that it was. No more nights in a bed that was unnaturally comfortable. Tonight, he was going home.

31

DARU WAS waiting for him at a table in the back. Among the rabble, he was easy to spot. He shone like a jewel in the mud, like someone who'd lost their way and stumbled into the wrong neighborhood. He was, as always, impeccably dressed tonight with a black and blue sleeved jerkin that was tailored perfectly to his lithe form. Despite his presence, he was completely at ease with a goblet of something and an open book on the table. His hair was free of his typical ponytail. Dark waves of hair hung to his shoulders. A spectacularly tall hat rested at his elbow.

Mouse weaved through a cluster of tables, fragments of conversations pelting him as he passed. The inane troubles and petty complaints he heard made him grind his teeth. If they only knew what real troubles looked like.

Daru glanced up from his book to catch Mouse's approach. He casually closed the book and slid it aside as Mouse stood opposite him. With a wicked glint in his eye and a gentle roll of his hand, he gestured for Mouse to take the seat. As Mouse seated himself, Daru leaned back in his chair while his thumb massaged the stem of his goblet. The lantern at the center of the table caught the fine brocade of his doublet and the aquamarine broach resting on his throat.

"I feel decidedly underdressed this evening," Mouse told him. "Off to a party after?"

"I dress for the occasion, and this, my friend, is a moment to celebrate." He lifted his goblet to Mouse.

"You could have warned me."

Daru's smile widened. "I prefer you as you are. There's a truth about you I welcome. Wouldn't want to spoil it with…an unsuitable costume."

A wench's hand swooped in from Mouse's side and a goblet was set at Mouse's wrist. Without a word, she dove back into the crowd.

"And what are we celebrating?" Mouse asked.

Mouse pulled out the chair and lowered into it. Daru waited with his goblet in the air. With a sigh, Mouse lifted his goblet, too.

"To new beginnings," Daru said. "To new partnerships. And, I might add, a successful rescue."

Mouse's lips pressed together. "Yes. I am in your debt."

Daru clinked his goblet against his. "That was, as they say, on the house. Though we did have the unfortunate loss of a few from our beloved family. But that won't factor into our dealings now." He took a sip of wine. "How does our friend fare?"

Mouse felt his insides tighten. "He'll be fine." He tried to keep the edge from his voice, but based on the slight tightening of Daru's eyes, he was confident he didn't succeed.

The corner of Daru's mouth lifted. "He'll be pleased when the package is delivered, I'm sure. It will arrive any day now."

Mouse said nothing. What happened to Tenric now was no longer his concern. Or interest.

"So…free of the guild," Daru prodded with a widening smile. "What now?"

Mouse took a sip of wine. It was the same velvety type of vintage he'd poured onto the street in Tenric's room. It worried him that he could tell that. "Still mulling that idea over. Seems rather unreal, if I'm honest. But I'll work it out. I always do."

First thing, before he did anything, he would have to pen a warning to his father and hire a trust-worthy messenger that would get it there quickly. Before the king's guard arrived to arrest him for his crime.

"Wherever you land, be sure to inform us. When Momma is in need of you, she will need to be able to locate you quickly. And without fuss."

"I will inform her the moment I know myself."

"Excellent," Daru said, and he took another slow sip from the chalice. His expression shifted to something more serious. He seemed to weigh whether he should continue. "A warning though, if I may," he said after a long pause. "As you embark on this new adventure, free of the guild's shackles. I offer this as a courtesy."

Mouse raised his brow at him.

"This comes not from Momma. This is from me to you. Because I like you."

"Go on," Mouse said.

"Caution is in order. The guild is in disarray right now, but it will not always be so. Someone will wrestle control of it eventually, and order will return, and the business of the guild will resume as it always has."

None of this was surprising or new. But Mouse remained quiet and listened.

"No one can say how long this will take. A moon. A year. But it will happen. And…" Daru tilted the goblet at him pointedly. "When that day does come, they will not take kindly to someone working independently in their city."

"I'm not afraid of the guild, Daru."

Daru smiled. "Of course you aren't. That's part of your seductive appeal. But guilds exist for a reason, Mouse. They prevent competition for the available work. All work for the guild, and the guild benefits."

"And I will be taking potential jobs from the guild."

"Snatching potential coin right from their coffers. I know you well enough already to know that you won't be surviving on petty crimes and picking pockets. Your talents will make you well-sought. And popular enough to gain the ire of the guild."

Mouse took in a full breath. "I appreciate the warning. I'll be fine."

Daru's grin widened as he leaned back. Goblet still in the air, he pointed with his forefinger at Mouse. "I believe you will. But stay in the shadows. And always watch your back."

Mouse nodded. "Self-preservation ranks high on my list of important matters. But I appreciate the warning, all the same."

Daru took a sip again as he leaned forward. "To be honest, I thought you might run off with that handsome merchant boy. But...I suppose this makes more sense. You don't strike me as one to take the easier path."

Mouse said nothing.

Daru drained the chalice and slammed it on the table. "Well, the hour grows late, friend. Time I return to the Cage. Momma always tends to worry about me. Gods know why," he added under his breath. He started to rise from the chair but threw up his arm. "But ah! I nearly forgot." He reached for something under the table. When his hand returned to the surface of the table, it was holding a box. It was simply constructed, made of a decent hardwood, and a bit smaller than a loaf of bread. He set it in front of Mouse.

"What is this?"

"Some gift, left for you."

Mouse raised an eyebrow. "A gift."

"Perhaps an exaggeration. Two king's guards

approached someone from the guild and told them this must reach your hands. Rather mysterious, don't you think?"

A stone dropped in Mouse's gut.

"It made its way to my hands, and now, here you are."

The box had a lock on the front of it.

"No key?"

Daru laugh as he straightened the front of his jerkin. "As if that matters to you. Be in touch soon, young Mouse."

And he launched into the crowd behind Mouse, who barely noticed. He couldn't take his eyes off the box.

He first inspected it, turning it about in his hands. No traps apparently. Just a simple wooden box with a straightforward lock on the front. He pulled out his tools and inserted them into the hole. It wasn't difficult for him, but beyond the skill of many. Whoever sent it knew he could unlock it, but others would not.

He lifted the lid. Inside was a single leaf of parchment, folded into quarters.

Frowning, he unfolded it, angled it toward the lantern light, and scanned the contents.

Jardem had been true to his word. Upon word of his death—which, he had to admit, the news traveled fast—members of the king's guard would be notified of Mouse's real name, the murder he committed, and the name and location of his father.

But, according to this crudely penned missive, the guardsmen involved had decided on a different course. The letter was a challenge to read, but the essence of it was easy enough to discern. The guards, two apparently, and presumably the ones who came to deliver the box, saw this as an opportunity. Instead of administering the king's justice as was their sworn duty, they would instead extort coin from him. Regularly.

A tavern name was given. Mouse knew of it, despite it being out of the way. The box was to be kept there, behind the bar counter. And Mouse was to leave a required amount of coin in the box on a regular basis…

So, he was being blackmailed.

Again.

It came, surprisingly, with a wave of relief. This was ultimately better than the alternative. And the requested amount wasn't so exorbitant that Mouse might worry about not making enough to cover it.

It did grate him—he was finally in a position where he could keep all his earnings for himself. But the cut these two were asking for was less than what a guild would take from him. Although, Mouse was now on the hook for his own lodging and his food.

Still worth it, he thought.

Another benefit of their extortion was it gave him time to locate them and take care of the problem another way. These two didn't appear all that bright, to be sure. He could bury this secret forever.

With a sigh, he folded the parchment again and returned it to the box. Then he drained the goblet and moved to the vacated seat across from him. He was more comfortable with his back to a wall in a place like this, anyway. He scanned the tavern, looking for a wench so he could order an ale and perhaps secure a room for the night. Finding a place of his own would be the first order of business tomorrow.

Gods burn him, living on the streets again had little appeal. Perhaps he had gone soft now, spent too much time in that river craft, but what he thought would be a nostalgic night turned out to be cold and miserable. The reality was he would have to resort to some old habits to build up enough to afford a tenement. He was down to nothing.

A figure approached from the side and stood a respectful distance from the table. Mouse shifted his eyes up to him. The man with a grey beard and rust-colored coat waited for Mouse to notice him.

Mouse eyed him. "Can I help you, friend?"

"I certainly hope so." He took a step closer. "I mean no

disrespect, and I had no intention of eavesdropping on your conversation, but if I understand the nature of your work, I might be in need of your services."

Mouse leaned back in his chair. "Go on."

"Appears," the man added nervously, "the traditional channels for what I need are closed currently. I don't understand what occurred, but the organization is in some disarray, I understand."

"That is an understatement," Mouse answered dryly.

"So, are you available to employ? I have coin with me."

Mouse gestured to the seat across from him, and the man promptly occupied it.

Mouse watched him silently a moment, pressing his lips together. He hoped it pulled off a look of consideration, but, in truth, he was fighting a grin. "A deposit would be required," he said finally. "And before I agree, I would need to know all the relevant details."

"Of course. Are you good at what you do? Are you experienced? Again, I mean no disrespect to you, but you seem rather…young."

Mouse smiled. "You are in the most capable hands, I assure you," Mouse replied, and he allowed the grin to escape at the corner of his mouth.

The man accepted the answer with a nod. "My name is Leveret Vasquey. And you are?"

"You can call me Mouse." He leaned forward and crossed his forearms on the table. "You are fortunate to have found me here, Master Vasquey. This isn't my typical haunt. Now, let's hear all about what it is you need me to liberate for you."

The man released a long sigh that was tinged with both woe and relief at having the luck to have found Mouse in this busy tavern. "I had all but lost hope."

"Fear not. All will be made right for you. Now, proceed. The job at hand."

Master Vasquey launched into his tale. Mouse listened

and fought the giddy smile that threated to split his face.
Maybe everything was going to be fine.

The End

Acknowledgments

I have so many people to thank for the creation of this work.

TJ Austin, Andrew Baus, Robert Black, Jimmy Brown, Nate and Rachel Martin, John Martinovich, Kiim Dwan-Collins, Kate Hutmacker, Dawn Kaminski, Beth Thorngren, and Tyler Ulrich for their continual encouragement and support, and for being truly fabulous sounding boards for my relentless deluge of ideas.

Thanks to Gabriel Hargrave for his phenomenal editing and insight. The story is so much better because of your keen eye!

Thanks to Acharius Fox, for his creative vision and attention to detail, helping me get my website to where it needed to be.

Thanks to Tim Barber for creating a truly spectacular cover design and being generally awesome to work with. I appreciate your patience.

Very special thanks to Suzy Austin, Jessica Trent, Tye Radcliffe, Maxime Jaz, Micah Weltsch, Gideon E. Wood, and Lisa Wasielewski for reading various stages of this work and providing brilliant feedback and notes. Your input has been invaluable.

MASON THOMAS is the author of three other novels of speculative fiction that center on gay protagonists. He lives in Chicago with two extremely spoiled cats. He enjoys anything nerdy and his list of fandom is too long to include here.

Website:
masonthomasbooks.com
Social Media:
Facebook: www.facebook.com/MasonThomas999
Twitter: @MasonThomas999
E-mail: masonthomas999@gmail.com

More From Mason Thomas

Scoundrel by nature and master thief by trade, Mouse is the best there is. Sure, his methods may not make him many friends, but he works best alone anyway. And he has never failed a job.

But that could change.

When a stranger with a hefty bag of gold seduces him to take on a task, Mouse knows he'll regret it. The job? Free Lord Garron, the son of a powerful duke arrested on trumped up charges in a rival duchy. Mouse doesn't do rescue missions. He's no altruistic hero, and something about the job reeks. But he cannot turn his back on that much coin—enough to buy a king's pardon for the murder charge hanging over his head.

Getting Garron out of his tower prison is the easy part. Now, they must escape an army of guardsmen, a walled keep and a city on lockdown, and a ruthless mage using her power to track them. Making matters worse, Mouse is distracted by Garron's charm and unyielding integrity. Falling for a client can lead to mistakes. Falling for a nobleman can lead to disaster. But Mouse is unprepared for the dangers behind the plot to make Lord Garron disappear.

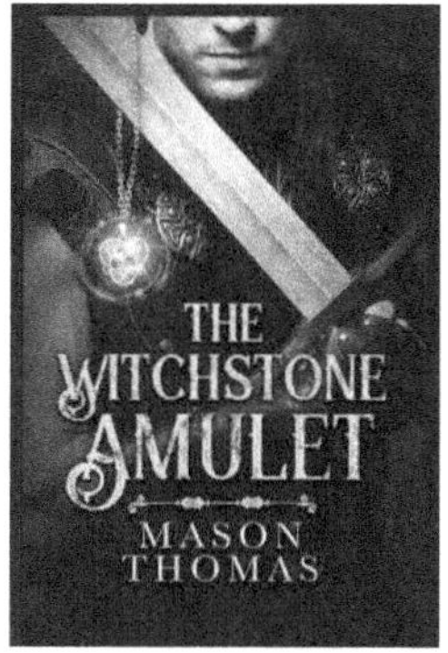

Protect it at all costs.

That's what rugby player Hunter Best's mother told him before she died. But when Hunter surprises an intruder in his Chicago apartment, he discovers her amulet missing. Hunter pursues the thief—all the way through a strange vortex. He wakes in a bizarre and violent world, a benighted realm on the threshold of civil war.

The queen has become a ruthless tyrant, punishing any who oppose her, and weakening the kingdom's defenses against the brutal Henerans. To survive, Hunter must depend on the man who robbed him, a handsome former spy named Dax, now a leader in the resistance and believes the queen is an imposter— a Heneran disguised by magic. She also happens to look identical to Hunter's mother.

There's no love lost between Hunter and Dax, and even if Hunter grudgingly agrees with the resistance, he just wants to reclaim what belongs to him and go home. But he might be the only one who can oppose the queen and end her reign of terror.